Mort

To my oldest and best buddy in the art & entertainment wars.

12/02/01

CONTINUOUS

THE

A Novel

Aloha & all the best to you and yours

MICHAEL ERIC STEIN

Michael Eric Stein

Dr. Leisure
Kihei, Maui, Hawaii

D0732887

Copyright 2001 by Michael Eric Stein

All rights reserved. No part of this book may be reproduced or transmitted in any form or by any means, electronic or mechanical, including photocopying, recording, or by any information storage and retrieval system, without permission in writing from the publisher.

Published by:

Dr. Leisure
P.O. Box 1137
Kihei, Maui, HI 96753
808-879-4160

Manufactured in the United States of America
www.drleisure.com

Library of Congress Cataloging-in Publication Data

Stein, Michael Eric,
        Continuous Trauma / by Michael Eric Stein.

"Pick up one end of the stick, you pick up the other end as well." – A Chinese Proverb

To Windy Russell and her courage

I've lost my inside person

-1-
a bad day at the orifice

It was sweat but not sweat. His skin was boiling and he...she...eyes shut but the light blasting through his eyelids...and what if his skin was cut... with all the things that had happened to her...black-and-white embrace...the light suffocated him...but now a strong hand led him to a bench, so kind amid all the shrieking...yes, I'm Charlie...Charlie Solomon...I know where I am and what happened....

They came, as they always did, in their neck braces and casts, with their crutches and their canes and their wheelchairs. They filed in sluggishly and plunked themselves down at the dirty white tables with skewed metallic umbrellas. As their numbers increased, they sat in rows on the benches and chairs and finally on the rims of the stone magnolia planters: a procession of the halt and the lame, scars ready to be bared, their faces assuming a purgatorial scowl in the relentless heat.

Charlie Solomon scrutinized the day's load of worker's comp claimants, then dragged his carryall heaped with legal files across the courtyard of the Van Nuys State Workers Compensation Board. He was still sore from a hard tennis game on Sunday, and the case files on the carryall today were so heavy that they had strained his back even worse.

He had spent ten minutes down in the garage loading the files from his car trunk onto the aluminum carryall, amid the squealing echoes of other lawyers' carryalls trundled across stone floors, beneath exhaust-darkened concrete beams and the incongruous warbling of finches. The pendaflex folders buckled and slid over each other. Papers leaked out the sides. Every attorney in the Los Angeles worker's comp system began the day the same way, dragging a load of files up to the hearing rooms. But usually it was the claimant lawyers, representing up to fifty allegedly injured workers at any one time, who had the mountains of files on their carryalls. Defense lawyers for the insurance companies like Charlie would tote to work maybe six or seven case files.

But Sheila Reed vs. the Bernard-Duvall Health and Wellness Clinic was hardly your usual case. Charlie steered the top-heavy carryall down the courtyard towards the waiting area. He noticed to his dismay that the wheel was catching and squeaking. The weight of the files was actually deforming the aluminum frame.

The morning had turned acrid and sultry, and Charlie blinked in its coarsening glare. The Van Nuys Workers Compensation building was three stories of jauntily angled stucco mezzanines, balconies, and exposed stairwells built around an atrium. It had been designed to be open and cheerful, but on the average San Fernando Valley day, with the sun blazing through that bright, happy latticework roof, it was a heat trap. Whenever you had to cross the courtyard to take a leak, or grab an iced tea in the cafeteria, ninety-eight degrees of smog-curdled Valley sun would slam you in the face.

A large group of lawyers gathered in front of the court calendar schedules posted on flats by the entrance doors. Chatting busily they looked like between-seminar conventioneers, until one would call a name - "Muldaur? M-u-l-d-a-u-r" - and dash off towards the claimants waiting on the benches. A spark of interest would light up the face of whichever injured worker was meeting his lawyer for the first time, as the other claimants watched with torpid indifference. They had all the enthusiasm of passengers squatting by a derailed Amtrak. The average disputed worker's comp claim, from the claimant's filing of the lawsuit to its resolution, took seven months to a year, and that was only if there wasn't the welter of disputes that marked the Sheila Reed case.

Charlie wondered if Ms. Reed was actually seated in the courtyard, waiting out today's events. He probably wouldn't recognize her. In the files he had found a photo that was clearly a "before" picture that would be entered into evidence by her worker's comp attorney. The actual appearance of Sheila in the court would be the "after" image of five years of untreated illness that the judge would be asked to consider in all its rueful decay.

Charlie remembered that Kodacolor photo. Three legal secretaries, arms around each other, enjoying a day at Zuma Beach. The young woman in the middle had bright, teasing eyes, straight hair halfway down her back, and a sensational body: lean, hard abs, the kind of thighs you saw in photos of exotic dancers from the Fifties, heavy but superbly toned. Sheila Reed had been a volleyball player for U.C. Irvine. He tried to spot her among the women carrying stuffed daypacks and Walkmans for their hours of bus travel to and from worker's comp court.

Sheila was now on welfare, living in a ratty apartment with her brother. U.C. Irvine, Class of '83.

Charlie really felt it now, a wave of anticipation laced with dread. The whole worker's comp judicial process was geared towards settlement, settlement, settlement. That was why, before any hearing on any worker's alleged injury was held, there had to be a Mandatory Settlement Conference. That's why judges would have a Mobius-loop of a schedule and be slated to hear five cases in four hours - because three would most certainly settle out.

But there were always the two that wouldn't, the exasperating, bewildering cases that fermented in "the System" for years in a mass of motions and counter-motions until they poisoned the attitudes of everyone they touched. No one was in the mood for artful compromises on the five-year Sheila Reed case. District Manager Ted Shackleton had instructed Charlie to repeat Hobart-Riis Insurance's last settlement offer to Ms. Reed, then fold the cards. If necessary, blow off Sheila Reed's case without any settlement at all. Nail her with a "take-nothing."

And Charlie knew that Ms. Reed's attorney, Elizabeth Worcek, would never agree to his bosses' token settlement offer. Not when she could argue at top volume that her client had been damaged for five years by an evil insurance company refusing to pay an honest worker's comp injury claim.

So today Charlie had something extra on his plate, a rare event in the life of a worker's comp attorney. Today would be an actual trial.

The clerk took the medical reports Charlie was serving on the Board and time-stamped them without so much as a nod in his direction. The waiting room was as busy and noisy as ever. Lawyers went down the row of chairs

3

talking on the fly with their claimants, or stood murmuring into the public phones like an order of cheap-suited supplicants at prayer. Charlie could already feel the sweat chafing at his neck.

He spotted a tall, ash-blonde woman with dry mottled skin, who was chatting with Ben Salerno, a claimant lawyer Charlie was acquainted with from a case two years ago. Her twitching hand held fast to a cigarette. She would light it the nanosecond she left the no-smoking building. Charlie knew about the blonde, a waitress at a low-grade comedy club. Some heckler had grabbed her ass. Trying to get away from him, she claimed, she wrenched her knee out. Completely destroyed her knee out of shock and horror at getting her butt swatted by a drunk at the Funny Farm. And then there was the psychological trauma the event caused this veteran waitress, who now claimed total inability to ever return to her usual and customary employment. Ben Salerno was putting on his best shrewdly sardonic masculinity for this client who, whatever her knee problems, had quite a rack on her.

"Yeah?" chuckled the blonde. "Who's worse mad?"

"It's bullshit. Dr. Mintz - the one who said you could no longer bend your knee past 90 degrees - now he says you can run marathons. We deposed him; he said what he said on July 15 and that doesn't go away."

"Some fuckin' bedside manner he's got, huh? Hey, so I can still exercise a little. You know, chronic pain affects another part of the brain in women, right?"

Exercise a little? Charlie couldn't help noticing she had the kind of deeply cleft, supple ass you only got from pushing major Stair. A word popped out of whatever memories of Yiddish he had. "Traife." Unkosher trash. This woman knows the game, and some club owner who at least ponied up for legitimate worker's comp insurance has to pay the price.

The whistling came from behind him. Charlie smiled at the melody, "Sealed With A Kiss", and looked over his shoulder at his fellow defense lawyer Jerry Kaukonen.

"What you think, Charlie? Ben's going to get over with her?"

When it came to women, Kaukonen had a one-track mind, and Charlie knew just how to talk to it. "Legally or sexually, Jerry?"

"Christ, Charlie, Ben's got no chance of getting laid here. Not without heavy equipment." They both gazed at the biker waitress in her knee-braced spandex and black leather jacket. "From what I hear, Ben might get her some p.d., even vocational rehab."

"You're telling me this woman could get permanent disability payments and training for a new job because someone made a pass at her?"

"That's why we insurance shysters are on the side of the angels, Charlie." Kaukonen whistled another tune, an old Beach Boys hit, "Little deuce coupe/ You don't know what I got..." An aging former beach hippie and d.j., Kaukonen used a cluster of '60's tunes to tag the claimants in the courtyard. Some were "Little Deuce Coupes," tasty settlements for his claimant lawyer adversaries. The opposites, claimants Kaukonen knew he could shoot down, were "Deadman's Curves" - a tune he also used for certain gorgeous female claimants. Then there were cases like the Sheila Reed case, the "Endless Summers" that dragged on for months or years towards a Compromise and Release settlement that would please nobody, and sometimes degenerated into "Nineteenth Nervous Breakdowns," when claimants would get a hearing and sob to the judge about how the damn system had denied their rights, ruined their lives...

"What the hell have you got there?"

"Oh," Charlie sighed, "a draw-the-short-straw ball-buster-and-a-half. Sheila Reed vs. Bernard-Duvall Clinic." Charlie looked at the column of files. "This case has been in the system since I was in law school."

"Wait a minute. The office manager, right? She claimed this one doctor drove her off her job and made her sick, they said she walked off the job, she said she notified them of her injury but they lost the files?"

"Yep. Not a promising beginning."

"I thought that case was safely in legal limbo by now."

"Liz Worcek got ahold of it. She shoehorned it back into the court calendar, just in time for me to inherit the fucker."

"Hoo boy. Worcek." He shook his head as if Charlie had just told him he had gallstones. "Well, gotta book, Charlie. Got three conferences, two trials, and a deposition in fucking Baldwin Hills." Kaukonen shook his head balefully. "Bad day at the orifice."

5

Kaukonen was pulling the cheesiest defense lawyer trick: sign up for an unworkable schedule. Two cases would be kicked over because Kaukonen couldn't show, and Kaukonen would arrive for the other so late that the court reporter (of which the system had short supply) would be yanked for another trial. The result would be three more free passes for Kaukonen, and three more six-month delays in the cases of three more injured claimants.

"Oh well," Kaukonen added, "I think I can settle Lanie Badham's broken hip pretty cheap. Her lawyer's Jag needs a tune-up." His eyes flicked sidewise. "Say hello to Miss Congeniality for me."

Vel was sitting at one of the tables in the cafeteria. Charlie could see her through the glass doors, sipping an iced tea as she leafed through her files. As always, she seemed to funnel a silence around her with her concentration, black hair swept back over her forehead in a barrette, index finger poised above her thumb as if drawing a silk strand out of the air.

"So, Charlie, is Vel playful? I mean, playing safely, of course. I hate to think either of you are at risk."

"Jerry, this is getting old. We go back. Not out."

Vel looked up at them. Charlie knew she wouldn't budge from her seat with Kaukonen behind him. He leaked little sputters of sexual avarice talking to Vel, and Vel couldn't stand his middle-aged horndog schtick.

"Good thing, Charlie. You don't want to catch what she's got."

"Don't you have fifty cases to go to, Jerry?"

"The master of space and time." He whistled another tune as a parting shot at Vel. "I Can't Get No Satisfaction."

Charlie had long ago noticed how he and his fellow worker's comp lawyers all had their game faces on the minute they walked into the hearing rooms. Kaukonen always played the reprobate. Charlie could feel his own pose creep up on him, the sleepy-eyed, silken charmer in tennis whites, baiting his opponent, waiting for the moment to pounce and drive home the best possible settlement.

His friend Elena Velasquez's working vogue was the prim Catholic girl armored with intellectual disdain, ruthlessly freezing claimant lawyers out of any easy deal making, forcing them to play on her own severe terms and lose. It was a successful enough facade that it had taken Charlie six months to get

6

past it and discover a mischievous, arrogant, yet thoroughly enjoyable personality.

"I got nabbed by a lien claimant. Right in the cafeteria over my bagel." Vel gestured towards a tall woman in a boxy plaid skirt. "The one that looks like a Scotch tape dispenser."

"What's the lien about?"

"Psych claim. She's got a serious Del Rio problem, though." Vel irritably skimmed the pages of her file. "Her boss, a psychiatrist, submitted a bill for treatment of Delores Jackson for depression. However Ms. Jackson did not claim she got clinically depressed on the job" - Vel's finger jabbed down on the notice - "until five months *after* this psychiatrist treated her."

"Not too clever."

"We set up a meeting with Judge Gelman. I should be able to send her packing about two minutes. It's a nuisance, though. I think the claim went back to file."

Annoyance came off Vel in waves. The shitwork of a defense lawyer's day was ridding potential settlements of encumbrances, getting frivolous or fraudulent lien claims from doctors and shrinks dismissed - and it was much worse when you had to go dig out the records from the file room. The County, always on the lookout for cheap labor, hired their file clerks out of a pool of petty criminals doing community service. Charlie had often gotten sullen glares from these shoplifters and barfighters turned civil servants, as they retreated into the back rooms to sluggishly comb through the files.

"I've got three M.S.C.'s today, and then I've got to go down to San Diego for my cousin's wedding. I didn't need this, Charles."

Vel was one of the only people he knew who called him by his full name. Charlie had long ago gotten used to being called almost anything. His name was that kind of all-things-to-all-people name. To his dad, "Charles" or "Chuck" sounded friendly, solid and bankerish, to his mother "Charlie" or "Chazz" sounded cool and jazzy. Still, it felt weird when Vel addressed him by his formal name, although Vel explained that was because she was used to the Spanish name, Carlos. A regal name, she told him - he should be proud.

"How's your day shaping up, Charles?"

7

"I've got one M.S.C., which I'm looking forward to, actually – I've got a bit of a surprise lined up, should be kind of fun." His eyes fell to the huge load of files. "And then on this Sheila Reed case a last gasp offer in chambers."

"Who's the claimant attorney?"

Charlie made a face that was the equivalent of a groan. "Worcek. You better believe she's going to shoot my offer down."

"You mean 'shout it down.' Always 'j'accuse' with her. You're heading for a trial, Charles."

"Yeah. Lucky me." Talking with Vel he found that sometimes the macho posturing that was part of the routine slipped away. "Hobart-Riis expects me to get a 'take-nothing'."

Her ironical smile and little intake of breath mirrored his own. "On a disputed case that goes back five years? That's too bad."

"Well, I am defending the Bernard-Duvall Clinic. The doctors we send workers to to prove they're not really injured. Our boys."

"Well," she sighed, "whatever you do - do it smartly."

She spiraled her fingers in a little wave, and headed off. Charlie watched Vel for a moment, her unruffled, plumbline posture as she confronted the fidgety lienclaimant, and as he left the courtyard, he could see Vel leading her away like a teacher about to give a pupil a difficult scolding.

"Can you believe this bullshit? My client can't grip a pencil, and Mr. Solomon over here says 'only 7% disability rating.' Seven percent!"

Charlie grinned as he busied himself with his papers, and replied "Bob, you're the only claimant lawyer I know who would try to sell an arthritic client as a fresh industrial injury. I'm impressed."

"You should be, you little pischer. Actually, you should get arthritis. You wouldn't speak so lightly."

Waiting for his M.S.C. to begin, Charlie got a kick out of Bob Barasch's fulminations. Barasch was a claimant attorney with a caseload of about six hundred clients, and enough compassion for every one of them. There was nothing in a worker's comp judge's hearing room to pump one's blood. There was only a conference table worn to grimy dullness by a million tweed forearms, the elevated desk where the judge sat, and behind his rivet-studded

8

leather chair, a California flag with the golden bear drooping to the ground. A hearing room was a haggleground rather than a battleground. To walk in with the daily load of files would be depressing if there weren't a few adversaries there to prick you to a sense of readiness. Meeting Barasch, the old crusader in his seersucker shirt and blazer scuffed at the elbows, was better than a shot of coffee.

"Remar, do me a favor," Barasch shouted. "Go into this m.s.c. and humiliate Charlie for me."

Dave Remar tossed off a sour grin. He was a late-thirtyish claimant attorney with close-cropped, bright reddish hair that contrasted oddly with his pinched, grave expression. Remar always seemed to have his gaze locked into his files, as if the people surrounding his paperwork were merely bookends.

Charlie turned away from Barasch and Remar, trying to spot the blondish man with the goatee that had been described to him, or the black ex-football player. He hadn't yet heard from either of them on his cell. Had his secretary managed to impress on them the importance of meeting Charlie here today? He was sure his secretary had provided and green-tagged all the evidence he needed to discredit Remar's client. But if those two guys didn't show up, Remar could still jimmy some real damages out of him.

"Good morning, barristers!"

A tremor of alertness went through the hearing room as Judge Pleskow appeared, striding through a volley of "morning your honor"s towards his chambers. As always, the little old martinet shut his frosted glass door just long enough to unpack his valise, and a few lawyers unused to his routine milled around the closed door, hoping that would gain them early entrance. Then Pleskow opened the door just a crack and barked "Ruiz vee Ishler's Carpets!"

Charlie and Remar headed for Pleskow's chambers.

"Look, Dave," Charlie asserted, "not only did Ruiz fall behind on his deliveries, not only did he get fired, but then there's the small matter of his previous auto injury in '78." Charlie laid out the forms generated by Hobart-Riis Insurance's staff. Like snails leaving accretions of slime behind them, no claimant could navigate the health system of California without depositing a track of medical reports and health insurance claims. Charlie could simply link up to the insurance firms' massive "Index" on computer and discover that in 1992, Enrico Ruiz, taking a load of carpets from Bellflower to City of Industry in a Dodge pickup, injured his rotator cuff in a $2000 accident.

"Your honor," protested Remar, "that was a shoulder injury. This is a back injury."

"No, Dave, there was lower back damage in that previous accident as well. Which now suddenly and mysteriously recurs in a brand-new slip and fall injury."

"Hobart-Riis accepted the claim, Charlie."

That was true. Some lazy examiner didn't "deny timely" on the injury, creating Remar's whole case.

"So far, gentlemen, you're both right." Pleskow's epiglottal buzzsaw cut through their argument. "You got a pitcher's duel going. No hits, no runs - we're all bored." Pleskow mulled over the file. A cloying odor of peppermint tea from the judge's PGA Golf Classic cup permeated the room. "I see that, regarding the disability rating....uh-huh, uh-huh....the Agreed Medical Examiner for both sides issued an opinion on the impairment scale of slight to moderate."

"Exactly," answered Remar. "The guy's really injured. There's a lot more to this case than depressive disorder."

Charlie's senses sharpened as they homed in on the question of the injured worker's disability rating. At the point doctors declared a claimant's condition "permanent and stationary" or "p. & s.'d" - stabilized for better or worse - the claimant would seek a rating of 10%, 20%, or, in more gruesome cases, 50% disability. The higher the rating, the higher the monthly stipend or overall cash award if the applicant won the case. That's when Charlie's real work kicked in: a hunt for the truth. Who was closer to correctly rating the claimant's condition, the claimant's doctor or the insurance company's doctor? How much of the injury was due to an industrial accident on the job, and how much due to all the slings and arrows of outrageous fortune that had struck the claimant before that accident?

"Dave," Charlie jumped in, "maybe the AME gave you an opening on the injury, but the records will kill you. Then there's the credibility issue."

"So he worked at a hotel for a year and stole some silverware."

"A tablecloth." Pleskow leaned over the table like some brooding Old Testament prophet, and nailed Remar with a reproachful glare. "I know what my wife would think about someone who purloined a fine linen tablecloth."

Charlie couldn't believe how incensed Pleskow was. The old man seemed to hold linen theft on a par with sodomy. "He did 240 hours of community service for it," Remar spluttered. "And may I remind you, your Honor, he's gone back to work for another company?"

"Why not?" Charlie replied. "It's not as if he was - *injured* or anything."

"Thank you, Mr. Solomon. You know, much as you'd like to apportion Ruiz' injury to a previous accident and save Hobart-Riis Insurance some spare change, the medical records show a fairly complete recovery from that injury. And the hospital records of the new injury show some restricted hip flexion."

Now it was Remar's turn to let slip a malicious smile. Charlie felt the conference slither through his grasp - damn, this pompous altecocker judge loved to fuck with lawyers' heads. He masked his annoyance as the judge continued. "Mr. Solomon, I'll grant you that the prior injury dictates a partial apportionment of the claim. Mr. Ruiz isn't going to win the lottery here. But I'd still like to wrap this thing up with a lump sum, if we can agree on a rating, take this case out of the traffic jam and park it. You ready to put an offer on the table?"

"I can't put a dime on the table, your honor. His client steals tablecloths."

Pleskow slid down in his chair with a throaty cackle that lasted long enough for Charlie to be pleased with himself. In a flash he had turned the conference around. With the judge briefly in his corner, it was the right moment for him to rise from his seat. Remar instantly rankled at his move. "Come on, Charlie. You're not going to the phones? Your Honor, he told me he had authority to settle -"

"Nature calls, Your Honor. Be right back." It wasn't much of a line, but at least it slipped him out the door where he could scan the hearing room crowd for a blonde man with a goatee or a solidly built black ex-football player. Nada. No calls on the cell either. What the hell had happened to them? He hustled out into the hallway, and tried to pick out faces in the hastily conferencing and cell-phoning throng – and found a solidly built black man checking the numbers on the hearing rooms with the air of a harried latecomer. He fit the description. The guy turned his back, headed for the exit.

Charlie ran up to the man and introduced himself at top-speed – the man turned out to be a lawyer named Arliss Jefferson, just who Charlie was looking for. Charlie steered him quickly through the hearing room and into the Judge's chambers. Pleskow squinted up at him.

"To what do I owe the honor of this visit?"

"Arliss Jefferson, Your Honor, from State Comp. I got a call directing me to a conference regarding Enrico Ruiz? He filed a claim with us for shoulder and back injuries last year."

Remar's usual sluggishness vanished in an instant as he leaped up and glared at Charlie. "What kind of stunt is this?"

Charlie was about to coin a reply when there was a knock on the glass door. "Y-e-s-s?" drawled Pleskow, and a blonde man with a goatee strode into the room.

"Don Showalter."

Oh this was good, Charlie thought, this was primo.

"You're here on the Ruiz case?"

"That's right."

"Let me guess. Left shoulder and back."

"He's had a claim with us since 1995."

Pleskow sank back in his chair, flexing his tented fingers as he savored the little brouhaha in front of him. Remar, to his credit, appeared unruffled, almost amused. "I assume Ruiz had a truck accident in the course of his employment?"

"Oh yeah," Showalter winked. "His brother did the bodywork on the truck and he swears to it."

Pleskow turned to Remar. "Maybe your client better stick to driving a truck. Because his shot at screwing the worker's comp system just went down in flames."

Back in the courtyard, Charlie watched Remar trudge across the atrium for an iced tea, purposefully striding past the claimants still marking time on the benches. Charlie had been gracious in victory, and Remar had conceded without rancor; after all, Ruiz had "a checkered job history, and holes in his memory you could drive his fucking truck through." Remar didn't exactly have much zest for the cause of his workers. Secretly, Charlie guessed, Remar hankered for the cleaner world of defense law that Charlie inhabited. Half the caseload and a well-ordered Century City command post where a lawyer's intellect and a few insurance company computers could search and destroy waste and fraud. But Remar's father had built up a thriving practice as a claimant attorney, and he had acquiesced to the guaranteed work. He was probably more bothered by the shouting matches that loomed with his client and his father than anything else.

The glare off the stucco walls abraded Charlie's eyes half-shut. This was the hour when the wait for the claimants on the benches hardened to a grim stupor that dulled their interest in their magazines, their Walkmen, everything but just getting through the day. If Enrico Ruiz was somewhere in that crowd fuming as he awaited the outcome of his case - was he that muscular potbellied claimant in the ochre-and-brown silk shirt? – it wouldn't be surprising that Remar would head right past him, putting off his client's inevitable wrath.

Screw Ruiz, thought Charlie, he was another lowlife whose scam Charlie had exposed with style. He strode back cheerfully to the hearing room to fetch his carryall, past lawyers who paced the waiting area sounding for clients - "Spradling? S-p-r-a-d-l-i-n-g?" – past slivers of scuttlebutt, murmured promises and trade-offs, claimant lawyers dispensing advice - " Take a card from every doctor you see. Engrave his questions in your head."- this was the yeast Charlie swam in every day, and he was no shuffling malcontent like Remar, he honestly enjoyed the whole fucking show. The show would no doubt be gossiping about his little coup this afternoon. He'd get a few pats on the back, maybe even impress Vel.

He slipped into the cafeteria for an iced tea and a tuna sandwich, and gave himself a half-hour to psyche up. Despite the heat of the day, he literally hadn't broken a sweat all morning. His hair remained in its usual lightly moussed waves, with one casual forelock dangling over his forehead. His attire was perfect. Judge Merrill was straight whitebread Valley, Panorama City and church on Sundays, so Charlie had chosen a plain white shirt, a burgundy fleurde-lis tie with a clasp, and the Gieves and Hawkes suit, gray with chalk-blue stripes. Everything was in place, clarity reigned, and Charlie, reviewing a few memos in his Palm Pilot, called up "Get Dana b-day perfume."

He flashed back to the morning, his car scuttling along the freeway with thousands the others. The descent towards the Valley had begun, a plain of tract housing that leveled off into a veil of blue and ochre smog. Charlie had crawled past an RTD bus and seen the perfume ad. Dana's birthday was in a week - he was notoriously weak on remembering birthdays – so he figured he'd quickly get her that bottle of perfume. Today. Effective advertising. He remembered the rest of the poster - the couple in three photos toggling his eye back to the golden vial. Nice design.

The couple falling into each other...locked in a black-and-white serial embrace...

He felt restored and ready for whatever the afternoon would bring. He dragged his carryall back into the waiting room, heading towards Hearing Room Number 5, where the main event of the day awaited him. He conjured up an image of Dana in her silk kimono, grinning lustfully, ready to show her gratitude at his birthday gift - and he saw another blonde woman, dirty blonde, tall – was that the defendant? Was that Sheila Reed?

He yanked the carrier towards the woman, and there was a creak of aluminum deformed beyond endurance, a sharp metallic ping, and the case files slithered to the floor. Pleated manila portfolios and legal folders, slippery inside and out, tobogganed over each other to fan out across the hall. They gaped open and discharged batches of loose notices at the feet of the bored, angry claimants packed into the waiting room.

Charlie shuddered as howls of glee in Spanish, chortles in Farsi and Russian, and straight all-American snickering erupted through the room. No help for it - Charlie crouched down, not quite willing to kneel, and duck-walked through the sprawl of the Sheila Reed case as he gathered up the folders as best he could. He piled a few on the spindly metal carryall, which clanged in sections to his feet and spilled them back on the floor again.

Now Charlie was sweating with embarrassment. He began to heave the files over to the nearby hearing room. "What's the matter, Esquire, some poor-ass sick sonuvabitch giving you all this work?" Great, someone knew he was

14

a defense lawyer and this was getting ludicrous. He crouched down and swept a trail of paper quickly back into his folder, and as he did he stared up at the boots and plumber's overalls of a huge black man, who, with a taunting grin, held over Charlie's head two square gray plastic cases.

There was a chorus of cackles at the sight of the cases, and at the black guy holding them over Charlie like bait. Everyone in the waiting room knew what those boxes contained. They knew that video investigations might be waiting for them at their hearing, proof on tape of the golf games a worker sneaks in with crippled wrists, the tennis played on knees allegedly damaged on the job. How could Charlie get his videos away from this behemoth, an instant hero to the crowd just for dangling them out of Charlie's reach? No way he could go to the trial without them. His thoughts swarmed in a flurry of exasperation, then congealed into phrases he might use to extract his videos. Nothing clever or witty came to mind, no, he would have to beg for his evidence before a crowd of horse-laughing claimants - but just then the black guy shrugged and handed the videos back to Charlie. Just like that.

Charlie nodded - he couldn't quite bring out a "thank you" - and slunk the videos into Hearing Room 5.

"Your Honor, that's what Mr. Solomon and Hobart-Riis Insurance are offering my client after five years? Five years? A thousand dollars, and have a good life?"

Elizabeth Worcek stood frowning over the conference table, a tall, zaftig woman with a slightly drooping peasant's face, shaggy raven-black hair streaked with gray, and canny eyes that knew how to mantle themselves in furious self-righteousness in an instant.

Officially this was a trial date, Reed vs. the Bernard/Duvall Health and Wellness Clinic. But there was still room for one more pretrial conference, one last chance to avoid the labor pains of a trial and induce a settlement. Charlie had promptly, blandly and reasonably proposed to Worcek a Compromise and Release based on paying Sheila Reed's travel expenses to and from her doctors and settling out the stress claim for a total of $1000.

Charlie knew he was pushing from the baseline to the opponent's backhand. If your opponent's any good she knows she's being set up. But keep pushing and her shoulders will loosen, her confidence imperceptibly surge, she'll see her chance, try to ram your shots back down your throat - and when she's over-committed and off-balance (and no one over-committed like Worcek) you rush net, punch in the half-court volley, and nail her. Charlie knew what his bosses wanted. He had proposed this settlement knowing full well Worcek wouldn't accept it, and knowing it now wouldn't take much now to goad Worcek into totally losing it, especially given the devastating piece of evidence Charlie had submitted two weeks ago.

"I can tell you right now my client is not moving off her stand on continuous trauma!"

"Sort of continuous, Liz. There is this one small break in the action."

Worcek's skin darkened. "You mean this spurious garbage about my client's so-called affair with Dr. Sandoval?"

"That 'garbage' is in Dr. Sandoval's depo. Under oath." Questioning two of Sheila Reed's fellow workers, Charlie had learned they too felt the stress of reporting to a high-turnover, rapidly expanding clinic. They also shared a keen resentment of "how Sheila got Sandoval off her back by getting him between her knees." Charlie had deposed Dr. Sandoval, a truly unctuous, devious schmuck, and had gotten lucky when Sandoval finalized his divorce and had no reason to perjure himself. Charlie had actually nabbed the whole truth about his night with Sheila Reed and nothing but.

He decided to push Worcek a little harder.

"Liz, if you need a delay to respond -"

"Charlie, this is such a transparent attempt to back me into a corner. Your Honor, my client can't take another delay. Her physical and psychological disorders make her life a living hell!"

Judge Merrill looked dryly at Worcek. "If that's the case, then why won't your client consider a settlement?"

"Not under these circumstances. For Mr. Solomon to bully us this way is virtually extortion!"

"Yes, and my son's new videogame is virtually a Stealth bomber cockpit. It's a legitimate issue, Counselor. If harassment at work is the linchpin of your psych claim, that claim rests on shaky ground if Ms. Reed was having consensual sex with her harasser."

16

"She was coerced, your honor. Harassment at work merely continued in the bedroom."

"Liz, you're saying the sex itself was injury 'arising out of or in the course of her employment?'" Charlie shook his head. "'AOE – COE' isn't gonna work here, Liz - unless your client was really in a totally different profession."

"That's enough." Merrill voiced her warning at Charlie, but aimed it at Worcek as well. "At the very least, Ms. Worcek, this throws into question your client's credibility and morality."

Charlie knew he'd scored a point without trying too hard. Poor Sheila Reed was losing without having even set foot in the hearing room. Here was the real contest: the give-and-take between people who had to deal with each other every day. Judge's schedules traded off against defense counsels' need to tighten files. Defense counsels' demand to get fines dismissed set against applicant lawyers' impending vacations. Somewhere in that grid of bargains and demands the worker's case, like a fleck of gold caught in dirty runoff, hit the mesh and bounced whichever way these conferences deflected it.

Worcek backtracked. "All I'm saying, your honor, is that stress is stress, harassment is harassment, and a psych injury is a psych injury. Not to mention the gastrointestinal complications. Not to mention my client's 132A claim for harassment after filing a worker's compensation claim. Defense counsel's sandbagging us? Fine. We're not backing off our stand."

Judge Merrill allowed herself a smile, which evoked an answering grin from Charlie.

"Come on, Ms. Worcek. I don't see Mr. Solomon all bent out of shape about your eleventh-hour tactics."

Charlie thought the judge was giving Worcek a little too much credit there. Effective last minute grandstanding, but not enough to break Charlie's stride.

"Maybe Charlie just figures it's a quid pro quo."

Charlie felt an unpleasant tingle, like a cold patch of alcohol vaporizing on the back of his neck. He knew he'd missed something. "Liz, what exactly are we talking about here?"

"You have reviewed Dr. Chesley's depo?"

Charlie took a wild stab at recognition. "Umm... Chesley...the primary care physician at the clinic..."

Worcek leaned forward, like a conductor inviting her woodwinds to sing more sweetly. "You have reviewed his testimony? That my client was so burned out she desperately needed time off, which the Clinic refused to give her?"

"I - I - Christ, Liz, talk about playing hide-the-ball! I was never served this document!"

"The file reflects a letter of transmittal," Merrill replied.

"Yes," chimed in Worcek, "and I kept a double letter to protect myself."

Charlie's mind raced through the scenario that had just ambushed him. Chesley - staff gatekeeper at Bernard/Duvall Clinic - Sheila saw him before she filed for stress. If she'd told Dr. Chesley she was severely stressed out, that was the same as telling her bosses. If they refused her time off and kept stressing her out, aggravating her psych injury – damn it, he'd thought the Clinic had relinquished control of Sheila's care at the outset! He'd never expected that some doctor on the staff might see Sheila on his own. Was she screwing him too? - come on, that was bogus - no, what was really, deeply bogus was that a whole report had slipped through the cracks! Maybe it was lost when Charlie inherited the case. Or when a secretary was fired and dumped it. What the fuck did it matter? The sheer mass of paperwork vomited by the system was impossible for any firm to channel efficiently.

This was one of those moments when his whole career degenerated to a spot in a casino, a turn at the roulette wheel, and this time the number had come up one lost report from one Dr. Chesley that could validate Sheila Reed's claim against her employer and sink his whole case.

Worcek was grinning, and Charlie knew why. He couldn't accede to a higher settlement now without looking like a total idiot - and also facing a potential cascade of penalties. Not paying Sheila's temporary total disability for related physical and psychological injuries for five years could mean a fat ten-percent retroactive penalty against Hobart-Riis Insurance right there. And any more significant settlement would have to factor in medical costs, above all the dreaded "future medical" - Hobart-Riis might be on the hook for Sheila's medical treatment for the rest of her life! The company had trusted Charlie to erase this smudge of a case, which was suddenly growing into a black hole that could suck hundreds of thousands of -

"Well, folks," Merrill waspishly interjected, "you're both facing this trial with certain risks."

Charlie realized a delay wouldn't help him here. What Charlie would later remember about his state of mind at this point was his absolute certainty that he had to fight this out. He couldn't look bad before Shackleton and the examiners by drag-assing back to the office and saying he'd have to settle because his staff had lost a key file. Sheila Reed and Worcek were suing Bernard-Duvall, Hobart-Riis Insurance's main defense clinic, where his bosses sent workers to to have their claims disproved. The Clinic was practically a part of the Hobart-Riis family.

Besides, Charlie reflected, calming himself, wasn't Sheila Reed's claim of extreme stress refutable based on the cunning and resilience she demonstrated in the affair with Dr. Sandoval? Carve the argument from that. "Continuous trauma" – that old bullshit that a client's everyday stress on the job could somehow amount to never-ending injury – couldn't he shoot that down? Charlie was at the height of his game. He could nail it. Besides, look at all those Sheila Reed records sitting there - did he really want to schlep all those miserable heaps of paper back another day? It was the broken carrier, Charlie would later remember, that locked him into the trial.

The volleyball champ had been worn down to a nub of herself, but there was still a tautness about her. Sheila Reed could probably could still muster enough energy to exercise like a prisoner. Poverty and desperation had left its mark: lipstick a little too paltry and red, catalog plaid shirt, torn jeans. Her nails were long, more like talons. An exception to the shabbiness was the leather purse that lay along her thigh like a big cat, soft and well-oiled, embroidered with purple and gold batik designs. Sheila had spent some time in Asia, and no doubt the purse was a souvenir of that pilgrimage.

She sat calmly and barely flicked a glance Charlie's way. Sheila had seen her share of lawyers. In the tremor of intent that followed her averted gaze, like the echo of a slammed door, Charlie felt the chill of her obsession and a twinge of sympathy for her. He'd known a few people who had, at some irrational moment, confused a deal with a quest. To lose all detachment, to take your eye off where the ball was really going, was terribly unwise.

Maybe Sheila should've learned that on a golden hill in India. It was Charlie's job to teach her that lesson today.

Judge Merrill, in one brisk motion, took her seat and called the court into session. Below her the court reporter's fingers began to flutter over the keys of the squat little steno machine like gears whirring on a clock. Merrill moved swiftly through her printed trial sheet with Charlie and Worcek stipulating to all the medical reports they would admit. Sheila leaned back with that ingenuous ease of repose true athletes had, but she listened anxiously as the judge rehashed the issues of her case. The main issue was compensability. Was Sheila really injured in the course of her employment? Was it up to the clinic and their insurance carrier to pay to restore her health? Did she have any rights in "the System" at all?

Worcek began her direct examination by briefly painting a picture of a woman who rose above poverty and parental neglect to win an athletic scholarship to U.C. Irvine. When a promising career as a legal secretary was cut short in the recession of the early '90's, Sheila became an office manager, landing a position at the prosperous Bernard/Duvall Clinic. She immediately consolidated ordering procedures for medical supplies, cut expenses by about 15%, and brought in a friend to implement new accounts payable software which improved billing by about five thousand dollars a month. Her initial evaluations were thoroughly positive. Sheila and her husband moved forward in their purchase of a home.

"Sheila, how long had you been employed when Dr. Andre Sandoval arrived at the clinic?"

"About six months."

Dr. Sandoval came on to manage the clinic's period of growth, and also serve as risk manager, dealing with the worker's comp carrier, Hobart-Riis Insurance. Sheila began reporting to him. Relations were cordial at first, but then came nagging criticisms of her performance. Files went missing.

"What course of action did you take?"

"I reported the missing files to my boss, Dr. Bernard. He told me it was a routine housecleaning Dr. Sandoval had undertaken, don't worry about it. Later I found out that Dr. Sandoval was blaming me for the missing files."

"And that's when the headaches and dizziness started?"

"Yeah, that's when the stress really kicked in."

"Was Dr. Sandoval's conduct a factor in your experience of that stress?"

She threw back her head and laughed. When Sheila had first asked Sandoval to sign a performance review to render her eligible for a pay increase, Sandoval had refused. He'd responded with words to the effect that the two of them should be "jointly compensated" for the office's enhanced performance. Charlie winced as Worcek let the implication hang that Sandoval was pressuring his poor office manager for a kickback. The man's name was definitely beginning to grind on Charlie.

"When did you first suspect Dr. Sandoval was going beyond harassment and trying to force you out?"

Charlie shot a glance up at the judge. "I'll have to object, Your Honor. Leading the witness, calls for speculation."

"Could you please rephrase your question, Counselor?" Merrill coolly asked.

"How did Dr. Sandoval behave when you first questioned his treatment of you?"

"He indicated it might be wise to start seeking another position."

Numerous petty harassments followed. Sheila's office was moved twice, and she had to move all her files herself. She was given the office's slowest, most temperamental computer, and when it broke down, she had no personal computer access to office records for a week. It was at that time that a truly alarming amount of patient files were misplaced during the office expansion. Dr. Sandoval stormed through the office yelling that he would hold Sheila responsible for the missing files.

"At that point I figured he was just moving the files around and hiding them while the offices were being rebuilt so he could blame me for it. I just couldn't take it anymore. I filed the DWC form claiming a worker's comp injury and decided to go through the system."

Dr. Sandoval did not relent. The man would charge into her office screaming abuse at her full blast, calling her a bumbler and a liar and a stupid cow. His abuse and harassment reached the point where Sheila figured he was snorting coke. After a day when he hurled a clipboard across the room Sheila demanded another employee be present at all their conversations. She tried complaining to Dr. Bernard, who glacially told her to work things out with Dr. Sandoval.

"Sheila - and I have to ask you this - if relations between Dr. Sandoval and yourself had deteriorated to this point - how could you have an affair with him?"

Sheila hugged her purse a little closer. "The man wasn't without charm. He would blow up - then ask for forgiveness afterwards. He would buy me drinks, and when he-well, showed an obvious interest - maybe I got into some kind of Stockholm syndrome. You know, falling at my captor's feet at the slightest kindness. Anyway, one night he walked me home - I lived right near the clinic - my husband was away, and I let him inside."

"How do you feel about that affair now?"

Like a struck tuning fork, she vibrated with an inner chill. "I can only explain it as a perverse reaction to the stress."

Charlie watched her as her momentary paralysis broke; her fingers splayed against each other in discordant patterns. Her halting voice only regained its cadence when Worcek guided her back to describing her medical treatment. The routinely commiserative staff psychologist had "washed her out" after three sessions. It was soon after that she came down with serious stomach problems.

"And what was the course of treatment?"

"I was sent to Dr. Marcus, who's on staff at the clinic. He prescribed a standard gastritis drug and a mild tranquilizer."

"Since Dr. Marcus treated you, what has been the state of your health?"

"Constant stomach pain and bowel disorders."

"How has Dr. Marcus responded?"

"He won't follow up now that I've sued. He cites 'conflict of interest'. Besides, he's rendered all the treatment he can justify to the bean-counters. My ticket's been punched."

"What's your current course of treatment?"

"Herbal teas from practitioners of traditional Oriental and Ayurvedic medicine. I get those from a friend. Also Tums and borrowed Tagamet. Vomiting sometimes helps."

That technique had come into play when Sheila and Dr. Sandoval had their final confrontation. This time patient files were missing from the computers themselves after a routine backup procedure and Sandoval accused Sheila of destroying them. Sandoval had learned that Dr. Chesley had recommended time off for her and that Dr. Bernard had refused her a vacation. With Sheila's nerves worn to the breaking point, Sandoval knew he had a shot at getting rid of her at last. When Sheila offered to immediately execute a LAN search-and-undelete procedure to retrieve the contents of the files, Sandoval screamed that this "stupid whore" would pay for her act of sabotage. Sheila was unclear about what happened next, except that it took three of her fellow workers to restrain her from repeating her game-winning corner spike against USC on his balding head. Weeping on the clenched forearms of her friends, she was racked with cramps whose bilious load she directed straight onto Sandoval's three-hundred-dollar cordovan ostrich-skin shoes. Her friend Theresa Calder drove her home. It was the last time she reported to work at the clinic.

Sheila duly filed a 132A claim charging that Sandoval had harassed her after she'd filed her worker's compensation claim. The Bernard/Duvall Clinic responded that Sheila had walked off the job. Finally Hobart-Riis, as worker's comp insurance carrier, initiated discovery in Sheila's disputed case - a process that took two years. Hobart-Riis blamed Sheila for the delays, claiming she failed to respond to notices of deposition dates and medical appointments mailed to her home.

The reason was she was no longer there. Her marriage, crippled by her affair with Sandoval, did not weather the strain of three years of headaches, sleeplessness, depression, ulcers and steadily mounting rage. Bought out of her share of their house by her soon-to-be-ex-husband, unable to work, she lived two more years on her savings, then went on food stamps and welfare. She now lived in a ratty apartment on Las Palmas Avenue in Hollywood that she shared with her younger brother, Brandon. It was that gray and squalid image that

Worcek left hanging in Judge Merrill's thoughts as she turned the hearing over to Charlie.

Charlie had to concede that Worcek knew how to tell a story in direct - or maybe it was just Charlie hadn't realized what a putrid case this was. As a former defense counsel for Charlie's company had once told him, "Sometimes you should just fix 'em up and get 'em back to work." If someone had listened to Dr. Chesley four years ago and given Sheila Reed time off, maybe she and Dr. Sandoval would've averted the confrontation that had cost Sheila her health and could soon plunge a fiscal knife into the belly of Charlie Solomon's employer.

That's what Charlie had to think of now. Disarming the knife. Outside the square of glass of the conference room door, lawyers' grey faces blocked the view, lips framing the terms of arguments, offers, deals. Their words could not penetrate the quiet of the courtroom, now under Charlie's command, the treacherous dough on the potter's wheel of his cross-examination. He could mold it as he liked for the next hour, but one false move and it would harden into a botched creation that would humiliate and damage him for months. Think of Sheila Reed's indefensible psychology, he told himself, the cracks in her sorrowful façade. Think of your job.

He began gently, asking her if she wanted a brief rest, a glass of water. He appreciated that this process had been long and burdensome for her, and he would try and make his questions as brief as possible. Watching her closely, he saw the clench lines in her face, the streak of hair clinging to her temple. He preferred that to meeting her gaze. That was like trying to outstare a cat.

Charlie moved quickly to the question of the files. Did she ever find out why they were lost? No, she had not. "But I damn well know I didn't lose them."

Charlie let her have that point – his strategy was not to belabor the question of the files. Even Charlie's boss had felt nervous about the missing files, what he called "Sandoval's shenanigans" in the office. But Charlie was feeling confident, and couldn't resist one jab at Sheila. Wasn't tracking the files and computer records her responsibility? Yes. Did Sandoval ever recover some of those files? Yes. Then when he referred to "joint compensation," isn't it possible he was referring sarcastically to his completion of her job?

"Objection! Asked and answered."

"Sustained. Try another, Mr. Solomon."

"Might Dr. Sandoval's subsequent refusal to sign your performance review have been a 'pocket veto' objection to your job performance. After all, the records -"

"Objection! Calls for speculation."

"I'll allow her to answer."

" My belief is that it was harassment," Sheila calmly asserted, "and my perception of harassment is what matters to this court."

Charlie smarted from the well-aimed remark. It was true that a worker's perception of harassment was all that was needed to initiate a harassment and stress complaint. Charlie realized he'd botched that line of questioning - but Sheila had now opened a door he was eager to enter.

"Yes, I agree with you. Perceptions are important. Would you say your perception of your health was good when you first reported for work at the Bernard-Duvall Clinic?"

"Yes."

In fact, Sheila had filled out an application for group health insurance in which she claimed no pre-existing health conditions except "occasional menstrual cramps." But wasn't it also a fact that, in 1988, she'd suffered from severe gastritis that had required time off from work?

"Yes. I suppose," Sheila wearily replied.

"So wouldn't you say your stomach complaints were a pre-existing condition?"

"Objection!" Worcek shouted.

Charlie withdrew the question, but he was pleased to see Judge Merrill assiduously making notes. His job was to keep her pencil moving to the rhythm of Sheila's misperceptions.

"Why didn't you feel it necessary to inform the Clinic's health plan of the illness?"

"I thought it was a transient episode and I was fully recovered."

good

"I see. You have rather strong views about your health care. Is it true you experiment with Chinese herbs?"

"Chinese medicinal herbs, counselor. It's all I've got, and it's my body. Besides, I'm not sure you'd call a five-thousand-year-old medical tradition an experiment. You're a college grad, I could recommend some good books."

Charlie heard the venomous edge of that reply, and his anticipation quickened. She was starting to look like the sort of ornery, unreliable claimant he wanted the judge to see. In any tennis rally, there was a moment when the point shifted in your favor, and you could read it in an opponent's lunge for a well-placed shot, or grunt of anger in the slamming back of a return. Then hints of the moves you were yet to make would flicker along your nerves, beneath your skin, the afterimages of your own strategies. You were diagnosing their game, they were responding, and your pulse quickened with the intimacy of control.

"It's my body" - the self-righteous complaint of another cheat in the worker's comp game. It might be her body, but that body was now moving to the rhythm of Charlie's case.

It was sweat but not sweat....

Now it was time to puncture that self-righteousness of hers, to break her down the best way he knew how - with the inescapable truth of her own lies. He popped the video into the courtroom VCR.

The monitor glazed over with snowlines, then flashed onto a scene at a community garden. There was the "exhausted and depressed" Sheila Reed working like a coolie. She was spading up hard dirt, hauling shrubs in burlap bags. Sweat shone on her bare arms as she turned the earth, and lifted up her face to the sunshine with a grin.

As he watched the video, Charlie marveled at the crisp images and sound obtained by his private eye, Rody Golan. He'd heard Rody had quite an elaborate camera and mike setup in his van, and he made a mental note to check it out someday. Charlie let the video roll on for another two minutes, just long enough to show Sheila and her friends buoyantly chatting away as they helped themselves to quesadillas and camarones at a communal picnic table.

"That is you in the videos, Ms. Reed?"

"Oh, without doubt."

26

"For someone who's too clinically depressed and racked with bowel trouble to return to her usual and customary employment, you have a hearty appetite for food and work."

"You're right. I never should've eaten that good hearty Mexican grub. I forgot myself, and my ulcer flared up for two days. I will never do that again. As for the day in the garden, I was dead on my feet for a week after that, but I didn't care. There are times you just gotta risk getting out of your apartment, Counselor."

Judge Merrill's pencil was churning again. Sheila watched her movements with a bemused curiosity that shut Charlie completely out of her attention. That rubbed him the wrong way.

"Ms. Reed, when did you begin your affair with your supervisor, Dr. Andre Sandoval?"

"October 10, 1994. 7:30pm."

"Thank you for your attention to detail. You say that on that night he walked you to your house?"

"My husband and I had rented a place near the clinic while we were awaiting close of escrow on the home we'd planned to purchase."

"And where was your husband at the time?"

"He was a sales rep for Novell. He was out of the city most of the year."

"Why did you let Dr. Sandoval into the house?"

"He wanted to talk. He said maybe we could discuss problems at work in a more relaxed setting, make a fresh start."

"So he didn't force himself in."

"No, he did not."

"Did he force himself on you later?"

"He made his move. But no...he didn't force himself on me."

"So basically, this just happened, and you went with it?"

" I suppose," Sheila muttered.

"Ms. Reed, you initially testified in your deposition that due to your psychological injury you became unable to have sex with your husband. I believe your words were 'You're lucky if you even like yourself enough to masturbate.' Is that correct?"

27

"Mm-hmm." Her lips were pressed into her knuckle too tightly for her to speak. She lowered her hand. "Yes."

"Given your actions with Dr. Sandoval, how can we believe that previous testimony?"

Sheila smiled grimly. "If anything, my self-loathing increased during and after that encounter. It was an awful mistake."

"During that period of self-loathing, did you receive any further performance reviews?"

"Yes."

"Were they satisfactory?"

"For a brief period, somewhat more so."

"And did Dr. Sandoval sign them?"

She sadly exhaled her response. "Yes."

A ticklish residue of aggression danced inside him, and it flared up in his next question.

"So if you 'perceived' Dr. Sandoval was harassing you by asking for a kickback - didn't you ultimately end that 'harassment' by giving it to him?"

"Objection! This is character assassination!"

"Withdrawn, Your Honor. I'll ask it another way. How can you testify your supervisor was causing you psychological injury while at the same time you were welcoming him into your marital bed?"

"Objection!"

Sheila's eyes seemed to empty of every emotion except a dry appreciation of an unknown joke. She had nothing to say. Charlie felt the utter precision and correctness of the point he'd scored.

Game. Set. Match.

But of course you never walked off the court with a clean victory in worker's comp.

After the recess Worcek came back with a terrific re-direct. To emphasize that the defense could never have established Sheila's illness was pre-existing, or even denied that it existed, she ran through the series of routine tests the Bernard-Duvall Clinic had never performed: they didn't even take Sheila's blood pressure for thirty days after her stress claim. Worcek hammered home all the delaying tactics that Sheila had endured from Hobart-Riis Insurance, like the endless postponement of an appointment with Agreed Medical Examiners in both the psych and gastro injuries. Finally Worcek limned the cascade of physical and economic hardships brought about by Sheila Reed's case, torments that had reduced her from productive middle-class office manager to welfare dependent.

A hell of a performance. And Charlie could hear in the gravity of Judge Merrill's expressions, phrases like "pyramiding stress", the measured tones with which she uttered the predictable "take this under advisement", that the case was slipping away from him. Keep a dignified silence, he thought. The impression of mastery. Ask for a delay, get shot down, and you're dead. Besides, he was just over-anxious. Merrill would reflect on the gaps in Worcek's logic, Sheila Reed's pre-existing health problems, the affair with Sandoval - still, how could he get the take-nothing Shackleton expected from him? And any stip and award from the judge might open the door to all those penalties...

....*10% penalty on all those retroactive temporary total disability payments, vocational rehab, future medical...Hobart-Riis on the hook for Sheila Reed's medical bills for the rest of her life...*

"Your Honor? We respectfully request a delay in your decision."

Worcek just grinned. "Charlie, I expected a little better from you."

"Just why are you requesting this delay, Counselor?"

"Your honor, we need a neutral, expert opinion on whether Sheila Reed's behavior during the course of her affair with Sandoval was or was not an outcome of stress on the job."

Sheila's absolute calm shattered. "Oh Jesus what a slimebag! He the one who dredges that shit up, and now he's trying to get another shrink appointment out of it?"

"Hold your tongue, Ms. Reed!" the Judge shouted.

Worcek took a beat, then calmly rose to the moment. "Your Honor, my client is correct. Mr. Solomon is not entitled to another bite of the apple. We've had our mutually agreed upon medical review of the psych."

Merrill's eyes beetled in on Charlie's. "I agree. Court can only make its decision based on records already submitted."

"Court *can* only make its decision based *on records already submitted.*"
There was an opening there, a window, if he could only see where that shaft of light was coming from.

Sheila calmly shouldered her purse and Worcek gathered her evidence and placed it on her carrier. Charlie would have to drag his paperwork down for about five humiliating elevator trips, and none of it had been worth anything except the Chesley report he never received. Ten lousy pages.

Ten typewritten pages. *Evidence already submitted...*

"Your honor!" Charlie cried out, "I need to see Dr. Chesley's handwritten notes!"

Worcek looked up from her carrier in sheer bewilderment.

"I respectfully request a continuance to subpoena and review the notes Dr. Chesley took at Sheila Reed's interview."

Worcek strenuously objected, but Charlie hammered on, speaking as fast as he could. "With every other report we've received handwritten notes. Now I assume these typewritten pages are reasonably accurate and authentic, but did Dr. Chesley type them? His secretary? We don't know the circumstances under which they were prepared, and we have a right to the doctor's first impressions. Here we have a purely informal session with a doctor whose later report could have been slanted, based on his friendship with Ms. Reed, to show greater job-related stress than was warranted by the evidence."

"It was all job-related, you little bastard! Why the hell else would I be here?"

Charlie was about to reply when he saw how Judge Merrill stared down at Sheila Reed. The staunch Valley conservative glowered at the hysterical claimant and Charlie shut up. He knew.

"I'll grant defense counsel's request."

"Your Honor!" Worcek bellowed, "this is absolutely outrageous!"

Judge Merrill was unmoved. Worcek pleaded that her client faced eviction from her home in three weeks. Judge Merrill coolly responded that if Worcek submitted the notes expeditiously, she would calendar the case as quickly as possible.

"Your Honor, please..." Sheila's voice seemed to echo from the bottom of a ditch. "Another delay will destroy me. I just can't take it."

Merrill busied herself with her papers. "Court has ruled, Ms. Reed."

Charlie braced himself for the caterwauling, a "19th Nervous Breakdown" deluxe, but Sheila stood there in silent bewilderment, cradling her purse against her hip. Charlie turned away from her and found a welcome distraction in his papers. The hearing room, as it sometimes did, throbbed with a residue of shame.

Charlie decided that he would roundtable the Sheila Reed case with Shackleton again. Make him see the ludicrousness and the meanness of going for a "take-nothing." The Bernard/Duvall Clinic should never have dismissed Sheila's complaints. Charlie would calculate a reasonable settlement for Sheila Reed, and enter into good faith negotiations to fix Sheila Reed up and get her back to work.

"Liz," he whispered to Worcek, "we'll work this out. I'll get some numbers."

Worcek wasn't listening to him. She was staggering like a marionette tangled in her strings.

Charlie instinctively moved forward to help the attorney, but then stopped - Worcek's panic was directed at him, freezing him in his place, and when he turned to see Judge Merrill she was also warding him back with her stare. A triangle of revulsion. Puzzled, he advanced towards Worcek again, until Sheila Reed ordered him not to. The stiletto edge in her voice spun him around. He didn't register it at first - but then he made out the purse sagging like some broken cocoon, and the dumb gray tube of metal it had produced, barrel pointed right at him.

"Over there." The gun spoke. "The corner."

Sheila was maneuvering him to the wall past the door. Making sure he could not be seen from the vantagepoint of the little window. Past that thick pane of glass two lawyers paused for a quick chat, rapid-fire grins vanishing like smoke. Frantically Charlie's gaze sought out Worcek and Judge Merrill, but, guarding their own lives with unforgiving silence, they had banished him to the barrel of that gun and the woman trembling behind it.

"Sheila!" Worcek at last cried out. " Please, look at me, Sheila." Worcek was half-crouched behind the desk, one hand tremulously reaching over her transcripts towards her client. "We'd talked about the rage. Sheila, we'd talked about taking a step back from –"

"Nobody talks anymore or this bastard is dead! NO MORE TALKING!"

Sheila's feverish grin sent Charlie's heartbeat blasting through his skull. The wall, the pane of glass, Worcek's feeble gestures, the color of Sheila's clothes all drained into a fog. Only the gun barrel floated before him.

"Three times I have to come back because my trial 'doesn't have priority'! Then I finally get a trial and it's a waste of time! What are you gonna do now, offer me two thousand dollars? Two-thousand three-hundred dollars?"

Any moment now, Charlie kept thinking, any moment someone will come through the door and end this, any moment - but the moments stretched into an infinity, from which Sheila's voice at last issued again, gravely quiet.

"I was just trying to do my job."

"Yes...yes, of course." Charlie could barely force the reply out through the freezing lassitude that gummed up his thoughts.

"Those files getting lost - that was out of my control. He made sure they were lost!"

"No one's blaming you for - "

"DON'T TALK! LISTEN TO ME FOR ONCE! Can't you understand, you stupid, worthless shits? They destroyed me with their schemes and their fucking lies and now you have to DEAL WITH IT!" She clutched the gun harder.

"Ms. Reed, please, you're only getting in bad trouble, we can talk..." Charlie found his voice again, though it sounded like the babble of a child.

Sheila slowly advanced on Charlie. "You all tell me the system's long. Complicated. You have to play the game by the rules. 'Court has ruled.' Follow the rules. Rules, rules, rules, rules. I understand rules. I wanted to be a lawyer once, Mr. Solomon."

Charlie could tell by her voice that something had wavered and relented. If before she was hectoring, now she was beseeching him, pulling back the rage, creating a space where he could reach out and draw them both from this nightmare. He could see her face crumple, her arm begin to droop.

"Sheila, listen. Right now nothing's gone wrong." He walked towards her as the arm continued down. "I'm still hearing you, you're still talking, everything's okay. We can work things out."

He could move for the gun.

"There's no rules," she muttered. "Not at work, no, not that place, not in this court, not anywhere." She threw her head back to take in Worcek, Merrill, and the whole hearing room. "What rules? Who rules?"

When her head turned and the tension on the gun arm slackened to nothing, it was as if a rope wrenched Charlie forward to pounce on her forearm and get a purchase on her weapon. In almost that same instant he realized he'd made a terrible mistake. Sheila's grip welded itself to the gun, her arm became a lashing cable as a woman who had once been in top physical shape regained in an adrenaline-charged second all her muscular fury. Charlie tried to hang on to the gun arm as it hurled him against the wall. He quailed as he saw her other arm rise, the hand clench into a fist. He heard Merrill and Worcek scream for help as they crouched under tables like kids in some earthquake drill, but it was too late. With both his hands gripping Sheila's gun, all he could do was crunch his face down towards his chest as the fist smashed his temple and then his jaw. The taste of blood turned his legs hollow, he had no more strength than an infant as the hand came back and rammed his head against the wall. Only that wall now kept him on his feet, his grip on the gun no more than the clasp of a prayer.

But his grip held. The metal tore at his fingers as he blinked up at Sheila.

He could feel her scalding breath. It was just the two of them alone in the corner, the whole world reduced to the gun that would never stop pointing at him. A cloudiness numbed his senses in anticipation of the bullet, but then, like a pale gray shard of light off the edge of that cloud, came the realization that his grip was still there. She had not dislodged their embrace.

With an expression that was almost piteous, she smiled at him. He felt the metal slither beneath his hand, the pressure of her grip angle the gun away from him...

Charlie heard his own scream even as the blackness came down when he shut his eyes. He put up his free hand to try and ward it off, but he could not stop the blast that roared through his eardrums. His upraised fingers caught part of the hail of bone fragments but some cut into his face along with the hot splash of blood. The impact of the shot drove him to the floor.

Charlie's limbs jerked spastically as he clambered to his feet. He groped and stumbled along the wall until his shoes came down on something thick and pulpy. He looked down and saw it was a neck, a face that had sheared to the right and ceased to make any sense where eye socket puckered into a gray horn of - and Charlie ran from it. Ran until the table slammed into his gut and knocked the wind out of him - and he knew he was breathing.

He had to get away from those clotted eyes stamped into his. He ran past what seemed a statue of Judge Merrill, half-frozen lips muttering senselessly. He grabbed the door and flung himself out into the babble briefly silenced in his wake - there were gasps, screams, but he could barely hear them through the ingot of high-pitched sound rammed through his ears by the gunshot.

As he charged through the noise towards the claimant waiting room, the late afternoon sun intercepted him and he could see his shirtfront soaked in blood. Flecks of purple gelatin and quartzlike fragments were embedded in his Gieves and Hawkes suit. They clung to his face like gluey coral with an acid burn. A scream erupted all around Charlie, the crowd abandoning their seats to back away in a spill of near-collisions and panic. One lawyer dropped his cellphone and collapsed into his chair.

Charlie smashed through the doors into the sunlight, where the applicants held to their interminable wait on the benches. And now he could hear it, he was hit by the full-throated howl of people who'd seen babies born and auto crashes, who had rescued the fatally burned or shot or mangled, reacting to him with all the anguish and horror that the signs of death can inspire. Charlie stumbled, fell to his knees, and vomited. Even as the stench enveloped him, hands clutched his suit, lifted him to his feet. Charlie looked up at stern but solicitous eyes, the sun glinting ivory off a halo of gray-blonde hair. Judge Merrill now had a steadying hand on his shoulder. Her eyes confirmed something permanent and terrible had happened, but that he was stable and intact.

The judge and the guard led him to the bench. He told them his full name, Charlie Solomon, where he was, and what had happened. Of course he would agree to go to the hospital and be examined. He could walk to the ambulance. He even remembered to ask that someone transport his files to the office. The carrier had broke.

-2-

the gift that keeps on giving

The new key rocked against the grinding wheel and Brandon Reed bore down as hard with his gaze as with his grip.

He liked the sparks that buffing of the metal drew on the edge of the key. And he knew he had to keep alert. One day Brandon had been working at the key machine, and his thoughts had drifted to the photos he could take in Barcelona, where stone buildings rippled like cream in the sunlight, and just when a gorgeous Penelope Cruz-type model had thrust her hip forward at his command the key had shot from his fingers and turned into a missile that nearly hit a woman by "Gardening Tools." He'd almost lost his job that morning and he knew better than to slip into the kind of stupor that would take that risk again.

Brandon enjoyed working at D & D Hardware. He'd gone for a sales job at the Cyber Circus outlet on Pico Boulevard. He could've gotten the gig through a former classmate. But the salary sucked. Plus the commission structure looked pretty bogus once he figured how much time he'd have to spend trying to sell each customer. He'd either have to babystep them through the choices of CPU, monitor and software, using whatever knowledge he'd picked up from two lousy junior college classes, or he'd have to put up with endless shit from the other type of smartass who had so many parameters in mind for his system that he just wore you out.

D & D Hardware was better. Not that the salary was an improvement, but at least it wasn't tied to the "incentive factor" - sales managers always said when they meant either sell our shit or get paid shit. And Brandon found reassurance in the very atmosphere of a hardware store. Those pressboard surfaces nailed with racks of tools and fittings chilled people out, made people think of how wood, rubber, metal and ceramic were meant to fasten together and make sense. Customers browsed through displays of tiles, extruded aluminum, and weather-stripping with the silence of visitors at a museum.

Brandon ground the key to a hard shine and then handed it back to the customer, a mildly unshaven old Elmer Fudd guy in a lumberjack shirt.

"That'll do it."

"Thanks, son."

People often called Brandon that. There was something of the perpetually towheaded Little League kid about him. Of average height, but with slim, narrow shoulders and long limbs, Brandon had a shy loping gracefulness that intrigued the girls he met and disarmed the adults. In a city where even the most self-assured darted like chipmunks, Brandon sauntered at his own pace. And he'd figured out that's what his customers wanted. Be cool and you had a good chance of receiving cool back, with good humor and gratitude thrown in.

Too bad that strategy didn't work at home, where he had to counter pissed off panic every day. Things had been especially bad in the week leading up to the trial. Sheila had torn like a crazy woman through her closeted shoeboxes of notes, records and unpaid medical bills. Brandon had sprawled on the rug with his headphones on, while good old Smashing Pumpkins clanged out the screaming of his sister, loose and loud and endlessly aggrieved, as she tramped through the apartment looking for that one scrap of paper that would leave the motherfuckers in the dust.

As five o'clock rolled around, Brandon copied his last key, smoothly manipulating the lever that rocked old key and new in their twin vises. The guide knob's resistance to the teeth of the parent key shaped the teeth that the wheel notched into the new key. It occurred to Brandon that this was the same principle by which a fax machine worked, but in the hardware store that principle had a heft and a resistance that you could feel. There wasn't some force out there running all the machines that never answered to your control. Maybe that was why offices and courtrooms gave Brandon that sour twinge in his gut he felt when a car shot forward too fast and he wasn't driving.

Brandon's Hollywood street was just a couple of blocks from the bus stop; it began as an alley and curved behind the parking lots that bracketed the local t.v. studios near Las Palmas Avenue. The four-story walkups, with their faded yellow stucco walls and unrepaired masonry cracks from old earthquakes, looked as fragile as movie set facades. Brandon's building had a stoop and a canopy, which only heightened the artificial effect.

He often sat on the stoop lingering in the quiet of the street, so well hidden behind the lots that it was usually deserted. But once he trudged up the stairs to their second floor apartment, he was assaulted by the thumping of guitarron strings mixed with the bellow and screech of r'ai music and Ofra Hazi tunes - the slovenly anthems of the Mexicans, Lebanese and Israelis across the backyard. Brandon opened the door and froze at the sound of a rifle shot - no, it was just the Mexican kids stomping tin cans. He heard their squeals of delight followed by a mother's tongue-lashing in Spanish. At the window he watched the kids sprint around a backyard fortified by huge slabs of plywood, beneath a Japanese-looking tree with flowers like orange lather. The makeshift walls below were strung with clotheslines and backed with redwood trellises overgrown with geraniums. Brandon liked the way the Mexicans were so creative with junk. Maybe he could be friendly with them if it wasn't for the fucking noise.

He grabbed his old Nikon camera. Framed their frenetic can-stomping jamboree. Click.

Turning his back on the window, Brandon plumped into the rocking chair. There was zero special about the furniture that came with the apartment, all the same nubbly slack-cushioned burnt orange and dingy brown castoffs, but one of the pieces just happened to be a rocking chair and perfect for watching t.v. The old nineteen-inch JVC was perched on a lowboy shelving unit which contained everything Brandon had brought to the apartment except his clothes: his baseball glove, his box of tapes and Walkman, the Nikon, and a glossy book, "Barcelona 1992 – City of The Olympics." He slid the chair closer to the t.v. to make sense of its green-ghosted picture and turned on the local news.

There had been a shooting at some court in the Valley. The usual bunch of shocked bystanders described how a man bathed in blood had staggered past them. Then they cut to the front of the building, and shots of some slick dude in a suit that the newswoman described as still bloodstained, though Brandon couldn't make that out through the set's cruddy green haze. Now the sound started to pop like some audio blister, but Brandon could hear that this lawyer had tried to take the gun from the killer, who then apparently shot herself. What up with those fools, Brandon thought. The foxy little Japanese reporter signed off from the "Workers' Compensation Court in Van Nuys."

Brandon jumped up and reached for the set as if he could snatch back that face and ask it a question, but the anchorman had moved on to some anti-crime demonstration in Compton.

He suddenly had to jump out of his chair and run into the kitchen to pour himself a Coke. Whenever he'd thought of Sheila's case, he'd had an image of her and her lawyers flinging themselves at a wall of a building in downtown L.A. It seemed so useless that he expected Sheila any day to walk in and announce she'd found a job, or that she wanted them to move to another city. He thought he could hear it in her voice that she was finally getting the pointlessness of it all. Nothing will happen out of nothing. Come on, he thought, this was ridiculous. Still his heart was pounding and his throat was so dry he drank half the Coke in one swallow. She'd been at that court. She was late.

Then he saw the answering machine. Kourosh, the Iranian salesman on the fourth floor, had let Sheila have one of his surplus old Code-A-Phones for twenty bucks. The machine took the endless harassment calls from collection agencies while Sheila and Brandon gave the phone the finger. Now it had taken three messages. Brandon jabbed the playback button. The first two were almost identical. "This is Sergeant Tom Ridley of the Van Nuys precinct, calling Brandon Reed, with regard to his sister, Sheila Reed. Please call back the station at..."

Brandon's stomach lurched as if once again he was suddenly careening down an icy road, brain numbing - he'd been on the passenger side, seen the guardrail veering towards him - only this time there was no sudden catapult into unconsciousness. This time he was wide awake, living the infinite seconds of first grief when the day crumbles into a void.

He ran to the drawer. Flipped open Sheila's hardwood box from India. How much money? One hundred dollars, enough for three days. But were there tokens? He might have to travel somewhere. Identify the - no - that was an image from a morgue slab filtered through a green broken television, not Sheila - but where was the gun? He yanked open another drawer and dug under Sheila's blouses, trying to tell himself he'd forgotten where it was stashed, but that couldn't be. He knew where Sheila kept that gun - he'd taken it out once and practiced the upsweep of the flat of the hand that knocks the clip into place. He'd gotten it down to the quickness and sufficiency of a baseball motion, just in case he ever needed it and was alone.

Now that gun was gone.

The phone twittered again. A woman's voice, ragged with exhaustion. "Hello, this is the office of Worcek, Nadjari and Bellis, calling for Brandon Reed. I'm Elizabeth Worcek. I was your sister's attorney. We – I wanted you to know how terribly sorry I –"

He ran down the stairs to the stoop, his breath scraping at his chest. Sheila had always been there, a tall girl towering between him and the desert sun or a father's drunken rage. Now he looked up through nothing to a pearl-gray dove wing of a cloud in a shell of lavender dusk. He stared desperately at the beauty of it, the luminous thread back to the day, but he knew the truth in spite of all hope, and with soft infantile sobs he cried out to the purple twilight.

When the same uniformed officer that had led Charlie to the emergency room opened the exit door three hours later to the hospital parking lot, Charlie remembered the last time a cop had been so courteous to him. It had been the week his father's life was threatened.

Jonas Solomon had speculated heavily in Manhattan apartment buildings in the mid-'80's. His favorite tactic was flipping properties that had ground floor retail space. You bought the building, cut services to the bone, then jacked up the rent and common area maintenance expenses on the old storekeepers until you drove them out. Once you replaced them with retail tenants paying 30% higher rents you either refinanced the building for 10%

more to get your hands on the bank money, or resold the cash-richer building for a 40% profit.

No one could ever sue his dad because with every new building came a new partnership or corporation, in which Jonas Solomon was merely a "general partner" or even a "manager." In those heady years Jonas put in many Saturdays doing deals, and Charlie's mother would take him downtown in a cab to meet his dad for lunch. Charlie remembered how the receptionist would interchange five or six names depending on what infuriated tenant or tenant's lawyer was calling. "No, I'm sorry, you've reached 235th Street Apartments, Inc. 150 East 175th Corporation is not at this address...No, I've never heard of 980 Lexington Associates, you've reached Sutton Development Partners."

Then one blazing hot week in August his dad evicted an Irish bar owner who decided to forgo the usual legal wind-pissing. Years later his father would tell Charlie that the "shanty Irish prick" had sent him a box of freshly butchered meat with a note saying that next time Jonas or someone in his family would be in the package. The way his mother told the story, after too many vodka tonics, that box of meat, swarming with bluebottle flies, was decidedly at the post-digested stage. Whatever the box contained twelve-year-old Charlie was greeted that Saturday at the door of his dad's firm by a huge black uniformed cop, who ushered him into an office that buzzed with paranoid activity. Two private guards sat alertly on the Barcaloungers. A blonde well-scrubbed FBI agent was interviewing Jonas Solomon about the bar owner, whom the Bureau suspected was running guns for the Irish Republican Army. Jonas, Charlie's dad, a balding, moonfaced man with the prowling gaze and quick gestures of a card sharp, sat behind his big stone-topped desk facing his corner view of 57th Street and relished all the attention. Only in his hectoring tone laced with obscenities did his anxiety show through. " We don't have to worry about that fat fuck showing up here. These Irish traife, they love to talk shit about kick England's ass, kick the kike's ass. I mean, the truth is they're fucking conquered peasants and who the hell's fault is that? You know what he's really smuggling? Nannies! He's getting these poor shit-for-brains colleens to sneak over to America for bullshit nanny jobs and shtupping them in the back of his bar. Guns my ass...ah, my son and heir, come on in!" Almost as an afterthought he waved Charlie over to the desk and patted him on the shoulder.

41

"Little bit of excitement here today. Agent Bradley, my son Charlie…officer, please, no keys on the desk, it's obsidian. "

His dad escaped the IRA's wrath and continued to amass a small fortune, which he then moved, along with his family, to Los Angeles, buying a three-bedroom house for seven figures in the Venice canals. Charlie lost every friend he ever had, but he quickly fell in love with his new neighborhood. On drowsy summer Sundays he would take the family boat and row his girlfriends around the waterways, past Tudor homes, mock-Venetian palazzos, bamboo and banana-tree sheltered bungalows. The sunbeaten lawns and fences glowed with poppies, torch ginger and skirts of bougainvillea with the bright colors of parasols on rum drinks. As twilight fell, Charlie would barbecue a salmon and pour the K.J. Chardonnay, or take his dates to the nearby hot restaurants like Fennel, Capri and Bandoneon. Even when the AIDS epidemic started, Charlie had the best sex life of anyone in his school.

When the real estate market crashed, Charlie's dad tried to restructure all his mortgages into short pays with lowered principal balances and longer maturity dates. His bank responded by selling those loans in a pool to a new lender from Dallas, who squeezed Jonas Solomon by his shrinking balls until, a condo auction, a foreclosure, four judgments, and one disastrous house sale later, Charlie and his family were living in a two-bedroom apartment off Fairfax Avenue. The blazing ginger and poppies gave way to ficus hedges and squat, peeling palm trees. Celebrity neighbors became muttering families of Hasidic Jews. His friends, male and female, found other friends.

But something kicked in that year for Charlie. He aced every course in his junior and senior year and nailed the highest SAT score in his class. The same motor churned in his gut all through his college and postgraduate years at Stanford. It wasn't until he found himself arrowing towards worker's comp law that he realized what fueled the engine. It was the stink of fraud. His father had built a business on paper equity, dominoed debt, and total bullshit, and had defrauded his family. For years Charlie heard that fraud in the snarling arguments over the phone when he called his parents. He felt it on his soapy forearms as he muscled dinner plates over to the dishwasher to work off his college loans. So when it came time for a career choice, Charlie made himself into a truth-seeker that would target the most massive fraud he knew: the looting of the Los Angeles worker's comp system by claimants with spurious injuries and the medical and legal mills that supported them. Against the universal drive to get something for nothing, Charles Solomon would apply reason, judgment, and finely sifted detail. If the claimant attorneys were fighters, he was a hunter, out to snare the truth and use it against their freeloading thieving clients.

But it seemed strange that, though so much had changed for Charlie since he'd left New York, the cop opening the door for him had stayed the same: a polite but disinterested black man doing another day's work tidying up after another violent disorder.

Didn't the cop realize what everyone else knew the minute Charlie, still dazed by the shooting, stepped gingerly into the ambulance? Charlie had undergone a peculiar metamorphosis. In the blink of a gunshot he'd become the daily hero. When the two sinewy young paramedics saw his face whiten as Sheila Reed's covered body was wheeled towards the coroner's van, they'd steadied him when he almost fainted, and assured him he'd done his best.

He'd tried to wrestle the gun away and save lives. Everyone knew that.

The pretty Latino nurse made references to his courage as she checked his pulse, respiration and blood pressure, and then cleaned up his cuts and gashes. When he winced at the sting of the disinfectants she suffered with him. Her sympathies were almost clumsily profound as she drew his blood for a routine AIDS test. Nothing to worry about, but there was a possibility that, through minute cuts, there had been contact between Charlie's blood and the body fluids of the deceased, by which Charlie supposed she meant *the ragged chunks of brain matter and skull that had stuck to his flesh....*

The nurses folded his suit and shirt into a box with assiduous care – as if any cleaner would ever be able to save it – and gave him not just scrubs but a warm-up jacket from the hospital softball team. And she gingerly made sure his Palm Pilot was okay.

"Get Dana b-day perfume," Charlie read.

The cops that arrived some time later were a little more cynical. They knew the difference between heroism and getting in the way of a bullet. And they had some pointed questions to ask for the upcoming coroner's report. So you were pinned against the wall, Mr. Solomon? Yes, of course, we understand, it's hard to think straight when someone's attacking you like that. We're just trying to get the facts as best we can, Mr. Solomon. *So you say your hand was on the barrel? Did your hand ever get near the trigger? Do you remember pushing against the weapon in any way? Were your hands sweaty? When did you close your eyes?*

Charlie appreciated they had a job to do, ascertaining the exact circumstances of the death, and they were almost deferential as they culled from him details that they assumed were still fresh in his mind. It was his duty to give as full an account as he could. Still, he was profoundly relieved when the questions were over, and the cop led him out the door.

The news media army pounced on him. Their lights blasted into his face. The whole blue-suited, tweed-skirted pack bounded out of their leisurely coffee break like small animals flushed from cover. It was as if he held a string that yanked them towards him and there was no way he could get away and hide.

"Mr. Solomon, how are you doing?"

"F-fine. Heading straight home to - "

"Did you ever get control of the weapon?"

"No, I tried, but she was desperate and - "

"How long have you been a lawyer?"

"Two years."

"How much money was at stake here?"

"That's a little complicated, but - "

"Is it true the victim was abused on the job?"

"I - I really can't comment -"

Charlie started to feel sick. The hail of questions, unlike the respectful police interrogation, was random and increasingly ferocious, like hands tearing at his suit to find his wallet.

"Did she ever aim at the judge?"

"Um - at one point she was covering the room. But she was mainly pointing at me."

Now another rapid-fire volley of questions backed him against a Mercedes. The car's alarm shrieked across the lot. Assaulted by white noise, he picked out one last shout.

"Charlie? When you were wrestling for the gun, did you ever anticipate the incident would turn into a suicide?"

The thundering senselessness of the question at last brought silence to the parking lot.

"Of course not!" Charlie shouted with indignation. Then, pleading a need for rest, he left the reporters behind him, and practically hurled himself into the cab the hospital staff summoned for his ride home.

He was worried when an echo of that car alarm persisted in his ear like a thin ringing burr. For hours after the gunshot there had been sound in his head, a grinding, electrostatic parody of the ocean noise in a seashell. The doctors had warned him the tinnitus might persist. But for now the noise had left him, and there was only the murmur of a lowing herd of cars making their way down the freeway. He could feel, as he never felt in the driver's seat with his tapes on, the throb of the engines swallow him and bundle him into the collective migration home.

He passed a point in the drive that he always relished, where the freeway picked up as it climbed through the Santa Monica Mountains, and where he passed the road to the hillside courts where he taught his volunteer tennis class every Sunday. Just this morning, on his way to the Van Nuys hearing rooms a century of a day ago, Charlie had gently accelerated the Infiniti through that last stubborn remnant of the undeveloped West. Hills overgrown with mesquite and chaparral, an elm or two perched on their crests. A strand of tile-roofed houses way above him had shone in the morning sun like an unclaimed bracelet - and for a moment, there had been a wild, untarnished silver light on the edge of the hills, ready to race off the treetops like a flock of birds, a light that pricked Charlie with a longing all the more delicious for being so unexplainable.

Now the sky flushed bitter orange, veins of fire through the big scudding clouds, which soon dimmed to the color of hot coals. A line from an old Shakespeare class occurred to him: the hectic of the blood. *The hectic of the blood. The blood everywhere...*

He would call Dana as soon as he got home, get away from these thoughts - but then he remembered she was on an agency retreat. He could call his mother - no, he thought, he would spend the evening alone. First, though,

45

he would pamper himself. He walked over to Mikita's for an early dinner because he knew the sushi bar would be nearly empty until ten o'clock. None of the itamae-san knew what had happened to him. After a flurry of "Arigatoooo!"s they quickly sliced him some yellowtail, saba, red clam and California roll. He ordered a plate of grilled squid and had an extra bottle of hot sake. A doctor had mentioned the possibility of nightmares and he knew he didn't dream much when he was drunk.

His apartment looked roomier minus the Sheila Reed files, which had been taken to his office. The last trail of dusk glowed on the two massive cream leather Italian couches, the halogen torchieres, the wet bar's glass block. In his decor, Charlie had followed advice a producer friend of his gave to screenwriters: leave plenty of white space. It calmed him to look at this smooth vista broken only by dracaena plants and a blue glazed vase.

There were eight messages on his machine, but he figured everyone would understand if he left them unanswered. He went to his CD spinner and picked out a jazz disc. The trumpeter blasting a long sweet note through the icy penumbra of the spotlight. That's what he needed - Chet Baker, whose music he'd discovered through his mother, warbling gently on the speakers.

But as soon as he lay down on the bed he crashed into sleep, and a dream floated up like smoke wraiths above the rubble. He and his little sister were walking amid pools in a garden, where fish hibernated, their scales glistening purple and green. Charlie and the girl walked towards the clear, bright streams that fed the pools. His sister wanted to drink but Charlie told her he knew from school show-and-tell that the fish glowed from radiation in the water. He begged her not to drink, but she put her cupped hand in the rushing water, sipped from it. He screamed as she smiled.

When he woke up he kept trying to remember the sister's face.

Liz Worcek crawled in her Volvo down Hollywood Boulevard, looking for the Denny's where she was scheduled to meet with Brandon Reed. The buildings, as always, were clownishly depressing, the traffic a disaster, but at least, she thought, this is purposeful action. I'm not staggering through this day anymore.

She had never felt so much like a ghost. For the first hour after the shooting, it was as if all the substance inside her had wound up on the wall with that terrible splash of blood that had exploded out of her client. She'd closed her eyes before the shot. She buried her face in her arms just like a little girl, and opened them to the sight of a bloodstained, panic-stricken little boy that five minutes ago had been a confident young attorney. He was scrambling to his feet. She'd beaten him out of the room, crying for help.

Help of course didn't come until after the fact, with offers of grief counseling, and a card with a number to call if she wanted to talk. But that's not whom she'd wanted to talk to. She was still, in the aftermath, a little girl, and she headed to where little Catholic girls go. A steeple that seemed almost laminated in sunlight flanked by orange trees.

When the priest asked her how long had it been since her last confession, she replied " It's been twenty years, father, but it's not every day that a client of yours – I'm a lawyer, father – a client of yours blows her head off right in front of you."

"How long ago did this happen?"

" Just two hours ago, and I…I…This was one of those days, Father, when you're gonna be tested. And I knew that. I mean, a trial day is always a test. But I didn't know just how…how much I was gonna be tested. You never do. There's no warning." She tried to stop, but the deliberate, poised silence of the confession box drew more truth out of her. "Actually – maybe I had a warning."

"What kind of warning?"

"The rage. The rage they all feel – the claimants fighting for compensation for work-related injuries. She had it worse. Much worse. And also – the other lawyer, the one defending the insurance company, he was trying to take the gun away from her, and I felt it coming right then, but I – I did nothing." The sobs came freely now in the tight, musty booth. " I couldn't do a damn – I couldn't do a thing, Father. I ran away."

"And now you feel remorse?"

"I feel – I don't know how I feel. This woman – she could have been one of my daughters."

The priest took a long pause. "Perhaps it was your daughters you were thinking of when your client pulled the gun."

Yep, this was a good priest. The pain began to recede, throbbing in the background, away from the core of Worcek's life. Father Johnston had definitely made the point that she had other things to do with that life than throw herself in the firing line of a woman bent on destruction.

When she walked out of the church, the bright late afternoon sun no longer seemed like an insult. But with a lighter step and a clearer mind came a thought that for a moment seemed so venal right after confession that she crossed herself again. The thought wouldn't go away.

"Burnight."

No, she realized, it was a perfectly natural reaction. The God who'd led her to Father Johnston, put her in the same room with a terrible tragedy, and made her a claimant lawyer in the first place would inevitably deliver to her lawyer's brain thoughts about the Burnight case. That case had established that, in the case of an employee's suicide, if, but for the industrial injury, the employee's mental state would not have resulted in suicide, the death would be held compensable under worker's comp law. Given that Sheila Reed had killed herself due to the strain of her injuries and her tortuous worker's comp case, that meant a potential death benefit for a partial dependent. And Worcek knew that Sheila Reed had a partial dependent.

Worcek's staff was astonished when she strode back into her office at four o'clock and, assuring everyone she was sound in body and mind, took her seat at her desk and made the phone call to Brandon Reed. She left a message on the machine expressing her condolences and informing him there were certain rights to benefits that he might not realize he had in this matter. When she hung up, she was hit by a wave of fatigue so severe that she finally conceded, yes, it would be best if she retreated to her home. Brandon certainly wouldn't call back anytime soon.

The call came within ten minutes.

"You were the lawyer for Sheila?"

"Yes I was, Brandon."

"Yeah. I'll talk to you."

"When do you want to meet?"

48

"Now's okay."

"I'm in Encino, Brandon."

"I don't have a car."

"I'll come to you."

By the time she was working on her second cup of coffee in the Denny's, Brandon finally shambled through the door, and Worcek called him over to her booth. The kid was wearing gray loafers and white pants, the cuffs of which had sustained grease spots on the street. Over his white tab-collar shirt he had thrown on a robin's-egg-blue blazer that was maybe a half-size too short for him - it had probably sat in a closet since his high-school graduation. But the awkward dress was of a piece with his slightly askew, droopy-lipped smile. The kid was likeable, plus he had all-American good looks sadly tempered by adversity. Worcek couldn't help thinking that he'd play well.

She once again expressed her condolences, then tried to make him feel comfortable. "What would you like, Brandon? I'm buying."

"Just coffee. I don't feel like eating much."

"Of course not, I understand." She looked at the Walkman in his hand. "Did you take a bus here?"

"No, but, sometimes I just feel like listening to music when I'm walking down Hollywood Boulevard. Sometimes I'm just not in the mood for all the creeps. They can really wear you out."

He laid his tapes on a nearby chair - Verve Pipe, Cold, Sublime - and Worcek mentioned that was the same stuff her daughter Becky listened to.

"She sounds pretty cool, Mrs. Worcek."

"I think so. Of course, all moms think their kids are too hip for the room."

Brandon grinned politely back at her, and she plunged into business. She explained how Brandon was a partial dependent of his sister – she had provided a home for him and other support. Therefore Brandon was eligible for $25,000 in partial death benefits and $5,000 in burial expenses. Brandon seem to flinch and shield his eyes from Worcek, guarding the pain any mention of his sister's death caused, but then his eyes grew calmly appreciative, as if you'd just offered him lemonade on a hot summer's day.

"Thanks, Mrs. Worcek. I could use the dinero. When do I get it?"

"That's not quite so simple, Brandon."

Brandon fingered the fabric of his pants leg. "There's a catch, huh?" he deadpanned.

"You might say that. Since Sheila's employer's worker's comp insurance carrier - I know that's a mouthful, but you'll get used to it - since they've denied all along she had a worker's comp injury, they'll obviously fight to deny any worker's comp death benefits. So you'll need to retain counsel to get these benefits. Now my firm has a long track record in obtaining benefits for - "

"You're telling me I have to fight in court for the money? Even to get my sister buried?"

"You won't have to do a thing but help us do our job." It was a good answer both for securing business and quelling anger.

Brandon slouched back into his chair. He rotated his wrist and extended finger in the air, as if trying to fit a key into an invisible lock. "Mom's taking care of the burial. She finally called me back about a half-hour ago. That's why I was late."

"Where is your mother, Brandon?"

"Somewhere in New Mexico. I only have her phone number. My dad – I don't know where he is. Nobody knows."

For the first time, Worcek winced with pity for Brandon. She felt the burning indignation she needed to go to the wall for a client.

"So I guess I got the burial money, Ms. Worcek. So maybe I don't want to go to court for the rest."

His voice emptied out to a wispy numbness. Worcek had the feeling he was trying to retain his tranquility of just ninety minutes ago, even though he didn't believe it anymore. Or maybe he was just totally wiped out and ready to give in. She had to jolt him past that incipient hopelessness.

"What problem do you have with that, Brandon?"

He mulled it over sadly. "I dunno, it makes me feel – it's too extreme."

"Brandon, I know legal action seems like some sort of drastic procedure. Unfortunately, we live in an irresponsible and adversarial society, which means lots of people have to fight in court to secure their rights." The

50

kid's stare was so intense she tried to defuse it. "Hey, lawsuits are like baseball in this town. Put me in coach, I'm ready to play."

The banter misfired. Brandon's eyes drew down hard. "I played Little League baseball, Mrs. Worcek."

"Um...sure. You know, my daughter's a pretty good left field - "

"Baseball's a beautiful game. And it's a fair game. Not like your fucking courts."

Worcek echoed that simmering outrage of Brandon's in her own voice. "You're right. It's not fair. That's why I don't play fair. That's why I win."

Brandon uncoiled from his slouch. He spun his finger back and forth again. The key was fitting into her eyes and trying to engage.

"I dunno. She fought this stupid case for five years. And then it killed her."

"Yes, Brandon. I know. I was there."

"You were there in the room with her?"

"I was representing her, Brandon. I was right there."

Brandon seemed stunned. "What did you do?"

"I told her to take a step back. Put the gun down. I thought she was going to do it. But then Charlie tried to take it, and things happened so fast I —"

"Wait, Charlie tried to – who was Charlie?"

The meeting had just careened out of her control. "Charlie was the other lawyer. He —"

"You mean for the insurance company? He tried to take her gun?"

"He was just trying to end the situation Brandon, he was just trying to help. But it didn't work. She fought him off."

"Yeah," Brandon grinned. "She was strong as hell."

"Well, that's certainly true. She pretty much beat him to the ground, and then she - it looks like she killed herself."

Brandon stared down into his cup of coffee. "I saw him on t.v. That lawyer, that Charlie whatever. He had her blood all over him."

Worcek had wanted to stoke Brandon's anger, but not this much.

"Brandon, I know your sister fought this case for five years. I've won benefits for clients after seven years. Ten years! I'm not telling you the check's in the mail. I'm saying I can get it."

"Yeah. You can get it." He rocked forward, and for a moment Worcek didn't know if he was going to cry, or retch, or leap across the table at her. "You can get your cut, right? Always about your cut."

Worcek, defending her professionalism, banished her fear. "What cut, Brandon? What will winning your case get my firm? Five, six grand tops? We have hundreds of clients. There's no way I can economically justify a case like yours. The money is meaningless. So let me repeat this in case you weren't paying attention. I was there. I couldn't do anything then, but I can do something now. Your sister was viciously oppressed in the workplace, and totally discarded when she ran up against the worker's comp system. At least with this case I get a second chance. No, I won't hide it, the reason I want your case is so I can retry your sister's case for everyone to see. They'll know it was abysmally neglected worker's comp-related injuries that drove Sheila to suicide! Someone will be made responsible for what happened to her!"

Brandon's voice quavered back to life. "I mean, she was a little off the wall, okay? But she wasn't crazy."

"Exactly."

"They're saying she was criminally insane. I mean some news person, some bimbo was saying that she tried to kill that Charlie – that fucking insurance lawyer."

"We won't let them get away with that argument, Brandon."

Brandon's grin suddenly broke out again, full-hearted, trusting. "Okay. Let's go for it."

"Fine. We're in business. Now what have you got from Sheila's case?"

"Endless paper. Shoeboxes of shit."

"Lay it on me. Wait a minute - you don't have a car. I'll have an assistant drive by and get it. Brandon, this firm has a long, successful track record. You're going in with the heaviest gun possible."

His grin faded. "Whatever...Look, Mrs. Worcek."

"Liz."

"I appreciate you're going to fight for me and all, Liz. It's just...I don't know much about the courts. They're just a big meat-grinder to me. Might as well be science fiction. I want to always know what's going on from you."

His request seemed so unnervingly intimate that she flinched from it. "Sometimes it's hard to even get me on the phone. I'm in court eight hours a day. Communication is difficult."

Brandon's stare was unrelenting. "I mean it. I know you've got to do what you do, and I've got to let you do it. But I don't ever want to be a mushroom."

"A mushroom?"

"Yeah. You keep a mushroom in the dark and you feed it shit. Not me. I don't want to get lost like my sister, Liz."

Until Shackleton led him into the meeting, Charlie's day had been as peaceful as the benevolence of a profession shocked into sympathy could make it. Like the gaily-winnowed sunshine on his wall that he'd opened his eyes to that morning, so unlike the specters of dread he'd anticipated, his duties had been light and evanescent, smoothed over by caring associates. He'd been on a post-traumatic holiday.

His car was waiting in his parking space, thoughtfully driven back to his condo by one of the Hobart-Riis staff, who had removed every last file from the trunk. His drive was smooth as his Steely Dan tape. Donald Fagen's uneasy but seductive melodies, the voice of the appalled gentleman – Don always seemed right for the slow, nervous morning commute. Stopped at a Century City light, Charlie could see the twin towers rise against the bright sky like two huge shiny silicon wafers. He was eager to get back to work.

As soon as he strode into the burnt sienna marble reception alcove of Hobart-Riis Insurance, Inc., the young Chinese woman at the voice terminal jumped up to shake his hand as if he were some head of state. Bert Silver, the slick, bluntly handsome litigator from Beverly Hills who'd just joined the company, barreled out of his office snarling about how the company's adjusters couldn't testify worth shit - but seeing Charlie, he dropped his kvetch as if some unearthly radiance had struck the room. "I don't know how you did it, Charlie - but good show," he intoned. Charlie found his desk swept clean of all

53

but essential files, a scone and coffee waiting for him. Mavis Thorpe, plump and smug, the canny old senior secretary with a deck of grudges she shuffled every morning for all to hear, practically wept when she saw Charlie. "You should be in seclusion," she muttered, clutching his hand.

"In seclusion" - wasn't that the phrase applied to mourners or criminals? It was the last place Charlie wanted to be. Maybe his colleagues were astonished he showed up, but he never doubted he would make an appearance. Fall off the horse, get back on the horse - that was how he told his tennis students to react to an unforced error. Or to a shot blown by them they didn't anticipate.

But the buzz of adulation made it hard for Charlie to transact his normal day. An applicant lawyer called to notify him he'd be reopening a case. Charlie used the old defense lawyer dodge of "I'll review the file and get back to you" - never let an adversary talk to you when he's prepared - and then the lawyer said of course, he understood, with everything Charlie went through and all. All that benignity threw him off his game. Finally Charlie decided to make an end run around his secretary and pull some files himself just to get his hands dirty. The iron phalanx of cabinets in the Hobart-Riis records department grounded him again. Charlie remembered when a veteran claims examiner, a puckish little man who wrote poetry on the side, first took him to the file room and quipped "Here's where they shoot the passenger pigeons." Charlie had been intrigued enough by that remark to research it on his Britannica CD-ROM. He'd learned that, at one time, hordes of these toffee and garnet-hued pigeons had swept across the American plains. Frontiersmen out to bag them for their plumage and squab meat had stood beneath flocks of thousands of the birds, raised their rifles, and kept on firing until they became extinct, in the same way workers, lured by promises of settlement bonanzas, had taken a worker's comp system meant to enfold them in its protective wings and released a fusillade of lawsuits, until a hail of claims had tumbled down into the files, crushed into a heap of rotting sludge. The great generous pigeon had been exterminated, and was now a billion chunks of dead paper, a swamp that sucked in everything it touched and poisoned it with lies.

Returning to his desk with fresh files, Charlie felt that once again he was on track, straining out the bullshit to distill the truth. His mind was further

54

sharpened by the unforgiving task that lay before him. The kindly colleagues who'd massaged his day hadn't quite hid the Dictaphone. There it sat, the black box on the cockpit of his desk, and it waited to record yesterday's crash.

Charlie got right to it. Sticking carefully to the usual phrases, he named the original adjuster on the Sheila Reed case (whom he would be having words with over the Dr. Chesley document), and all the parties involved. He summed up the principal issues. Then, like a driver putting pedal to metal, he shot through his own argument for a delay in Judge Merrill's decision. The jade-colored motor light winked at him like a coolly appraising eye. "After Judge Merrill ruled in favor of a continuance so defense counsel could obtain and consider evidence not yet submitted, claimant produced a weapon. Defense counsel attempted to..."

leap in the dark towards the fury...

"...intercede. In the resulting struggle, claimant once again obtained control of the weapon..."

Whose hand? Whose blood?

"...and killed herself."

Charlie realized he had drifted. How much tape had rolled, how many winks had the green eye shot him? He appended some final matters relating to the Sheila Reed case, including a lien claimant's unresolved psychiatric issue. "Well, it sure as hell resolved itself, didn't it?"

He couldn't believe that line was now on the tape. But almost as soon as he said it he felt a voluptuous relief. He could be permitted a sick joke - in fact, at the thought of a lienclaimant in her boxy plaid skirt trudging up to the judge with her little psychiatric claim only to learn the patient had blown her head off (not real effective psychiatry there, was it?), Charlie laughed out loud, and he only stopped when he turned to see District Manager Shackleton looking directly at him.

Ted Shackleton had one of those parchment-dry faces that seemed cast in a rictus of disapproval, and so for an awful moment Charlie thought his boss was glaring at him for inappropriate behavior, but Shackleton's jowls creased into a smile, and he took two magisterially large steps forward to shake Charlie's hand.

"Good to see you this morning, Charlie."

"Good to be here, Ted."

"Yes. Yes it is. Charlie, I - I don't mind telling you this shows character, this really - will you walk with me to the conference room? - this shows a steadiness that, well, I truly appreciate. We all do, Charlie."

Charlie grabbed his attaché case and rushed to keep up with his six-foot-four boss as they headed past the examiner's area. The big fluorescent-gray room was subdivided into beige cubicles thumbtacked with Far Side and Garfield comics and personal souvenirs. Through the partitions Charley got scattered glimpses of the examiners hunched over their computers recording their case diaries and delay-deny schedules. Shackleton always gave a friendly nod to the examiners, for he'd manned one of those workstations many years ago. Charlie found it hard to imagine Shackleton's hulking, spectral presence cooped up in one of those boxes. In Charlie's mind, his boss had always had an office similar to the conference room they were approaching, with its massive oak table inlaid with a green marble top, teak cabinetry, plush davenports and armchairs.

"Charlie, I just want to have a brief meeting - get some issues squared away - but I want you to know I've contacted a very fine man - Dr. Westphal - he's had experience in treating...I believe it's called post-traumatic cases, and he would like you to go see him. I'd recommend it, and please, any assistance you may need, all the resources of Hobart-Riis are at your disposal, Charlie."

Charlie appreciated Shackleton's almost surreal delicacy in broaching the subject of therapy. That showed a respect that Charlie welcomed at this moment, for he was a little nervous at being confronted with a meeting so soon. It wouldn't be just a pat on the back - the presence of Supervising Attorney Maxine Bunning and Bert Silver guaranteed the meeting would have some teeth to it. Bunning, as always, looked polished as a diamond - a woman in her early fifties, she had the fine complexion, lustrous bobbed hair, dimpled chin and racehorse poise of a Beverly Hills leasing agent ready to show you a split-level ranch-style home with gold faucets. She was at her warmest and most genuinely cordial as she expressed sympathy for Charlie's ordeal and welcomed him to the meeting. She left it to Bert Silver to bring the bonhomie down to the problems at hand.

"Charlie, I should mention that we're only having this meeting because you've shown such a willingness to get back into the hurly-burly. If anything we discuss here causes you any uneasiness - "

"Oh, I think I can take it, Bert." A gratifying ripple of laughter filled the room. Charlie breathed a little easier.

"The Sheila Reed case isn't over, Charlie."

Charlie visibly quailed. The words drained the blood from his face, and it was almost as if that gun was once again zeroing in on him. Bunning jumped in to calm him down.

"It's her brother, Charlie. Brandon Reed."

"Her brother - um - y-yes, I remember - "

"He's suing for death benefits as a partial dependent."

"Partial dependent?" Charlie's lawyer reflexes took control. "He's suing under Burnight."

"You got it," Bert chimed in.

"Who's the attorney?"

"Who else would have no problem troubling the bereaved before the corpse was cold?"

"Worcek."

Bunning politely winced. "Yes, that – that harridan has found a way not to let this case go."

"Well," Charlie quipped, "she's not the letting go type, is she?" He folded his hands and let them fall on the table – the thump rang through the suddenly silent conference room. His eyes roamed the group nervously. The table's sheen threw back his reflection. "She was in there you know, Worcek. When it happened."

"Charlie", Bunning almost whispered, "we'd like to ask you some questions regarding the incident - but if you feel uncomfortable, it can wait at least until tomorrow."

"No. I'm ready."

There was a brief glow of approval around the table, and then Shackleton inched forward on his elbows, perched to strike. "Actually, it may come down to one issue really - what prompted Sheila Reed to take out that gun in the first place? It's our principal clue to her state of mind. That may be all we need from you, Charlie."

"Well - I got a continuance, and she was very disappointed. I believe she was facing eviction."

A deadening void opened up around the words Charlie found. He could feel anxiety curdle at that blankness' edge, and a vibration peel off of it that started the ringing in his ears. He concentrated on remembering the circumstances, the external events beyond his control. "I remember she said when she pulled her gun that I was just trying to do my job."

"She understood that?" Bunning interjected. "That you were just trying to mount the best defense - "

"No. I meant she was just trying to do her job. She said the records getting lost wasn't her fault. Sandoval - her supervisor – planned it that way. Then she...she went on about no rules, no rules anywhere...and I figured I could jump in before she..."

"Look, it's obvious!" Bert interrupted. "She was on a crusade. She was going to bring that gun into the courtroom and take somebody out."

Shackleton didn't buy it. "She could've been carrying the gun for protection. Fear of getting assaulted on the bus. The poor creature did have to take the bus every day."

"Besides," Charlie added quietly, "I don't think she would've used the gun if she hadn't thought she'd lost."

Shackleton let Charlie's reply hang for a moment. Charlie could tell his boss was readying a statement of incisive clarity. "Let's leave aside for the moment whether Sheila Reed was suicidal or homicidal or just trying to make some pitiful statement when the gun went off by accident. The coroner has yet to make a decision on that aspect of the case. The poor woman was deluded. She was never injured in the first place. Her financial problems were her own concern. Her profoundly neurotic relationship with her supervisor and the guilt and rage that set off in her must not result in this company having to pay one cent in worker's compensation or any other damages."

Bunning echoed Shackleton's response, and proposed a review of all the evidence gathered in the Sheila Reed case, along with a deposition of her brother.

"And the handwritten notes of Dr. Chesley."

Everyone stared at Charlie.

"I asked for the delay based on the need to examine those."

"Oh yeah - the clinic gatekeeper," Bert explained. "We'll have a meeting on that, Charlie, when it crosses the transom."

Charlie drew a blank until Bunning slipped in the explanation. "We think Bert should handle the case from now on."

"With all due respect, Maxine, I'm prepared to continue. In fact, I very much want to pursue this case."

The conviction he heard in his voice was a surprise even to him. The room was silent – even the ringing in his ears was gone. Charlie could feel Shackleton take a moment to calculate his response. "Charlie, reviewing the material inevitably means re-examining the event."

"Ted, it seems to me I have such an intimate knowledge of this case now – I am the point man, so to speak - I really should follow through with it. And for all sorts of reasons, I'd like to be the one to close the books."

Tentative glances ricocheted around the room. Finally Shackleton scrutinized Charlie once more, then smiled with what seemed a touch of pride in him.

"If you feel up to it, the case is yours."

"Thank you, Ted. I'll get started on it right away."

"Please, Charlie, take the rest of the day off. I think it's fair to say you've earned it." The meeting broke up with a general nervous sigh of relief. Charlie was on the whole pleased with his performance.

"If I might make one suggestion, though," Charlie added, "perhaps we could offer a payment of one-thousand dollars for funerary expenses? Without admitting any kind of guilt. The kid's so poor – it could be a real easy fix."

His suggestion drew blank stares all around the table and for a moment there was a gnawing queasiness at the pit of his stomach – but then Shackleton nodded in assent.

"Actually, you're right Charlie. I'll modify slightly my previous statement – it seems a proper thing to do."

Bert smiled in agreement. "That's good. We make nice – then we let Miz Worcek know how rough we plan to play later. Carrot and the stick. Way to go, Charlie"

Laura, Charlie's secretary, was driving to meet some of her friends for lunch, and Charlie offered to walk her to her car. As they headed for the elevator, one of the other secretaries walked out with Jim Cotner, a young Brentwood lawyer who'd been at the company for about a year.

"Was anyone else there to take the depo?" Cotner barked.

The secretary lowered her eyes. "They were all in meetings."

"Damn it! I told the office I'd be taking the morning off. How'd the guy react?"

"He's a fireman and had to swap a shift to meet you. He was kinda upset you weren't there."

"Well - if the depo's important to the guy, he'll make time next month."

Missed depositions, missed shifts...if the depo's important to the guy...Charlie's head began to throb as a squirt of adrenaline coursed through him. When Cotner buttonholed him at the elevator, the throb became piercingly insistent.

"Charlie, I heard all about it. That's showing the right stuff. Good man."

"Thanks." Charlie wanted Cotner to just go away. The guy's disdain for the poor fireman, his Mr. Status-Points arrogance wore him out. But Charlie's gaze was riveted by Cotner's silk tie and its pattern of green and blue splotches beneath a drizzled web of gold.

"Some neckwear, Jim."

"Hand-painted. By a guy who did a whole section of the Berlin Wall. In fact, I think this pattern was on the Wall somewhere."

The blotches and streaks lost color, like *dried coagulated bloodstains* - and Charlie bolted for the rear of the elevator. The doors closed on Cotner's astonished face.

Laura looked him over anxiously. "You all right, Charlie?" Charlie realized he was suddenly pressed into the corner of the elevator, as if some invisible editor had just cut three frames of his life.

That night, Charlie drove over to the apartment of his friend Ellis Landorf, a short, square-jawed entertainment lawyer, whose lightly mocking eyes seemed at odds with his solidly-muscled frame. As Charlie walked in Ellis was pouring the first of the night's Rolling Rocks for Jack Hansen, who, as an actor/bartender, appreciated being on the other end of the service. Ellis was indulging in his favorite complaint and trashing L.A. nightlife, to which Jack had a standard response, "I dunno. I only feed it." Jack was so slim and cherubic-looking, with melancholy hazel eyes, that you could tell he needed all the detachment he could muster to deal with the oafs and goons that bellied up to his bar.

Ellis and Jack quickly polished off their assurances of support for Charlie. The three friends had spent more time sharing their feelings on Kurt Cobain's suicide than they devoted to Charlie's brush with death, which was just the way Charlie wanted it. Charlie had already spent an hour on the phone with his mother, repeatedly assuring her he was okay in body and mind. All he wanted to do now was simply go with his pals to dinner.

Above Melrose Avenue's neon boutiques the edges of the sky glowed rust and sodium pink, and a trace of ghostly blue twilight sank beneath the wake of a slivered moon. Ellis steered his Lexus into one of the last parking spaces on the sidestreet, relishing the way he beat out an SUV for the space. "Up yours, Stupid Ugly Vulgar!" Ellis shouted, and Charlie and Jack chorused with their own epithets for the van, "yuppie sarcophagus...nerd-herd thinner!" The three young men joined the throng of strollers keeping pace with the headlights. Two dreadlocked girls in black vinyl materialized from the shadows, their high-heels stamping out cigarettes in a trail of sparks. Charlie and Jack eyeballed the girls, Ellis made some remark loud enough to almost get them in trouble, and Charlie laughed and eased into the night's careless mood as they sprinted across the street to Orfeo.

Orfeo had been Ville Grille, a restaurant that had followed the Sino-French tic in food fashion and had resembled a blank trapezoid plunked down from a graphics board, too minimal even for Charlie's tastes. Orfeo's owner, Marcello Giametti, had now brightened the toneless rear wall with Malibu lights and mounted a row of Greco-Roman pillars and a faux-marble statue of a discus-thrower. The tableau was meant to evoke Hadrian's Villa in Italy.

Fountains sprang from clusters of greenery or from cherubs on the walls that poured water into scalloped bowls above the diners' heads. That the waitresses were dressed like cigarette girls from the '50's lent the final touch of retro goofiness to the place.

But the main draw was that the carpaccio, calamari, spaghetti bolognese and gnocchi in pesto sauce were some of the best in West Hollywood for the price. After two glasses of Chianti, Charlie's thoughts were as pleasantly warm and mottled as the earth-toned gesso surfacing of Orfeo's walls. He lay back and goofed on Jack and Ellis' descent into the usual horniness.

"I dunno. I'd vote for 'Indecent Behavior 2'"

"Nope. 'Scorned' is the all-time Shannon Tweed classic. Tweed's playing pool with Andrew Stevens, right? He's the director-actor, sort of Tweed's Josef Von Sternberg as it were. Anyway, Stevens knows his son hates him for being hot for Tweed. Tweed knows the son's in the next room and that he can see both of them, and Tweed's out to destroy the family...plot point. So Tweed lets Stevens lift up her skirt. He takes one look at Tweed's thighs, her ass, this sunburst of sex, and his face just...unnnggggh. Just total abject depravity. He starts banging away at her and it doesn't matter that his son can see everything. He'd bang Tweed in the middle of Thanksgiving dinner."

"So you'd say that the essential theme of a Tweed movie is male humiliation?"

"Exactly. But also female empowerment - of course."

"What about 'Body Language 4'? " Jack chimed in. "Tweed lifts her skirt and this poor schmuck of a lawyer starts banging her in a garage with half his office watching."

"I enjoyed La Tweed's complete subjugation of an attorney in that movie," Ellis echoed. "Especially since our firm might land Tweed as a client."

"I don't think you'll get laid that way, Ellis. You might get laid off."

"Ah, for Tweed..."

"I dunno, guys," Jack demurred. " 'Supermodels in the Rainforest' is far more socially relevant."

Charlie finally jumped in. "Maybe you guys should try steadier relationships."

"I'm planning to, Charlie!" Ellis shouted. "I've got all those movies on tape!"

They subsided and watched the waitresses skitter by in their tight black skirts. Charlie grinned momentarily at the thought of how detached he could remain from talk about soft-core porn and from half-serious pickup lines aimed at the waitresses. *The black and white couple in their serial embrace. Honey-colored perfume.* Dana and he would have a good hug after she got back from her corporate retreat, he'd give her that perfume as a gift, tell her about his deflection of mortal peril, and she would lavish on him all the comforts a frisky, large-breasted, short-waisted young woman could -

"You have to admit, Jack, technology stocks are over."

"Come on. Infrastructural Internet, B to B – that's still solid. Even if the mom-and-pop mutual funds don't agree."

"Fuck the mutuals. Trading on automatic pilot. Family values gambling for people who should put their pennies under a mattress. Holds the rest of us hostage to the dumbest bunch of consumers in the world."

"Actually," Charlie replied, feeling a sudden drop in energy, but wanting not to fade out of the conversation, "American consumers have got to be the smartest in the world. I mean - it's what we do. It's our...reason for being."

"Yeah," Jack grinned. "And it's all in the credit cards. You think they're stopping 'cause of a little recession? Amazing the tabs that get run up every night on those Visas. Beats any slot machine. Last night I stopped a guy, this sales convention Neanderthal, because he was clearly way fucked up, and he gets all outraged and waves the Visa card at me, like it makes him Tom Goddamn Cruise." Jack mused on that as he speared at his penne with his fork. "Compared to credit cards, the stock market's bullshit. You get an interest crunch on the cards, the economy's toast."

"Yeah, maybe. But the real stock market's moved way beyond Joe Six Pack or even the Net." Ellis got that same hungry look in his eyes as he had talking about Shannon Tweed. "We're talking globalized engines of investment. When you talk about what the herd does with their two-grand limit Visa cards - I mean, what's that compared to the capital generated by investment in the Chinese market, or by the digitalization of the planet?"

The waitress sauntered by. "Another Fume Blanc?"

That was not the choice Charlie would be making. Suddenly Ellis' high finance groupie babble was grinding like a screw into his brain. He was about to beg off the rest of the evening, since Ellis and Jack were planning a club night, but his friends sensed Charlie's growing exhaustion, and in deference to him they opted to catch a movie instead.

They were drunk enough to choose the latest wildman comic's "heartfelt" film, "Losing Face." A chemist, rejected by the woman he loves, discovers a formula for instantly transformable flesh and uses it to give himself the face and body of the man of her dreams. Of course the ectoplasm runs amok, adhering to his body and copying the shapes of everyone and everything he runs across, throwing the nerd into all sorts of disasters. Twenty minutes in and it was clear the movie was idiotic. Charlie waited for one of Ellis' famous blurts - when they'd seen "Kiss The Girls," during the scene when the killer surrounded himself with his kidnapped women wrapped in sheets and made one play the violin, Ellis had shouted "Christ, the laundry bills!" Now Ellis and Jack were annoying the crowd by trading mock-high-flown film rhetoric - "An unsuccessful blend of the physical tableaux of Shadyrac's "Ace Ventura" movies with the more distanced approach of early John Turtletaub." Charlie just thought the movie sucked. About the time an abortive nose-stretching flare-up caused the hero to get stuck facefirst in a toilet, Charlie was struggling just to pay attention - and then the crying baby shot that all to hell.

This was a loud little bastard. Although the movie's soundtrack was cranked to the max, it was still rent asunder by the screeching. All over the theater people hissed at the baby to shut up, but the infant only squalled louder. Charlie decided, since he wasn't at all into the movie, to try and handle the problem.

"I'll get this," he told Ellis.

"Wish he'd pick up a check that fast."

Charlie squirmed past the other moviegoers. The popcorn-and-soda-encrusted floor gripped the soles of his loafers like tar. Finally he made it to the aisle. Dark faces swiveled towards him on what seemed like an endless trek to the usher in the back.

The kid was dressed in a red suit and a fez just like the ushers Charlie remembered from old Hollywood photos. Modern multiplexes packaging nostalgia. He stood nonchalantly in the corner while somewhere nearby the baby kept bawling its head off.

Charlie offered to help the usher evict the mother and the baby. The kid seemed annoyed. "She's been trying to take care of it, sir."

"Well, it's not working very well, is it?"

"She's holding the baby up, talking to it." The usher grinned. "I've seen 'em start nursing if you let 'em alone."

"Look, your customers are getting angry. If you don't watch out, people will start asking for their money back."

That remark at last stirred the usher to action. He led Charlie to the row where the mother, a fat woman in a kerchief who looked Russian, was cooing to her relentlessly screaming child. Charlie asked her politely to leave. The woman frowned, lowered her head and shook it angrily.

"Just until the baby shuts down, ma'am," the usher pleaded. She let loose a guttural stream of Slavic expletives, even as the seething moviegoers all around her finally snapped, and one by one demanded that she get out.

Now her anger crumbled. She hugged the baby tighter, and in broken English begged them to let her stay. She had a right, she had a right - her chest spasmed and she was crying as loud as her child was.

This was getting impossible, Charlie thought, now they'll have to shut her up along with the baby. He bent down to talk to her when something skittered past his ankle. "What the hell?" he shouted. A rat - a rat in a Beverly Hills multiplex! Then he noticed it wasn't a rat, it was black-and-white, pointed ears - a kitten that looked so familiar...

"Here! Here!" the woman shrieked, and Charlie turned to see the woman, heartbroken, thrusting the baby at him. He reached out to prevent the child from falling and suddenly it was in his hands, weeping and sobbing with all the shock of its abandonment. What could he do now? Take it from its mother? He was stuck in the back of the theatre holding the crying baby while all the faces upturned from the shadows glared at him like he was some sort of pariah. He tried to rock it, but it yowled, wheezed, a tiny baby that appeared truly sick and tormented.

What did he know about babies? He tried to pet its face as you would a cat - and the baby bit him hard. Charlie tried to yank his finger away but the infant's teeth dug in viciously. Now the mother was pleading with him with incomprehensible cries of despair. The infant's little hands clung to Charlie as it screamed in sheer panic. He tried to shake the baby off, and its clothes peeled away, its tiny pink body vibrated until it liquefied to a bloody pudding, face dripping away from the crushed eye socket in the skull.

Charlie howled at what he'd done, and as the clown's obscenely grinning face above him exploded into a hundred morph-masks, Charlie beat at it and yelled for it to get away from him. Even after they woke Charlie up his buddies had to pin his arms to the seat to get him to stop.

-3-
lie support systems

After Brandon had his second meeting with Worcek, he grabbed his camera and took a long walk.

He headed west on Hollywood Boulevard, following the line of grimy brass stars past the corner of Highland and Hollywood. On one side was Ripley's Odditorium, its plastic tyrannosaurus head chewing a clock. Above him the big sporting goods building, windows like cheap green sun visors, glinted with a gray patina of sky. He loitered by the movie palaces where, he'd been told, his grandfather had seen the old black-and-white movie stars wave to hysterical crowds. In the wake of those Babylonian relics trailed the other stores, like tics nibbling on the belly of a great cat - the massage parlors, tarot readers, sex paraphernalia outlets. A little gray-haired loiterer in a beret shambled to a window to gaze with tired longing at the chains and pushup bras. Brandon raised his camera. Click.

When Worcek had finally made some time for Brandon on her schedule, on a day his boss had granted him as bereavement time, Brandon had started riding buses at the crack of dawn. He had to hook up with about three different R.T.D. bus lines to make it over to her office. By the time he got there, she was running around making grunty out-of-breath noises as if she'd just cut short some exercise to force herself to meet with him.

"Brandon, let's get right to the point. We've received an insult, and it's my duty to pass it on to you. They're offering you one-thousand-five-hundred dollars."

"What? Out of twenty-five thousand? That's bullshit."

"Yep. Basically, they're willing to chip in for the funeral and pay your groceries for a couple of months. It is real money, Brandon, but it's – "

"No way. No fucking way!"

Worcek sat back and grinned., "Good. I was hoping you'd say that."

Having shot down the offer, Brandon felt a recoil of uncertainty. "Liz, how can they get away with that? They really think they can get away with it?"

"Well, that's what we have to talk about, Brandon. The coroner's ruling was not what we had hoped. Basically they ruled Sheila's death was a death by gunshot wound." Worcek spread her hands with resignation. "They didn't find evidence of suicide – or so they said. We'll now have to demonstrate that ourselves, Brandon."

Brandon felt a queasy outrage stir within him. Some city agency he'd never dealt with before, some arm of the law he'd only known through television had come into his life and robbed him of a truth.

"And there's some other stuff we need to talk about. Your deposition will be coming up soon."

"How soon?"

"Well, 'soon' is a relative concept in this system, but let's say a month or two. So I've got to give you some information to get you prepared, and I'll tell you right off the bat, you're not gonna like it. But better you get pissed off here in my office than flustered and confused before opposing counsel."

Brandon continued walking west and south. Fountain Avenue echoed with the squabble of Russian immigrants and their radios, but up near Vista and Franklin was peace and beauty, where stucco apartment complexes gave way to private homes and gardens. There were Spanish courtyards that sheltered lemon trees and rosebushes, blazing sunflowers, lush peach and white hollyhocks. He walked along rows of calla lilies with petals like red and yellow starbursts of confetti, deep blue lobelia sitting like jewels in the ground, sprays of pink cyclamen. Brandon knew the flowers' names from his talks with Sheila. He saw that someone who was as smart a gardener as she had been had laid in those spiky purple flowers, a kind of garlic, that Sheila had always planted to drive whiteflies away.

Sheila could make a garden anywhere. She knew how to cook a delicious meal out of what to Brandon looked like rabbit food. She could organize a whole office, she had such good sense - how could she do what Worcek said she had done? Whenever Brandon thought of Sandoval, that prick with his foreign name, he pictured him with a barb of a goatee, vaguely Oriental eyes glinting with malice. Dr. Sandoval – that was the name of the rich evil suit in the martial arts movies who'd check out Bruce Lee or Don the Dragon Wilson in the fight ring, then turn to the other heavy and say "Can your man handle him?" That kind of dickhead. How could Sheila have let the man who abused her at work - did he even know his sister at all? What kind of stew of self-hate and skanky female lust was kicking up inside her back when Scott, who wasn't a bad guy, kind of a nerd but at least friendly, funny in a nerdy sort of way, and still keeping a roof over her head - why didn't she rush to her supposed mate, tell Scott how twisted the job was making her?

Worcek was kind, he had to give that to her, easing him through it, going slow enough so that he felt like saying speed it up. I'm not a baby. I know what's going on. My sister fucked the guy who fucked her life.

Up near the Hollywood Hills long white walls shone behind stands of juniper and cactus, and guarded - he heard it in the soft jazz sax echoing from a stereo - a hive of unseen treasures. Sex, money, music. Click.

He followed Vista Avenue to a fire road that climbed towards the Hills, and ducked past wild cedars to a meadow overgrown with purple iceplant. Dry grass crunched under his toes. He smelled menthol and he gazed up at a grove of eucalyptus trees filtering the sunlight on his path.

What if Sheila and he could've just walked here together?

Brandon fled south into the grunge again. Stores hawked used furniture, athletic shoes, the "new horizons" of a "multilevel marketing company." The buildings were the color of newspapers left in the trash too long, and above them rose cheap signs and world globes and swamis and ten-foot frankfurters. Brandon walked faster, into West Hollywood, passing old crones "talking Jewish" (as a neighbor of his had said) and a gay couple walking arm-in-arm. He didn't like the glitzy restaurants, or the vast dull stretch of Wilshire Boulevard heading towards the museum. He kept shooting photos, but now it was almost a reflex, to tamp down the fiery churning in his gut.

The more he thought about it, the more he couldn't get the taste out of his mouth - the acrid taste of betrayal. He could hear it in Worcek's voice. Could he ever rely on her? She was his attorney, working for him, but he could hear her distaste not just for what Sheila had done but for what she was, what

Brandon was. White trash assholes from north of the Valley. The kind of people who only got into college playing ball and who worked at gas stations and hardware stores. He'd said as much to Worcek. "Sheila had a hell of a kill shot, or you all wouldn't 've cared about her when she was alive, and she shot herself in a way that could make you some bucks, or you sure as shit wouldn't care about her now that she's dead! I mean, if you see so much difficulty because you think she was a slut - "

"No, Brandon, I don't see difficulty because I think she was a slut. I don't think she was a slut. I believe she was – she was just trying to manipulate a truly horrible situation the best she could. I see difficulty, Brandon, because there's always difficulty. It could be anything, Brandon. You wouldn't believe it. I have a client – a teacher. She saw a boy shoot another boy in class. Then the killer pistol-whipped her to the ground. When she couldn't go back to work the school and the insurance company denied her worker's comp claims of physical and psychological injury. Know why? Because they said that when she tried to cool out the two students after class she was 'volunteering her time'." Worcek raised her hands almost prayerfully. "Look, you wanted me to teach you okay? Then calm down a minute and learn. This whole system is supposed to be about an employer being obligated to 'cure and relieve' the effects of an injury on the job. And that should be between the claimant, the doctor, and the employer. But these days when the case gets in the system it's no longer about the injured party and the employer - it's all just a battle with the insurance carrier from that point on. I mean, Brandon, this system has a law that states that when the insurance company is late on benefits, or is illegally denying benefits to injured workers, you know what happens? They're supposed to "self-impose" penalties. Punish themselves! Guess what - they don't do it! They pull all sorts of tricks and delays, and sometimes it takes years! I don't think it will take that long in your case, Brandon, but it will be as long and hard as they can make it. And they'll throw whatever shit they can at you and your sister's memory to see what sticks."

At the Tar Pits, Brandon suddenly stopped, amazed. He was standing on the sidewalk peering through a chain-link fence at an enormous sculpted mastodon, its tusks glowing feebly in the twilight. The animal collapses into the muck with a dying roar. The little elephant on the embankment reaches out with its trunk and screams. But its one surviving parent - for the other is as good as dead - stands despairing on the edge of the pit. There's nothing it can do for its child. The Black Tar has claimed its mate forever.

Brandon stared for several minutes at the mighty elephant soon to be crushed by the pit. At least this was a righteous death, the raw power of nature, the dark force of the ages, not some idiots spitting out paper, not these asshole lawyers...no, it can't be, they can't have killed her...and he pressed his face to the chain-link fence to hide the tears that splashed on the rusty metal and bit into his skin. In the musky twilight air, the shadows exhaling off the sedge by the tar pools, Brandon gazed at the baby elephant so utterly bereft, and his chest rippled with sobs like the methane that burst out of the black ooze.

He could not get away from his loss - not now, not ever. He would never see Sheila again, and he'd been warned that the casket would have to be closed, so he would literally never lay eyes on her for the rest of his life.

She was already beneath the pit, a fossil and a memory.

He left the Tar Pits and walked slowly back home, watching the tarnished sky fade to pale violet, fingers of sunset glowing like cinder-streaks over the Roosevelt Hotel. The hookers and skateboarders and "midnight rambler" homeless, faces glowing like pale watch dials in the sodium light, reclaimed their chunks of the street. Brandon instinctively reached for his Walkman, but he'd taken his camera instead – so he just kept walking faster, trying to shut out the headlights, the cherry-top flashers, the asphalt babble of the zombies and the snarls of bikes and dying blue smoke car engines.

He lay on the rug of his apartment, curled up in the shadowy residue of the twilight. Like firecrackers the sound of the stomped cans rang through his window, like a hail of bullets. As the purple dusk settled on the alley the laughing Mexican kids outside were a thread of rude sonic vitality he couldn't let go. Brandon sat and watched them as his walls grayed out, as his couch, his rocking chair, even the tree outside with the orange flowers hunkered down into shadows.

"Look, Brandon, nothing you've said in this office can't be unsaid. If you want to take their offer."

"No, Liz, I can't do that. It's bullshit."

71

"Brandon, I'll keep shoving this in their faces every way I can. You should be getting a call soon from a reporter on a Valley newspaper. I'm gonna keep this story in the media, Brandon. I'm gonna embarrass them, frighten them, drag them to the table."

Yeah, yeah. Brandon shut his eyes, tried to numb his thoughts, so he wouldn't hear Worcek's endless pitching, and so that he could rid himself of a massive jumble of images. Sheila's anguished eyes and Sandoval's ghostly hand reaching for her breasts and Charlie Solomon and the gun - it was all skittering through random moments like a broken filmstrip, all torn and burned through with images of Sheila in some raw, dark, trapped place Brandon couldn't understand, going down with some coke-snorting vicious -

The kids were called inside, their laughter swept up into the darkness. Brandon's cold blue apartment seemed thin and porous as a sponge. Shitty as Sheila's welfare check had been, without it all that was standing between him and the street was a nine-dollar-an-hour hardware store job, and Brandon could do the math. He could look around the apartment and imagine how and when everything would disappear.

Brandon cracked open a can of Chef Boyardee spaghetti and threw it into a pot on the gas stove. He put on Nirvana's "In Utero." Asshole, asshole. That's what Courtney Love had the crowd chant after Kurt Cobain's death - and the crowd had built it to a cheer. A burning, gut-spawned rallying cry that welded them together. Assholes, assholes. Why'd Brandon even have to think about all this? Why did he have to make Sheila's case his? Maybe the real betrayal came from Sheila – how could she leave him this way? No, he wouldn't cry again, he would not cry. He cranked up Nirvana on the speakers, the pillowed sound of the headphones weren't good enough now, fuck the neighbor's complaints, he wanted to feel waves of feed-backing guitar swarm out of the speakers through the floorboards. He succumbed to a wave of fury that disoriented him, and was so sunk in it's backwash that when he reached for the phone he found himself gasping for breath.

Mindy Crawford from the Pasadena News introduced herself. She was shouting over the music. Inquiring if they could meet and discuss "the tragic death of your sister."

Things instantly made sense again. The call re-adjusted Brandon's reality. He turned the music down, made the appointment, hung up the phone, and turned the music off to make room for his new thinking.

Worcek had delivered. A newspaper wanted to write Sheila's story, his story. Turn the heat on the insurance company. That fact alone hardened his sense of purpose. In telling this Mindy Crawford what she needed to know, in the same way Sheila had once safeguarded him, he could protect Sheila's old obsession and make it mean something. And that obsession, which had been so bothersome to live through with Sheila, had its fascination for him now - the spurts and torrents of energy it recalled had the heightened edge of a landscape you wanted to capture on film and have for your own.

At least that bastard that got her blood on him would feel that blood again.

Mira Halperin had only been with Hobart-Riis about six months, and Charlie could see her narrow little frame quiver at the slightest criticism of her work. So with as much tact as possible he made a fairly damaging observation. She had failed to spot, in one of the depos taken in her case, an admission that the injured worker had gotten into "dust-ups" with other employees. That was rustic San Bernadino-speak for brawls. She could now raise the affirmative defense that the claimant's injuries were caused either by horseplay or out-and-out fighting on the job, and therefore were not compensable. Charlie let her get away with some joking about how she'd have to brush up on her hick talk. It was lazy of her to miss the obvious, but Charlie knew she was a tireless worker and would become a solid attorney.

Christ, he thought, this conference has me feeling like one of my seventy-year-old law school teachers. No, he wasn't taking that well to being sidelined. Shackleton, in what Charlie felt was an overabundance of caution concerning Charlie's mental state, had grounded him from going to the hearing rooms for at least a week. Four days had passed in which he'd assisted on everybody's grunt work, helping to locate a "custodian of record" of patient documentation, doing some index searches, cleaning up some liens.

He'd wound up with so much trivia piled on his plate that the Sheila Reed files remained ominously uncracked. Now that Brandon had officially rejected the offer, he had plenty of work to do, but all he'd accomplished was prepping the subpoena for Brandon. Yes, he had to admit it, at the thought of questioning the nineteen-year-old ex-Little-Leaguer (as a local paper had dubbed him), Charlie felt squirrelly. That reluctance to pry open the sandy-haired head of the all-American boy had led to an avoidance of those files. They were starting to seem like props in one of those schoolroom nightmares where every test you ever faced in your life had to be taken over again.

Well, at least Charlie knew what he'd be talking about with Dr. Westphal. Charlie had never had therapy. This was his parents' territory, zones of elaborate complaint, and he distrusted it. But he sensed it would be like any other meeting. A focused conversation with an agenda whose angle of deflection was up to the person who wielded the power: patient/customer/client Charlie Solomon.

Even with traffic it was only a short drive from Century City to Dr. Westphal's private office on Rexford Drive. Charlie coasted through the patrician heart of Beverly Hills, rows of stately homes where every lawn had its rosebushes and manicured banks of impatiens and petunias that hugged the twilight beneath balloon-curtained French windows. Dr. Westphal not only owned one of those homes, but also had a separate office in a two-story apartment building right near Wilshire Boulevard.

Charlie pressed a knocker on an oak door and was greeted by an elfin gentleman with fluffy gray hair, whose face softened into a tranquil smile and whose long fingers took Charlie's hand briskly. The high ceilings, the furniture with its hand-carved moldings, and the polished hardwood floors reminded Charlie of his old apartment in Manhattan. Charlie complimented Dr. Westphal on his office. The doctor's smile widened.

Charlie wanted to begin the session with his squeamishness about grilling Sheila's brother, but as he relaxed into a plush armchair and saw how relaxed Dr. Westphal was he responded more naively than he had planned. Once the doctor merely told him the same thing everyone else had told him, that he was impressed by Charlie's quick return to work, Charlie came right out with the crying baby dream. Even the most embarrassing part, when his friends not only had to restrain him, but retrieve the loafer he'd kicked off while his

74

legs were thrashing. They'd had to crouch down and peer under half the aisles in the movie theatre before they finally found it.

"You can see I feel pretty stupid talking about this."

"How did your friends react afterward?"

"They joked about it."

"They didn't sympathize?"

"Well, sure they did." It was humiliating for Charlie to recount his friend's concessions to his damaged state, but he mentioned how Ellis had said he had a "license to vent" and Jack had said it would be kind of spooky if he didn't have a few moments like this.

"That's good," the doctor muttered.

"Oh yeah, I mean, we're not exactly a sentimental bunch. If someone were to overhear us talking about, oh, I don't know, just about anything, and they didn't know us, they'd think we were the most - the most insensitive, sexist, nastiest pricks they ever met. But it's all just joking - and we're basically very good friends."

"What kind of joking?"

"Well, for example, they joked about my loafer being a Bruno Magli shoe. That was what O.J. Simpson wore, y'know, the footprints. Anyway, Jack said 'Bruno Maglis. You don't want to leave those behind - haven't you drawn enough attention to yourself?' and Ellis said it was a tragedy, if O.J. hadn't been wearing those shoes, he'd be even more innocent."

"I have a lawyer friend," the doctor replied carefully, "who's still so angry about that case. For certain people, that case has become a code about social breakdown. My friend called it the wheels of justice running off the tracks."

"Well, at least in my branch of the law that doesn't matter."

The doctor paused to isolate Charlie's remark. "You say justice doesn't matter?"

"Well - no. Not really. Doesn't rear its ugly head on my beat. No - worker's comp law doesn't deal with crime and punishment. It's all about the Red Thread, as one of my old law school professors would say. Somewhere beneath all the tangles of exaggerations and lies there's that red thread of the truth, and we just try and dig it out. What's the true extent of the injury? Did

75

it really occur on the job? What compensation does the injured worker deserve, if any? It's that simple, really. Dollars and cents - well, more than that, but -"

"You enjoy your work?"

"Yes. I've always enjoyed it. I plan to enjoy it still." He could feel the anxiety mounting within him. "That is, as soon as I finish dealing with Brandon Reed's suit. Sheila Reed's brother sued for death benefits. The same Sheila Reed files are back on my desk."

"You chose to stay with the case?"

"I didn't want to run away from it. But I...I haven't touched the files."

"It's natural you don't want to reconnect with the event."

"But it's also natural," - Charlie couldn't keep sarcasm out of his voice - "that I want to stay connected to my paycheck."

The doctor seemed unfazed. "You're doing it already."

"Excuse me?"

"Reconnecting with the event and staying employed. Your dream took you past the blackout of your memories." He took a delicate pause. "The image of the skull of the baby. It's possible you may have seen something like that in the courtroom."

Charlie thought he was going to be sick, and inhaled the nausea down. "That's...that's what I thought."

The doctor offered him a glass of water. Charlie took it gratefully. While he drank, the doctor gently told him that the nightmares would be helpful if they dredged up material that would then be subject to his conscious acceptance and control. "We can then proceed by certain techniques - 'exposure' is one word commonly used - to perceive and analyze these traumatic events. It's the unconscious and uncontrollable that's the enemy here." Westphal leaned back and spread his hands to underscore his point. "What we're looking for, you see, is the return of the repressed."

"Tell me about it," Charlie muttered.

"Perhaps," Westphal dryly echoed, "you should tell me about it."

So Charlie told Westphal about volunteer tennis class at the Moreno Tennis Club. The oasis of his week, a row of clay courts in an enclave of silver sunlight and menthol-scented breezes right beneath the Santa Monica

Mountains. He had come in early last Sunday morning to make extra time for Randy Kellerman, who had a tennis tournament coming up.

Randy, with the weakest backhand in the class, is tapping Charlie's drives back into the net, dragging his feet and pinching his swing as usual….Charlie goads Randy a little until he finally steps into the ball. Charlie shouts "Wings! WINGS!" the way his own tennis coaches had once shouted at him… and then Randy at last concentrates on that good uncoiling of his backhand stroke, both arms extended front and back like the wings of an airplane…and then the gunshot rings out.

Of course it was only the backfire of a car, but Charlie had hit the deck, fully flinging himself into prone position on the court and eating clay. He could actually remember the rust-red powder on his gums and its chalky taste. He'd stared up through the mesh of the net at the petrified face of his student.

"What did you say?"

"I covered it. I rolled around, grabbed my calf and started cursing. They know what sudden cramps are like. I did a little performance, made like I was walking it off and lectured him on cramp massage, and then we resumed the lesson. No questions asked."

"Charlie, that's what we call a startle reflex. Perfectly normal under the circumstances. This sort of reaction will lessen in time. The main thing is not to fear anything that's happening to you. Recover the memories. Face the freakouts, learn from them. Gain control."

"Fall off the horse, get back on the horse."

"Exactly."

Charlie knew it was a stupid question, but he asked it anyway. "Any idea how long it will take? I mean - case depos, hearings, this case will really get cranking in less than a month. I myself - I might be deposed fairly soon."

"We'll get you ready. I think you'll find in a week you'll be cracking those files."

"A week." Charlie was pleasantly startled at the doctor's prognosis. "That's great. Unless of course - "

"Yes?"

Charlie spoke carefully. "There's always the possibility I'll go back into the files and find out, I don't know," he smiled weakly, "something that doesn't fit. Something new."

"Well…that will give us something to talk about next session."

Charlie tracked Dr. Westphal's eyes to the clock. He actually had two minutes left on the hour, but he wouldn't quibble. After all, he wasn't the one paying for the time.

"These guys are like every other salesman. They tell you what you want to hear!"

"Oh please, Jonas, psychotherapists have many years of training!"

"I'm not saying they're not skilled salesmen!"

Charlie's parents, Jonas and Beryl Solomon, had been divorced for over five years, but the rhythms of their spats were still finely honed as vintage comedy routines.

"Charlie, tell him. The session was helpful, wasn't it?"

"Maybe a bit more - demanding than I thought."

Beryl smiled. "You know what Freud called psychotherapy? The 'awful conversation'."

"You bet it's awful. Ninety-nine-dollars-an-hour awful."

"Jonas!"

How often had Charlie watched them in the living room in their bathrobes quarreling about his mother's shrinks. At least here at the Camelot Inn, the arrival of a red-haired fiftysomething waitress in a quasi-medieval dirndl cut short the argument. Like all the waitresses at the Inn, she fussed over Jonas, a regular for over ten years, and still a commanding, elegant figure, even with a shiny bald head and a back torqued sideways with a flare-up of sciatica. When Jonas had heard from Beryl about Charlie's "terrible incident", he'd decided the best way to ease Charlie's mind was to summon him and his mother to dinner at the Inn. Charlie had wanted to spend the whole evening with Dana, but Beryl had pleaded with him to make some time for his father. "After all," she'd sighed, "he's making the gesture, and we should both just go and appreciate it."

So Charlie, a fan of sushi bars, and his mother, a coffee shop habitue, were both dutifully seated in a pseudo-medieval dining hall poring over a mid-

1960's meat-eater menu. Jonas slipped on his bifocals and announced with an imperious wave of his hand that, while he loved the New York steak, he would order the Prime Rib Special to save money. In the same way Jonas had once flaunted his wealth he now broadcast his relative penury. He still bought a new suit every year, but his newest one had been acquired, he proclaimed, at a bankruptcy liquidation store ("mostly shvarzes buying sneakers, but you can get some great deals"). It was an excellent light gray worsted wool suit ("you can touch the quality") and all he'd had to do was instruct the tailor to cut off the fake silver cuff buttons engraved with hunting dogs, replace it with something more dignified, and presto - he defied Charlie to tell the difference between this suit and some "overpriced European schmatta."

"There's no way, Dad," Charlie tactfully demurred.

His mother moped over the menu. "Steak, prime rib...nothing but red meat."

"Look, Mom. You can always have the chicken...fried steak."

"Yeah. Cute, Charlie. Oh, this is better - fish of the day."

Once the waitress had taken their order and retreated into the busy semidarkness, Beryl gently reminded Jonas about his eating more fish and chicken, and Jonas snapped "I have news for you, Beryl; the ulcer's probably gonna come back anyway. Might as well enjoy my beef, 'cause you never know." He slapped Charlie on the shoulder. "Charlie just found that out."

His mother winced, but Charlie realized his dad, in his own way, was acknowledging him as a comrade in the manly skirmishes of life.

"Yep. It's a jungle out there."

"A cesspool," Beryl glumly added. "They say this woman was suing over stress, right?"

"Yes. That was the basis of the suit."

"It's lunacy. Lunacy that these people get to make a court case about stress. Life is stress, for Chrissake!"

Charlie began to feel like some fan belt had gone slack in the motor of his brain. He was in no mood to match wits with his father tonight. "There's such a thing as compensable stress, Dad. That's the law. Nowadays they've tightened up the rules on how much you can claim for stress, so most of these cases settle out for five grand. But this was an older case."

Beryl could sense Charlie's weariness. "Jonas, don't badger him."

"I'm not badgering him, Beryl. I'm proud of him." He emphasized the point with a stabbing forefinger, which froze in midair as he contemplated Charlie with paternal fondness. "You got balls on you, son. And don't let 'em tell you didn't do the right thing. I mean, for Chrissake, the one time that a tenant came into my office with a piece - "

"Jonas, PLEASE! Always bringing it back to yourself."

Charlie had never realized his father had actually faced a gun. "How'd you handle it, Dad?"

"Oh, this was a different kind of confrontation - an old storekeeper renting from me who was just bluffing. So I told him he could cause a lot of trouble for himself, and I quietly asked him to put the gun down. He did, I took it and put it in a drawer, he cried a little, then I called the police and they jailed the schmuck.... Ah, that's the way I like it, with plenty of horseradish!"

The arrival of their dinners briefly silenced Jonas, until his cellular twittered from his briefcase. He yanked out his Motorola to take a call from his partner in the management firm. Jonas still owned a couple of Hollywood properties, including a fire damaged fifteen-unit building in El Centro he was renovating, and he managed a few others. Charlie doubted that a property management company would have business to transact this late at night, but he figured Jonas had had someone call just to check in - he still needed to feel in the thick of the kind of action that overflowed normal business hours. The news from one of his assistants - that he'd gotten a water heater at a dirt-cheap price - buoyed his spirits. "You checked on installation? What about delivery, for Chrissake!"

Beryl wilted over her trout as nearby diners glared at Jonas, but Charlie enjoyed watching his father hammer away at the conversation. For a moment his own energy resonated with his father's raw animal vigor, which matched the glistening pink heart of the prime rib on his plate. But the moment quickly passed. Numbing fatigue again slid over Charlie and the heaviness of the trout and baked potato and overcooked broccoli, the drone of his father's shoptalk, the turgid lighting, all conspired to smother his energy. Beryl eyed him with concern, patting his hand, and her attentiveness kept him awake. Through half-closed eyes, he watched his mother, her hair threaded with frizzy gray streaks

80

but still tied in a girlish ponytail, her figure's tidy way of sagging beneath its slight, fine-boned contours. She still fit the mold of a 1950's Barnard College girl, and somehow her good taste and basic kindness had remained, pickled in the liberal wit and compassion of the best years of her life.

He still couldn't understand how his mother had wound up with a man who liked to sum up the 1960's with the phrase "What's new, pussycat?"

Finally Charlie, despite his best efforts, began to nod out at the table, and Beryl persuaded Jonas to call for the check. She gently pleaded with Charlie that maybe he could take a sick day or two, and that's when Charlie revealed that he was still working on the Sheila Reed case.

"Those bastards!" Jonas roared. "They just want to milk the legal fees! All of them!"

Charlie was suddenly wide-awake and furious at his dad for reducing all the complexities of the case to a grab for more shekels. "Look, I don't like it much either, but the truth is, there are points of law here, dad! It's not just your usual backroom conspiracies!"

Jonas stiffened, and Charlie instantly regretted his use of a phrase that had come to signify Jonas' real estate speculations. He apologized and his dad coolly shrugged it off, but even after he'd hugged Jonas at the valet booth and watched him drive away in his old Volvo, Charlie was angry at himself for having ended the evening on such a dissonant note. Jonas had built a sleazy paper real estate empire and paid in full for that. On a night he'd at least tried to be a caring father, Charlie could've let the past remain the past.

But Charlie was resonating with all sorts of submerged resentments he could barely control. Gobbets of shame floated up in the soup of his memories, bubbles of pure rage. Westphal had warned him there would be moments where his brain would seem an open wound. Silence gripped Charlie and his mother as he drove her home. At last, after they'd found a parking space and Charlie was walking her down to her apartment, Beryl shrugged and said, "You know, he really is concerned about you."

"Yeah. He says it with steak." Charlie and his mother laughed, a weary sort of chuckle, and then she glanced at the waxen yellow glow in a nearby shaded window.

"That house is almost all Hasids now. The way they look at me sometimes. I mean, you go out to buy a quart of milk on the Sabbath you're the scarlet woman around here. I'm serious."

"Hey mom, you can get a great lawsuit out of a stoning."

"Cut it out, Charlie." Beryl grinned, but only for a moment. "I dunno, it's just really weird. I've got two degrees, I've been around the world, and now I'm living in a shtetl."

"I like this street. It's funky. It has character." Charlie wasn't kidding. The street had a flavor and a smell, not the vaporizing stucco and car exhaust odor of the usual L.A. block, but the warm breath of freshly-cooked challah bread and the scent of night-blooming jasmine. "Besides, mom, there's lots of coffee shops around here. You should feel right at home."

"You hated this neighborhood growing up, Charlie," Beryl whispered. "I could feel that for five years."

Silence slipped back, and they lugged it between them through the street's echoes of shouts and television shows. Finally they came to the door of her apartment house, and she pressed his hand warmly. "Your therapist - he seems like a good man?"

"I think so. He's been pretty helpful so far. I mean, I've had bad dreams - no surprise there - and there's the recurrent tinnitus – my ears ringing like crazy - and sometimes I have moments where the littlest thing can get me really angry or afraid. But he's helping me deal with it."

She squeezed his hand again, then put on a heavy Jewish accent. "You can always talk to your old mother, bubbalah." They both smiled at the corny term of affection. Then she abruptly leaned against him and hugged him hard. It was strange to feel his mother's heart beating so anxiously.

"Why did she do this awful, awful thing, Charlie? Does anyone know?"

He patted his mother on the shoulder. "Not really, mom."

"And to do it right with you there. Like it was meant for you somehow. Like she was trying to tell you something."

Charlie cut her off. "Mom, the coroner didn't even rule it a suicide."

She squeezed his arm. "Are you going to see Dana now?"

"I think that's the plan."

She whispered, "My baby...", kissed him on both cheeks, and hugged him tighter. In the clench of her embrace he felt the echo of Sheila Reed's gunshot. He went numb even as he hugged her back.

Dana flung herself at Charlie at her door, heartbeat galloping, cinnamon scent of her hair musky with a faint panic. She was dressed in a yellow pullover he'd given her and a pair of distressed jeans. She'd planned as easygoing a night as possible, but now tears trickled between their cheeks and he clung to her until her shaking stopped. Finally, still unwilling to let him go, she led Charlie into her apartment.

"Oh God, Dana, I forgot your present."

"Charlie, please..."

They walked out to her patio, four floors above the beach, and into the tranquil echo of the moonlit waves below. A moonlight snack ordered from Mikita's of California rolls, baked sea eel, and sliced oranges and kiwis waited to cool his palate after the ridiculously heavy meal at the Camelot Inn. "Perfect," Charlie whispered gratefully. After they devoured the sushi and the fruit and tongue-kissed luxuriously, mingling the tastes of soy and ginger, they relaxed over some rum-and-Cokes and Charlie confided to her in greater detail about Sheila Reed's suicide. Dana simply held his hand and whispered "I'm so glad you shut your eyes."

He loved her for that remark, not just because there was a world of caring in it, but because of its sagacity. He knew a little more now about the power of dreams and memory. Had he seen the moment when Sheila Reed had pulled the trigger, his hold on sanity would be a lot more tenuous than it was now.

"So enough of me and my near-death experience. What was the retreat like?"

It took some pushing on his part, but he finally coaxed Dana away from her pity for him and back into her mode of proud businesswoman, whose confidence and zest for her work had slowly captivated Charlie when they were just friends. Charlie had met her after she had broken up with a buddy of Jack Hansen's. She had helped Charlie upgrade his computer, they'd surfed the Net for hours as she demonstrated some then-cutting-edge applications, and by the fourth session they were on the couch groping.

"So basically it was all about taking us through the merger. We design and market shopbots and they have a bunch of Net guides….it's a great fit…"

She began to sway in his arms, and Charlie guided her to the bedroom. But then she playfully stopped him. There were dishes to wash, and she wanted him to hear all about her new duties: she was the point woman for liaising with the new partners. Every so often as they loaded the dishwasher she would brush her ass or rock her thigh against him until he was almost dizzy with exhilaration. Nothing like sheer lust and the promise of its immediate quenching to drive the shadows from the brain.

"Is Microsoft targeting your market yet?"

"They're making some moves."

"What's your strategy for that?"

"Pray." She laughed heartily. "What the hell - we'll deal with that when it's breathing down our necks."

"Speaking of which…" He bent down to inhale the scent off the curve of her throat, and kissed the little hollow above her chest. She slammed the dishwasher shut and laughed softly as he lifted her up and carried her to the bedroom. Dana was the biggest computer jock he knew, with a truly scary pile of hardware in her den, but her bedroom was a sanctuary of rose-tinged warmth and gentility bequeathed her by her family's old California wealth. He carried her past a 19th-century Mission style hutch and cabinets, where Dana's antique doll collection sat and watched them with mischievous eyes as they tumbled onto her four-poster bed.

She mock-wrestled him, giggling with enjoyment of her strength, her legs almost lifting him off the bed, until his hands slipped beneath her shirt and his fingers spanned her breasts, stroking her torso into a slow ripple of pleasure. The muscles in her belly fluttered as she wriggled out of the pullover and he tongued her nipples. Her thumbs went to her belt and he promptly rolled off her as she peeled her jeans off. He always shuddered with pleasure as she bared those horsewoman thighs of hers, the curves of muscle swelling beneath the elastic of her pink thong panties.

Charlie was instantly sprawled on top of her. She was guiding him to the foreplay she wanted, but doing it in fast-motion, like some herky-jerky silent movie. He tasted her skin, the honey and the salt of her, and as she pulled him closer he yanked out the condom, tore the wrapper to shreds, slipped it on in a flash. Now he was inside her and the groans came.

Dana was a screamer. She could get so loud that when they once went to an adult motel as a goof they actually got complaints from the next room. Charlie had told her he couldn't take her anywhere. Now, as the smothered gasps bled into piercing groans, his groin coiled and his heart raced. By now he knew how to time himself to the sharpness and pitch of her sexual arias; he would wait for the moment she was ready and they would cling together until they both burst.

Only this time, Christ, he was really hearing the screams. Traces of archaic agony at being rent asunder - he heard that *distant wailing. The gun spoke to him...*

His force drained away instantly. Dana modulated. She rolled her hips, pumped him slowly. Finally he pulled off the condom and she ground herself against him, but it didn't help.

Like clockwork came the phrase "You must be so tired...," but Charlie actually was scared and furious. How much of him had been stolen by that moment he could never erase? Dana stroked the nape of his neck, and for the first time Charlie felt truly crippled by the burden of his memories and the blank spaces gouged between them.

How much would he lose? How much of a putz would this catastrophe turn him into? Like that lawyer in the Tweed movie - his brain idly and miserably fell upon the casting of that soft-core porn film. Whoever that actor was, he was perfectly cast to play a putz, with his hangdog babyface that went sick with lust as Tweed leaned against the car and bared one long golden flank, and then he was grabbing for her in the garage, moaning like the stupid degraded asshole he was as Tweed let him glimpse that tender pink skin on that unbelievable six-foot rack...and now they were in bed, Tweed looming, blonde hair tumbling down over enormous breasts, and Dana was shouting, trying to keep up as Charlie thrashed and shuddered. She yelled "Pull out!" and he did, speared with luscious pain, gushing over and over.

Afterwards, warm and sweat-scented, Dana told him he really shouldn't forget like that. "Where did that - that rashness come from, Charlie?" He tried to chuckle the moment away, but then he could tell she was nervous.

"I'm sorry, Dana. But I feel like…so wasted sometimes, so completely unlike myself. I…I guess I just wanted to prove I still had a pulse."

"You don't have to prove anything with me, Charlie."

He watched her lie there, one bare leg lazily curled over the other, and he felt desire take him again like the first undertow of sleep. In a little miracle he'd remember for a long time afterwards he reached out to her. "No matter what's happened to me, Dana, I love you." He mounted her, she sighed gratefully, and he surrendered to one more fervent, gentle spasm in her arms before he sank into peaceful dreams.

Next morning at work, Charlie's "Far Side" coffee cup (a herd of a thousand penguins, one breaking out into "I JUST GOTTA BE ME!") was steaming on his desk. His scone was soon chomped down to a pile of crumbs. Those fearsome Sheila Reed files were soon quickly ingested as well. Nothing like a night with the woman you love to clear your head.

Charlie realized that most of his work on this new Brandon Reed case would only have to recapitulate his argument before Judge Merrill. The evidence of Sheila's prior mental and physical illnesses would undercut Brandon's claim as surely as it had hers. Her lies damaged her as much dead as alive. Of course he'd have to counter once again the testimony of the abuse she'd suffered at the hands of Dr. Sandoval. And there was that wretched Dr. Chesley's report on her stress burnout - although Charlie's theory was the doctor had slanted that report to help a co-worker he sympathized with, and the handwritten notes would show a more cautious -

bone chips lashing at his skin...

He shut that mental circuit off. That sound, that grating of bits of skull against his cheek - that might never go away. He had to draw the line in his own head. Crack the whip in the cage of his thoughts.

Above all, he had to isolate his main problem: what was missing from the Sheila Reed file was just as important as the paperwork in front of him. No DWDC form provided by Sheila's employer. No defense report. No evidence whatsoever that the Bernard-Duvall clinic had complied with worker's comp procedures.

They'd simply blown off the law.

And as part of that they'd washed their hands of Sheila Reed, never tried to treat her, and thus her whole state of mind between the time she left her job at Bernard-Duvall and the time she killed herself in the hearing room was a mystery.

His mom had asked the right question. Why the hell did she do it? And why didn't anyone even try to find out what was ticking in her head before the bomb went off? That's what really made this the ultimate legal sewer detail, and what put him alone in the dark.

Charlie could feel the anger backing up, clouding his thoughts. He wanted to wheel his swivel chair back from his desk and take a breather, but it's not as if you could grab a walk around the block in Century City, a hive of skyscrapers, walkways, and boulevards whose thin slivers of pavement discouraged everything but the most rapid and purposeful motion. Besides, he had a conference coming up just after lunch, and he knew that while Shackleton and Silver would be tolerant if he didn't have a fresh angle of attack, they wouldn't exactly be pleased.

So he focused again on the key period between when Sheila left work and when she killed herself. Over three years when this woman's life wasn't even a blip on their radar screens. When her life didn't matter.

Who could know when a life would matter?

It had mattered to Theresa Calder, a secretary-receptionist at the Bernard/Duvall Clinic who became Sheila's good friend. Charlie unearthed Theresa Calder's depo and turned swiftly to the page where Theresa had let slip that Sheila felt she was "doing something wrong" in filing a worker's comp claim in the first place. Much had been made of that remark, although Charlie knew that it was a common enough reaction among claimants facing the system for the first time. Suddenly, after a lifetime of clocking in to their job, they're pleading in a court of law for the right not to go to work.

Theresa had put Sheila up at her apartment when she needed it. She'd also steered Sheila towards Chinese medicine and let her borrow Tagamet for the pain of her gastritis.

Possibly untreated ulcers. Possibly colitis. Charlie had read an unbelievably pompous article about Kurt Cobain's suicide, which claimed that the lead singer of Nirvana, the biggest band in America, who went home every night to a little baby girl and to Courtney Love - this man had killed himself because he couldn't regain his sense of "authenticity." Bullshit. He killed himself because colitis was poisoning his guts and only heroin could stop the agony. If you're carrying a leaky vial of hydrochloric acid in the pit of your being, day and night, it doesn't matter if you come home to a woman who Ellis had said had "one of the best racks in Christendom."

Why the hell was he thinking of Kurt and Courtney at a time like this?

He lashed his gaze to the depo. Theresa had said she let Sheila borrow medication. The attorney had asked her what she meant. She'd told them about the Tagamet.

He looked at that phrase again. "Borrow medication…" The attorney questioning her had stopped right there. But other stuff had come out in Theresa's deposition. A burglary at the clinic where drugs went missing. Employees possibly lending each other anti-depressant medications. The fact that Theresa Calder herself suffered from manic-depressive states…

"Oh come on!" Charlie shouted, banging the depo with his fist, part with disgust, part with the sheer relief of finding a possible way out.

Shackleton waved Charlie into his office, and he saw Bert Silver seated at the swivel chair by his side, a mirror image of poised attentiveness. The room exhaled the starchy cocoa scent of Shackleton's afternoon cup of Postex. Charlie could tell the meeting had gone on some time without him. For a moment, as Charlie took his seat triangulated by two pairs of watchful eyes, he wished that Silver and his relentlessly pleasant smile could vanish from the office. When would he be able to have private meetings with his boss again without being backstopped?

Charlie shook off his mild flurry of nerves by plunging right into business. He had reviewed the files and he intended to depose Theresa Calder once again. Shackleton directed what seemed a vaguely approving glance at Silver, who dutifully caught the glance and rebounded it towards Charlie.

"That's reasonable."

"Theresa loaned Sheila medication when she couldn't afford it? Worcek milked that for all it was worth at the trial."

"Yeah, Calder," Bert muttered, "the office flake."

Shackleton mused on Charlie's information without comment.

"The one question I'd love to ask Ms. Calder is just what other pills did she get for her friend? It came out that Theresa Calder had symptoms of manic depression. We know Sheila Reed liked to self-prescribe medications. What if her friend got her the wrong kind of anti-depressants? Prozac, for example?"

Shackleton didn't budge. The glare beating against the black Venetian blinds in back of his chair made it difficult to read his features. Then he leaned forward, and Charlie could see that the stern gaze had lightened a bit. Silver picked up on that.

"Attaboy, Charlie. Looks like a live rabbit to me."

Shackleton was puzzled, and Charlie and Silver quickly spun out the story of the judge who, faced with an attorney springing a particularly lame argument on him, sneered that he'd pulled a dead rabbit out of his hat. The term quickly leaped into the worker's comp lawyer parlance.

"Ah yes," Shackleton muttered blandly, "shoptalk." But Shackleton had warmed up to Charlie's analysis. What if Sheila had been self-administering Prozac, among whose potential side effects were suicidal impulses? It would be a lot more difficult to argue that her suicide was actually caused by stress or stress-related injuries sustained on a job she'd ceased reporting to years ago. Charlie watched Silver and Shackleton embroider his argument and sank back into a delicious sense of well being.

"You know, Charlie, that could also explain why she was so incredibly violent."

Shackleton's point threw Charlie off-guard. "What do you mean, Ted?"

"The way she hit you - my God, you still have the bruises."

"Well, I - I did go for the gun, and she fought like hell to keep it."

Silver leaned forward with that look of gentling a child through bad news. "You know Worcek is going to depose you, Charlie."

"Well, that's no shock."

Shackleton pursed his lips and shook his head. "The press seems to like this story. Have you seen this?" Shackleton held up page two of the San

Fernando Valley's top newspaper. There was Brandon Reed seated on the stoop of his Hollywood walkup, his childlike face heavy with bereavement. The story's accusations snapped at Charlie even in the few seconds it took before Shackleton pulled the paper away. "We've been told that a lawyer for Hobart-Riis Insurance, Inc., tried to take her gun away. Wouldn't a fair hearing and an equitable settlement of her case have been the better way to do that?"

"Christ," Charlie fumed, "some little light news reporter from the Valley trying to make her bones off of this."

"It's in the paper that the funeral will be tomorrow. Can you imagine? And with that kind of attention they'll calendar the Brandon Reed case fairly quickly."

Silver leaned towards Charlie. "And Worcek made sure to tell me that this article helped Brandon get a job. Apparently the reporter introduced him to some grade-Z--movie producer who sympathized with Brandon's plight and needed a photographer on his movie. So we can expect Brandon to keep holding out for awhile."

Charlie felt it for the first time, like some sour stench emanating from his body: his responsibilities. The post-traumatic holiday was over.

"No problem," Charlie promptly shot back, "I'll be ready for the deposition." Silver conceded a tolerant smile, as if he were granting some kind of benefit to Charlie. The Beverly Hills import was really getting on his nerves. "Bert, I can assure you, my deposition will be no problem for me. I can deal with this."

"All right, let's deal with it. The fact she was so violent - what does that suggest to you, Charlie?"

Charlie was pissed off at the patronizing tone in Bert's voice, but he had no comeback for his question. He knew they'd politely considered his "Prozac scenario", but now, on the eve of his deposition, they were after something else. Oh yeah, the ball was in his court now - and he couldn't move his racket. He drew a blank as first Silver's and then Shackleton's gaze pinned him to his seat. "Well, I - she was freaking out. This was two minutes before she killed herself."

"Do you really think that's what she intended?"

"Bert, what's your point? That the suicide was an accident? Or that she-"

Sheila's eerie smile as she angled the gun away from him...

"Look, if she wanted to kill me - she had me. I was almost out cold."

"But your hand was on the gun."

Charlie froze, remembering the grips lashed together by the blinding panic and fury.

"Judge Merrill did see her elbow pull back," Shackleton quietly interjected.

"She was yanking on the gun, clearly trying to get control," Silver continued. "And then what happened when the gun was fired? Judge Merrill's view was blocked. That's what she told the police. You're the only one who can say what happened, Charlie."

Charlie was conscious of a dry flap of skin in his throat. Like a piece of rope or a little fist. He tried to swallow, but the leathery obstruction was still there. It had started to go for his breathing.

"Wait a minute, Bert. I - I'm sorry, but I need a minor reality check here. This conversation's getting a little too close to a request that I tailor my depo."

"I don't understand, Charlie."

Charlie instantly was appalled at his own words. But something else was supplying the words now - the little creature scuffling in his throat. Bert's stare glittered coldly. "Charlie, are you telling us that you saw the moment the gun was fired?"

I closed my eyes.

"Exactly," Shackleton replied. "So no one saw the gunshot, did they? How can we be absolutely sure it was a suicide?"

His boss had spoken. It was a suicide no longer. It was the moment the gun was fired. An explosion, a chance encounter of metal and flesh, the moment of intention being reversed....

Sheila's smile. The gun angling away...

"She intended to kill you, Charlie. But in the struggle, the gun misfired. That's the testimony. There was no suicide. There can be no death benefits."

"Ted, I - I just feel I need - I need to raise the red flag here that - our speculations on her state of mind don't have the probative weight of evidence even in..." Shackleton and Silver's hard, smooth stares were the face of a cliff, and Charlie was plummeting, clawing for handholds, basic law precepts in a fog of memory and terror "...and after all, there were others there in the room, and if we're wrong and they clearly saw a suicidal move...if I say I saw what I didn't see...if I...I'm sorry, I have to get a drink of water."

He slipped out of the room with as much dignity and poise as he could muster, grabbed the doorknob, and could barely turn it from the sweat on his palms. He felt a backwash of troubled murmurs about the case, or about his behavior - he couldn't tell because that mosquito whine in his ear was back that he couldn't swat away, and now the tinnitus became a rapidly ascending siren of protest as his head echoed from blows that came straight from his wildly accelerating heartbeat. No, Charlie instructed himself, this is not a coronary, this is a panic attack, just like Westphal warned me about, and I don't have to have someone drive me to the emergency room at Cedars, beg someone to watch over me and help me, just head for the water in the kitchen, and SHIT - don't slam into Carol, just smile, excuse yourself, the office kitchen is deserted thank God there's your water. He drank Dixie cup after Dixie cup of Arrowhead Mountain Spring water, fascinated somehow by the little emblem of the pristine rills trickling down into the peaceful valley. What he really needed was some Jack Daniels, he thought, but he clenched the sink until he felt calmer, though the ringing in his ears persisted, along with the echo of an undeniable conclusion.

She could have killed me.

Brakelights lit up all down the stretch before him, and Charlie muttered a curse as he downshifted into a glut of traffic. Nasty orange diamonds. "Road Construction Ahead." Static gnawed at the corners of the Tom Petty tune on the radio and Charlie instantly popped in a Steely Dan tape. He slid the a/c switch up a grade as much for the noise of the fan as the cool air.

He wanted all the aural and climate control possible. He was on the San Diego 405 Freeway heading north.

No question about it, he was en route to "deepest 405." Not the 405 to the Marina Del Rey Freeway and a day at Venice Beach with his buddies. Not the 405 to the 101 to get to Universal Amphitheater for a rock concert, or to a day at work at the Van Nuys hearing room. No, now he saw ahead of him a parched Valleyscape where corporate complexes and malls swarmed over the hilltops. The San Gabriel Mountains had grayed out in the smog, the resinous sunlight bearing down hard as emory to grind all the color out of their surfaces. He was passing Panorama City, home of colleagues like Judge Merrill, who, no doubt, was praying comfortably in church this very minute. To his left was Van Nuys Airport, and an odd WWII-themed restaurant, the 92nd Aero Squadron, where a little-known but sumptuous champagne brunch could be had for only twenty dollars – but no, he would have to keep driving.

Saugus. Newhall. The exit signs passing behind him threw out city names he only knew from mass murders and natural disasters. Castaic - was that a plane crash or a brushfire? The foothills took on a defiant green in the face of strip malls dug into their flanks, and the scars of red clay excavations fronting bone-white gated communities whose pennants spasmed in the wind.

Charlie was getting hungry but the thought of grabbing a burger at one of the local fast food dives kept his foot on the accelerator. Sheila Reed wouldn't touch that crap even down to her last few dollars. She would scrounge up vegetables somewhere for herself and her brother. Make her own macaroni and cheese.

But for...the short, sharp phrase bubbled up in Charlie's thoughts whenever traffic congealed on the hot, stifling freeway...*but for* the industrial injury, suicide would not have occurred. Charlie would not have flashbacks to a gun barrel and black streaks of blood out of nowhere in the middle of the day. He would not have an ear alarm that rang when no intruder was in sight. His kitten Gaucho, squashed in the road six months ago, would not have appeared last night mewing at his bed, one eye crushed, his legs metal pincers clicking on the floor.

He would not be driving on this hundred-degree Sunday morning to visit the grave of a total stranger.

Now he was traveling the 14 Freeway. Here-be-dragons territory as far as he was concerned. The hills all around him became steep canyons encysted with boulders. The map indicated old mines, rifle ranges, and a string of lonely private airports, gliders parked at dusty runways.

*But for...*but for the fact that a meaningless creep named Dr. Sandoval took over the risk management activities of one of a thousand clinics in L.A. County...but for the bastard's petty cruelty and lust...

Charlie exited the Antelope Valley freeway at the outskirts of Palmdale and promptly got lost. He drove empty boulevards past furniture warehouses, gun shops and car lots. He trolled for any hint of directions, squinting towards a horizon where telephone poles sawtoothed into a bleached haze. Finally he pulled into a KFC for some extra crispy with coleslaw, and then got directed to another highway, but as he headed for the 138 he was boxed out of the left lane by a horse trailer, shot past the merge, and was soon humping a dirt road through vast fields of broccoli and strawberries. The pickers pointed him towards a community of ranch houses that shuddered in the heat, shrunken roses holding fast to brown lawns, American flags limp in the dead air.

Finally, after several cul de sacs, Charlie broke through to a road that whipped him past a ridge of barren mountains. Their slopes were nothing but scree and clusters of dry shrubs, but houses still clung to them, each with its own cactus garden and fresh coat of paint. The woman whose fingers had entwined with Charlie's in her last moment on earth came from this dusty place, where you dug into the ground and always turned up sand and rock, but tried your best to make a garden out of cactus. In the shelter of one of those mountains, a mile off the road, the ground was watered enough to support a stand of willows, a meadow and some pastureland, and it was here, next to a horse farm, that Charlie finally found the cemetery.

The stone walls reminded him of New England somehow, but the dry patchy grass was definitely southern California. A group of mourners were concluding a service a hundred yards away and the reverend's murmur pulsed like the sound of a cricket in the dry air. Charlie felt obliged to take off his sunglasses and put them in his pocket. As he walked among the graves he realized he'd made a stupid mistake. Sheila Reed's grave would not yet have any kind of marker or stone. He'd come to pay his respects to her and he had no idea where she'd finally been laid to rest.

He spotted one of the cemetery workers returning from lunch, and asked him if he knew where the grave was. The old Chicano looked him over as if he'd dropped from the moon.

"Es la familia." He pointed to the mourners. "La familia aqui."

Charlie was stunned. He'd made a discreet call to the funeral parlor to make sure he'd be an hour late, he was in fact an hour-and-a-half late, but there was the family of Sheila Reed right where they could see him. He quickly slipped his sunglasses on and nodded pleasantly to the Chicano, took a few steps in the direction of the service, and then, when he was sure the worker's back was turned, he stopped at a nearby grave and lowered his head, hoping desperately to remain unnoticed.

It had been a busy Sunday, and numerous grave sites were spread with the artificial greensward used to cover freshly dug pits. The cemetery grounds were dotted with wreaths and bouquets. Charlie averted his face from the Sheila Reed service, but drew a little closer. Now he could dart sidewise glances and make out their faces. There was Brandon Reed, stiff, almost soldierly, and very clear-eyed, intent on the preacher's every syllable. Charlie wondered if the kid had ever been to a funeral before. At Brandon's side was his mother, a woman with red hair, pale complexion and bleary eyes. She had the premature jowls of an alcoholic. The mother stood next to a pale blonde, emaciated man with thick glasses. Charlie had heard Brandon's father had vanished, so this was possibly a second husband or a brother.

These were Sheila Reed's people. Yet none of them had been with her when she died. None had seen her or been able to call to her at the moment she had decided there would be no more cactus gardens for her, when that smile had floated up like smoke from the fire of her despair. "I am the Resurrection and the Life." Charlie listened to those words never heard at Jewish funerals. A huge mystery, centuries old. A door that opened two ways. He wondered what Sheila Reed saw when she slammed the door shut. He knew that his face was the last thing she saw behind her. And what had happened to him at that moment? Suddenly Charlie knew that the Charlie Solomon that had existed that day, the Charlie heading for another case, or a tennis game, or a purchase of perfume for Dana, had vanished into a shadow beyond reclamation, joined with Sheila Reed behind that forever darkened door.

The service was over. The mother and stepfather bent over the gravesite and tossed their lilies into the pit, and then it was Brandon's turn. He squatted over the grave, elbows on his knees, gazing into its depths. Then his face crumpled and squeezed out his tears before he finally tossed the flower onto the coffin.

Charlie felt a terrible cord of grief lash through him. He too wanted to toss a flower into the grave and comfort the boy. He wanted to tell Brandon how he had thought his sister was smart, beautiful, resilient and brave, that he'd truly wanted to avert that terrible moment, to help her, to help them all. There were tears scalding his eyes now, and he reached up to wipe them, forgetting he still had his sunglasses on.

He smacked the glasses off his face, and the moment shocked him so much that he almost tripped on one of the naps in the greensward. His leg shot out and knocked down an urn of lilies and snapdragons with a clang that echoed through the eucalyptus trees.

When he looked back up, one of the mourners was meeting his gaze. Dressed in a black skirt and white blouse, she had a face of startling clarity, with flushed skin, darkly piercing eyes, and the thin, slightly drooping nose of a woman in a Renaissance painting. Her gaze was tranquil but faintly amused, as if even the gravity of this moment couldn't dent her awareness of the absurdity of Charlie's presence.

"Theresa, who is that?"

Now they all spotted him, and he saw to his horror that Brandon was staring at him. The eyes held his fast and he felt himself and all his reasons disappearing into the question in that kid's stare. Lost in that juncture he felt he couldn't move, couldn't even breathe - but somehow his feet were already backpedaling. "Look, I - I wanted to say - I'm so sorry for your loss. I - I'm very sorry." As he made a stiff bowing motion and walked back faster he realized he had muttered the words so low that they couldn't possibly have heard them. All that they could see or hear was Charlie Solomon running away.

"No, I saw him on the news," Charlie heard Brandon shout behind him. "He's the insurance lawyer, still fighting the case, he - Hey, what the *fuck* are you doing here?"

"Brandon, please, son!" That sounded like the priest. Charlie heard clothes rustling, footsteps racing towards him through the grass. This had been a terrible, terrible mistake. Charlie took large contorted strides that finally verged on an uncontrolled sprint to his car. There was an old Lincoln Continental parked nearby, but at least the driver was turned away, moving a parcel to the passenger seat, and couldn't see him. As Charlie jumped into his car, his vision seemed to blister, like a strip of film melting on a projector's hot lamp, from the blaze of shame rising up within him.

The cry came through the windows as he slammed the door shut. Brandon's yellow hair flared in the sunlight. His spit flew onto the glass, flecks of it bubbling before Charley's stunned glance. Then the blow from Brandon's shoe slammed through his car door just before the ignition kicked in and Charlie sped away.

"Where are you running, you fucking talking head?"

Rodion "Rody" Golan spread the pictures out on Shackleton's conference table. There was none of the usual joking around that accompanied his sub rosa videos of crippled roofers playing softball, or horribly injured gaffers dancing at wrap parties with porno queens. This was very different. Rody had disliked this assignment intensely, and all Shackleton and Silver had to do was read his stare.

The p.i. had one of those broad Slavic faces, with a heavy forehead, a blunt spigot of a nose, and close-set eyes beneath thick straw-colored eyebrows. Kids had called him "Wolf" at school, and Rody had learned way back then that all he had to do was nudge those eyebrows together, and the man across from him would know he had to leave Rody alone, back down fast, or prepare for a fight.

Shackleton looked at the pictures of Sheila Reed's funeral, realizing that Brandon indeed had a support group that might help him fight his case, one that might even include Sheila's inconstant friend, Theresa Calder – and then he winced at the shots of an anguished Charlie Solomon running for his car.

Rody at this point felt an explanation was required. "I did not know Charlie is there. I like him, work with him. I take picture of a man running, then see who it is."

"Of course, Rody, I understand. Believe me, we had no idea he'd be there either."

Bert Silver picked up one of the pictures. "We have got to know where Charlie's head's at. If Worcek gets him to say the wrong thing at his deposition it could open up a whole can of worms." Silver slammed the picture down. "What the hell was Charlie up to?"

Shackleton studied the photo of his employee, then looked up with a rueful smile. "Oh, poor Charlie - he's not up to anything, I'm afraid."

-4-

the whole and nothing but

The rain was hammering down hard enough to overflow the gutters by the time Charlie arrived at Dr. Westphal's office. The ground of Beverly Hills, the whole asphalted desert basin of Los Angeles shrugged off its failure to absorb the rainfall, which glutted the antiquated storm drains, gushed up through the streets, and pooled on the crosswalks. Lawns were impastos of trodden mud, and even the bright day lilies that flanked the entrance to Westphal's building were drained of all their color.

Charlie shook out his umbrella on the second floor landing as he greeted Dr. Westphal, who was serenely dry in a black pullover and smiling non-judgmentally as ever. Today Charlie wanted to get right down to business. Get a grip on some problems, parse them out, solve as much as he could with Westphal in the allotted hour. Only when he was once again facing that impish, half-expectant smile, and hearing the rain's drumbeat on the windowsill, he couldn't make up his mind what to prioritize.

So he simply complained. First he vented his anger at the freak late summer rain, not to mention all the tiresome Mexican hurricane coverage in the local news. Then he talked about trying to organize his fellow condo residents to get the building's exterior repainted. The garish pink façade was an eyesore. Long ago it was meant to resemble adobe, and now it had faded to the hue of whorehouse chiffon. But no one but him seemed to want to make the effort to choose a new color, arrange a schedule, get a price. His fellow association members were all flaking out on Charlie, but of course, Charlie muttered, "... what do you expect from the people who let Gaucho lay out in the rain for two days?"

99

The doctor raised his eyebrows to let Charlie know he'd leaped past the limits of coherence. Charlie was embarrassed, but by now he knew he had full license to ramble as long as he could explain himself afterwards.

So Charlie told Westphal about the little black-and-white kitten he'd picked up from a pet adoption agency for fifty dollars and a promise to have him fixed but never de-clawed. His only pets growing up had been birds and fish because of his father's allergy to animal hair, but a girlfriend had just dumped him in a particularly noxious way and he'd finally decided to become a cat-owner.

He'd named the kitten Gaucho after one of his favorite Steely Dan albums. At first his pet had been a poolball of anarchy and diarrhea caroming through his shelves and closets. The low point had been when he'd caught Gaucho shitting in his indigo-glazed New Mexican Indian bowl: the kitten had freaked and scrambled away, and only a diving catch from Charlie had saved the ceramic from total destruction. But gradually Gaucho had calmed down into a non-stop grumbling and chattering playfulness and Charlie had become very fond of him.

Gaucho picked that month of awakening tenderness to squeeze out the front door on a day Charlie had carelessly failed to lock it. Charlie had always kept his neighbors at a courteous distance, but the next day he managed to approach a few of them and admit his cat was lost. They promised to keep an eye out for Gaucho. One of them, a fortyish divorced graphic artist, did a little missing cat leaflet for him, and even followed Charlie around the block, calling out for the kitten in a piercing Texas accent that roused every cat or dog in the neighborhood but Gaucho. But somehow no one from the building but Charlie noticed the squinched mass of black and white fur by the curb near the intersection, wrenched into a grimace of open-jawed agony as if the kitten had vomited out his life beneath the car's tires. There Gaucho lay in runnels of water on a pissing rain day like this one, with his soaked Xeroxed photo on a nearby streetlight, and a heart-shaped collar i.d. with Charlie's phone number on it for anyone to see.

He told Westphal the dream that he'd had just a few nights ago. The paramedics led Charlie to that spot near the intersection. Gaucho was still alive, thrashing up towards Charlie's face with his bloody little paws. Charlie

100

had begged them to save the cat. The paramedics took Gaucho into Charlie's apartment and Charlie had called the vet, but after hearing Gaucho's injuries described the vet had hung up on him. So the paramedics had thrust a large tweezer into Charlie's hands, and muttering garbled instructions, they'd taught him to insert tiny metal joists into the cat's legs and wrap his stomach with bandages. Once they were out the door, Charlie, lying in his room, had watched Gaucho feebly cross the floor on his new pincer legs, his fur matted and bloody, one eye crushed. He'd wanted to call the paramedics back and tell them he'd screwed up. Now with the same loathing he felt after that dream he lashed out at his neighbors again, a tirade that only stopped when Westphal pounced on one of his phrases.

"You felt they were irresponsible?"

The remark surprised Charlie and he retreated into lawyerliness. "Well, technically it's not as if they had any 'good Samaritan' obligation here, but come on, if I saw someone's pet lying in the gutter - well, actually I'm not so on fire to leave 'Your cat is dead.' messages myself - "

"Charlie, I'm not asking you to be analytical or reasonable. How did you feel?"

"All right. I was outraged. I mean, someone's pet is lying half-squashed in the road. My cat, Gaucho! For people just to ignore that, to not even *contact* me and –"

Charlie stopped. The sound nicking at his ear had lengthened to a high-pitched whine.

"Damn it! Fucking tinnitus again."

"This question upsets you?"

"No, the tinnitus upsets me, Doctor! I'm not getting rid of it." Charlie laughed painfully. "It's like a guest you can't throw out."

"Would you prefer to talk about that, Charlie?"

Charlie looked up at the diamond-shaped panels of Westphal's mullioned windows. The pelting storm had fogged them up as if the glass had been bruised. Every plash of rain on the glass left a rivulet that traced a plumbline down through the metal frames, each one stark and clear.

"I'll tell you what upsets me. I went to Sheila Reed's funeral."

101

Westphal leaned forward and paused for a few careful seconds. "Really...."

The whine in Charlie's ears revved up and he spoke louder.

"I didn't mean to be seen, of course. I just wanted to pay my respects, but I didn't get there late enough. I figured there would be an empty grave, I'd be there alone, but what the fuck was I thinking? I'm the lawyer defending my company against her brother's death benefit suit, for Chrissake!"

"Your work doesn't exempt you from your humanity."

"Yeah, but it does make it a low-percentage choice." Charlie tried to force out a chuckle but nothing seemed very funny. "The brother remembered who I was. I wind up running out of there, literally running to my car like a thief. I was so exposed, such an idiot! And I'm sure it's gonna get back to Hobart-Riis. Oh this one will come back and bite me in the nuts!"

Westphal leaned back in the plush armchair. "Remember what the main enterprise is here. Reconnecting to the event. Restoring control. This was a very positive step. Going to the grave, acknowledging the death."

Charlie knew Westphal was right, which only sunk him deeper into confusion. "So if I'm on the right track, why the tinnitus, the awful dreams? If I'm feeling violated, betrayed - where's that coming from?"

Westphal let the question echo in the office, giving Charlie room to continue.

"Yeah, I know. The medicine, the white-noise generator by my bed, they'll help me sleep, make the tinnitus manageable in time. It will probably disappear - though it may not. The dreams scare the shit out of me, but they may be, along with our "exposure" and "restructuring," oh, signposts leading me back to a nice calm state of mind. Little billboards. 'This way back to normalcy.' I may be sane again, I may be a functioning lawyer again, after three years of law school and three years of clawing up the - Jesus," he cried out, "what was I doing going for that gun?"

"What did you think you were doing, Charlie?"

Charlie didn't even think about the answer. "Trying to save my ass."

Westphal spread his hands. "You don't think that was a sufficient reason?"

"Of course, of course..,." Charlie muttered, briefly exhausted, feeling a mild sense of relief and trying to hold onto it.

"The tinnitus is merely a symptom of the havoc this event has caused in you. The misery, the sense of betrayal, where that might come from..." Westphal let the sentence quizzically trail off.

"I suppose that requires poking around in my memories, right? We talk about my family, my early sexual experiences."

"Did I say I was a strict Freudian?"

"Well, I just assumed as a therapist, you - "

"Talking cures that take forever - that's okay if you're an hysterical 19th-century Viennese heiress, but this is modern day Los Angeles, Charlie, and we both agree you have to get back to work."

Charlie felt re-invigorated, as if the session had briefly become a doubles match and Westphal, his partner, had just fired a winner down the alley. The main thing was not to slipslide into boring counterproductive victimhood. And when it came to that he and Westphal were on the same team.

"You know, one reason I'm getting so stressed out is my upcoming depo."

"This is something to do with Brandon Reed's case?"

"Well, yes. Basically, I'm going to be asked if Sheila...I mean, if what happened with the gun...was really a suicide."

"So you feel now that maybe it wasn't?"

"Well, my boss sure would prefer I come to that conclusion...I mean..." - but Charlie didn't mean anything more than what he said and he knew it. His feelings of reassurance dried up and blew away like flecks of dead skin. He glanced up to check the time. Two minutes on the clock, but this time Westphal wasn't stopping the game.

"The truth? The truth is – the truth is, I don't know what to think!" The feeling of sheer wretched remorse washed over him. "Sometimes - I even wonder if I accidentally pulled that trigger. But no - she was in control."

Charlie could see in Westphal's face a radiant moment of discovery - he did everything but cry "Eureka!" as he leaned excitedly towards Charlie. "There. What did you just say? 'She was in control.' Had you gotten hold of the gun, no one would've died. But she was in control. This was a very strong, stubborn woman Charlie. It makes no sense for you to blame yourself for anything that happened to her."

"But - there was this look she gave me - just before..."

"And then she moved the gun. Again, she was in control. And you closed your eyes and you didn't see what finally happened, did you? And don't you think the fact that you blame yourself might be distorting your memories of the struggle?"

Charlie felt once again, fighting to the surface of the black waves of his anxiety, that bubble of absolution. He tried to dredge it up to the light. "I wanted to stop it all."

"Yes, but she was going to do what she was going to do. She was going to pull that trigger. And now you have to do what you have to do. Move on and do your job."

Charlie had slipped backwards in the session, and the doctor had put him right. Two professionals solving problems. Just the facts, Mr. Solomon. As he took his still dripping wet umbrella out of the vase, Charlie shook the doctor's hand warmly and felt a genuine strength in the elegant fingers that resisted his own.

Westphal watched Charlie race through the puddles the short distance to his car. Clearly this was a kid who hated getting wet. His nervous sprint reminded Westphal of the image of Charlie running from the funeral, and he decided to take care of the business at hand right away.

Mavis Thorpe had him on hold only a second when Shackleton came on the line.

"Yes, Dr. Westphal. How are you doing on this totally wretched day?"

"Keeping a busy as possible. Listen Ted...", and Westphal took a pause, trying to shape the phrase as delicately as possible, "I was wondering if you could let me know a little bit about Charlie's movements over the past few days."

"Well, he seems to be showing up to work, attacking the case strongly. But we happened to find out that he was present at Sheila Reed's funeral. No doubt he was looking for some kind of closure, but – well we're all concerned about him."

By now this sort of conversation was like a practiced dance routine, with Westphal introducing no phrases that could be construed as breaching doctor-patient confidentiality. "Does he have any – particularly stressful situations coming up in the next couple of weeks or so?"

"He'll probably be deposed in the Sheila Reed case."

"You should be concerned, Ted. Very concerned."

The Santa Monica Workers Compensation hearing rooms were the perfect arena for Charlie's return to his daily rounds. The downtown L.A. branch, located in a pockmarked old building on the fringes of Skid Row, was definitely too creepy, while returning to the Van Nuys hearing rooms might have left him literally gun-shy. Charlie parked a couple of blocks away and enjoyed the brief walk to work, relishing the cool snap in the air.

The hearing rooms were located opposite a pleasant industrial park near the Santa Monica Airport, on whose baseball and soccer fields Charlie had played many pickup games while Bonanzas, Cessnas, and Piper Cubs roared off into the bright sun. The layout was similar to Van Nuys: two levels of busy hearing rooms built around an open courtyard with a few ornamental shade trees. An elevator column discharged new arrivals onto the second floor, where lawyers popping and unpopping cellphones held the usual bazaar of swaps and deals, and claimants, tired of their long sit in the waiting room, paced blindly back and forth through the verbal sparring that would determine their fates.

"Hey, it's the Master of Disaster."

Only Kaukonen would lead off with a wisecrack like that, and then have the chutzpah to whistle the refrain from "Spirit In The Sky." Charlie saw genuine affection spark behind his usual wiliness, and was soon in the grip of a hug and a couple of back slaps. When he broke the embrace he was greeted by Remar and a couple of other claimant lawyers he'd tangled with over the past year.

"Welcome back to the monkey house, pal."

"Good to see you again, Charlie."

"Glad to have you back."

Their greetings were warm, even ebullient, but Charlie could also hear in their voices the shadow of the ordeal he'd endured. It was an

105

acknowledgment that took the form of neither praise for a winner or consolation for a loser - more like a mutual exhalation of "There but for the grace of God..." and a loyal seal of approval from the fraternity. And it was a fraternity after all. A few hundred men and women trying 95% of the cases, the fifty judges they appeared before every week, and they all knew each other by name. And while they fought each other hard over their cases, they fought the caseload together. They were brothers-and-sisters-in-arms against the same confusing, ball-busting system, cutting red tape, cutting deals, cutting through the bullshit as much as they could and laying it on each other as little as possible. No other specialized branch of the law had as little backstabbing among the brethren and as much camaraderie for a fallen comrade returned to the fray.

Another arm corralled him, another fervent embrace. Bob Barasch could be always counted upon for a little extra intensity. "God bless you, kid, you've come back from more tsouris in a week than some guys come back from in a lifetime."

"Well, hey, the thought of never doing another MSC again just broke my heart - "

There was a chorus of laughter, and Kaukonen brought up a case of his he considered "aggravated attorney abuse," and Barasch told Kaukonen "hey, sometimes a fucking predator has to eat crow...", and Charlie knew they were onto the usual war stories and off his trauma for the day. Thankfully, he would neither be praised nor judged. These men and women were too alert to the shifting points of view in any catastrophic event, and too savvy about the messiness of people's behavior in a crisis.

Charlie savored the congenial workday conversation, and then out of the corner of his eye he caught sight of Vel standing by the railing gazing at the group of men. He could tell that, having been gone for ten days, she was anxious to speak with him.

The others noticed Charlie noticing Vel. Barasch quickly excused himself for a scheduled appointment with Judge Maitland, while Kaukonen begged off for his meeting with a lienclaimant, and soon the whole crowd broke up with a last round of sympathetic glances his way.

Vel's ironic gaze was still trained on the departing men as Charlie hustled to catch up with her. "I couldn't have broken up that meeting any faster if I had leprosy."

"Vel, we'd all finished shooting the shit for the day. And since when would you want to join in?"

"But Charles," she mock-sighed, "I so want to be back in their good graces again. Smoke cigars in the club car."

"You can probably get a date with Kaukonen."

"Please, my grandmother has spells for encounters like that." She ceased smiling at Charlie, and leveled at him a gaze of penetrating intimacy that only a woman friend could muster. Her pale white brow actually showed a tiny wrinkle of solicitude, like a fingerprint on porcelain. "Charlie, I'm so sorry I didn't call you before. I was off for a week in San Diego and I never got near a t.v. or a newspaper. How are you holding up?"

Charlie leaned against the railing and looked out over the courtyard. Vel didn't bother to wait for an answer. "For what it's worth, you're showing good form. That's important."

"I'm trying, Vel," Charlie replied sadly. "I'm glad others are impressed."

Vel turned to him. "You've just been close to death. It will take awhile to feel - intact again."

Her words speared through Charlie with their unflinching compassion. Charlie wondered for a moment about the mind that worked behind that high, well-scrubbed forehead, of the heart beating under her tidy little blouse. What was it like growing up in Mexico? Charlie had a sense that for all Vel's exquisite manners, he could talk more with her about scenes of blood and darkness than anyone he knew. But he doubted they ever would have that talk and they certainly wouldn't begin it now.

"I've got an MSC coming up, Vel."

"I'm finalizing a C. & R.... Oh, look at that. The daily drama."

The crowd in front of them was parting as Liz Worcek chased down her latest defense lawyer adversary and made a scene.

"I will go down in flames, Stan! I will be a kamikaze in there for this woman and -"

107

"Oh, for Chrissake, Liz, it's just a postponement!"

The defense lawyer was trying to shrug her off. It was like trying to brush away a badger.

"Yeah, Stan, right, the computer's down, another bill for another delay. Go ahead, ask for a continuance and sign the damn blame sheet. There's gonna be no settlements on this case. No deals! Know why, Stan? This woman tried so hard before she fell apart and they fired her. She tried to cram the medical technology for her new assignment but they gave her only three weeks. A dyslexic, Stan!"

"Never proven!"

"Yeah. You don't believe it. I guess that's why you sent her requests for documents and insulting letters until she broke down and cried in my office! Because you feel she has no case. Or maybe you wanted to send her a lot of reading material because you know how wretchedly hard it is for her to read!" The lawyer stormed off in a huff and Worcek cast a brief glance at the ripples of laughter left in his wake. "You keep treating her this cruelly and we can't lose!" Slightly out of breath, she turned to Charlie and Vel. "Well, we can lose with Judge Hartley, stupid Encino whitebread prick, but clients don't need to know the politics.... How are you doing, Counselor?"

"I'm making it, Liz."

"Vel can give you moral support. She knows something about carrying heavy baggage."

"You're discreet as always, Liz," Vel replied, but not without a trace of affection. Worcek's utter lack of inhibition about embarrassing herself or others should've disgusted the glacially proper Latina, but Vel seemed fond of her, within strict limits. Vel had once told Charlie that Worcek reminded her of old widows in little Mexican towns who bark their way invincibly through life from behind their veils.

And Worcek respected Vel. She'd once told Charlie about Vel's exploits at the much-loathed downtown L.A. hearing rooms. Worcek could never run the gauntlet of bums flanking the entrance there without a queasy sense of fear and revulsion, but Vel seemed to welcome confrontations. Once when four unwashed transients had blocked Vel's path, figuring the pale, demure princess would be cowed into a big handout, she'd let loose a volcanic stream of Spanish curses and sent them scuttling back to the corner. Another time Vel had actually handed a bum a dollar only to have an adjacent bum try to grab the prize. The two had furiously quarreled and would've slugged it out had not Vel plucked the dollar from the second bum's hand, torn it in half, and handed one-half of the bill to each of the combatants. "Now you have to be friends," Vel had sweetly told them.

"So tell me you two," Worcek asked worriedly, "you think I can exercise a peremptory? If I try to shoot down Judge Hartley and I lose, I'm screwed."

"Were you the original attorney on the case?" Charlie asked.

"No."

"You can do it. Challenge the judge. Get him removed."

Worcek grinned at Vel. "Man's such an iron-butt when it comes to procedure, I love him. Thanks, Charlie. Makes me sorry I have to depose you in a week."

The edges of the courtyard suddenly whited out. "What? A week? It's coming up that fast?"

"No one wants to linger on the Brandon Reed case, Charlie. Calendar it fast, move it the hell out of the system - I'm sorry, Charlie. You'll be noticed today, but I wanted to warn you."

"And it's going to take me a month to get Brandon Reed on the stand," Charlie snapped. His annoyance quickly soured to cruelty. "Think he can wait that long, Liz. Think he's going to be the next Quentin Tarantino before then?"

"I suppose it's possible he'd consider a bona fide settlement offer instead of the kiss-off Hobart Riis is throwing at him. Any chance you might work some of that Charlie Solomon gentle persuasion towards that end?" Worcek looked Charlie over shrewdly. "Could save us both a little trouble."

"And how far up in dollars do we have to go Liz?"

"I don't know, Charlie. That depends on how much trouble you want to save."

"I suppose," Vel added, "you should factor in how long it'll take the kid to starve."

"Yeah. I guess I just get too emotional, I never learn. Go along to get along, right, Vel?"

Charlie saw Vel's eyes grow hard as little sheets of mica. Worcek had transgressed their mutual courtesies, and Vel instantly let her know it. Worcek turned quickly back to Charlie. "Stay in play, kiddo. And tell Shackleton and the rest that I'll be very happy to depose you and fight this Brandon Reed case to the end, with every iota of indignation in my body. But if you can make it worth our while to settle...anyway, wish me luck."

"Good luck, Liz."

"Back at you. Really." She patted Charlie on the shoulder and hustled off to her next case.

"What exactly is she deposing you about?" Charlie didn't have to explain very much before Vel grimaced in disgust.

"Oh Christ, Burnight. Look, just argue suicide isn't compensable and that's that. Burnight's only meant to apply in the most extreme cases."

"Like shooting yourself after you get screwed on a worker's comp case at the worker's comp board?"

"Was it a suicide? Do you know that for sure?"

"Well...obviously our defense will be that – that nobody knows, and thank God the coroner didn't rule one way or the other. See I'm the only one who can really say..." Charlie's fingers laced around the bright red railing. What, he wondered, was the reason for that tinkertoy kindergarten color? He gripped the rail until his fingers whitened. "My upcoming deposition - it's a big deal, a very big deal, and I don't know why, or how..."

...what he saw, what he did at the moment his life was torn asunder, that blur of events would be teased apart for every advantage that Worcek could uncover. And no one knew its precise articulation, not even Charlie, because each moment had been filtered, and would once again be refracted, through his bewilderment and horror...

"Well, if you say it's a suicide," Vel finally ventured, "you just better be sure you're sure, Charles."

What Charlie always found truly weird about the Sunset Strip was how many chaste and sober places of business fronted the Boulevard right next to the garish rock clubs, video stores, and a five-story high babe in purple leotards caught in mid-leap like a startled deer. In one such small building, fairly

110

nondescript except for a facade of Ionic columns, the Bernard-Duvall Health and Wellness Clinic had set up its new headquarters. Charlie cruised past the walls of the manorial Chateau Marmont - hotel of choice in cocaine Hollywood's dark glory days - and pulled into the clinic's small and chronically packed parking lot.

He'd had to draw on all the sympathy that Shackleton, Bunning and Silver had for him in order to get this interview. From the beginning of their association with Hobart-Riis the founders of the Bernard-Duvall Health and Wellness Clinic had avoided interviews regarding worker's comp cases, had claimed as part of their privileged status as the "house clinic" that they be exempt from legal prying. Bunning had even repeated a point Bernard had made on the phone: that any testimony from Bernard or Duvall regarding the Sheila Reed case, given their business ties to Hobart-Riis Insurance, Inc., would be worthless. Charlie knew that, of course, but had basically begged permission to try to glean some evidence for his "Prozac theory."

He wasn't too surprised when, after being briskly escorted through the spanking white clinic rooms to Dr. Larry Bernard's office, he spotted the doctor rapidly packing his attaché case. Small but barrel-chested, heavily jowled, Bernard always reminded Charlie of an aging gnome, especially when he was grimacing and moving as quickly as he was now. "Terribly sorry Charlie – I have to run to lunch with one of our investors who's just in for the weekend."

Charlie just as quickly took a seat, glancing around the elegant office with its parquet floors and comfortable-looking furniture. On the cabinet behind Dr. Bernard's desk was a large aquarium, where angelfish with gossamer fins trailed each other in a graceful limbo.

Bernard shot him a surprised look, then drank down a cup of tea on his desk. It looked suspiciously like he'd ordered a relaxing cup from his secretary before he'd realized he would just have to duck out on Charlie's appointment.

"I'll cut to the chase, Doctor. Liz Worcek is suing Hobart-Riis for death benefits for Brandon Reed, Sheila Reed's brother. She's going to be arguing that Sheila Reed committed suicide as a result of her worker's comp injury."

Bernard shook his head. "Terrible thing, that incident. Poor misguided girl. Very sad."

111

"Yes it is. Anyway, what Worcek has to establish is a very tight lock between the suicide and stress generated by Sheila Reed's worker's comp case. I have to break that lock." He was about to summarize his theory at top-speed when he realized that if he mentioned Theresa Calder to the doctor, not only might Ms. Calder get in trouble, but she could get him in terrible trouble as well. "Theresa, who is that?" *The funeral. His run to the car.*

"Yes, Charlie?"

He found his footing again. "Now as I understand it, some drugs were once stolen from the Clinic?"

"Oh, yes. We filed a police report. Nothing ever came of it. And about a year ago, we had also had some pills disappear from the office, if that helps you. But frankly, we suspected that that might be Dr. Sandoval. That's one reason he was terminated."

Maybe it was the doctor's mile-a-minute indifference that provoked him, but Charlie couldn't resist a small jab at that reply. "Sheila Reed said he was a cocaine abuser. Did he pop pills too?"

"We think so. But I'd let opposing counsel bring that up if I were you."

The meeting was not going well. "Look, we know Sheila Reed experimented with alternative medicine. How about pain pills, anti-depressants?" Charlie was finding the man's polite excuse for attention more and more irritating. "You see, if we can establish that, perhaps by obtaining anti-depressants, she altered her own mental state unwisely, and that that was behind her suicide…"

Dr. Bernard threw his tabletop a look of deep contemplation.

"Doctor, that's what the case boils down to. Why'd she do it? Was she getting pills here from a friend? Perhaps you observed or heard of something a little more specific, let's say some connection with other office personnel. Or maybe she was just getting treated here and overmedicating herself." He knew his voice was rising but he didn't care. "Doctor, we need some answers!"

The doctor finally deigned to reply. "I understand your reasoning. Someone helps Sheila get some pills, the pills have side-effects, like suicidal tendencies…but I have no proof. None whatsoever." He spread his hands to express his disappointment. "And I certainly don't think she ever sought

112

subsequent treatment here, once she started to fight us." He clicked the attaché case shut and grabbed his windbreaker from out of his closet.

Charlie realized the interview was over, but one last question leaped out of him. "How could Dr. Sandoval – how could he have remained on staff, kept treating Sheila Reed like – well, kept letting that friction in the office continue? I mean - " Charlie flailed for a safe way to proceed, "I mean, she was the office manager, right? Mavis Thorpe, who's our secretary-office manager-whatever, she knows where all the bodies are buried. You want to be nice to her."

Bernard had the look of a teacher having to drive a point home for an obtuse child. "Charlie, actually it was Dr. Sandoval who had all that knowledge. Once he came in, Sheila pretty much was reduced to ordering the paper and pencils - which, you might consider, might've made her a little resentful, a little more prone to hysterical charges against the man."

"Especially when he started deep-sixing those files and blaming it on her?"

Bernard's jaw tightened. "Charlie, I admit it took us too long to realize he was out of control, and I'm sorry about that." The doctor stood up from his chair while still musing on the problem. "You've made an investment in a person, you see: your money, your time, your professional judgment. You don't want to throw that away. And even then, it's more difficult to terminate a fellow doctor than you think. You're a boss, but you're not God - what a disappointment! You know, when I hired him, I couldn't imagine he'd be a threat to anyone. Did you ever read Machiavelli's 'The Prince'? 'A wise leader appoints his inferiors.' I thought Sandoval was pretty stupid, actually." He chuckled at the humor in the strange turn of events, then clapped Charlie on the shoulder. "Look, why don't you stay awhile, have some tea, and I'll have the staff bring you that police report. I'm sure you'll find something, Charlie." Bernard jabbed brusquely at the air with his pipe. "But here's what I think. Sheila Reed was homicidal, not suicidal. You're lucky to be alive, my boy." He said those words as if rendering a professional diagnosis, then wished Charlie a good day and headed for his car.

"Well, that does seem to be the party line," Charlie muttered in the wake of Bernard's retreat. He decided to try and salvage the day by having that cup of tea and reviewing the report. But even though there were anti-

113

depressants among the missing drugs – even the magic word, Prozak – and some suspicion an employee stole them, there was nothing there he could use.

Still he remained in the office. He soon realized why – he felt as if he were observing the scene of a crime. Sandoval and Bernard meeting here every day, Bernard knowing how fucked up his colleague was, probably knowing the routine savagery of the way he treated a key member of the staff...

A heavy object smashed against a wall. Charlie rocked back in Dr. Bernard's swivel chair and almost smacked into the fish tank. He heard a muffled male roar, then the sounds of a frightened woman's protest. Then it was over. Charlie remembered all the things Sheila Reed had said about this place. He walked over to the edge of the door, peered down the hall, and was immensely grateful to see nothing broken, nothing that would call for his intervention or confront him with a glimpse of pain or panic.

Another woman stepped lightly out of an adjoining office to check the halls. Charlie lingered in the hall and let his eyes roam over her trim calves and her wide-hipped but beautifully formed legs poised alertly in a tweed skirt. Then she looked in Charlie's direction - and he instantly recognized those eyes that hung before his stare like calm little pools of darkness, the elongated chin, the pursed, dark lips and swarthy skin - suddenly he was once again standing on the parched grass of the funeral ground, and he couldn't begin to explain himself. A disdainful smile flicked across Theresa Calder's lips and, tilting her head with a dismissive motion, she slipped back into her office.

Charlie knew it was time to retreat. If Charlie's presence at the funeral could be used against him, Sheila's good friend would use it - there was no reason for him to walk by her open door, watch her look up at him with mild annoyance. She flexed her fingers together impatiently, and the turquoise rings and silver bracelets she wore gleamed in the fluorescent light.

"Can I help you?" she coldly asked.

"No, I, um - I heard a noise, I wanted to make sure everything was all right." She looked at him as if he were a burglar, waiting for him to explain himself. "My name's Charlie Solomon, I'm counsel for Hobart-Riis Insurance Company, so I doubt there's much we have to talk about at this juncture. Sorry to disturb you."

"I'm Theresa Calder, the office manager. And don't worry, I didn't mention to anyone that you were at the funeral."

Damn, simply by peering in her door he'd asked for that. "Well, that should be my business alone," Charlie curtly replied, but then he added "Thank you anyway." His eyes evaded hers and surveyed the office. Between a corn plant and a ficus were what looked to be southwestern Indian relics.

"Those are beautiful. I should think you'd keep them at home."

"They're good luck charms. They go where they're needed."

Charlie smiled uneasily, but Theresa wouldn't smile back. He redirected his attention to the hallway.

"Looks like there's no problem here."

"Oh, these little storms pass quickly." She leaned towards him with an expression of sarcastic curiosity. "You ever work with doctors?"

"Can't say that I have."

"They can be like children. Temper, temper. But we all try to adjust. Comes with the territory."

Charlie desperately wanted to break off this conversation, but he knew he couldn't dare be the least bit hostile. And he also wanted to terminate the lingering, unsought-for connection that had been forged by his own stupid actions. "Theresa, if it's of any interest to you - I was at the funeral because I felt I should be there. Pay my respects. I didn't mean to intrude on the family. I figured everyone would be gone by then, I'd have a moment alone - anyway, I might have handled that poorly, but I hope you understand."

Theresa's expression hardened. "Sheila didn't shoot you. So I guess that makes her an important person in your life."

The rebuff chilled him back to reality. "I really shouldn't be speaking to you. The Reed case is continuing, and - "

"What? What are you talking about?"

"Brandon Reed, Sheila's brother. He's suing for partial death benefits. Anyway, I can't comment further, I'm running late - take care, Ms. Calder."

"Just a minute. I didn't mean to be rude." She rose like a ballerina would, tautly composed. "This was her office, you know."

Charlie gazed at the room. Not a trace remained of Sheila's presence, but Charlie was newly fascinated by the office, and what seemed equally intriguing was how little Theresa had added to it. Just those New Mexican feathered idol masks on the bare walls.

"So you took over her job?"

She gave a little toss of her head. "Lucky me." She sat back down, and Charlie could feel the weight of her stillness - except for the legs, gently flexing within the sheath of the skirt, the hem drawn along a glissando of a knee movement.

"I hope you're being treated better."

"They're more careful with me."

Charlie wondered briefly why he was still asking questions. Was it reflexive curiosity, or the enticement of a secret he'd be better off not knowing?

"How were they ' careless ' with Sheila Reed?"

The minute he asked that he recoiled from his own question, and braced himself for a shutdown, a "save that for the deposition, Counselor."

Instead, she told him a story.

"Sheila had pictures on the wall of her college team's championship game. Well, Dr. Sandoval one day storms into her office, and says that we have very conservative female workers and patients of the Muslim faith, and those pictures were offensive to them."

"Women in volleyball uniforms on the beach?"

"He said they were out of keeping with the tone of the office and demanded they be removed."

"How many patients would ever see the manager's office?"

"None ever come back to see me. No one on the staff minded Sheila's pictures. But she told Sandoval she'd agree to remove them, went to lunch, and Sandoval had them thrown out."

"In the garbage?"

"He said that he assumed that's what she meant."

Charlie shuddered at the cruelty of it. There was a look on Theresa's face of grim indifference to the story's impact, as if she could tell a hundred stories like these. Charlie expelled a breath and his eyes dropped to the ground.

"I'm glad they fired that bastard. At least you don't have to deal with him."

"He did his damage, though."

Now that they were talking to each other, Charlie suddenly realized why he'd sought Theresa Calder out. He could mention now that he was reviewing the police report, seeking evidence that Sheila had possibly overmedicated herself and succumbed to the medicine's side-effects. He could watch her reactions, hope for a crack in the wall. But the impulse died just as soon as he called it up. This woman, the so-called office flake, was more watchful, cautious, compassionate than you might expect. She'd protected Sheila, and she'd still protect her. Besides, she and Charlie now shared secrets that it would be very unwise to breach. Charlie backed away quickly. "Anyway - sorry for your loss, Ms. Calder."

"Likewise, Mr. Solomon." Her eyes glittered, brutal and unforgiving. "By the way, I was the one who dug up that police report for you. If you're looking under every rock, better be prepared for what might crawl out."

"What do you mean by that?" He nerved himself to continue. "If you feel there's anything we should talk about -"

"Have a good day, Mr. Solomon." She turned back to the paperwork on her desk.

There would be no further questions, unless she was compelled to answer under oath. No one in this place would help him avoid his deposition, or mitigate its importance. Charlie could only the hope that Brandon would get desperate enough to accept the crumbs they were tossing him, otherwise....*What might crawl out? Oh god, what if Worcek brings out I was at that funeral? No, that wouldn't help her, she wouldn't....*Charlie rushed down the hallway from Theresa's office. He was suddenly aware of the furtiveness of his actions, worried that someone would observe his erratic behavior and report him to his bosses, or that some article of glass or china thrown in a fury would smash with a woman's cry of pain into a nearby wall.

The air-conditioning in Hobart-Riis' office went down on the day of Charlie's deposition. Charlie, seated at the conference table, drank his glass of water quickly. Everyone waiting for Charlie's deposition to begin had a glass, and there was a pitcher of ice water set on a paper mat on the adjoining cabinet. Two floor-standing fans retrieved from the storage room were blowing at Charlie as he tried to compose his thoughts.

He exchanged sardonic glances with Silver that simply meant "This day of all days." The building had been impregnably efficient since Charlie had started work for Hobart-Riis, and now, for the first time, the HVAC system had broken. Out in the lobby several pails collected the steady drip still leaking from the ceiling, and the carpet stank of the torrent of water and coolant that had unleashed itself onto the floor just before Charlie's arrival. The walls echoed with metallic clangs as, somewhere above them, mechanics busily wrestled a new part into place.

Worcek rushed in, followed by her partner Roman Nadjari, a swarthy thirty-year-old with a hawk nose and the subtle sharpness of a pickpocket. They piled their documents on the table and Worcek shook hands all around with Charlie, Silver and Shackleton.

"Bummer about the a/c, huh?"

"It appears the difficulty's in the compressor," Shackleton replied.

"Well, gentlemen, and lady," Worcek announced, glancing sideways at the stenographer, "if there's no objections, let's get started. I can see we're going to need some breaks for fresh air."

"This is Century City, Liz," Silver drawled, and he distilled into those few words all his thinly-veiled scorn for a slob of a Valley claimant lawyer who thought you could just take a walk around the block in this all-business neighborhood. Silver also conveyed that he wanted to move along quickly as possible. Maybe he didn't want to give Charlie time to think too much about his answers. Charlie couldn't agree more.

Shackleton, having impressed the shadow of his presence on the proceedings, withdrew to carry on the day's business. The four lawyers turned to the stenographer, and instantly her fingers began their spidery ripple on the keyboard as she intoned Charlie's name and address. Charlie was briefly fascinated by the responsiveness of those fingers, by the speed and precision with which this young woman would engrave his testimony into the permanent record.

"Do you swear to tell the truth the whole truth and nothing but the truth so help you God?"

Charlie watched the fingers embody the words, and then the fingers stopped. He'd interrupted the machine. A shudder of chagrin went through him, and then the cold taste of fear.

"I do."

Worcek began with the basic parameters: how long he'd been a worker's compensation lawyer, how long he'd been working for Hobart-Riis, how many claimants and claimant lawyers he had, to the best of his knowledge, gone up against. The usual lawyerly fishing and futzing tolerated in all depositions as long as it had a vague thread of a purpose - and in this particular case, Worcek was out to show that Charlie's answers to questions about claimants and hearings would have genuine validity. Next she began to focus on that percentage of cases Charlie had encountered where the claimant had been fighting her case in the system for a long time. Both Charlie and Silver knew what she was going for: the "Nineteenth Nervous Breakdowns."

When Worcek asked if, as a rule, these clients often were agitated and distraught, Silver finally disentangled his hands from off his belly and played his ceremonial attorney's role; he objected that such a question called for speculation. Worcek dug down into more specific territory. Can you recall more than one such claimant raising their voice in the courtroom? Yes. Verbally confronting the judge or opposing counsel? Yes. Threatening violence? Once or twice. Crying in anguish?

Silver again objected, and Worcek moved on, unearthing a case Charlie had worked on where Nadjari had repped the claimant. With stabbingly precise questions she and Nadjari took Charlie through the woman's plea to the court: how her slip and fall in the restaurant had activated a degenerative hip disorder, how the worker the company claimed she'd confronted in a shoving match would have testified on her behalf but was threatened with dismissal, how other co-workers couldn't be located after two years, how unfair it was that, because she'd tried to continue to work, the company claimed she was lying about the extent of the hip disorder. Charlie began to put images to the memory: red, very Irish freckles, pasty skin, gray weeping eyes. He took

119

another drink of water, while answering Worcek's questions as minimally as he could.

"What would you say," Worcek asked quietly, "if I told you this woman committed suicide three months ago?"

Silver leaped out of his chair. "That's an absolutely outrageous question, Liz!" Nadjari also instinctively got up, which only heightened the absurdity of the moment for Charlie, and made Charlie feel almost sorry for him. The man had spent most of his life in Bucharest, where a spat with the wrong person could mean a beating or much worse. For just one atavistic moment he'd forgotten that in his new land of freedom and opportunity low blows were hardly a punishable offense. The important thing was to get up from the canvas holding your balls and come back fast. Charlie knew just how he would answer Worcek.

"I'd ask, Liz, why aren't you suing for death benefits for her relatives under Burnight? Or is that case even weaker than this one?"

At Charlie's icy reply, Silver took his seat again and gave Charlie a well-concealed pat on the back. Worcek was one of the hip-and-lip shooters of the profession, and Charlie had just punished her soundly for it. He smiled at Worcek, who flicked her eyebrows skeptically, as if to assure him victory was short-lived.

"Was Sheila Reed vs. Bernard/Duvall Clinic your case to begin with?"

"No, I was assigned the case when another attorney left the firm."

"So you'd never discussed Sheila Reed's case with opposing counsel prior to the pretrial conference?"

"No, I had not."

"And you never had a personal encounter with Sheila Reed."

"No."

Charlie knew where Worcek was going. Sheila had never met Charlie, she had no particular animus against him, no personal motive to pull a gun on him and try and kill him. When she asked if Sheila was completely neutral in her feelings towards Charlie, Silver was about to object, when Charlie pulled his own countermove. "Well, she is on record as saying in her previous depo 'You goddamn lawyers are all the same'"

"Meaning any lawyer connected with her case?"

"Well - yes."

"A fairly irrational claim, wouldn't you agree?"

Charlie silently cursed his stupidity, knowing the damage was done. He'd put on the record a hint of how obsessive and paranoiac Sheila was about her battle with the system, and how her worker's comp injuries and subsequent case had mentally damaged her. Silver's indrawn breath, the mild disgust on his face, certified the setback.

Suddenly Charlie hated the Beverly Hills bastard. The crow's feet under the eyes pursing with every complacent little grin of contempt. As if Charlie had never fenced with a claimant lawyer before, as if you didn't sometimes take a hit in the parry-and-thrust, as if he needed a fucking minder in a deposition. His flash of anger was suddenly extinguished by a dull clonk from the ceiling. The lawyers watched in horror as a panel buckled and split and a jet of water gushed down onto the faux black marble credenza top.

Workmen's curses reverberated through the walls as Silver rushed to the door and shouted for more pails. Within minutes, office assistants had moved the credenza out of harm's way and, after a volley of accusations and rebuttals of incompetence in Spanish, the invisible workmen's hands had stanched the cataract to a trickle. Still, everyone agreed the depo would have to be moved into Silver's office.

In this smaller space the fans blustered so close to Charlie he could see the dirt crusting on the metal grill. Around him were pictures of Silver and his family. His three-year-old girl playing with a dog. A little white fence drank in the sun. Silver relaxed and calmly scrutinized Charlie from within his pride of place, his comfort zone. Worcek barked "Back on the record!" The centipedal fingers ran along the keyboard. Charlie poured himself another glass of water, and felt that taut astringency in his gut, that overcharge of adrenaline that he knew would key the damn ringing in his ears.

"You interrogated Sheila Reed about her affair with Dr. Sandoval pretty extensively during her hearing, didn't you?"

"I suppose I - Yes, I did."

"You assumed it was a weak point in her case?"

"Liz," Silver snapped, "we all know it was a weak point in her -"

"I'll ask and he'll answer, Bert."

Yes, Charlie finally replied, he was exploiting a weak point in her case. It was a fulfillment of his professional duty in doing so, he asserted, trying to make his point clear above the tinnitus, and a headache shooting its first pincers into the base of his skull.

"Isn't it true that you repeated to her her own words 'You're lucky if you like yourself enough to masturbate?'"

"Yes," Charlie replied, and he did it to point out the contradiction between her previous testimony and her actions in sleeping with Sandoval. And as he did he remembered Sheila coiling in on herself, biting her knuckle, like one of those flowers you find shriveled on its stem after a freezing night.

"So you were trying to cast doubt on her perceptions of being harassed and being so depressed she couldn't work?"

"Compound question - but I'll answer yes."

"So it's fair to say you were trying to prove she was a liar and a cheat. Wouldn't this make her feel frightened and even more depressed?"

"I was trying to win the case! Do my job!" He was shocked at the reaction around the table. Figuring he was merely being emphatic, he could see from their faces that he'd roared out the response. *Well, what else could he do, trying to make himself heard over the fans, inept plumbers crawling through the ducts, the siren in his head?* Worcek asked him if he needed a rest. He self-consciously relaxed back into his chair, trying to summon up his usual nonchalance, and declined the offer.

"When were you first aware Ms. Reed had pointed a gun at you?"

"When everyone was staring at me. That's when I turned around and saw it. I- I was going towards you and Judge Merrill, and Sheila told me to stop. Then I turned around and saw the gun."

"Well, which is it, Charlie? You turned around and you became aware of the gun, or she called to you?"

Charlie knew he was flailing. The ball shooting past him over and over. Get behind it. Dig in.

"She called to me. She specifically told me to get in a corner away from the others." He could see Silver's infinitesimal smile of approval.

"But she didn't call you by name?"

"No."

"What did she do next? Threaten you specifically?"

"Yes. She had a gun on me."

"What did she say?"

"Oh, she went on about her job. About being blamed for lost records. I think she even said she wanted to be a lawyer."

"In short, she didn't threaten you specifically, did she?"

Charlie drew a blank. *Does my headache know the answer to these fucking questions?*

"Um...not in so many words. No."

"So, Charlie, when you tried to grab the gun, what happened?"

"She hit me."

"She didn't shoot you?"

"Everyone knows she hit me, Liz!"

Silver tried to whisper into Charlie's ear something to calm him down, but the buzz of Silver's whisper scratched like an insect leg on the tinnitus' shriek. What did I do next*? I shut my eyes.*

"Yes," Worcek replied softly, "we all did. But in your own words – can you tell us why?"

"Why? Because I was terrified, I thought I was going to be shot to death."

"Can you tell us what you saw before you shut your eyes?"

"I don't understand the question."

"Do you need me to repeat it?"

I don't understand the question. No, really, I don't understand it. Can I remember or am I able to remember? "There was a struggle. Our hands were clenched on the gun. I shut my eyes. The gun went off..."

"Before you closed your eyes, Mr. Solomon, where was she pointing the gun?"

That look of hers. That angle of - where was the gun? It was a lascivious smile wasn't it? The pleasure of dealing death. The Red Thread. I misunderstood it before. Just remember, the way you just discussed it with your colleagues...with Westphal... her wanting to beat you, to kill you...she had control...the gun just - between my desperation and her fury - but what about that smile? Was it sorrowful? No, contemptuous. No, it's - I've got you, you

123

bastard – no - what's the use - to hell with it - Oh God, what have I done. Oh God, I know it's all over for me - Sheila's face and the angle of the gun fighting for definition, as if his brain suspended it in a gray sac of an egg, wove it in the glue of a cocoon...

"I can't remember."

"Let me clarify this, Mr. Solomon. You're saying at the moment you were engaged in the climax of a life and death struggle, before you closed your eyes for what might have been the last time, you can't remember if the gun was pointed at you or back at Ms. Reed?"

We had our hands on the gun. I closed my eyes. The gun went off.

The gun angled away from him. Her look, so tender, a breath of forgiveness...

"Yes. I mean no, I can't remember."

Silver fiddled with his papers, a sullen look of disappointment on his face. Worcek, deflated, moved through her last questions, and then looked up at the ceiling with a faint smile. They could hear the air conditioning kick in, but it was a few moments before Silver at last got up to switch off the fan.

There's a certain safety, Charlie thought, when no one is satisfied. Charlie clung to the assumption that neutrality was the same as truth. Sheila's last pitiful gesture on earth was neither homicidal nor suicidal. Just a messy nervous tic with a fatal bullet attached. Such was his testimony.

After Worcek and Nadjari had left, Charlie told Silver that he felt nauseous, really terrible. Silver put a desultory hand on his shoulder. "You should go home, Charlie. Everyone will understand." Silver looked like a man with a long, tiring, dirty job ahead of him, who was just disposing of one of its more trivial tasks.

Charlie was too exhausted for anything more than a mild suspicion of Silver, or for even the slightest attempt at damage assessment over not having given Hobart-Riis Insurance, Inc. exactly what it wanted. It was a compromise, he thought. Like it always is, a compromise.

He practically sleepwalked off the elevator at the first floor. The sandpaper glare of the white courtyard stonework blasted at the uncertainties in his brain. A sputnik-shaped fountain shot out an endless geodesic burst of water, wheels within wheels of superbly efficient spray glittering with harnessed sunlight.

He wanted water. He bent over a water fountain in the lobby by the garage and drank for five minutes. When he got back to his condo, he put on his dark mirror shades, poured a thermos full of icewater, and went out to sit by the pool. His brain was one long scar still vibrating with the echoes of his headache. Above the empty row of lounge chairs a pianist was running the scales, and the notes drew his eye to the rim of the pool where a blonde woman in a T-shirt let her dog run out its leash to trot into the grassy shade. Charlie felt as dry and hollow as he ever had in his life. He drank his water, rested the cool glass on his stomach, and watched the chlorine green ripples of light dance on the pool's surface.

A bunch of kids played the old "Marco Polo" game at the shallow end. He watched them splash wildly and disperse, stopping whenever the "it" cried "Marco!", dutifully squealing "Polo!" in return. A tiny girl with an ecstatic smile couldn't stop giggling with excitement when the "it" got too close, a sure sign to him to lunge out and tag her next time. The boy blundered vigorously through the cool water, trying to sort out the voices, leap through the water with his hands open. The others tried to elude the call, but through some surface tension in their fractal course never drifted too far. Their closed eyes glowed red with warm buffered sunlight. They navigated subtly through the pool, off the slightest inflections of Marco's cries, you saw how sensitive they were. Yet there was the girl cornered by the "it", the cries came impetuously faster, until, with peals of hysterical glee, the touch was passed.

125

-5-
breaking eggs

The best moments on the set of "Nightwinders 2" were when Brandon made his own pictures.

Not that he didn't enjoy working with the camera crew. Color temperature - that was a great secret. To know color wasn't just a blaze of blue sky and red clay hills at noon or a streak of gold in the sunset. Color was a secret code, blue and hot in daylight and cool and orange indoors. Your vision broke the code in daily life, but when it came to colors on the screen, cameraman Lonny Hirzfelder, his two assistants, and Brandon filled in for the brain. If they didn't slap the correct filters on the lenses, load the right film stock, and lay gel sheets on the windows, skin tones would gray out or glow like a jack-o-lantern. Color temperature took Brandon deeper into the camera and the pleasure of control.

Then someone would shout for him to haul ass to the honey wagons. He was, after all, the production assistant. Drag the dolly. Tuck the cable under garbage in the street. Stand on a corner at two in the morning, walkie-talkie in hand, to stop a club-crawler or trucker headed towards the warehouse district that was the main set. For about a week he'd tried to work both his hardware store job and the movie, but then came night shoots and nodding out in the D & D basement, and he'd finally had to quit on his kindly hardware store boss. The "prod ass" stuff really wore him out sometimes – and he wasn't getting paid that much more than he got to lug boxes of nuts and bolts at D & D.

But then, at last, would come the order to grab his old Nikon and shoot production stills. Brandon loved the time when he stood right behind the director, Barry Pelz, to record the scenes as they were filmed. Pelz, who was also co-executive producer, a choleric little man with a thick black beard, snapped at just about every crew member, but he'd quietly let Brandon trail the action, gauge when the light was right for his picture (sometimes the gaffer would angle a spot for him), and fire off candid scenes for the production album.

Of course, the reason Pelz tolerated him was because producer Nate Wesserman genuinely liked him. Wesserman, a large but quick-moving man with a grubby salt-and-pepper beard, had taken a shine to Brandon the minute Brandon had walked into his office for a meeting that Mindy Crawford, after regretting that her paper didn't need photographers, had set up. Wesserman had been sympathetic to Brandon and his ordeal right off the bat. "I had a key grip once on a film had a worker's comp case. Insurance company cut off his benefits, he had to fight in court for a year to get them reinstated, a bunch of bullshit. You hear about this crap happening to good people it makes you sick."

Wesserman had looked over Brandon's photos, told him he had "a hell of an eye", and had sat Brandon down in his cluttered movie office with his assistant, Jana, to explain his "female vampire genre" movie NIGHTWINDERS 2: THE STALKER'S RETURN. "These are contemporary vampires. Smart, like Lara Croft." They'd originally been bit by The Stalker, nasty lord of the underworld's party scene, and imprisoned in his harem of killer succubi. They'd escaped the Stalker's seraglio and set fire to him on the way out, but because of terrific Asian presales and a box office bonanza in Latin America, the Stalker had patched himself up like Tom Cruise in INTERVIEW WITH A VAMPIRE, in an oozing burn-encrusted sort of way, and was now back and really pissed. Wesserman had a New York cop show rasp that broadcast the same message to a worker or a casual listener: you're mine, so relax and enjoy it. Brandon, entertained, listened.

But then the woman playing Ligeia, Soleil, had walked into the meeting, and Brandon had found it hard to keep his eyes off anything else. Wesserman seemed to take that in stride, and with a little smile he'd asked Brandon. "Sound like something you're interested in?"

Brandon had nodded fiercely.

"Yeah, you seem motivated. Look, I have a feeling about you, and I always trust my gut. That's why it's so big, right? It's trusted. It's interesting to me to have someone work as a production assistant and a stills photographer. Two for the price of one."

"Or one half," Jana had chimed in. Brandon, stealing a little glance at Soleil and getting an answering smile in return, didn't think about the money.

Tonight the crew was filming the "Ligeia Takes A Yuppie" sequence. Soleil waited in the middle of a blocked-off intersection draped in a long cloak, under which, as Brandon knew, she had nothing on except a G-string. She shivered and churned her arms under the cloak to keep warm as Hirzfelder lit the scene and Wesserman screamed "Someone paint her fucking claws!" Brandon helped set up the flags that would mold the light on the various marks she would hit, and relished the chance to stare at her until Pelz ordered him over to the honey wagons with Keith Mondaro's dinner. Mondaro was playing Bromley, an obnoxious leering partygoer who gets bit by a Nightwinder in the first ten minutes of the movie, after which - in the movie's big running gag - he gets a weird allergic reaction to vampirism that causes him to rot. Naturally, since he can no longer see himself in the mirror, he doesn't know that his face has become a pustulent slab of goo, and he can't understand why girls puke at the sight of him. Mondaro had to have grotesque latex makeup plastered on him every night, which meant he had to wolf down his food before the makeup made it impossible to eat. So Brandon rushed Mondaro his meal, then ran frantically back to watch the key shot, though he needn't have worried. This was a scene where Pelz definitely wanted a production still.

The shot was tricky. The yuppie in his Miata, dressed in your basic all-black club mufti, rolls up to the deserted intersection, scoping the derelict warehouses for the underground club, painfully aware that, in his little convertible, he's perfect carjacker meat. "Got a light?" Soleil calls out, and saunters up to the Miata.

As they set up the shot, her shaggy auburn hair caught the backlight in a spray of iridescence. She had pale amber skin, blue eyes so widely set she looked almost Oriental. She was so graceful that by the third take she was hitting her marks flawlessly, the boom mike swinging like a compass needle, the dolly trailing her like a bass line as the focus puller's hand spun in rhythm to her steps.

The yuppie of course is totally gone on her. When Ligeia asks for a ride, he starts grinning like a fool - but then he gets hinky, realizing gorgeous women don't normally just hop into his Miata. He starts to refuse...and now it was time for Brandon to cock his shutter. The spring ratcheted and advanced the film and Soleil, with the aid of a concealed platform, leaped onto the edge of the yuppie's driver's side door with a balletic ease that took the crew's breath away. As the dumbfounded yuppie gaped at her, she dropped her cloak. She stood perched on the Miata, long and sleek, her ass round and hard to hold her steady, thigh muscles like silver ropes, her back floating up into the light that just caught the sweep of her breasts. Brandon could barely steady the camera against the pounding in his head as he fired off the shot.

"Yep," whispered the boom man behind him, "that's a Kodak moment."

Pelz yelled "Cut!", the crew roared with approval, Brandon lowered his camera and Soleil was looking at him. She gave him a little wink as she jumped off the car. He stood in the street gripped by sheer "cock shock" as he and his buddies called it, a seismic rift below the waist, groin full of smoke and hunger.

Next day he was still on a high from that moment, still spinning fantasies off of it as he drove the writer's new pink pages to the director's house. As Brandon drove down Olympic Boulevard in the company Toyota, he cast a glance at the cellphone on his belt that kept him linked to the action on the set. Wesserman always made him feel a key part of the picture, even if Brandon was just manning the phones at the "Nightwinders" offices. The producer could make a command like "Conference me to fucking Pelz!" sound like the whole movie depended on it. Brandon rode on surges of adrenaline, especially at the end of the night's shoot, sometimes two in the morning, when they'd pack his car trunk full of film cans, the whole day's work, Soleil's every invitation to the camera, and he'd drive down the freeways to the lab.

Stopped at a light, he dialed in for his messages, got one from Worcek's office, and called her back. When they put him right through without dangling him on hold, he knew there had been movement on the case.

"Hey, Liz, what's up?"

"Brandon, we got a crack in the wall here. I deposed Charlie Solomon and he fell apart."

"The lawyer fucked up? A'right Liz! I woulda liked to seen that."

"There's no way they can dare argue that your sister was out to kill Charlie Solomon after what Charlie said on the stand today. And he pretty much put on the record that the shooting was a result of the continuous trauma she'd gone through over this case."

"Continuous trauma? What the hell's that?"

"You know what Chinese water torture is, Brandon?"

"They drip a little water on your head every minute until you finally go batshit?"

"She had all the classic symptoms. Showed them right there in that courtroom during her case, and now we've got it on record."

"So that nails it, Liz? She committed suicide because of continuous trauma?"

"Well, now Solomon's claiming it wasn't suicide."

The glare off the windshield exploded. It filled his eyes like dust.

"He's fudging it," Worcek continued. " A loss of memory."

"The other people who saw it - they know he's fucking lying!"

"Actually, Brandon, Sheila blocked everyone else's view. Charlie Solomon was the only one who could've seen the gunshot."

"He can't lie about that! He - OH SHIT!"

The stupid tourist fuck in a white sedan and Kansas plates slowed down on a green. Brandon slammed the clutch and brake down, yanked the wheel to the right, and barely had time to register the Camaro now coming up beside him half out of the parking space - horns screeched, front bumpers converged, and Brandon saw the driver's horrified face just before he found the clutch. He stomped on it, downshifted to second and roared back into the left lane just in time to evade the Camaro and cut off the Kansas car, whose horn blared behind him.

"Sorry, Liz, almost crashed the company car."

"Christ, Brandon, car phones are dial-ins to an accident. I'll hang up and _"

"No!" He ordered Worcek to tell him what their next move was. Nothing, of course. Charlie did such a pisspoor job of lying that the insurance company would slow the case down to a crawl. When in doubt, delay.

130

"Something you could do for me, Brandon. I hate to ask, but - we could use more of an indication she was suicidal. If she had any letters, a diary -"

"Liz, why do I have to dig up her goddam diary?" he screamed. " The guy's full of shit, okay? If she didn't kill herself, if he didn't feel guilty, why was he at the funeral?"

"He was at the funeral?"

"Yeah, he was. What was he doing there, then? Was he spying on us?"

"No, Brandon, calm down, I don't think it was that –"

"Then he felt guilty! He knew because of what he did she killed herself!"

He could almost hear the gears churning in Liz' brain. "Brandon, you have to understand, Charlie might go there even if he didn't feel guilty, because of the traumatic nature of the event. The bottom line is, it doesn't help us Brandon. But it is interesting -"

"Liz, he's got to take back his fucking lie!"

"Yes, Brandon, I understand. And ultimately I think he may do that. He wasn't exactly cool, calm and collected, Brandon. For now, what he said is on the record and I'll have to deal with it. But I'll also keep the pressure on him."

"Yeah yeah, whatever." Fucking lawyers. He saw he was going up the steep hill towards Sunset. This was such a bad hill that once he stopped he knew he would have to use the handbrake in order to start up at the green without clonking the car behind him. He just wanted to concentrate on his driving.

"Liz, I gotta go."

Worcek purred sympathetically that they had them on the run, that they'd win this thing, before she finally hung up. The car engines rumbled at the light, a placid herd of exhaust-spewing cattle. Then, at the green, Brandon, distracted, released the handbrake too late. The engine revved up and he lurched and bumped the car in front of him. Fortunately, the guy just blew him off, leaving Brandon behind with his humiliation.

He backslid into thoughts of Charlie Solomon, the lying, squirming sack-of-shit asshole who was a blot on his sister's name, on his grief, on his hope for the future. A different kind of quiver rocked his loins, not the lust for Soleil he'd been feeling all morning, more like the hunger of a heightened sense of purpose. He would have to take more control of events. That was all there was to it. He remembered almost catching up with the prick as he ran for his car at the cemetery – but then, simultaneously, he remembered how embarrassed he'd felt about the shockwave that he'd sent through his sister's funeral, how he'd sunk into a black hole of shame the whole drive back to Los Angeles.

For now hold back. Let Worcek do her thing. Maybe she could deal with the prick a lot better than he could. He downshifted, breathed out with the thrust of the accelerator. That's it. Slice through the traffic. Concentrate on the driving, the work – and the other thing, hold it back for now. It would be better to try and get back the calm he felt buffing keys in the hardware store. But the radio played Rage Against the Machine, then "On A Plain," one of his favorite old Nirvana tunes, and he didn't want to turn it off. Brandon had been thinking of Kurt Cobain a lot lately. Raised in some hovel on pop tarts and beer and Doritos. All his life his stomach boiled itself raw with the crap he ingested. That's what the suicide was about, he said it in his note, "the pit of his nauseous stomach." But something had lurked in that pit he could use, and it made guitar strings crackle like green wood in a fire. Asshole, asshole...no, their lies only make sure I can't let the fire go out.

The more Charlie looked at Bert Silver's family pictures, the more he saw the appeal of having a child. That little girl toddling after a white blur in the grass. A pet rabbit that she knew in all her innocence she could catch and embrace. The barbecue with family friends, Bert in the floppy chef's hat spearing the hot dogs and honey-mustard chicken. Among Charlie's buddies, the idea of having a family was so distant and yet so unsettling that the one friend of theirs who'd had a baby girl tossed off the whole experience as lightly as possible. "This age, she's like a chimp, really." They could all be at ease with that. Tim Sandler had picked up a big, goofy pet that kept him running. Not a lifetime responsibility, a road down a chasm of awe and love. But as Charlie looked at Bert's pictures, those tranquil and affectionate moments, he felt how comfortable it could be to slip into the paternal barbecue bib, hoist a laughing new baby in your arms.

Charlie had seen a lot of Bert's family pictures lately. Ever since Charlie's deposition Bert, on Maxine Bunning's instructions, had scheduled twice-weekly informal conferences with Charlie to provide a "fresh perspective" as Charlie went through his "readjustment period." Translation: all his cases had to go through Bert.

On the table this morning, along with Charlie's customary scone and coffee, was the Cavanaugh case, a combined carpal tunnel and stress case brought by a secretary whom (everyone had to admit) had been overworked by an abusive supervisor. Charlie considered it quite a coup that he'd bargained away the whole psych claim, given that the company shrink had legitimized it. In return, Charlie was willing to accept therapeutic pain management, as long as that was coupled with a modest buyout of any possible future medical care. As for the job disability rating on which any benefits would be computed, he got the applicant attorney to agree to a lowered rating on the right upper extremity, due to Ms. Cavanaugh's history of bursitis, as long as Charlie accepted the carpal tunnel syndrome portion of the claim. An elegantly parceled-out and crafted settlement, on which Bert, the Beverly Hills genius, had only one comment:

"Jew them down more."

"Bert, I've totally negated our exposure to the psych claim."

"We can settle out any stress claim for five grand. You know that. Let 'em have the psych. Lose the pain management."

Charlie took a swallow of his cold coffee. "You want me to go back to Hoffman and undo the swap? The whole settlement could unravel. Bert, we know the woman had depressive episodes in the past. But the pain is purely a result of her job."

"Hey, carpal tunnel, ergonomics – the new administration has buried all that shit. Say it's all a flare-up of her bursitis. Or psychosomatic."

"Psychosomatic? Bert, she's put in this workstation. She has to constantly shift files back and forth just to use her desk. She's not a very strong woman. Meanwhile, her supervisor is on her ass all the time, showing hostility that's way beyond the bounds of acceptable workplace conduct."

Bert's eyebrows arched and he smiled. "You paint such a vivid picture of her plight, Charlie."

133

Charlie felt a flush rise to his face as if he'd been slapped.

"Limit the number of pain management appointments."

"I already got them to agree to a buyout on the future medical," Charlie protested. "She's going to need at least six months - "

"I have an aunt on Medicare. They limit her physical therapy. Surely we have the right to do the same."

Charlie wondered if Bert occasionally brought his aunt some extra pain treatment, or if she just sat in silent agony in the midst of those family barbecues.

"Try it my way. It's a manageable case, Charlie."

Charlie knew better than to challenge Bert's usurpation of his case. The settlement offer was a memory. Soon Charlie's reputation among his fellow attorneys would be a memory as well.

"Maybe you should keep your eyes on the road."

The Pacific Coast Highway was one long bottleneck. The Santa Anas had recently scorched Calabasas with brushfires, the flames had roared down almost to the beach, and partial roadblocks somewhere up north were still backing up traffic. Normally there would be a gorgeous sunset as tons of finely sifted chaparral ash, vaporized ornamental shade trees, and incinerated multi-million-dollar estates, one huge particle track of desire and terror, swirled together in the air to refract and distil an image of those fires over the Pacific. But tonight a mist hung low over the northern promontories, and the sunset was no more than an apricot glow that blanched over a leaden ocean. The engines idling all around him, the thud of the bass sounds leaking from the nearby Izuzu Trooper, all magnified the sullen churning of Charlie's guts.

"I just try and find a balance, Dana. It's that simple."

Dana sat uncomfortably erect in the passenger seat, hands folded on the navy blue skirt that matched her blazer. She was wearing a ruffled blouse and a cameo that practically screamed "family reunion." She looked like a china doll. "You don't get a balance by being too adversarial."

"I can't see you being anything but diplomatic, Charlie."

"Exactly. Hey, I always want to win, always, but - that case where I warned Seidel about his client's prior auto injury? Got a great settlement just

134

like that! And I won! I didn't nuke my fellow barrister, I even helped him - but I won. You know that's the one case this week where Bert didn't interfere. All this fucking micromanagement."

Every so often he shot a glance at Dana and saw her eyes fixed on the oncoming traffic. It seemed she was listening patiently to him, but he could smell she was tense, even through the perfume - an acrid edge to that flushed corn and honey scent of hers. Like a cat fixing every aspect of a fence in her mind before a leap, Dana was pondering every possible scenario of the upcoming dinner, in which Charlie would meet her entire immediate family for the first time.

Charlie knew he should reciprocate her silence, but he'd picked up a new habit. When he got on the subject of work, he couldn't stop talking.

"I mean, if Shackleton and Bunning really think about my deposition, they'll realize I gave Worcek no ammunition."

"Of course not."

"I've been told repeatedly by experts - although admittedly these experts have never actually experienced a moment like I went through - that my memories are going to be untrustworthy. I merely conceded that at the depo...Fuck, look at this traffic!"

"It's what we expected. We'll get there on time."

Charlie exhaled away the tightness in his gut. "You're a real diplomat, Dana. You have the nicest way of telling me to shut up."

Dana smiled wearily, and Charlie finally found his silence. He calmed down once he made the right turn at Topanga Canyon Boulevard and began climbing the hills towards the Juniper Heights Inn. Weathered hippie era bungalows and antique shops hunkered down beneath willows and eucalyptus trees in the twilight. They hugged the silence to their porches and wooden frames with an ornery determination. Out of it and proud of it. The old Topanga mall flashed by, the signs above its trading post waving in the breeze. Badges of old psychedelic glory.

Steely Dan formed its glistening bubble of sound between Charlie's car speakers, luminously detached. So many of their songs, coming in the wake of the '60's, were both wistful and cynical about people needing to be cheated by beauty. He turned up his "Countdown To Ecstasy" tape.

Why did you need to be cheated by beauty? Why were you disappointed when the twilight didn't set the sky ablaze?

At least for a few hours the tinnitus had vanished, and he could listen to his old favorite band without the high whining tone lodged in his ear that tore to shreds the fabric of their silken harmonies. Sometimes the tinnitus got so bad that Charlie had turned back to guitar-driven bands like Radiohead and Soundgarden - the power chords at least fought the tinnitus to a draw. Then his neighbor had told him with dismay that he was the last person she'd expect to be playing rock music through her walls at night. Forty thousand down on a two hundred grand condo and you still had stucco wonder walls that leaked your habits to your neighbors - *gouts of blood littered on your face -*

Charlie shuddered alert. He realized he'd been driving without attention on a mountain road. He turned to Dana, who gave him a reassuring pat on the hand. She hadn't spotted his lapse. Above him, misty trails of cloud swagged across the hilltops, and in their silver wake the groves of pine trees emerged with brushstroke clarity. This was better. Dana at his side, her family waiting at the big cozy restaurant on the bluff of pine trees. Just ahead - that was where he should be.

In Los Angeles, you knew you were in a privileged place when you stepped out of your car and looked up at green mountains, a winding road stretching below you, the scent of laurel and menthol floating in the air. The Juniper Heights Inn was an L-shaped tile-roofed hacienda with an imperturbable reticence. Its guests, mingling in the white gravel parking lot, chatted in hushed tones, sensing that any loud or brash talk would mar this perfect union of nature and wealth.

But the atmosphere inside was almost boisterous. The lounge was done up Art Deco-style with chevron lamps, fan palms, and Sydney Greenstreet ceiling fans. Waiters serving canapes and highballs threaded through customers who stood at the two full bars or relaxed on the plush divans and armchairs. In the corner by the dining area Dana spotted her family getting fawned over by the maitre 'd and proudly led Charlie over to greet them.

Bob Brandt, Charlie could see, had taken full advantage of the Juniper Heights' eccentric dress code, which mandated jackets and ties but welcomed Western-style flourishes like capacious silver buckles and hand-stitched leather boots. Charlie winced in the grip of Bob's handshake and returned the big man's efficient grin. Dana's dad had inherited an agricultural machinery company that supplied the great farms of the Coachella Valley. He liked to accent his wardrobe with touches of sodbuster California, but he was a Los Angeles business magnate through and through, living in Holmby Hills, golfing at the Brentwood Country Club. Charlie found him glacially remote, but at least he told good stories about the financial and real estate deals he'd been involved in at Charlie's age, including the one that had brought the Dodgers to Los Angeles.

Dana's mother, Lisa, was far easier to take. Still brash and auburn-haired and showing off a voluptuous figure in cocktail dresses, she'd had an eight-year run as a daytime soap actress. She and Stefanie Powers had once been up for the same "Rockford Files."

Soon Glen and Bill Brandt sauntered over from the bar to join them. Glen ran the family's Sacramento headquarters, while Bill was pre-law at UCLA. Charlie looked at the shades of blonde hair that surrounded him. Dana's fine, sun-bleached straight hair, Glen's ash-blonde curls, Bill's more stylish reddish-blonde buzz cut. The movie "Village of the Damned" flashed through his mind but he quickly suppressed the thought.

Once they were seated in the Juniper Heights' enormous southwestern-style dining hall, beneath a wrought iron Mexican chandelier with copper-tinted glass bulbs, Charlie at last managed to relax. Dana had warned him that Glen was ponderously all-business, while Bill had a definite appreciation of irreverence and style; he'd even managed a grunge band in high school. So Charlie deftly talked music to Bill, business to Glen and Bob, and old Hollywood with Lisa. He noshed on a baby green salad (remembering to use the right fork) and an appetizer of New Mexican squash with acorn dressing, washing it down with a killer pinot grigio from the Juniper Heights' own vineyard.

By the time the medallions of venison in raspberry sauce, sliced ostrich in pomegranate sauce, trout amandine, prime rib and filet mignon had arrived, Charlie felt that, if he wasn't glowing with conviviality, he was at least basking in the warmth of this family's acceptance. He was blending in with the business scuttlebutt. He joined the family's praise of the decor - an impressive mix of

Indian masks and relics with boldly un-p.c. stag and bears' heads mounted on the walls. He could easily ignore Mr. Brandt's ironbound right-wing politics when the man so generously ordered a third bottle of wine. Charlie had to pass after two glasses, since he had no chauffeured limo waiting in the white gravel parking lot. But he relished seeing this family hang loose. He could trust that future family gatherings would be lubricated by tolerance, goodwill, and plenty of pinot grigio and merlot.

Charlie was working on his third slice of ostrich steak, which tasted appealingly like London broil, when his knife hand was clutched by Mrs. Brandt's warm and urgent grip. He looked up at her, her skin flushed with martinis and wine, and for one bewildering moment thought he saw a flash of lust in the old soap opera star's eyes. He gulped down his morsel of ostrich and tried to frame a response, when the corners of her lips turned down with sadness.

"Charlie, I just wanted to tell you how well I think you've handled all this."

"You've made it easy for me, Lisa. I'm having a marvelous time."

"Oh, I didn't mean this dinner, Charlie." She laughed a little too heartily from the wine, and Bob Brandt quickly jumped into the conversation.

"So, Charlie, dinner with the 'other family' isn't quite the trial you expected?"

"Bob, I don't mean that," Lisa almost shouted. "I mean that terrible case of yours!" Charlie saw the eyes of everyone at the table dart to their plates. They all knew exactly what she meant and had clearly dreaded that the right blood alcohol level would bring it out of her. It was up to Charlie to smooth things over.

"Well - you do what you can. You get some therapy, you go back to work, you move on."

The family as one smiled with approval. "Way to be, Charlie," Bill interjected, and Dana threw her arm around him. "I think Charlie was very brave."

"It was an accident, Dana." The words leaped out before he could think them through and he was confronted by puzzled faces around the table. "I mean it never should have happened. Any of it. But it did. Main thing is I'm still here. Enjoying this excellent dinner with excellent company."

"I raise my glass to that," intoned Bob. They all toasted Charlie, and Bob grabbed the bottle out of the standing bucket to pour his family a refill.

"You know," Glen pronounced, "it's really sad how these workers misread the system. Hell, before Sacramento tightened up on the stress rules, they'd sue for anything."

"I know what you mean," Charlie replied. "Back when you could sue if you proved your job caused more than 10% of your stress? I mean, if your job's not close to 100% of your stress, you're probably not showing up."

The whole table laughed, and Lisa leaned forward, staring at Charlie. "You don't know stress until you've worked on a daytime soap. You not only had to know your lines every day, but who had what disease, and - I played the temptress of course, and one time I forgot who I was seducing that episode, I kept calling him Fred instead of Donny, and they had to change the whole plot!"

"Well, the old worker's comp rules were ridiculous," Glen persisted. "Every lazy sonofabitch who wanted a ticket to Hawaii was suing the system. God, between the worker's comp and the disability laws and the damn unions it's amazing anyone in this state can run a business."

"Actually," Charlie said, laying down his fork, "I've always felt more unions could help the worker's comp situation."

Glen shot him a suspicious glance. "More unions?"

"Take this woman, Sheila Reed. She had a cocaine-addicted nut case for a supervisor, and he pretty much drove her off the job. She wanted to work, no question about it. If she'd been in a union, they might've protected her, and none of this would've happened."

"Charlie, they would've taken her union dues and gone to Vegas."

A part of Charlie wanted to laugh, concede the point, and segue into stories about Walter O'Malley or "Green Acres," but he felt he had one more observation to make. "You know my dad - was a thief."

The whole table froze. Dana's eyes were fastened on him, blazing with alarm. "I don't mean he was arrested or anything. He was a landlord in New York."

139

Bob grinned. "I think what Charlie's trying to say is that he was a successful landlord in New York."

Glen laughed heartily. "They're all thieves in that town. Rob their own mothers."

"Anyway," Charlie continued, "if you'll briefly excuse my language, my dad would fuck over anybody to nail a deal or save a dollar, but he wouldn't mess with the union. If his building workers threatened to go to the local, he'd say 'aah...the union', but he'd back off. So I'm just saying - if workers here were protected like that, they wouldn't have to sue in the worker's comp system over stress for what's really a question of harassment."

Now it was Glenn's turn not to let go. "What protection do workers need, Charlie? If we have a bad supervisor, we kick his ass out."

"I'm sure you do, Glen." Charlie began to feel his appetite draining away, the clutch of adrenaline in his chest. " I'm sure you also give them decent health care. But not everyone's as enlightened as you are."

"So that means that this woman can pull out a gun and threaten you?" Glen barked, his six-foot-two ex-linebacker's body slouching forward as he jabbed the air with his fork. "Because it's a little tough out there?"

The menace in his pose startled Charlie. "Well - let's just agree that there are problems that need to be solved."

"Far as I'm concerned, that crazy bitch solved her particular problem just fine for all of us."

Charlie took a deep swallow of his wine, hoping to drain from the glass some of that goodwill of the past half-hour, enough to quench the acrid taste that signaled the arrival of Mr. High Note - but it was too late, the ringing in the ears had already started, goading Charlie's thoughts towards malicious directions.

"You know, this is actually starting to remind me of some talks I've had with my father."

That was enough for Dana to shoot him a warning glance. He ignored it.

"You always have to flip things around a bit. It's not enough to say that, well Dad, when the city's stricter on building codes it helps keep tenants from being squashed in an earthquake. I've got to remind him, Dad, if you're held to a higher standard there's more protection against you being sued in a quake-related death!"

Bill smiled. "Yeah, that's kind of interesting. Turning it around like that."

"Exactly, Bill! Let's say you're talking about people who can't afford health insurance, you don't say, well, those poor bastards could get t.b. You say, what if they get t.b. and don't go to the hospital? They're on the street where they can give it to us!" Now Bill wasn't smiling, no one was smiling, and through the wail in his ears he could hear Dana calling his name like a foghorn, but the words were unstoppable now. "I mean especially when I'm talking to someone who's all business, some gung-ho, no-nonsense guy like you, Glen, I can't get all sentimental about people dying or going crazy because no one will treat them! Hey, no problem, survival of the fittest, that's the way the cookie crumbles, that's what makes horse races, can't have an omelet without breaking eggs! But if I say that when we have to have all this expensive emergency care for these people when they're on the point of death, who pays the premiums, who pays the higher insurance rates - that's you and I, Glen! Now I've got your attention! We've got to treat these people in order to keep our premiums down! People like Sheila Reed create all sorts of expensive difficulties! But you know, Glen, maybe you're right. So what if they drop dead? That's the way the ball bounces! Fuck 'em, right? Fuck 'em all!"

Charlie finally stopped when he felt the depth of the silence around him like an icy well. At the adjacent tables, diners were staring at Charlie with disbelief. The only movement came from their server, who, with practiced cheerfulness, wheeled a pastry tray up to the table.

"Anyone for sweets?"

"Hello, Dr. Westphal? Sorry to call so late."

"How can I help you, Charlie?"

"Well, I - it's not an emergency, but - I was wondering if we could squeeze in one more appointment before your vacation."

"I leave tomorrow, Charlie."

"Is that morning or afternoon?"

141

"Morning, Charlie. We're driving up to Tahoe."

"Sounds excellent. A little skiing?"

"Skiing, fishing - mainly a lot of rest. Charlie, I'll refer you to Doctor Kamens. He'll - "

"No, it's all right, I'll be fine. Maybe we can have that extra session when you get back?"

"You are aware we have only two more sessions?"

"No, I wasn't aware of that."

"That was the agreement with your employer. But regarding supplemental therapy, Dr. Kamens is definitely - "

"I'm fine. Have a good trip."

Charlie gathered his papers in the empty hearing room. He was grateful that at least the claimant attorney had accepted the about-face in the settlement discussions as "business as usual." Good thing he wasn't up against Worcek on this one. The attorney would dutifully take to his client the more unpalatable settlement Bert had forced down Charlie's throat. Charlie almost wished the claimant would shoot the settlement down just so Bert would have to explain that to Shackleton. But he didn't want to harbor disloyal thoughts - best just to forget about the case and get on with it.

Get on with what?

His cases were dwindling down to nothing. For the first time in months, Charlie was uncalendared for long stretches of the day. He paced aimlessly before the claimants until he was sure he was attracting their torpid stares. He felt himself sinking into the miasma of heat, smog and seething idleness in the Van Nuys courtyard.

"Slow day?"

Kaukonen, itching to waste time as always, found him by the stairs.

"My MSC went sour. I got another one at two in Santa Monica."

"How about we hit one of the local greens, Charlie? Ventura, maybe?"

"It's too early. I might get paged, a lien case might come up."

"We can play nine holes. Or just go to Los Robles and hit some balls."

"It's just too early, Jerry. I think I'll go back to the office."

"Watching your back, huh?"

142

A thin filament of dread prickled within Charlie. Was that remark the blurt of an aging hack who needed to believe every lawyer was equally expendable? Or was the threat to Charlie's job really that obvious to everyone but himself?

"Just kidding, Charlie." Charlie could see his own disquiet bounce out of Kaukonen's gray and bleary eyes like a last glimmer from the clogged wick of a candle. He quickly ducked away, knowing his lack of a nonchalant reply would prompt some gossip around the hearing rooms. But he didn't give a damn. He craved a long pointless walk, a drive down an endless boulevard.

With your hands on a steering wheel, you clutched to yourself inviolable silence. Especially on a foggy night on a canyon road, every headlight an ambush out of the mist. Dana had said nothing until they were back down at sea level and stalled in PCH traffic, the wraiths of taillights and high-beams flickering like the frayed nerves of a hundred lost travelers. When she no longer felt that she had to avoid distracting him from his driving, she'd talked without interruption. Hadn't she told him Glen was a bear when it came to business? He wasn't supposed to pay any attention. Why couldn't he just let it go? What did politics have to do with a family dinner? He could see her fingers meshing furiously in her lap, as if weaving her words of shock, outrage and betrayal.

She was right of course, and Charlie was welling up with the most sincere pleas for forgiveness for his outburst – and then she had to make the soccer team analogy. "Charlie, when I was on the bench recovering from that injured knee, don't you think that, once it stopped hurting like hell, I wanted to get back in the game right away? Every day they kept me off the field, don't you think I worried they might not put me back in? But that was foolish. I healed, I got right back into the - "

"A soccer team?" Charlie finally shouted. "You're talking to me about your college soccer team?"

"I'm talking about your fear that your position is somehow eroding at work. Your irrational resentment of your employers!"

"Dana, this is not some coach making a decision about whether I can play goalie for the junior varsity! This is Hobart-Riis Insurance and my weekly paycheck! These are bottom-line guys!"

"Your job's not in danger! It can't be! I know you did everything right, Charlie!"

"Oh, I see. I executed a nice pass off the wing? I scored on a penalty kick?"

Dana sullenly retracted towards the passenger door. "I'm sorry. It was inappropriate of me to bring up the soccer."

"No, it's totally appropriate! You're going to go play for the Cup!"

"It's wrong to be so paranoid and hateful! There's no reason for it!"

Her knuckles flew to her lips. Oh shit, Charlie thought, I've driven her to tears. He could see them form in the light glazing off the fogged windshield, and when he touched her fingers they had already splashed them. Instantly miserable and contrite, Charlie talked as fast as he could. "You're right, Dana. I am being hateful, and I'm sorry – look, that stuff at dinner was totally off the wall. It was my case talking, not me. I guess I just need to burn off a little more anger in therapy. I can't believe I did that. This whole night I've been behaving like a jerk, Dana, and I – I'm so sorry if I offended your family. Please believe me, I wanted so much to get to know them, and I – I hope I get another chance to get to know them a lot better."

Charlie could see what he called Dana's "smile crinkles" flutter at the corner of her eyes. She relaxed a little. "So when do I meet your father the bandit?"

Charlie laughed with relief and advised her to first meet his mother. "She's much easier to take. Perpetual old school college girl with a vintage vinyl collection. Joni Mitchell, Cat Stevens - pre-Muslim fanatic, of course." He squeezed her hand again. "Nice to know your knee healed up. You'll make a great soccer mom." It was a shameless and smarmy remark, and it worked perfectly. Dana beamed with relief and they made the rest of the drive in contented silence. The fog thinned, a mist flecking the windshield like silver pollen, and occasionally he would feel Dana's hand resting on his knee, a narrow highway line through the uncertainty that enveloped him.

Now in the middle of this shitty morning, having finished off a quick sandwich in the cafeteria, he held fast to that memory, the talisman of Dana's loving little clasp, as he sipped his iced tea, and he didn't let the memory go until Worcek sat down beside him.

144

"Charlie, do you mind?"

Charlie, with a wave of his hand, acquiesced.

"Listen, if I rode you a little hard at that depo - "

"You were in good form, Liz. Rules of engagement. No harm, no foul."

Liz had a bear claw on her plate and she started munching on it, chunk by bite-sized chunk. Charlie realized this would take awhile.

"The job doesn't exempt me from caring." She tore at her pastry and shoved morsels into her mouth with little finger flourishes, as if she'd found a stylish way of cramming breakfast food down her throat.

"Liz, touchy-feely doesn't suit you."

"How did your bosses react, Charlie?" When he didn't reply right away, she gave him one of her "got you" looks. He rolled his eyes, an attempt to deflect her inquisitiveness, but Worcek could not be silenced. "Come on, Charlie, they wanted you to say Sheila was homicidal and the shot was meant for you. Tweak your memories a little. Hey, to those guys perjury's no biggie, especially in a situation where you're expected to be confused." She daintily licked her fingers.

He could've told her what she was doing was totally improper, but he chose a less heavy-handed reply. "Right you are if you think you are, Liz."

"What do you think you are, Charlie?"

"I'm fine. Fine with what I said at the deposition, fine with how the case is progressing."

"Even though you went to Sheila Reed's funeral?"

The time had come. He'd expected it. "Liz, I hope you don't plan on publicizing that. Not only would I ruin your reputation, but if you bring that up to my bosses, I can –"

Worcek flashed him a look that was almost contemptuous. "I'll respect your privacy, Charlie. And don't worry, I know what helps me and what doesn't help me." She nibbled at the rest of the bear claw. "Well, I'm sure you'll be happy with how the case is progressing, because now we can all say goobye to progress. I scored at your depo, which means you guys will just stall, stall, stall..."

145

"You don't think I want this to be over with?" Damn it, he thought, I did it again. Sometimes now he anticipated the tinnitus, raising his voice, and suddenly he'd encounter the disdainful glances of a whole roomful of people.

Liz wolfed down the last of her bear claw and looked straight at him. "Know what, Charlie? You should file."

"File what? No one wants to re-open discovery."

"I meant you, Charlie. You should file. Worker's comp."

Charlie almost choked on his tea, then spluttered with laughter. "Liz, you're phenomenal."

She serenely drank her coffee. "Charlie, I can't believe you've been in the system for three years and you think that it's somehow shameful or grotesque to file for benefits. After what you've been through - "

"I can't believe it, Liz. You're ambulance-chasing me in the fucking hearing room cafeteria!"

She demurely wiped her hands on her napkin. "In case you haven't heard, I'm no shrinking violet." Worcek leaned towards him with professional solicitude. "Come on, you weren't aware of the severity of the injury is all. You're within the year to file, what's the problem? By all rights it should be an accepted claim. And if it isn't - "

"This has gotten ridiculous enough." Charlie got up and pushed his chair in with as much emphasis as possible.

"Charlie, I know it's not my business, but you must be having some sort of post-traumatic stress disorder therapy. I know I am. Stuff comes out, new facts come to light about what you saw. If you really had to lie in that deposition about this woman's last moments on this planet, Charlie, if they really made you do that, you can offer to revise your previous testimony, clear your conscience, and especially if you file as an injured worker, no one can ever say that - "

"Liz, you're right about one thing. I'm having p.t.s.d. therapy. Through my employers. And whatever 'stuff' comes out is between me and my therapist alone."

Worcek wiped her lips with her napkin. "If you're satisfied, Charlie."

He got up, slammed his chair into the table, and turned his back on her.

146

"As you know, this isn't my case," Judge Miraflores announced. "Given that it's not my case, I'll give it all the attention it deserves."

"Do we get kissed or what, Charlie?" Holzman, a veteran applicant attorney with a bulbous, chafed nose that made him look permanently drunk, tried to smile away his fear of the Judge's crankiness.

Charlie merely flipped serenely through his document files. He had shaken off Worcek's unwelcome lunch break intrusion, and was ready to put Ms. Candida Borchert's claim to bed. Mrs. Borchert had denied that she'd ever previously injured her back. Her case had dragged on for a relatively modest two years, but that had been long enough for her to forget what she'd told a doctor about her previous auto accident back injury. Charlie patiently thumbed through his documents, ready to expose her lie to her lawyer and the judge.

"You do understand, your Honor," Holtzman intoned, "that my client hasn't worked for three years."

"Maybe she didn't want to work," the Judge snapped.

That was an understatement. Charlie also had in his voluminous case files a report on Mrs. Borchert's trial for embezzlement, at which she'd received a sentence of five weeks in a county jail and 240 hours of community service. As if that weren't enough, there were summary reports of an earlier worker's comp injury. An injury that she'd recently denied ever having, but which in fact generated a case that had been c. & r.'d at three-thousand dollars. All Charlie had to do was lay out the evidence of all this woman's lies under oath for the case to collapse into a tidy and tiny settlement.

There was only one problem. Charlie didn't have the papers.

He thumbed as calmly as possible back and forth through the green-tagged sections of his files. There was no way his normally indefatigable secretary could have mislaid all those reports, and yet he could not find any of the key case numbers.

"There were no objective findings of injury, Your Honor. It's basically a soft tissue and psych case."

Charlie didn't really know why he'd burped those completely routine phrases out. He'd heard Holzman trying to inflate the case to involve genuine orthopedic injury, but that wasn't the point of his reply. He just wanted to show

Judge Miraflores he was in the game, not just sitting there like a schmuck holding in his lap a potential disaster.

Miraflores sneered at Charlie. "I think we've established your point-of-view, counselor."

Charlie was suddenly on his feet. "Your Honor, if you don't mind, I'm going to have to leave for a bit. Can we take a short break?"

"Nature calls, Charlie."

"More like stomach flu."

Holzman immediately made way for him. Charlie bolted from the room, and once he was on the mezzanine, he kept on running, down the staircase and out into the street, down two blocks to the trunk of his car which, as he dreaded, contained none of the missing files. A clammy unease percolated through his skin as he charged back up the stairs, whipped open his cellphone, and called Hobart-Riis. His secretary picked up the line and his panic spewed out of him. "Carol, I'm here at the fucking MSC and I don't have any of my reports on the Borchert case!"

She insisted that everything had been there before she left the previous night, and the quaver in her voice only aggravated his own. "Then who took it back this morning? Did someone throw it away? What the fuck's going on?"

"Nothing's been thrown away, Charlie. Maybe I - no, I couldn't - where are you?"

"I'm heading for the waiting room. Find the documents now and fax them to me!"

He gave her the number and settled in to the waiting room for as long as he dared. Any document a lawyer served after the MSC usually got discounted on the grounds that opposing counsel had not had sufficient time to review it and thus had been shortchanged on due process. But right up to the end of the MSC, an attorney could present a document and claim he met the deadline. Charlie and the other lawyers constantly groused about idiot lawyers who had to bolt from judges' chambers to go to the phones, desperately trying to get some document faxed to them. Now it was Charlie's turn to play the greenhorn. Twenty minutes passed, and still the "public communications center," the waiting room's one forlorn collective fax, was silent. He wondered just how much longer he stall, when at last the fax chattered to life. This time

Charlie recognized his firm's fax cover sheet. He hovered over the machine as it squeezed out a couple of pages.

Part of the record of Candida Borchert's embezzlement trial. Nothing more.

"That was a long sit!" Holzman bellowed as Charlie returned.

The judge turned to Holzman. "Maybe you scared the crap out of him."

Charlie grinned and bore the joke as he bent over, unsnapped his attaché case, and pulled the fax from out of the inner pouch as if he'd had it all along. The judge and Holzman gave the fax due consideration. The judge warned Holzman the fraud conviction raised serious issues of his client's credibility and demeanor. But he also acidly reminded Charlie that even if someone has been convicted of fraud in the past, *in the absence of evidence to the contrary*, her current complaint could still be believed.

What galled Charlie the most as he drove back to Century City was that a woman like Borchert, a flagrant liar, had gotten a free pass, whereas Sheila Reed - no, he thought, don't take that route, don't go down that path - but Sheila had crept into the junction between damaged eardrum and frazzled psyche, and once again the phone was ringing in Charlie's head that he could never answer, never put on hold. The tinnitus broke free, squealed with the tires as he ran his car into his parking space, rang with the elevator buzzer as he headed upstairs to confront Bert Silver.

He charged past the receptionist without even a nod, and rapped sharply on Bert Silver's office door. Silver, scrubbed to the point of glossy pinkness, was wearing a Jerry Garcia tie with his usual white shirt. He waved Charlie genially to his desk as he juggled three phone calls. Occasionally he rolled his eyes Charlie's way. How busy we are, the gestures read, how much in demand.

When he finally hung up, Charlie dispensed with all the pleasantries. "Bert, the Borchert material? Her 1988 injury report and her 1993 case summary? They're missing. Have you seen them?"

"I reviewed them. Then I gave them back to Carol."

"Are you sure? Because I've never known Carol to screw up like this."

"Charlie, no one's perfect."

Charlie was trying to harmonize with the tinnitus, dampen his anger along with his volume so as not to spit out words that couldn't be unsaid.

"Bert, I can understand why Shackleton might want - might ask for a provisional review of my performance. But with all the paper going back and forth between us we're having some real organizational difficulties."

"Charlie, I don't have your papers."

"Then Bert, where the hell are they?" Oh Christ, thought Charlie, he'd said it, just with the one word and the intonation he'd accused him. "I'm sorry, Bert, it's just that - they were absolutely crucial --"

Bert spread his hands placidly. "I don't take it personally, Charlie. There'll always be another day."

"Yes, and a better one." Charlie echoed his bland smile and backed away towards the door and the barbecue snapshots, relieved that everything had been smoothed over. Then Bert had to add one more remark. "Now I suggest you go have a talk with Carol."

Maybe it was the dismissive, patronizing tone, but Charlie felt that he too had one more remark to make.

"This is fucking sabotage, Bert. I'm going to Shackleton."

The tinnitus kept Charlie up all night and stalked him through the next day. It didn't subside until two in the afternoon.

The beveled dune of a beach that stretched twelve stories below Charlie in the twilight was empty of all but a few strollers, the surf lapping gently in their wake. Charlie sipped his glass of wine, and, as Dana listened patiently, he told her that when he'd reported back to work that morning, he'd submitted the DWC1 to his employers. He'd officially filed for worker's compensation benefits, claiming psychological and physical trauma on the job due to the Sheila Reed incident. The explosion at the Brandt family dinner, the snarling at Bert – it had all finally made him aware of the extent of his injury. Everything had been completely civilized, and Shackleton had accepted his filing in a gentlemanly fashion.

What he didn't tell her about was how he'd felt when he'd accused Bert Silver of fucking him over. In the synapse between the moment of a planned, civilized exit from Bert's office and that savage blurt - it had only been a few seconds, but a blinding rage had seized him so completely he hadn't even realized what words had leaped out of his mouth. He'd fallen down a rabbit hole.

Charlie had made a decent recovery from his "unforced error" when he'd instantly snatched back his accusation of sabotage, and invited Bert to come see Shackleton with him "to clear the air." With Shackleton watching Charlie had begged for an end to the paper-shuffling between them, told Shackleton of the incident with Bert straight out, and profusely apologized. It was the tinnitus talking, that was all…all apologies, all apologies…

And he'd heard no reassurance that Bert would not be handling his papers. No reassurance about anything. And that was the real reason he'd finally filed. He needed protection …He needed to hold back somehow a dark wave of unpredictable changes….

"I told them I needed more treatment. Especially for the tinnitus.…"

"I'm sure it'll all be handled in house, Charlie. When you're inside the system, what the system does comes easier."

"I told them I was sure we could work out further therapy. I mean, they control treatment in the first ninety days, but I thought I'd make sure to phrase it that way, that we'd both work it out, that I'd accept any therapy they suggested."

"Of course, Charlie."

"I wanted to make sure they knew I was cooperating. It's right to make sure of that - don't you think?"

"I think you said the right thing."

"Of course."

He and Dana stared down at the deserted beach. Dana's voice was on the edge of exhaustion.

"Everyone will understand, Charlie."

-6-
what to do when you don't know what to do

When Rody Golan was beeped he'd just managed to squeeze himself between the cinderblock wall and iron pillar of a Hollywood garage, where he had an excellent view of Mrs. Rachel Tejada confronting the flat on her Chevy. This was the second time the private investigator had slit one of her tires. Only this time, with a moment to spare in the empty garage, watching the tire hiss away to a rubber husk, he'd rolled a broken bottle under the trunk of her car. To mislead her a little.

It worked. The Tejada broad, big and muscular, a real moose, figured this flat was just an accident, and was opening the trunk and going for the jack. The first time, in the lot at Pic 'n Save, she'd gotten somebody to help her change the flat. This time, disgusted, figuring she was alone where no one could see her, she was going to put that supposedly injured back to work. Golan was ready with his camera.

Golan was not ashamed of this job. The workers were cheats and liars and fair game. Tejada had claimed she'd injured her back during a slip-and-fall while unloading the company truck. Naturally no one saw this accident. In the hearing she dragged her leg stiffly, but now she was squatting on her haunches as she guided the jack under the car. If you can change the tire, you can go back to work and drive the truck. Case closed. And he was just about to snap the first picture when the damn beeper went off.

Golan knew he was blown. He strode briskly across the garage, chin buried in the turned-up collar of his suede jacket, the walk he'd learned long ago from THE THIRD MAN and who knows how many other old crime movies in the basement theaters of Prague. The woman peered at him

152

suspiciously. Golan heard her toss the jack into the trunk and slam the lid down.

Nothing more he could do. He could always harass her and make her jumpy the way that p.i. Ballesteros did with his cases. Tell Tejada's neighbors he was from the F.B.I. investigating Tejada for insurance fraud. But the kid's tactics were crude and stupid. Golan didn't like them at all. The kid was on drugs, probably.

Golan thumbed the beeper, flashed Shackleton's number, and struck back at Hobart-Riis for screwing up his job by ignoring their page. First he dropped in on his favorite grocery store in the Pico-Robertson area. The store served mostly Jews, and Golan enjoyed soaking up the muttered Hebraic bargains over cuts of meat and fish, so much like the finagling in the markets of his Prague childhood. Red-sequined streamers with a cheery rhinestone glitter broadcast Hebrew and English holiday wishes - not that Golan had ever celebrated Succoth, but it was nice to keep tabs on it somehow. He bought a fresh chunk of halvah crumbling like mica at the edges, and a bag of dates, which he munched greedily as he left the store. Good for the heart, dates.

Then he decided to pay a visit to Yossi Metz at his Connection Central pager and cellphone store. Yossi and his brother Jake were now known by their first names to anyone who watched Channel 5 very late at night. Their garishly over-lit commercial featured Yossi in his loud silk shirt turning to the camera with a big grin and shouting "You want to be Connected?" With his accent, it sounded like an invitation to the Russian mob. Yossi thought of that phrase as a slogan. He would've put "You want to be Connected?" on billboards if he'd had the money. Golan thought Yossi and Jake looked like monkeys on t.v., and the stupid commercial had cost them so much they were having a 40% off sale.

Still Golan wanted them to beat the local competition, Cell Power, run by the Bagdagnesan brothers, a couple of slimy Persian Azjerbaijani that Golan loathed. And he had a real affection for Yossi and Jake. After all, Golan and the Metzes, though they'd never met, had shared Prague. Fed the swans off the Charles Bridge. Hung out with friends in the Jewish Museum cemetery, where the horde of toppling graves heaved out of the ground like a chorus of groans, and you could talk politics and be unheard. Prowled the beer gardens for one of the few approved forms of entertainment in Communist times, shtupping tourists.

For now, though, Golan gruffly accused the brothers of being the lowest form of gonifs for holding out for three hundred dollars for an old Sony monitor. After twenty minutes Golan haggled them down to two-hundred. Only after he had the Sony in his van did he place a call to Hobart-Riis.

A short drive later he was sitting in Shackleton's office. With Golan, the District Examiner felt free to lounge on his couch and throw his arm on his cushion where it hinged like the limb of a marionette. Shackleton responded to Golan's rough physicality by trying to be one of the boys, which only made Golan feel like one of the servants. So Golan acted like a servant, watching Shackleton with a truculent silence. Their conversations galloped towards the moment where orders were given or money changed hands so they could be rid of each other.

Shackleton was worried about Charlie Solomon again. "Oh, I'm sure Charlie will continue to soldier ahead. He's very loyal, and trying to – well - get on with it, but - you understand, he did file. He is a worker's comp case now, and he has been acting somewhat irrationally lately."

Golan had the option of refusing any task a client might offer him, especially a time-consuming tail job, but these days money was tight. He was setting up a new apartment in the Fairfax area. He'd limited the damage on the t.v., but he suspected he'd be getting fucked on furniture in Koreatown.

Shackleton let Bert Silver brief Golan on the details. Golan liked Silver's attitude. The guy was a pudgy little mascher but he didn't hand you any shit. The point wasn't that Charlie had a worker's comp injury. The point was that Charlie was a good lawyer, whose instincts might lead him to poke around into the events that led to his injury. Sheila Reed vs. The Bernard-Duvall Clinic - Golan knew how hinky they were about that little fiasco. And you couldn't bet the farm on Charlie's loyalty. If there was one thing Golan knew from his days in Soviet Eastern Europe, and even more from the days right after Soviet Eastern Europe, loyalty was a thing of the moment. Charlie was slipping off to the other side. Don't get hung up on the "tragic circumstances." Just fix the problem.

Charlie looked at the photo the claimant attorney had just handed him. A portrait of a retired LAPD officer with two ghastly scars on his cheek. Each scar represented a bullet.

The man had been moonlighting as a security guard for a videogame parlor near Florence and Normandy, the infamous ground zero of the L.A. riots. A Latino-black scuffle had broken out and the guard, trying to intervene, had been shot twice. Before his bosses cleared out of California, they refused to give the guard or the guard's attorney the name of the worker's comp carrier. So the guard had lost every cent he ever had on the surgery before the applicant attorney had located the carrier of record: Hobart-Riis Insurance, Inc.

Hobart-Riis, while regretting the incident and its aftermath, had denied the claim, because they had not been notified in a timely manner. Bert had assigned the case to Charlie.

Charlie inspected the gouges in the guard's cheek. Time to pull out that "live rabbit" that would save the case. *Let's see, an ex-L.A.P.D. officer fucked over on surgery to remove a bullet in the face who would no longer chew or talk correctly - what beast could he pull out here that would not immediately throw an embolism and expire, floppy ears twitching, on the judge's desk?*

In the cafeteria, Charlie grabbed another iced tea. He was wasted. Since the day he had filed his claim the tinnitus had really started to kick. It liked to go really full out at three in the morning, a banshee rising out of the shadows by his futon. Naps at his desk were becoming frequent and perilous. He would lurch awake and grunt an answer to his secretary on the intercom, trying to blow off the miasma in his head before Bunning or Silver walked in. But he was determined to stay off the benzodiazapines. He needed no chemical crutches to complicate his life. He gazed out the window at the bustling throng of lawyers that he could no longer join without strain and awkward silences, so lost in dejected contemplation he didn't even notice Vel glide into the seat opposite him.

"How are you doing?" Vel softly asked.

Charlie just shook his head and glumly recounted to his friend the sort of cases the firm was now handing him. Vel steepled the tips of her fingers together and took a deep breath, and Charlie let his horror stories trail away,

155

waiting for Vel's reassurance. Instead, Vel assumed the kind of clinical stare that he himself often used to take a client's expectations down. "I can make a few inquiries, Charles. I've heard Lasser and Vogelstein are hiring, and - "

Charlie cut her off with a wave of his hand. "We're not at that point yet, Vel. They're just giving me garbage disposal cases until the treatment's done."

"They're giving you laughers, Charlie."

"Yeah. This thing with the ex-LAPD officer – I won't even get into it. But they've been treating me, okay? Even before I filed the claim. I've been getting therapy"

"Up until now, it's cost them nothing. Charles, this new supervisor, Bert Silver - he does seem to be boxing you in. I'd at least investigate other options."

"Shackleton and Bunning are still in my corner, Vel. I understand that it threw them – I mean, first I said I was fine, I could do the job – well, I mean, of course I could always do the job, but I said I'm okay, I'm okay – then I filed. But they know all I need is a little more treatment. They know I've got the therapy and the medication for the tinnitus and I'm staying on an even keel. My personal life - such as it is - is just that. I mean, no one needs to know about the clanging in my head, the rotten dreams - as far as anyone needs to know I'm on the job!"

Vel looked at his glass, following Charlie's fingers as he ripped another pack of sugar. "There's nothing in there but icewater." Charlie poured the sugar on it anyhow and slurped the mixture down.

"Charles," Vel told him with studied gentleness, "I'm not saying you're not making it through the day, and I don't know what your particular alliances are at Hobart-Riis, but you can't pretend nothing is happening. You might want to try a pre-emptive strike."

"Oh. I see. The burn-the-bridges approach. That worked wonders for you, didn't it?"

Vel lowered her eyes with a coldly wounded smile and picked up her purse. "I suppose this isn't the best time for a chat. I'm sure you'll find your own devious solution to the problem."

Charlie apologized, he tried to call her back, but it was too late. He'd offended her, not so much by what he said as by the nasty tone of it. As if

Charlie, of all people, believed that the angriest and most overtly confrontational move of Vel's professional life had been a blunder, and not a decision she'd taken with the full knowledge of the personal consequences that might follow.

Everyone had known about Judge Ronald Minkin's little weakness. He'd presided at the Santa Monica hearing rooms for over thirty years, the slyly ingratiating fixer who could charm the most belligerent lawyers into a settlement. And if, in the afterglow of accommodation, a hand snuk out to caress a female attorney's waist - well, everyone knew what to expect.

But Vel would have none of it, and maybe it was because "the fixer" couldn't reconcile Vel's supple walk with her icy scorn, maybe he was getting old and foolhardy, but whispered provocation and taunts soon sank to muttered abuse. Vel was reminded of how easily stips and awards could go against her clients. When the Fixer's touch finally wound up on Vel's breasts, and Vel pointed out how he'd really and truly crossed the line, Minkin grinned and kept stroking the fabric of her blouse - and the crackle of static on the wire Vel was wearing got the Fixer a dismissal and a new title: Mentally Disordered Sex Offender.

In the collegial world of worker's comp, Vel was never totally shunned by lawyers who knew they'd have to work with her another day. But her firm was thick with Minkin's cronies. Soon she had to pack her files and become an "outside counsel," a free-lance litigator, hooking up with whatever clients she could attract. Mischievously relentless and brilliantly thorough, Vel fought back and after six months had a healthy clientele. But she still ran up against dinosaurs who wouldn't deal with her. She could still pass a congregation of the old boys in the courtyard and leave a wake of unforgiving silence.

Charlie desperately wanted to find Vel and apologize and tell her how he admired her courage, how he wished he could borrow some of it for the days ahead. But when he looked for Vel in the courtyard, he met only the curious stares of the workers who wondered why he seemed to be lost.

He turned to the sleepy gaze of a Hispanic woman with a child on her lap. The woman reached above her to the branch of a wilted magnolia. She bent one of the blooms down to her daughter, who gratefully took a sniff.

Charlie smiled at them, and the little child smiled back. It was hard to look at them and not feel uncomfortable. This woman, who simply wanted to one day go back to work to support that child, or hold up her end of a paltry two-income family, had to obey a day-long summons to come down here, explain why she couldn't work, what that was doing to her family....

What about Brandon and Sheila Reed's family? How had they divided up the bills?

Charlie saw in a flash the angle he could use to destroy Brandon Reed. He'd get Bert Silver off his back, guarantee his medical treatment, and save his job. He ran from the courtyard, drove back to Hobart-Riis as fast as he could without pushing the legal limit, and rushed to his office with an enthusiasm he hadn't felt in weeks.

The sea foamed against the rocky shore, tossing up a mist with a hem of pale rainbows. Brandon stared at the gleaming surf, not even noticing the pretty young girls in their bikinis who traipsed along the tide pools. Brandon lived in Los Angeles, and he hadn't seen the sea in months.

Then he remembered that he was, after all, working at the party, taking photos of the guests. He snapped their picture, and the click of the shutter made him feel even lonelier. When the waves curled back and grew silent, Brandon could hear the party behind him.

By now a reggae band was playing, and about two-hundred people had gathered to honor Jack Graebner. Nate Wesserman's idol. The king of low-budget direct-to-cable filmmaking. Wesserman, through his friendship with the host, had with typical low-budget finesse arranged for Graebner's party to also be the wrap party for NIGHTWINDERS 2.

Brandon could see Soleil's turquoise dress lighting up a corner of the crowd. The offshore breeze kicked the fabric up the back of her thighs. She was mingling with her agent's friends. Brandon stayed back, for he knew if he drifted nearby, just to be close to her, she might cast him that look of amused impatience that always unnerved him.

He took another slow walk across the grounds of the Malibu estate. The sun beat down so brightly that the thin white eucalyptus trees seemed to tremble in the heat. In the patches of orange and lemon trees the light burned

158

the green of the foliage into the shadows and the fruit glittered like jewels in the seams of that darkness. Whites were dazzling - the shirts of Graebner's young friends playing a game of tennis, the crests of the waves below. Daylight in Brandon's neighborhood was hexed to a stupor by pollution, smudged with the grim routine of poverty. But here above the ocean the day was as gorgeous and bright as it should be.

Brandon glanced over at the llama pen. The two llamas, Gus and Murray, with their thick, uncombed brown fleece, pudgy lips, and sullen stares, struck Brandon as two of the stupidest and most worthless beasts he'd ever seen. But Graebner had probably paid a fortune for Gus and Murray, and his guests got a huge kick out of them. Parents lifted their little kids up to pat them on their ungrateful snouts, and a procession of the gorgeous young women who populated the party would cluck and coo at them. When the girls petted them, even the dirty llamas took on an almost painful allure.

Brandon stood at the llama pen beside two buff babes who had played space commandos in "Denaris Nights," talking about the wire work in their battle scenes until one of the girls passed him a joint, warning him he shouldn't take too big a hit. Brandon sucked on the joint a couple of times - and turquoise sea ran into gray-blue sky like a polarizing filter had been slapped on the world. The distractions of the party took on velocity and luminescence. Randomness was radiant, and every furtive tic of the eyes promised a new thrill.

Soon Brandon's bout of sadness was pleasantly ambushed by the munchies. He took another turn through the buffet, and it wasn't until he was at the end of the line, chomping down his jerk chicken, that he lowered a drumstick to gaze in awe.

Busey stood alone, perched on the tussocks of grass at the edge of the bluff, taking in the ocean view. Brandon recognized even through the glare of the sun the actor's straw forelocks and hound dog eyes. The man looked almost mournful, as if the party had passed him by. Maybe a fan's admiration would cheer him up.

"Gary Busey?" he exclaimed. The actor responded with a smoothly courteous smile, and Brandon, after he introduced himself, had no idea what to say. Then he grinned at Busey.

"Out-standing!"

Busey chuckled. "You liked that one, partner?"

"Yeah. Well - you say that in almost all your movies, right?"

"It's become a trademark. You need one these days."

"You know the line I really love?" He puffed himself up as arrogantly as he could. "'Do I look like I need psychiatric help?'"

"Yeah, that role was a trip, wasn't it? Glad you enjoyed it." Brandon told him he was a longtime fan, and Busey gave him a friendly pat on the shoulder and thanked him, then waved to some old guy in baggy swim trunks and an aloha shirt, excused himself, and was gone.

Brandon's gaze hung by inertia on Busey working the front yard, until he abruptly realized Wesserman and Soleil had come up behind him.

"So, Brandon, enjoying Estancia del Graebner?"

"That was Gary Busey!" Brandon exclaimed to Wesserman.

"You like Busey, you should rent 'The Buddy Holly Story'. See what a hell of an actor he is."

"Is that the one about the racecar driver?"

Wesserman shook his head and chuckled, and Brandon quietly flared up with resentment over how much more Wesserman was in the know about Busey, about this whole world Brandon had hurtled into like some fragment from a bleak and dirty moon.

Soleil laid a hand gently on Brandon's shoulder, and pointed to the guy in the Hawaiian shirt. "Busey is talking to our host - do you see?"

"The little old guy?"

"That's Jack Graebner, Brandon." Wesserman intoned. "A trailblazer!" Brandon studied Graebner, trying to extract more majesty from the image of the potbellied man ladling conch fritters into his mouth.

"The man saved my life, Brandon." Brandon, now deeply wasted, tried to focus on Wesserman's story of personal salvation. "Back in the '80's I was trying to shop a military project to Fox that Kevin Bacon was interested in, I had another script with Michelle Pfeiifer's agent, I had this serious Chicano family drama, really A-level ensemble piece - and the bank was ready to take my house. That's when I met Jack. He introduced me to a Brazilian trying to get blocked capital out of Sao Paulo and his Japanese partner. These guys were

160

very specific. 'You got a "Lethal Weapon," you got "Fatal Attraction?" ' So I came up with both."

"What?" Brandon tried to catch up, realizing no one's life would be saved in this story.

"Guy has a one-night stand with an Asian woman, a female killing machine, dumps her. She's kills everyone he knows with her bare hands - until he joins forces with a female CIA agent who's been tracking her for years. Catfight at the end is unbelievable. Anyway, Graebner exec produced, we pre-sold it to the Far East, I was in the guns-and-honey business and I never looked back." He threw a paternal arm around Brandon. "See, you do the deals you do, find the action you can, then walk your walk and talk your talk like a motherfucker. You make something happen. That's what it's about. And when it all works out, it's magic, Brandon, magic." Soleil eyed Brandon in a way that flustered him deliciously.

"You going to shoot another picture soon, Nate?"

Wesserman looked almost insulted. "Hey, I make three films a year! You got a future with us, Brandon."

Soleil turned impatiently to Wesserman. "Nate, don't you think it's time to introduce Brandon to Monsieur Graebner?"

They came up behind the man of the hour, who turned from three of his aging colleagues to backslap Wesserman and voraciously hug Soleil. Wesserman introduced Brandon as one of his crack assistants. Brandon took Graebner's hand - it lay in Brandon's grip and impassively absorbed submission. Brandon groped for a few opening words. "Nate was telling me all the movies you produced. Awesome. I mean - I don't think I was born when you did the first ones."

Instantly that seemed the wrong thing to say, but Graebner roared with delight. "Yeah, I've been around a coon's age. So how old are you, pischer?"

"Twenty," Brandon answered.

Wesserman gave Brandon a paternal smile. "Brandon's on the camera crew."

Graebner seemed relieved. "That's the way. A kid with a skill. Below the line - that's where you want to be." Graebner grew meditative, even somber. "You get those big eyes..."

Brandon, puzzled, intoxicated, couldn't keep the words from springing out. "You had big eyes."

"Aah, it didn't seem big at the time. Booking drive-ins, selling syndicators in Albuquerque. I crept in from the desert like a fucking iguana."

"First you're underfoot," chimed in Wesserman, "then you're biting the dinosaurs on their asses."

"Exactly. I tell ya Brandon - you get that high and mighty syndrome, this is the City of the One Night Scams, you'll be lucky if you get fucked while you get fucked, right?" Everyone around them laughed at Graebner's drunkenly bellowed wisdom. He looked around at the gathering crowd of sleek and glistening young people. "Main thing is to enjoy the scenery, huh? The passing parade." Tanned red, shirt opened over his belly, he spread his arms wide, like a forgiving tiki-god. "What a pretty day! What a goddamn pretty day!"

Soleil took Brandon aside with a gentle pressure on his arm. "So what do you think of the wise man?"

Brandon saw Graebner wrestling with a Rotweiler, mimicking its slurps and roars. "The wise man's talking to a dog."

"His dog. The wise man's talking to his dog so he can show it off." She mimicked Graebner's stubborn Brooklynese. "'Fucking great dog, huh?' Like his girl that he's showing off. I almost go up to her and say 'Hello this-year'. Ooh, that's bad." Brandon laughed, then stopped as Soleil surveyed the party wistfully. "This is all just to impress. All of it."

"Yeah, well, it is impressive. It's great to know if you make the right things happen, you can have all this."

"In University we study all this...American pop and politics of the image. You serve the image, you feed the image, the *mechanisme*. I'm not sure I would like that that much."

Brandon peered into the center of her olive-green eyes, and saw tiny red flecks there, like strands of agate. "If you don't like it, what's the point?" he murmured. Their faces leaned towards each other. The spasm of desire raced up to his lips, he was ready to try to kiss her, when Soleil's hands flew to her mouth with a peal of laughter.

162

Brandon was shocked, but then he saw it too, the commotion at the llama pen. Someone had opened the gate, and Murray and Gus now cavorted freely on the lawn.

Graebner rushed to the pen, while curious guests ambled over in his wake. Two of the brasher ones, middle-aged types, shouted "Free the llamas!" At first, the beasts fled captivity with a tame, stiff-legged gait, and Murray, cantering towards the barbecues without much conviction, heard a cook shout at him and froze. Graebner and a servant quickly flanked him and urged him back to the corral. But Gus was hearing the call of the pampas. He charged across the lawn as Graebner called to him soothingly, "Come on, Gus, come on pal, you've had your fun...", and recruited some of the other guests to form a shoulder-to-shoulder ring around the animal. Gus butted his flank through the line of lawyers and starlets effortlessly. He trotted onto the tennis court and froze the game in its tracks. As three of the guests began snapping pictures, Graebner totally lost it. "You MOTHERFUCKER! After all the money I spend on you, you're embarrassing me, you PRICK!" He unleashed a storm of obscenities on his exotic pet, which, now bewildered, ran back and forth alongside the net, leaving a spatter of llama turds on the mid-court line.

Soleil giggled. "I guess Gus is walking his walk and talking his talk."

Brandon quickly fired off two pictures. "Yep. Like a *motherfucker.*"

The two threw their arms around each other and laughed as they watched Graebner chase his llama.

At sunset, Brandon told Soleil his secret. Barcelona and the buildings that rippled like smoke.

He had been ready to bag it on the party once the light started going. Time to drive the company car back to the office and catch the bus. But Soleil had come up to him, buzzed from the wine and the weed, and had led him down the stairs built into the side of the cliff.

As they descended towards the shoreline, Brandon's eyes parried the dazzle of the sun and lazily hovered on two women, one playing with a child, the other, a blonde in a straw hat, pointing to a distant sail. He seemed to float with them into a calm, still picture, a beautiful seaside painting, everything, for once, right where it belonged. Soleil chattered about all the ideas that had come

163

to her that day. The Graebner party had worked up a lot of those French ideas about "le program de pulp cinema" that made no sense to him, even though she said them mostly in English. To Brandon, it seemed she was playing with the ideas, as freely and carelessly as the feathered clouds tossed strands of gold, apricot and crimson from the diamond point of the horizon to a centerfield sky over the hills of Malibu.

He loved listening to her play as they walked alongside the surf. And all the while other words that crouched inside him were gathering force, the words that would stop her in mid-flight and keep her at his side. She had dropped hints that she was sick of shuttling between hotels and friends' apartments when she was in town. Brandon knew he couldn't offer her a stay at his place. The thought of Soleil sitting on his nubbly couch while the Mexicans stomped their Coke cans made him squirm. But if Worcek could just get some of that money from that insurance company and that lying wimp of a lawyer he could rent a place she'd be happy to stay in when she made the move to L.A.

She walked ahead of him barefoot on the rocky beach, carrying her pumps in her hand. Her hips swayed as they tugged the silk of her dress, cinched with shadows in the lengthening sunlight.

"You know, I'm going to miss this Brandon."

"You're leaving?"

"Oh, just awhile. I have a job – to make a movie in Spain."

"What part of Spain?

She looked quizzically at him, surprised. "You know Spain, Brandon?"

Brandon told her how he'd always wanted to go to Barcelona. Ever since 1992. "I picked up this book in a store when I was out walking. I had some dead time before I had to go to my weekend job - and anyway, I thought this book was about the Barcelona Olympics. See, I knew a guy on the baseball team. So I'm looking at it and I start getting into it. I actually bought it, and I never buy books. I mean, this city looks really old, but also pretty cool, like it's all old stone buildings and flowers. All these people in these nice outdoor restaurants eating these dinners that look like Mexican food. And then I see these pictures of buildings that were just like - melted cake. Or waves on the beach. This one house, it was called Casa Mila - I mean the walls looked like -

it looked like an earthquake hit and the whole building was going to fall down, but instead it just stayed put." He made an S-wave with his hand. "And it blew me away."

"That was Antonio Gaudi. He's the one who built it."

Her reply sank into him like a stone in a pond, the ripples overwhelming him. She hadn't laughed or given him a weird look like any of his friends would've done. She'd given his image a name.

"I didn't see the name. I mean – I was just skimming it, looking through the pictures."

"He has a whole park like that," she continued. "Guell Park. Full of cake buildings. So what is it, you think..." she asked, smiling teasingly at him, "... that is so beautiful about them, Brandon?"

Brandon stared at the sand beneath his feet, not knowing what to say. He thought again about stone melting and flowing like the waves, about iron gates carved with dragonheads, about the wild musical pulse in those Spanish walls and all the feelings it stirred within him. He didn't know where it came from, he had no name for it, this intimate code that filled him up like ringing guitar chords, but even better. A baseball diamond, that was dusty, solid, he'd got it all down to a sure thing. But this other - this was a yearning so strange that his friends would laugh at him, bust him, maybe even desert him if he confessed his feelings. He could only tell them to someone like Soleil.

"I mean to see something like that, and then get in a picture..." - his voice grew soft, abashed - "that's when I started wanting to be a photographer. I couldn't ever pay to learn to be an architect and build buildings like that - and anyway, nobody except this Gaudi builds buildings like that - but I could shoot it, right? The guys I played ball with couldn't understand. So I talked about fashion photography."

Soleil pouted, mock-tough. "Getting laid."

"Yeah, that's it. They got behind that okay. But for me what photography was always about was - cameramen can get close to the world. The most amazing stuff in the world. And then it's...", he raised his camera, "click the shutter, and you have everything in balance, no matter how crazy it is – just like that Gaudi with his buildings. And you freeze that moment and it lasts forever and - and it rules, y'know? Even in a war zone. Hell, cameramen

165

can walk through a war zone, and just capture it, like" - and the excitement of conveying these thoughts froze him up like a sputtering car engine, he almost couldn't speak - "those soldiers raising the flag, that's World War Two, and that line of children running from the napalm - that's Vietnam. That kid standing in front of the tanks in China. He's the man – but only because a cameraman shot it. So now everyone else has it, that kid just holding up a line of tanks. They have the power to make that completely intense moment last forever. And they're fearless. You know, cameramen in a war could walk through a firefight shooting their pictures and feel like they couldn't be touched. Some of them died taking pictures - but most of them just walk through it, like they've got a force field around them or something - and they come back with a gun battle in a jungle. Or something as beautiful as stone flowing like it's changing into water...I dunno, it's...photography is – you see a picture, press a button, and you've got hold of lightning, Soleil, you've got hold of lightning!"

Soleil smiled at him. "I think you will shoot Barcelona one day, Brandon."

Her remark was so gentle, like one you'd make to a child, and Brandon suddenly felt stupid and almost apologetic. He needed to make it make sense. "Main thing about photography, though, is that it cools me out. And I need that. I mean, I've always been surrounded by crazy, out-of-control people, and especially now - I can get pretty wired lately."

"This is difficult time for you. This case of yours..."

"Yeah, and – I don't know, sometimes it feels like I just have to do it, I have to fight it, and sometimes I feel like it's just bullshit between the lawyers, really dirty bullshit, and I should get what I can and walk away from it. Sometimes I don't know where I am with this."

"Brandon, that's because you're changing. This fight with the system, this will truly change you." Her strong little handclasp took his. A thrill shot through him as her fingers melted into a velvet caress, and danced in his hand like mercury. "You fight this case, you are strong, you will win. Then you will transform, you will have money, get to Barcelona."

"Yes. I'm gonna do it, Soleil. Join you in Spain, huh? On a beach."

She laughed. "We're on a beach, Brandon." His heart raced – but then her fingers were twirling in the air again, she was playing with her theories, slipping into that queenly voice she used for her scenes. "These lawyers, they are so oppressive, corrupt and you are very pure, *primitif...*"

He wasn't sure he heard her right. "What?"

"I'm sure sorry," she giggled. "I mean...more like...*naturel*. You are very natural, Brandon. I think now you are in just the right balance. Someone should take your picture, Brandon."

She suddenly grabbed the camera off his neck, and laughed at his surprise. She backed off and aimed the Nikon at him.

"Wait a minute! You're aiming right at the sun. I'll turn black."

"Come with me!"

She led him to a cave a few yards down the beach. The sun bathed the rock wall its glow. As Brandon backed up his feet crunched on twigs, and then he almost tripped on a beer bottle and a paper plate.

"Hold still!"

Brandon grinned and Soleil snapped his picture. Then he managed to perch the camera on a pile of rocks and set the timer. Soleil threw her arm around him and they both grinned as the Nikon fired away.

Brandon picked up the camera, turned, and for a moment it seemed Soleil had vanished. But the cave turned a corner. He found Soleil there, shafts of light from cracks in the wall playing on her hair. It seemed to him that she was deliberately catching the light, staging the moment. She turned to him with a drunken, inviting smile. "Amazing isn't it? Three meters from the beach, maybe – but so alone from everyone."

It seemed like he floated towards her, and the slow kiss he'd imagined for hours, nights, detonated into a clumsy leap, burning hands all over her waist, lips smothering hers. Her smile hardened, he heard an airless titter of a laugh, and he felt ridiculous, he was a slob, a geek, a loser with her, but then her lips yielded, her gums rubbed against his and her tongue was romping all over his mouth. Brandon couldn't even tell when they sprawled onto the sand, what his arms and hands were doing, but in the midst of it she pulled away from him.

"In a dirty little cave, Brandon?"

He was desperate to apologize, but then he heard something else in her laughter, and maybe, he thought, she was chuckling at the way he looked as she started to take off her sundress, because he knew he looked powerless, whatever was cool and had any style about him just melting away. "You are so young, strong, but I bet you are a virgin, aren't you...aren't you?...", and he wasn't, but he said yes, and he might as well have been, because he'd never seen a body like this, gymnast muscles, ripples on her belly like the wet, loamy ridges the surf carves on the beach, the legs so toned and golden and aloof in their symmetry. He was lost in frantic awe, a convulsion of joy on the edge of panic, as he heaved himself on top of her with one long shudder of abandon. She let him inside, groaning, then cried out in triumph as he came splinters of fire.

The interrogatories are irrelevant. The request for production of documents is too broad. Just the kind of objections you'd expect, Charlie mused, as he munched on his scone and sipped his coffee. Yes, Worcek would do what she was expected to do, but Charlie knew the damage to Brandon Reed's case had been done.

The sun slowly lengthened with a faint rainbow sheen across Charlie's polished desk. By five o'clock he felt a comforting sense of validation - this was the first time in weeks he felt useful again. He reviewed the new file: the interrogatories, the request for production of documents, the list of witnesses to be subpoenaed in Brandon Reed vs. Bernard-Duvall Health & Wellness Clinic. The cornerstone of a new narrow defense against Brandon Reed.

Hobart-Riis would argue that Brandon had never been, by any definition, a partial dependent of his dead sister, and thus was not entitled to death benefits. To that end, Charlie would depose a representative from Brandon's junior college to show that, even when he was in attendance and supposedly supported by Sheila, he was attending only a few classes and holding down a job. He would interview the landlord to ascertain how the rent was paid. He would request copies of all utility bills, and all grocery, laundry and other receipts, to determine how much Brandon contributed to the upkeep of the household. He would demand access to all the details of Brandon and Sheila's household budget-keeping.

Not that he'd get it. But the strategy was solid, and the psychology of it was devastating. Brandon Reed would soon realize they were dead set on investigating every nook and cranny of his life. Grocery receipts and checks stubs - with such trivia would Charlie destroy their claim and save his job.

There was a discreet knock on the door and Maxine Bunning slipped into his office. As he hurriedly composed himself he noticed she was looking especially Martha Stewart today, with her hair coifed and her pale mauve, ruffled organdy blouse tucked into a tweed skirt. She looked cheerful, refreshed, and ready to host a festive family dinner or birthday party. Soon she was amiably chatting with Charlie about the affairs of a busy afternoon.

"Charlie, I really like this new tack on the Reed case."

"Thanks, Maxine."

"Do you know what it is? It's a 'paradigm shift'. You're familiar with that phrase, right? You just look at something from a whole different point of view – in this case, the whole question of dependency, and bingo, it all clicks."

"We'll have them on the run with this."

Charlie drank in the reassurance of normal closing time conversation and didn't even notice when her gaze lost its cordial warmth and became the lawyerly Kabuki mask for imparting bad news. "Charlie, you're as resourceful as ever. And it's your sterling performance in the past couple of days, the way you've come up with such a handy solution to the Reed case, that was one factor taken into account by the examiners."

"Excuse me, Maxine?"

"I did want to tell you before you left for the day that Hobart-Riis, unfortunately, has decided to deny your claim. After a thorough review, we simply don't feel there's a compensable injury here."

Charlie knew at that moment that, however much he'd denied it to himself, he'd expected this decision all along. Maxine took advantage of his silence to lean towards him almost beseechingly. "Charlie, understand our position. It reflects our positive evaluation of your efforts. We're all very impressed with how well you've done since this tragedy. There's no evidence of mental or physical impairment." Charlie felt his throat drying suddenly, that panic attack dryness. Maxine's brow furrowed with sympathy. "I'm sure this awful event has had a continued effect on your life. I've gone through some hammer blows myself and I know, believe me. But surely as a lawyer you can

169

appreciate the difference between adverse reactions to the sort of misfortunes we all go through, and compensable injuries."

"Maxine," Charlie quietly replied, "when was the last time someone blew their brains out over that silk blouse of yours?"

Maxine involuntarily swallowed, as if Charlie's remark were actually going down her throat, and then continued gently. "You have a right to your anger. But perhaps I'm not the best target for it, Charlie."

Now Charlie knew he was facing the wall. He backed off and played the supplicant. "But what about my tinnitus?"

"You'll continue to receive all current medication through the health plan."

"So the psychiatry continues?"

"Well, as you know, ten to twelve sessions is the prescribed regimen for this sort of syndrome. You yourself argued in the case of that teacher who witnessed the gang shooting -"

"Yes, I know," Charlie muttered wearily.

"But believe me, we're very concerned about what you're going through, and we feel perhaps we could be doing more."

"I appreciate that." But he didn't, and he knew it, the wariness already growing…

"We really should farm out this Brandon Reed case, Charlie. You've done so well for us so far." She actually reached out and touched his hand. "Let someone else carry the baton now."

Charlie was trying to scrape up something to say when they both jumped at a rattling bang like the thump of a fist on the opposite wall. The sound was so invasive that for a moment all conversation died. Then Maxine laughed with a kind of relief. "Goodness, what a banging. It must be Bert nailing up another family picture. Look, Charlie, one thing I pride myself on is not being a hypocrite. I won't pretend I know what you're going through. But give yourself credit, you've proven you can carry on successfully and keep moving forward. I admire you, Charlie, I really do."

Charlie wasn't paying attention to Maxine now, but watching a Hispanic workman who had entered his office. He listened as the worker's helper in Bert's contiguous office rammed the wall. Charlie understood what they were doing. He'd done the same when he'd moved into his condo. They were testing the wall for studs.

"Maxine, is Bert expanding his office into mine?"

She turned to the worker and snapped at him angrily in Spanish. Charlie imagined her using those curt, icy phrases on a gardener who'd trampled her nasturtiums. As the worker ducked away, Maxine turned to Charlie and spread her hands helplessly.

"Oh, Charlie, we were going to tell you tomorrow in a meeting. It's just that Bert's responsibilities have increased so dramatically..."

"And where will my new office be located?"

"The room catty-corner to the examiner's area."

Charlie instantly had a mental picture. The old Xerox room. Windowless. Not much bigger than the den in his condo.

"It's only temporary, Charlie."

"They're taking the Reed case from me. They're denying my claim. And now they're - they're moving me into this goddamn cubbyhole!"

Dr. Westphal leaned forward, his elegant hands clasped around each other, studying Charlie's agitation. "That's a serious issue for you, I take it."

"Oh yeah. At Hobart-Riis, getting your parking space changed can reflect on your status. They're putting my office in a supply room! Like I was a fucking clerk!"

"I mean emotionally. Perhaps we should talk here only about your emotions."

"I'm pissed off! That's my emotions! In a fucking nutshell!" The doctor's face was blank, demanding precision. "Of course, my pride is hurt. And I'm scared. Really scared. You can fall off the hill in this business and find it's a mountain."

"In any business," the doctor replied.

"But mainly I'm angry. I mean, I just came up with a breakthrough on the Brandon Reed case, and they tell me this? I'm fighting real hard to keep up my performance."

"By all appearances you are, Charlie."

Charlie stopped dead. "By all appearances." The words were meant to comfort him. Instead they knit together his tangled thoughts. "By all appearances." Was that all it was? The past few weeks he'd felt that his most reliable moves were only gestures, his intuitions imaginings, his instincts deceptions. He was struggling to make himself known where once he'd effortlessly known himself.

"I came this close, Doctor, this close to literally taking a bullet for Hobart-Riis. I need help. I'm worth help."

"Of course, Charlie."

"Then again," Charlie whispered, his voice crepitating with shame, "that bullet was never meant for me."

The doctor leaned forward. "You're sure of that now, Charlie?"

"Yes. I lied for them. I mean...maybe not totally...but so far as I can tell. I lied under oath about...another suffering human being's...last moment on earth...oh God."

Charlie reached for a glass of water and smashed it across the table. In that part of his consciousness still unfazed by his emotions, he was amused by how quickly the doctor sprang up and grabbed the glass. He went back to the water cooler, refilled it and handed it to Charlie.

"Thank you, Doctor." Charlie drank down the glass in one gulp while Westphal studied him intently.

"Are you all right, Charlie?"

Charlie composed himself and put back in its cage the pain he'd just let loose.

"I feel fucking awful."

"Your memories are becoming clearer now. You mustn't blame yourself for that."

"No, no. Can't blame myself for anything. That wouldn't be productive. Productive..." Another word whose meaning slithered away. "What does that mean? What was I ever producing?"

Westphal inclined forward and cornered Charlie's question. "You know, Charlie, I think your awareness is taking a painful but very significant turn."

"You mean I'm finally getting past all the bullshit?"

A smile crinkled on Westphal's elfin jowls, like a seam on parchment. "That would be presumptuous of me to say. But I will say there has been progress." He settled back in his chair, in the splash of hazy light from the Tudor windows. "I'd recommend you continue some form of private therapy."

The words jolted Charlie. "This is our last session, then? You're sticking to that?"

Westphal sadly admitted he knew that was difficult. "If you like, we can talk about that difficulty."

"Doctor, I just had an anxiety attack right here in your office. Clearly some work remains to be done."

"We've reached the end of your prescribed course of therapy, and - "

"And my claim has been denied. Shall we talk about that, doctor?"

"I would not be competent to render any judgment in that arena, Charlie. You know that." Yes, thought Charlie, of course I do, I could practically have put those smoothly turned words in your mouth, Doctor. Then he briefly wondered if he'd actually shouted that out loud. He'd felt lately as if his brain were becoming weirdly permeable, and it was hard to distinguish the words that lurked behind his inner ear from the ones that made it to the surface. Up to this moment, Charlie had felt that in this room he didn't have to do that. Here the barrier in his brain could tumble down without fear of blunder or reprisals. But now he once again felt self-conscious, now that Westphal had officially dropped the role of his confessor and become just another devious prick.

"You know what's truly priceless about this situation, Doctor? Now that I'm sick enough to say I'm sick I can't get treatment. If the money is an issue, I can pay you privately."

"That's not the issue, Charlie. Frankly, if I continue treating you, it might be construed as a conflict of interest."

Silence pervaded the office, the silence of Westphal realizing he'd made a huge gaffe. Charlie could see it, the smile curdling on Westphal's face. From somewhere outside a car alarm began to blare.

"It would only be a conflict of interest if I sued the company. Are Shackleton and you anticipating that, Doctor?"

173

Westphal was silent. Charlie felt suddenly drained, but his legs got him up from the sofa, powered by nothing more than contempt.

"Charlie? We still have ten minutes."

You're lucky if you even like yourself enough to masturbate. Westphal had taken copious notes on him. In a disputed worker's comp psych case, Charlie knew, you waived your right to confidentiality. Your psychiatrist can testify about you. Your life's an open book, and it can all be read aloud in court.

Charlie felt nauseous. He hurried from the office without saying goodbye, and emerged to the glow of an evening sun that kept a chilly distance above the Beverly Hills street.

The skinny pimply-faced runt of a defense lawyer ran after Worcek through the courtyard. "Ms. Worcek, no one's ruling out a settlement. I'm not saying 'not a penny'. If you go with our rating, your client still gets the psych, the ortho."

Worcek spun on him, one big unladylike fused synapse of outrage. "I want my diabetes!"

"Mr. Cozen's last exam three years ago showed no sign of –"

"Oh for Chrissake! A pile of carelessly stacked plates falls on the man's right foot. A serious but not devastating injury which results in gangrene and amputation! Now absent flesh-eating bacteria, 'Doctor,' what could that be but 'lit-up' diabetes?"

"Look, it's an admitted injury. He'll get treatment. Can I get a response just - reasonably soon? I'll accept your timeline."

"The only line you're willing to accept from my client is a flatline!"

The lawyer now showed a bit of cohones, telling her he was offended by her rudeness. Worcek apologized without conviction and sent him on his way – then felt disgusted with herself. She'd just pointlessly alienated another colleague. Yeah, this was one of those days, framed by menstrual bloat and metaphysical disgust, when Worcek's methods would earn her the names given to her by her enemies, the Mistress of Stress, or, more pithily, Workers' Cunt Law.

Out on the mezzanine, lawyers with their cellphones ambled through the stucco glare like fat lazy spiders. There was at least twenty or thirty more of them today, a fucking plague of them. The Board, in its inscrutable wisdom, had temporarily closed the Pasadena office. Two of the old conference areas in the east wing of the hearing rooms had been combined to accommodate the overflow. She'd haggled it out with this last idiot with the cross-talk of thirty other lawyers and complainants assaulting her ears, only to get screwed in the MSC by one of the most pro-insurance judges in the system.

Was she truly losing her edge, or had she become that obnoxious to the rest of the fraternity? How could that MSC have ended so appallingly? Send Mr. Cozen in his wheelchair and his oxygen tank to another AME exam. To a doctor's office in the Valley, no less, when he lived in Culver City. Then wait another six months for a trial date, during which, Worcek was fairly sure, she'd be taking Mr. Cozen's deathbed testimony. She could settle, forget the permanent disability, grab something for the psych and ortho, but Mr. Cozen wouldn't hear of it. His injury had aggravated his diabetes and that had put him in a wheelchair. The bastards were ducking their legal responsibility. He would have just and full compensation no matter what it took.

And to top it all off Brandon Reed had called her – and for the first time she'd heard from him all the usual crummy uncertainty. Once so zealous to defend his sister at all costs, he was now hinting that "well, if it could be a fifty-fifty settlement, maybe…" Worcek had thought it was the request for production of all the household documents that had shaken him. Don't worry, she'd said, they'll never prove the primary burden of the household was yours. They'll never disprove Sheila killed herself over her worker's comp case. But then he'd finally admitted he now had "someone special" to think about. What he had, it seemed to Worcek, was the sexual nirvana that adolescents dream of. A French actress on a Nate Wesserman shoot for direct-to-video - try to tell a kid swept up in that kind of erogenous joyride that it's a big step to come-live-with-me-and-be-my-love. In Brandon's mind, he would soon need a better apartment for him and his bimbo, and while he wouldn't take a thousand-dollar insult – Soleil would surely understand that - a quick twelve thousand-dollar fuck-off might be just the ticket. Screw it, Worcek thought, it was a five grand case, now it's a two grand case, wrap it up and kick it out the door. But it was a case she would find hard to let go.

Besides, Worcek's pride was rankled at the thought of begging for the settlement from Charlie Solomon. Charlie could be easy to take, self-consciously clever, but fair-minded in his own way - and he'd taken a much harder knock than her in the Sheila Reed case. Still there was something rancid and slippery at the core there, if only because he continued to work for Hobart-Riis. There we go, Worcek thought, there's the jolt of sheer loathing that could get her through this day, even through this latest cramp savaging her loins. Hobart-Riis Insurance, Inc. Maxine Bunning and Ted Shackleton, pillars of their church-going community, their prosperity built on thousands of crippled workers delayed and denied their rights under the law.

Speak of the devil, she thought, there's Charlie now. Standing on the opposite railing in the midst of the lawyer's hubbub, looking utterly distracted and lost. Worcek now felt a surge of fellow feeling for him. They were both having one of those days when you just want someone else to take the wheel, pilot you through the standard operating procedure so you don't drift backwards in your own bitter wake.

"That kind of morning, huh?"

Seeing Worcek over his shoulder, Charlie jumped as if someone ambushed him, and felt so exposed, so ridiculous, that he needed to attack that innocuous remark. He told Worcek he'd cleaned up a lien case, convinced a lien collector to knock a grand off her bill. "The morning's actually been pretty productive, Liz."

"So Charlie, what do you think about a fifty-fifty split on the Brandon Reed case?"

"I think your client's getting a little more in touch with reality."

"He's had a change of heart. Well, maybe that's not the right organ, but the point is, maybe he'll settle for twelve thousand. You think the grand poobahs over there will go for that?"

The tiny surge of gratification he'd felt at the news Brandon was caving in, a purely professional reflex, was instantly extinguished.

"Yeah, I suppose it can be worked out."

176

Charlie's deflation suddenly pissed Worcek off. "What the hell is this, Charlie? You have no authority to settle anymore? Is that it?"

"Liz, you're putting words in my mouth. What a surprise," he muttered dryly. Charlie stared at the concrete, its obscenely bright sparkles of mica. "Actually, I suppose you might want to talk to Silver about settlement. No use either of us wasting our energy."

Worcek was instantly advancing on him. "Charlie? Did you file?"

"Give it a rest, Liz," Charlie snapped, and was sidling his way towards the stairs.

"Just tell me." Charlie stood on the edge of the steps and visibly paled before her. For a moment Worcek was worried he might pass out from the effort to compose himself.

"Liz, I'm not getting involved with this. I'm not going to resort to yet another fucking lawsuit."

"Then you've been denied. Is that it, Charlie?"

Charlie was more enraged at himself for his indiscretion than at Worcek for her persistence. He desperately needed to drive her away. "That's none of your business. I'm not getting down in the mud with you, Liz!"

He tried to flee, but now Worcek was actually chasing him down the stairs. In the courtyard lawyers' heads swiveled off their cellphones, nicked by the quick turbid passage of Worcek and Charlie's flare-up. "Charlie, do you think any of my clients want to get down in the mud with me? Miss Congeniality here? This poor diabetic with a crushed foot, you think he wants to wheel himself down to my office to have a little chat? You know what they all say? In my presence? Why, Lord, why am I here? And then they say - it makes no sense. I worked hard. I got along with everyone. How could they not want me all fixed up and back to work? They could never mean me any harm. Charlie, you were damaged goods as soon as that gun went off, and now they're dumping the merchandise!"

Charlie turned on her. "I am still on the Brandon Reed case, Liz. They're using my strategy!"

"So why do they have to keep you, Charlie? Come on, you know how it works! Do you really believe that 'No, that can't be piss on my head, it must be raining?'"

Charlie stiffened up, managed a grin, and patted her on the shoulder. "Actually, Liz, the reason I reacted with indifference to Brandon Reed's offer to settle is that we're going to bury the little bastard. Now if you'll excuse me, I have work to do." He headed back upstairs, and Worcek realized there was no point in following him. Besides, down in the courtyard, Mr. Cozen was waiting. She could see him in his wheelchair, his tube up his nose, oxygen tank braced against the struts behind his foot prosthesis. His eyes were closed, trying to dream an escape from the terminus of the system, the courtyard, his ruined body.

Down amid the normal hubbub of the courtyard, Worcek could hear a weirdly discordant shrieking. A woman sitting on the bench had become hysterical. She was saying she wouldn't go up there to the hearing rooms. Something about they wouldn't do it to her again. The words snapping loose - now she was screaming they wouldn't rape her again, her or her child. There were always psychiatrists on hand to testify and two were trying to calm her down. But her panic had leaked out, and little involutions of it played on the crowd, ripples of half-chuckled wrathfulness, sarcastic dismay, building, cresting, at last petering out again. Worcek, like so many other workers comp veterans viewing the restive crowd, let a tense breath finally escape. It was like an earthquake - you never knew when it would go a second or two past rattling cupboards to crack the glass, the furniture, the walls…

Not today. Not this morning.

Just two hours ago, Worcek had snapped at Olivia, her eldest, about her staying out late with her boyfriend. Her daughter had fidgeted on her sunlit bed and mumbled some excuse, lazy in the morning's careless radiance. Worcek retreated to the breakfast nook with the taste of failure in her mouth. She'd meant to measure out her concern and had spilled her anger. On Olivia's radio a Joan Osborne song had been playing. "Babies will put things in their mouths…Never heard of sin." That's what she always worried about with Olivia, her oldest daughter, that she might take the wrong fruit, the wrong swallow.

But what if Olivia shed her virginity with no more than the usual disasters? She could marry safe, sound and happily. She could make Worcek a grandmother.

And then, one day, trying to help her family, Olivia goes to work. And she runs afoul of a drug-addicted supervisor. Gets into an accident some insurance carrier just doesn't want to pay for. In one of the workers comp judges' offices was a map of all the fault lines in southern California. The state looked like a windshield hit by a rock. The judge hung the map so that quarreling lawyers in his office would have a "sense of perspective." But to Worcek, that map incarnated all the cracks her workers were falling through, fissures of winked-at lawlessness in a social contract that came apart more and more every day.

If her old adversary Charlie Solomon could fall through one of those cracks, who was safe? If her own daughter fell through, could she protect her? Worcek's case-hardened heart went milky with dread.

Charlie hadn't realized how dusty his books had gotten. Somehow he'd felt his law library had an immutable dignity, but as he picked up one of his books from the piles shoved against the walls of his tiny new office, lint and grime stuck in a ball to his fingertip. His bulwark of wisdom and strategy looked sordid and frail.

When would the bookshelves come? The longer it took for this office to really look like an office the more vulnerable he felt. He could hear the drills and hammers pulverizing the wall that had separated his previous domain from Bert Silver's. A similar boundary had just crumbled in the examiner's office. Henceforth all case files pertaining to Charlie's cases would be shown to Bert first. Just until Charlie "fully recovered."

Charlie could muster no protest to this edict. Since he'd turned his back on Worcek at the hearing rooms he'd felt as if every dust mote in the air lay heavy upon him. The normal ambience of his day had a blunt, alien glitter, like the water of a poisoned stream. He stared dully at the wires trailing from his CPU and his monitor, which looked discarded and ready for storage, then sat on his swivel chair in the midst of his junk and rocked with the forward motion of his day.

Into this torpor bustled Carol with a smile of genuine pride.

"I heard that strategy you worked out with Bert is really turning the Reed case around. Congratulations." Her lips pursed and her childlike face became solemn. "You know - we're all rooting for you. The secretaries, I mean."

He didn't have the heart to tell her he'd been relieved of the Reed case. "Just don't place any bets," he cracked, and then, seeing her uneasiness, immediately regretted it. "But I'm very grateful, Carol. Really."

Carol relaxed and handed him his mail. She indicated a thick manila envelope on the bottom. "I think that's what you've been waiting for."

"What is it?"

"It's from Dr. Chesley. Looks like his handwritten notes on Sheila Reed."

Charlie took a breath. He reached for his ever-present glass of water. He told Carol to take a little break. She thanked him, told him she'd submitted a second time for a new surge protector for his computer, and twisted past the pile of books on her way out.

Dr. Chesley's handwritten notes had been printed neatly on a regular legal pad, then photocopied. They betrayed the carefulness of a man being asked to step into a swamp. "Patient presents as agitated…appears to be deeply ashamed...speech almost incoherent...", words swathed in clinical caution, but Charlie's detachment was wire-thin and even those muffled phrases resonated deeply. Sheila's burning despair was once again alive within him. Charlie soon realized that Dr. Chesley hadn't slanted his typewritten report in Sheila's behalf - he'd softened it for the benefit of his employers. Here he'd put the truth in Sheila's exact words.

These notes I'd asked for, Charlie realized, would've killed us.

"Like a red curtain over my eyes...then it turns into this inner loathing...I try to meditate but it's all for shit...I could grab the Drano off the sink and drink it but I don't want to leave a mess. My husband yells at me, but he doesn't want to face the fact his contacts are drying up and I have to work in this shithole. Why doesn't he see? Why doesn't he see? I'll have to let Sandoval in the goddamn door. Sexual harassment suits in L.A. - take a number and wait ten years. I'll have to let him do the nasty. I want you to know that. I can't lose this job. I can't."

Charlie skimmed along the words on the pad, wanting somehow to both know and evade. "Maybe Sandoval's right, maybe I did lose the files, I fucked up, I'm a fuckup." This was a woman "mildly depressed"? Theresa Calder's description. Sheila's best friend at the office.

Another burst of vitriolic accusations leaped from the pages. "Friends? Family? They just turn their back on things. We all do. The abuse of people, I... I should've known they'd all blame me for the missing files. They'll have to blame somebody."

"I wish I was dead. I wish I was dead. I just wish I was dead."

The doctor had written out the repetition.

Charlie sat at the desk, hollow as a drum, resonating with the hammer-blows of those words, but he forced himself to read on. The doctor prescribes a mild tranquilizer, and a support system of friends and family. What else can he do? He's a gatekeeper.

I'm the gate-closer.

That look...the gun angling away...

I should've known.

"I should've known they'd all blame me for the missing files. They'll have to blame somebody."

Carol barely jumps back from him as he runs out the door. He hears books slam to the ground. He's sprung loose in the disorder of his thoughts, but driving reflexes hew to the road signs. Olympic Boulevard. Beverly Drive.

On Sunset he drives into the teeth of a relentless Santa Ana. The glare on the Boulevard is weirdly hectic, an amplification of blind white dust. It brightly polishes all the Day-Glo colored husks of the music clubs. Pages of a wind-ripped newspaper knife down the pavement. He can feel it come through the vents of the car, into his sinuses, his throbbing brain, whatever it was the hot winds ripped off the desert and blew into the city. Rock dust. Spores. He raises his bleary eyes to the billboards. Universal Citiwalk. A mall with fake city towers. A faint urban stencil of bright fuzzy skyline. He reads the billboard's slogan as he drives past. "What To Do When You Don't Know What To Do."

He was a few blocks from the Bernard-Duvall Clinic's parking lot before he realized he hadn't even made the call. He yanked out his cellphone. Fought his way past the receptionist.

"This is Theresa."

181

"Ms. Calder, it's Charlie Solomon. We have to meet."

"Really? When did you want to schedule a meeting?"

"Now. On the corner in front of your office."

"What are you talking about?"

"It's important."

That was brilliant, he thought, as he pocketed the cell. I'll be lucky if she doesn't call the authorities. But a few minutes after he parked the car and took his spot on the corner, he saw Theresa hurrying across the Boulevard, with a kind of half-trot to beat the bated traffic and the gusts of wind. She was wearing a white blouse and a tan pantsuit that the Santa Anas were rippling like a sail. There was a graceful vigor in her walk that mocked the ringing in his ears.

Leave now. Brandon will settle. The case is over.

"Theresa?"

She took Charlie in uneasily, and then at last dropped some icy words into the long, painful moment of recognition. "How can I help you, Mr. Solomon?"

"Maybe it's more about helping yourself, Theresa."

Theresa's vestige of cordiality vanished. "How so?"

"Theresa, I was going over the case files, and - quite honestly I've come to warn you, if the Brandon Reed case continues and you're deposed -"

Theresa raised her hand to her eyes to block the wind and sun, but the gesture couldn't mask her hint of derision. "If I'm deposed I'll say what I said before. It's not going to change. Why are you talking to me about -"

"There's new evidence."

The silence was full of the noise of the wind, the growl of the traffic. Theresa's hand involuntarily clutched her lapel.

"Dr. Chesley met with Sheila. She really – unburdened herself to him. He took careful notes on what she said. I subpoenaed them."

"Why the hell did you do that?" A cry of pure exasperation. Charlie didn't know how to answer. He felt the blustering winds stiffen him, but also strip bare all his niceties down to raw emotion.

"It was a delaying tactic. I figured we might lose the decision. I couldn't let that happen. So I asked for the notes to - to cause a delay. Then Sheila shot herself. So case closed, right? I should just throw out the notes, to hell with them! Only what they say...she talks about how all of you knew it. She says Sandoval and the staff teamed up to blame her for the missing files."

"Maybe she really believed that," Theresa hissed. "This conversation is over."

He grabbed her arm. She turned on him in disbelief. He released her instantly, but his words wouldn't let go. "Theresa, if Sheila was deluded, then that bastard and this job made her literally paranoid. If she wasn't deluded, and there was a plan to drive her off the job, then she was injured by work-related harassment. Either way, her case was valid." The words kept heaving out of him. "Did you really not notice anything? You said she was 'mildly depressed'? You were supposed to be her friend!"

Theresa's disbelieving smile was laced with contempt. "You've pulled me out of the office to tell me your remorse."

"I'm trying to warn -"

"Jesus Christ, what do I have to do to get rid of you? Get another lawyer, I suppose!"

"Theresa, I'm convinced there was genuine wrongdoing here. She was driven off the job, she killed herself, and I'm going to learn how and who and why!"

"You know, Mr. Solomon, if you're so hung up on it, tell your rabbi, you stinking hypocrite! How dare you come to me? How dare you?"

"Theresa!" But she hustled up the stairs in two long strides. She slammed the door shut behind her, and in the freakish microclimate on the Boulevard the wind sucked at it so hard that it doubled the door's impact and the glass smashed to pieces. Charlie barely ducked out of the path of the serrated fragments that scattered at his feet. He and Theresa stared at each other amazed through the hole in the door and its web of hanging glass shards and crazed sunlight.

Charlie heard tires scrape the pavement. He turned around to see a black van heading down the Boulevard. No, he thought, it couldn't be, there were plenty of vans that looked like Golan's. But he couldn't stop staring as the van disappeared – and by the time he turned back, Theresa was gone. He nudged a piece of broken glass with his feet.

The cellphone rang through his suit.

When Charlie saw Shackleton waiting for him in his "office" he realized how small it was. His boss' lanky frame seemed to swallow up all the space within it.

He also realized the size of his office was irrelevant. He wouldn't be needing it anymore.

Shackleton kept a cold silence all through the walk down the corridor, his crisp smile only for the benefit of the examiners who watched them pass by. Charlie saw the same expertly prepared masks on the faces of Maxine Bunning and Bert Silver as they waited on Shackleton's couch.

At first they congratulated him for his work on the Sheila Reed case. Charlie knew their praise was honest, and it was an eyedropper's worth of hope. A moment lit by the sun glistening warmly on Shackleton's oak and mahogany furnishings. If he could only freeze this moment, and believe that, now that they were saying they'd take over the case from here, that he could go back, back to his desk, back to a life expunged of any memories of Sheila Reed.

Silver cut off his hopes. "But we can't tolerate the unprofessional conduct you've displayed."

"Specifically," Bunning echoed, "the outrageous - well, there's no other word for it - the outrageous indiscretion of your visit to Ms. Calder. An unstable woman we might have to depose again."

"You had Golan trail me," he finally spat out in disgust. But his indignation had no force behind it. Of course they'd had Golan trail him. Probably for weeks.

"How we discovered your misconduct is irrelevant, Charlie." Shackleton took over the meeting now, in his disappointed avuncular mode. Mr. 1950's Dad. They appreciated Charlie's years of service to Hobart-Riis. That's why they were handing him an envelope with one month's severance pay. And there would be no negative repercussions when Charlie sought future employment. He had their word.

"I appreciate that," Charlie replied. "And I'm glad that - that you appreciate that I remained 'productive' to the end."

184

They conceded that to him, while re-emphasizing that unfortunately Charlie's careless and - Shackleton dare said - thoughtlessly impulsive response to recent events left them no other choice. Charlie rose from his last meeting. "Thank you all for three years of a very rewarding professional association, and...all I have left to say is...I'm going to press my claim immediately and sue the shit out of you."

Bunning and Shackleton recoiled, and Bert took up the cudgel. "Bad idea, Charlie. You accepted the prescribed treatment, you'd have difficulty fixing the time your injury became compensable -"

"And while I'm at it, you pompous-ass shit, I'll take another form to file a 132A. Harassment of an injured worker filing a claim!"

"Charlie," Bunning calmly interrupted, "we don't want to go to war with you."

"Then accept my claim! Accept your responsibility under the law!"

"It's a post-term, Charlie." Silver snapped. "You know the ride you're in for."

Post-termination. They're already claiming he'll be suing because they fired him.

The disdainful phrase walled him off from them once and for all. "Goodbye, then," he muttered, and headed for his desk. As he left the office and strode past the first of the examiner's cubicles, he heard Bert Silver padding behind him. He couldn't believe it; Bert was following him to his office to make sure he wouldn't steal or damage company property. Now the humiliation flooded over him. In their glum procession to his office, watched by all of his former co-workers, he felt the aura of a little death on him, like a man who'd just euthanized his cat.

Bert stolidly observed Charlie's every move as he unloaded his desk. "Forgive the formalities," he at last told Charlie with a wisp of a smile. And then, shuffling back and forth, he asked "I understand you want us to settle with Brandon Reed? Why is that?"

For a moment, Charlie thought of denying him an answer, just to strike back at him. Then he was seized with his own moment of curiosity. "Bert, do you ever take a look at that waiting room? Ever really take a look at those people?"

185

"See, Charlie, that's the trouble. That's what you started doing. Ever since Sheila Reed killed herself. And now you take your cues from them. You look into their eyes now." He leaned forward with an almost malicious intensity. "You know, you were a damn good colleague, Charlie. I don't like what that common little bitch did to you. I don't like her brother profiting by it. He has no case. You've spent the last week proving it. And now we're going to finish it."

Charlie could tell that Bert, in his own way, was offering an apology, and Charlie simply turned away to let him know that his sympathy was unacceptable. Meanwhile, he stuffed the last of his small personal knickknacks into his valise - and registered at the corner of his peripheral vision Dr. Chesley's photocopied notes, facedown on his desk.

"You still didn't answer my question, Bert. How do you feel about all those claimants? Or don't you even have the balls to have an opinion without checking with Bunning and Shackleton first?"

Now he knew he'd got him. Bert had the look of a man about to blurt out something definitive to someone he'd never see again.

"It's a free country, Charlie. The poor shitheads can get sick waiting for the system to treat them, or get better on their own. It's their choice."

Charlie held Bert's stare, and casually as possible reached for the Casey notes to slip them into his valise - when Bert's hand immediately tapped his forearm.

"For Chrissake, Bert, I'm taking my personal notes home!"

Bert withdrew from the notes a page of company correspondence that Charlie had used to mark his place. With a show of disgust to mask his relief, Charlie took the pad back, and then snapped his valise shut on his life with Hobart-Riis. He spoke his final words to Bert. "And I thought you assholes wanted me to recover."

Silver shrugged. "There's only so much recovery to go around, Charlie."

As Charlie left the office, Mavis Thorpe, senior secretary, waddled over to him. No use asking how she'd caught on, she could pluck office news out of the wind. Her usual expression of tired cunning melted into solicitude; the woman who knew where all the bodies were buried seemed to genuinely

186

lament Charlie's joining the graveyard. Then Charlie spotted Carol in the hall and wanted a moment alone with her, but Silver remained in the doorway of the old Xerox room. Charlie realized the bastard was going to watch him all the way to the elevator. He said a quick, almost embarrassed goodbye to his secretary, wincing at her anguish for him. She squeezed his hand repeatedly until he finally slipped it free.

At last he was ready to leave. But before he could get to the glass doors he saw Vel exiting the elevator. He stood and watched as she gingerly approached him. There was nothing to blame her for, really. Of course they'd assign her his work for "cover", and she needed all the work she could get.

"So you inherit the Brandon Reed case?"

The cleft in her chin tightened. "Lucky me."

"Wait until the Charlie Solomon case comes up."

"Charles, I - look, if there's anything I can do. You know I'll put in a good word for you. Wherever I can."

The whole idea of Vel helping him network suddenly nauseated him. He was tearing himself loose from the whole web. "Don't waste your time," he muttered coldly, and left Vel in the doorway.

"Charles?"

Outside, the sun lay crisply across the concrete like the bright pulse of a metronome, ticking everyone else into their lunch hour. Charlie headed across one of the bridges that spanned the big avenues intersecting Century City. He wanted air and solitude. In an isolated plaza, he plucked out his cellphone and called Worcek.

"I'm fucked."

"Then let the games begin."

-7-

in spite of the tennis

Daylight squatted on Charlie's brain and his first waking thought was that Calvados should not be drunk from the bottle.

A typical evening with Ellis and the guys. First a desultory low-stakes poker game. Charlie, heart pounding through the comradely ritual, was, fortunately, up. Then came that bottle of Calvados more properly sniftered than swigged. Prosciutto on melon, some crackers with some kind of white cheese, crumbly and very tasty, good old plain old Tostitos, some wine, some grapes, Brownies - and more Calvados. He and his buddies obscenely reviling clients, customers, and superiors. Then the downshift to real trash talk. Dave Sisley was headed for Loreno, Mexico for a week. "Bring it or buy it? I'd pass on the 'Midnight Express." Notes were compared from the last time one of the guys took a Mexican holiday. Golf vs. tennis, yep, tennis was better for meeting the Texas college babes - but which region of babes? "Austin - strictly nerdessas....low-hanging fruit...No, you want a woman from San Antonio, bilingual, great ass…."

Of course all the talk was bullshit. Sisley would probably take his new girlfriend with him to Mexico and never get near any herbs except chile. But Charlie jumped on that good-humored bullshit like it was a life raft. It didn't even matter that he could no longer afford vacations. The thought of Dave or Jake or Ellis trying to "get some" south of the border and landing in an Oliver Stone movie was just the amusement he needed to keep him in the room and get him through the night.

Yep. Time for the Weather Channel. The forecasts bubbled brightly in the shadow of his hangover. Sunny and mild. Haze at the beaches. Why do they dress their good-looking weather women in pink cardboard? Charlie had

188

always hated the color pink. Outside his window the morning light smacked the condo's bordello pink walls. At least his neighbors didn't expect him to get the repainting done anymore. How did the news osmose through the condo community about late payment notices? Or maybe it was on weekday mornings like this, when Charlie waddled squinting to the pool, over and over, that the neighbors could observe him and figure it out.

"Why do you dwell on it?"

Nope. Put that voice, that clear little bell of anguish out of your head. If there was one genuine, verifiable fact he'd learned from Westphal and the other bogus doctors, it was that your own thoughts could victimize you, fed by the panic buried in the empty moments of the day. The bottom rhythm of defeat. Time for a walk. Charlie ambled through the courtyard, head throbbing, dry-mouthed, at least no longer nauseous. His hip collided with the flanks of banana leaves and the blades of fan palms and rhododendrons that spread along the pool. Fresh golden day lilies, arching over the concrete buttresses, winked at his shambling fatigue. Charlie gazed at the lilies and his mood eased. He wanted to enjoy his surroundings while they lasted.

He opened the mailbox and adrenaline surged. Not enough to race his heartbeat- he knew the worker's comp drill well enough to know how elusive an actual event was in the process - but when he opened the letter there was no muting the uptick of excitement. The Mandatory Settlement Conference in his case was scheduled in seven weeks.

Four months had passed since Charlie had filed suit. What was another seven weeks?

He shut his mailbox cover, tugged the key out of the tight little lock, straightened up, and felt the pain sear down from the back of his neck to the center of his scapula. In his initial excitement, he'd bent down the wrong way to peer at his mail, and would pay for that error with twenty-four to thirty-six hours of neck pain until he could get to his chiropractor.

It had taken forever to find a chiro who would treat him on a worker's comp lien. There was an irony, Charlie thought. Because of the effectiveness of defense lawyers like Charlie in shooting down worker's comp liens, medical practitioners who'd once taken worker's comp patients by the truckload now routinely refused them, and so Charlie had gone through a week of agony

189

trying to find treatment. At last he'd found a compassionate and as yet unburned chiropractor in Silver Lake who made so much money on whiplash cases that he was willing to take one on a green lien. To reach him Charlie had to drive forty-five minutes, the last stretch up hot, snarled, construction-trenched Western Avenue, but the relief was worth it.

Charlie walked back to his room balancing his neck on its bent hinge of anguish. Work with snakes, his dad had once told him, you get snakebit.

Dueling doctors. Two weeks after he'd filed suit against Hobart-Riis, claiming physical and psychological injury, Worcek had arranged an appointment with a Qualified Medical Examiner. Our side. He'd put Charlie through a battery of ear tests that confirmed residual damage to the tympanic membrane and cochlea from the close-range gunshot blast. Then Hobart-Riis' defense QME a month later. Same tests but at light speed. Charlie could almost hear the meter running. The stiff cone with its fiber light poked in and out of his ear like a latch key and the doctor detected no impairment to his auditory organs whatsoever. Purely psychological, this tinnitus that still yanked him awake at night.

Over to the psychiatrists and the Hamilton ratings scale. Charlie knew these questions, designed to measure extent of depression, and he knew them so well that he worried whether any of his responses would be accurate. The lawyer in him judged the patient mercilessly and threw such a filter of cynicism on the exercise that it clouded all his attempts to answer the statements accurately. "I am especially concerned about how my body is functioning." Well, yeah, got to answer "Yes", that's a no-brainer, of course I want them to think I'm a hypochondriac...well, what if I really am a hypochondriac...well what if I'm not a hypochondriac but I really am sick? "I can concentrate easily while reading the papers." Honest-to-God no, and that truly spooked him. "I am being punished for something bad in my past." "Much of the time I am very afraid but don't know the reason."

He would've loved to answer that one "yes", more proof of paranoia demanding treatment. The trouble was he did know the reason. He knew he knew the reason the day he got the letter from Hobart-Riis scheduling him for two defense examinations thirty miles apart within three hours. Most claimants would be bewildered by the insurance company's stupidity, or enraged at the bad luck that jammed in two appointments on the same day. If they missed one of the appointments due to wait time or traffic, their T.T.D. payments might end and their whole case might be jeopardized. Charlie knew that was exactly the point. Bert Silver and his cadre of examiners knew all the dirty tricks, and they would subject Charlie to every one of them.

The defense psychiatrist's offices were in an old brick building on a drab stretch of Venice Boulevard. Charlie once again checked off his responses to the Hamilton test, one eye on the relentless clock. Again he trotted out for the opposing shrink's benefit the nightmares he'd carefully logged for the past six months. Earthquakes, freezing to death, being cornered by large insects that exuded a foul-smelling paralytic venom and then - a particularly nasty touch - pissed on his head. Or the most unnerving dream, his "vampire dream", when he looked in the mirror and saw no face.

The doctor, a bald Latino with a bristling mustache, interrupted Charlie's dream diary. What he wanted to know about was the gun. Whatever made Charlie think he could grab the gun? Why did he do it?

"What are you trying to say, Doctor? That I brought this on myself? Is that the game?"

"There's no game here. Do you think it's a game?"

"I think I was badly injured during the course of my employment."

The doctor's gaze was unwavering. "Your employment did not include wrestling for a gun, Mr. Solomon."

Charlie got up and walked out, sick to his stomach. Nothing more to say to this flunky. Especially since he had only an hour to make it to downtown L.A. There an AME, an Agreed-Upon Medical Examiner, waited to try and reconcile the two conflicting ear examinations. Traffic lumbered down the 10, and choked the long whorl of the cloverleaf to the Harbor Freeway. The blue-brown smog coated the skyscrapers with the patina of unearthed ruins. Charlie hated downtown. A warren of endless street repair, bordered on one end by the faceless office and court buildings, and on the other by warehouses whose broken windows and tagged brick walls screamed robbery and assault. As he looked for the AME's office, tunnels ingested him, spewed him out and launched him down one-way streets that spun him past blank plazas and endless parking lots. Infuriated by a traffic jam, he broke free to make a right

191

turn, any right turn. He picked the street in front of him and saw it was headed straight for a freeway. With a shout of disgust he slammed on the brake - and quailed as he heard the screech of louder brakes, the crescendo of squealing tires.

The Jeep Cherokee smashed into his driver's side rear bumper. Charlie felt the crunching thump blast through his back and snap his head. The car spun like an amusement park ride, careening endlessly, it seemed, thought it only fishtailed about thirty yards. Charlie later realized his good fortune at having been on a one-way street where he couldn't have been knocked into opposing traffic. But at that moment he only felt violated, the length of the street a membrane that pulsed with his humiliation. He took his hand off the gearshift and saw to his horror that his grip, contending with the force of the spin, had twisted it out of shape. The gearshift housing of the Infiniti now looked like a huge fist had smacked it, along with Charlie's pride and a good chunk of his remaining bankroll.

Out he trudged to exchange snarls and cards with the Jeep driver. Fender-bender etiquette: two nitwit motorists bobbing up and down as they checked the damage like toy birds on the rim of a water glass. Then the pain erupted in his neck and he realized that this accident was one up on the Richter scale, a body blow, a dent in his life.

Worcek, of course, was cheery. "Going and coming between doctor's offices, whiplash, ba-bing! - don't worry, Charlie, we'll just add this injury to the case."

"Why do you dwell on it?"

Why do I dwell on it? Shit, there's all this time on my hands. Time to watch LAW AND ORDER, neatly enclosing crime and justice in under an hour. There's a fantasy for you. Time to read classic novels again, bang out old rock tunes on the guitar, do some minimal gardening - not much luck with bulbs, but his blue hibiscus and a hardy cluster of geraniums were faring well.

By about two in the afternoon, though, after he'd worked out at the gym, trying to use his last month at the club to build as much sinew as he could, he could no longer forestall the dead time. All his ingenuity couldn't combat that sunny trough of idleness in the middle of the day. On this afternoon the biggest event was a doubling over from the night before, a sudden expulsion of the toxins of the body. Bowels purged in the worst way, he sprawled on the couch, glazed eyes on the ceiling. This was smellier, sweatier downtime than most, but not that different - the same limbo, the same dead weight. No way he could feel as he used to on his best days at work or at play, that he was a bright synapse of information and activity, a lively current of air.

What was happening to his tennis? With a burst of longing, he thought about his tennis class. He hadn't realized before how satisfying it was to teach kids so much like he was at that age, middle class kids without enough money for tennis pro classes, and watch them shine as they learned the game that Charlie enjoyed as much as he enjoyed anything. That class had perhaps been the most worthwhile thing he'd done since he left law school. He'd fought so hard to keep it going, but after the fender-bender, Charlie found he couldn't demonstrate proper serve pronation without dropping his racket in agony. He took a month-long leave of absence, knowing that he would never return. This was the sort of volunteer job so rife with networking prospects that it quickly vanished.

What he missed most was the path he would take back to his car from the courts, every part of him still notched and ready and pleasantly defined with sweat, the kids better tennis players, the eucalyptus trees vaulting towards spindrifts of sunlight.

Why do you dwell on it?

Dana loved her dolls. So once every couple of months, Charlie and Dana had dinner at Madeleine's Cafe Provencale. The bistro was set in an old apartment done up like a 1920's French salon, and every dining room had shelves of dolls: china and wood and straw dolls, Raggedy Ann dolls, Indian prince dolls on elephants, African and Samoan dolls - wherever you sat you were calmly watched by an audience of the little fuckers. Definitely on the precious side for Charlie, but the food was great and Dana adored the dolls.

They were halfway into a duck a l'orange, when Dana began to cut the crisp brown slices finer and finer and worry them with her fork. Her nervousness infected Charlie instantly. Without much enthusiasm she asked how his case was going, and hearing her impatience he decided to give her the short answer. The only thing now was - he tried to summarize - he'd heard that

Westphal, the shrink, hadn't filed his report within the ninety-day limit, so he was worried that Westphal had disappeared the reports, reports on which he'd probably labeled Charlie's psych injury "occupational stress syndrome" or even post-traumatic stress disorder. Did they really think they could stop his case that way? And Charlie and Worcek also needed to know if Westphal had p. & s.'d him, that is ruled his illness "permanent and stationary", because if he had they could file the declaration of readiness now and -

"I think I get the idea, Charlie."

She'd never cut him off that abruptly before, but he understood. His attempts at synopsizing had been pathetic. Charlie's mind now raced the loop-the-loop of his obsession endlessly and Dana was a captive audience finally rattling her chains. He apologized to her and she smiled wanly and patted his hand. He cherished her at that moment, gazing at her as she contemplated her slice of duck, the pale tendrils of her hair framing her small, delicate lips.

"Charlie, I'm going to be taking over an office in San Diego."

"That's a hell of a commute," he muttered. He tried to chuckle, but he felt the coziness of a moment ago blow out of him and snuff any laughter.

"I'll be moving there. To my parent's place in La Jolla."

"They're letting you have that place?"

"Well, kind of on a temporary basis. Greg will still be there sometimes."

"Uh-oh. We'll have to make sure the bedsprings don't creak." Dana smiled and shook her head. "You know, I always wanted to check out the Wild Animal Park," Charlie continued. "Greatest zoo in the world." He stopped talking about zoos and Gastown and the Padres when the weight of her hand on his began to tremble, and the shake of her head became a painful roll hitched to emotions too heavy to bear.

"Dana?"

She bit her lip, then finally got it out. "Damn it, Charlie, we started out as friends!"

Charlie stared at the rest of his duck, which now looked as appetizing as wallpaper. "Look, I know I've been a little distant lately. Part of it is this - de-sensitization I'm going through. We talked about -"

"Yes, of course. Your feelings are a little - shut down as you recover from the trauma."

"It's just a recovery stage. I'll get through this, Dana. And I'm going to win."

"I'm sure you will, Charlie."

He felt a bead of hot malice well up within him. He wanted to make her say it, that she didn't believe him, he was now a liability, a loser. But inevitably, he instead pleaded his case - only it was his fucking worker's comp case. He told her that there was no way they could deny injury, and he was about to embroider the legal argument when Dana's hand slammed on the table.

"Charlie, please, don't you see? I have to move on, and - and you won't even be there!"

Suddenly the moment seemed deeply perilous - even the little row of ornamental dolls seemed to peer at him with unusual solemnity. "You know what? I can move with you. Hell, I can't afford the condo anymore. San Diego rents are cheaper, and -"

"Why don't you just not have an answer for once?"

She was crying now. The waitress was in the corner trying to look preoccupied with the order pad. Charlie haplessly took Dana's hands, two limp, nerveless sheaths from which all sympathy had fled. "I - Charlie, I – I need people with me all the way, do you know what I mean? I understand why it happened, and I know it's not your fault, but - it's like I can't rely on you anymore. You were so solid, and now -"

"Dana, once this is over, I'll get a new job, replenish my bank account-"

"It's not that! It's not the money, I swear to you. It's like - you're not attached. You're away. And I don't know how long you'll be away, Charlie."

She turned up to him the tear-stained face of an abandoned child talking gibberish. That's what he was seeing now, he knew it, the face of a five-year-old whose go-go actress mother, after a skiing accident, had developed a discreet little pill problem. Nothing wealth and a fairly luxurious course of detox couldn't cure - but not without a year of a child seeing her mother fade to a specter of hostility and verbal abuse. Charlie was somewhere in that phantom zone now, where slipsliding attachments can't be trusted. The

195

enormity of the space he had to cross to get back to her drained the resolve out of him.

He tried one more time. "I won't lie to you, it will take some time to fight this out. I didn't ask for this, Dana."

"Then why do you dwell on it?"

The cry was short and sharp as a beak pecking into his soul. It still rang within him as they sat parked outside her building, and Dana quickly whispered to him that she wanted to be alone to think about all this. She would call him soon. She kissed him on the cheek, then ran for the cover of her lobby.

Charlie drove back to Beverly Hills re-rehearsing all the moments in the conversation when he could have deflected her pain, refuted her panic, found some argument to defray the judgment that had passed between them. But there remained the obstinate fact of his own case, which he couldn't reason away, along with the blind selfishness of her question.

Why did he dwell on it? Because it now dwelled in him. The case had taken possession of his brain and sunk its corded roots into his heart. The hobbled rhythm he moved to could no longer sync up with the pace of tennis, or the hoofbeats of the smart little bay mares Dana rode in Will Rogers State Park. He thought of her riding, of her skiing, of how proud he was that ski bums called her a TLU, "tight little unit", as she raced down the moguls, how happily they'd discovered each other. Now the discovery was undone, now he was so much less than the man Dana had loved. In spite of the credentials and degrees. In spite of the tennis. And all these truths had to be admitted.

Brandon hoisted yet another cardboard box breaking at the seams out of Wesserman's office. He'd never realized before just how much movies were paper. Not just the scripts. Budgets. Contracts. Location spreads. And the crumpled, angry sheaves of paper wedged in the inactive files. Fossil records of unborn films, abandoned films, legally disputed films. Dead and draggy as the shipments of bolts and screws he used to lug up from the cellar at the hardware store.

He was worried he might soon have to tote boxes of film out to the trash. NIGHTWINDERS 3: THE STALKER'S LAST STAND had been halted with twenty pages to shoot three months ago. No editors had been called.

196

Brandon had taken calls to the production office threatening various organs in Nate Wesserman's body. None of this was any good.

Brandon felt really down fetching loads of cinema refuse out of Wesserman's office, where'd he'd first taken professional camera equipment into his hands, where he'd met Soleil. But he needed the work, and Wesserman had assured him he'd get paid, in fact he'd passionately sworn it to Brandon, leaning so close he could see the milky fatigue in his boss' eyes, the tiny unrazored hairs anchored to his jowls. "I'm emphasizing this, Brandon, because maybe you hear the words 'Chapter Eleven' and 'bankruptcy' and you figure there's some big problem, like, what, am I supposed to work for this deadbeat schmuck for free? Bankruptcy's just a tool, Brandon. A way to protect your assets."

Wesserman had confided to Brandon that he was partnering with some guy from Milan with deep pockets. Brandon would shortly be going to the airport to pick up this guy's son, who was his advance man, and soon after that the deal would close. The partner was also behind the move to the new office - Brandon knew that because every hour or so Nate would shit on the new office. Too small. In the wrong part of town. Lousy a/c. And there were other complaints, something to do with development funds and an Italian television deal. Brandon heard snatches of a quick phone call to Nate's lawyer. "They call this a licensing fee over there? I could beat this deal in Krakow! The greaseball's fucking me up the ass so hard I'm spitting olive oil!"

Brandon gently lifted off its wall-fasteners the poster for NIGHTWINDERS 2: THE STALKER'S RETURN. It was the one designed from one of his photos, the naked vampiress perched on the car, the yuppie gazing with awe and delight and not seeing the talons on the hands folded behind her back - hands clasped just below the perfect cleft above her buttocks that rose in a long supple arc to that golden hair where Brandon buried his cry of ecstasy.

The memory coiled in Brandon like the spring of a second sharply beating heart...

"Brandon, wake up! Change of plan. I want you to go to my place in Malibu. Pick up the hotel bag."

"Nate, I gotta get to the airport!"

197

"You'll have time if you hurry. And for Chrissake, leave the company car in Malibu. Take the Jag."

"Wo! No problem there, boss."

"Got some other interesting news. You'll also be picking up Soleil."

Brandon swallowed hard on his excitement. "She's back in L.A.? Just like that?"

"Yeah," he mumbled, "looks like quite awhile. Anyways, you gotta move."

Brandon grabbed the keys to the company wreck and to the Jag and raced off to his errand. Traffic crept through Santa Monica to PCH in the last gluey heat of a yellow L.A. sunset, but Brandon was flying. Stuck at a light, he looked out past the grey bunker of a lifeguard station, the fading beach and darkly silvered surf, to the burst of day's end joy that sent the clouds feathering up into the crimson twilight. The softness of that hotel pillow. Brandon had never before been anywhere classier than a Best Western. Taking buses to Sunset Boulevard to meet her in that silly artsy yuppie hotel. Then that stolen luxury in Soleil's room, honey-porous and slithery with sweat, tasted in a stroking of moist lips, damp throat, the flush of warmth at the navel. Her pale green eyes oscillated between tease and trance as knowing muscles flexed up to him and sheathed him so close, peeled him down to a stalk of incandescent longing until the fluid burst from his hips and raced to his brain. The delicious current relinquished them only to snare them again and again before the daylight seeped through the curtain and found them loose and drunk on the warm scent beneath the hotel bedspread.

Brandon's car seemed to float past hills that swooped down to the crashing surf, on a ribbon of highway whose hold on the land was so tenuous that every year it cracked or sagged beneath rivers of mud. He gunned the car up Trancas Canyon Road, past the green bluffs overgrown with bougainvillea and wild white ginger kindled by the sunset, until he reached Wesserman's hillside bungalow. As he sprinted inside his glance briefly skittered across the last track of dusk embracing the windows, the faint violet luminescence on the glass table and the white rug in the step-down living room. There he spotted Wesserman's big leather bag, draped over the couch like a glossy seal pelt. He grabbed it and flopped it over his shoulder and all the bottles and vials spilled out.

Brandon gaped at the carpet. Christ, that had to be an ounce of coke, he knew what a bottle of roofies looked like, some X maybe, and what about the other pills, in plain bottles - and him in his Pearl Jam T-shirt and torn jeans driving the Jag!

But the thought of Soleil whisked away his fear. He tossed the leather satchel into the back seat and jumped into the Jag, inhaling the upholstery scent and running his finger over the walnut panels. Mellow indicator bells rang and dashboard lights flickered busily as he started up the engine, and when its silken purr was full-throated he eased the car down the driveway.

The L.A. climate was banished by a finely-tuned a.c., and in that smoothly temperate bubble he made sure to drive with concentration, newly auto-sensitive, feeling his every nerve the difference between a Jag and an old Toyota. He checked his watch periodically - only twenty minutes to get to the airport - but mindful of the bag in the back, he eyed the speed limit signs as often as his watch. Any cop catches him driving this fucking pharmacy.....At least PCH was humming, right through to the freeway exit. Turning onto Lincoln Boulevard, he deftly bobbed and weaved through the traffic and drove with a quiet elation that lasted all the way to the airport.

Soleil waited with her luggage at the curb and Brandon, exhilarated to see her, allowed himself one moment of automotive bravado. He niftily cut the Jaguar in front of a slow-moving station wagon with a screech of tires that had Soleil jumping back from the curb. Before she could fully recover he bounded out of the car and hugged her, and he felt her promptly embrace him back, but with an unsettling retraction of her chest, so that he almost stumbled into the awkward gap between them. A brief peck on the cheek, and then her arms perched gently against his ribs before fluttering away.

"Brandon, I'd like you to meet Silvio Glaudini."

Brandon turned to face the outstretched hand of a Mafia enforcer. At least he fit the t.v. movie type, a block of lithe muscle in a dark turtleneck and a sharkskin suit. But his face was laughing, open, with the wily but easygoing grin of a shrewd rich kid. Brandon winced at his powerful handshake and, as he helped load his luggage into the car, he immediately felt like a servant.

199

Soleil then introduced him to Inga, a dewy, leggy blonde friend of hers. Brandon glanced at Inga and then at Wesserman's bag, which Soleil was tucking down under the back seat. He sized up the contours of the party. And as he watched Silvio's hand cup the small of Soleil's back, he knew he wasn't invited.

On the drive back to Wesserman's office he kept calm and polite as he answered Silvio's questions about the "Nightwinders" shoot, asked mainly to evoke images of Soleil as a vampiress. Otherwise there was no way Brandon could jump into the conversation, which was conducted in French, liquid incomprehensible vowels with a nasal sting that ricocheted between bouts of laughter and an occasional salacious giggle from Soleil that pierced his sinking gut. Inga teased Soleil and Silvio, whose words melted into breathy whispers. Brandon's hand floated with the wheel, necessary adjuncts of another's car, the rest of him settling into ghostly misery. He glimpsed Inga in the rearview mirror, his nastiest thoughts oozing to the surface as he wondered if the pills were a fix or an ambush, but he kept silent.

None of this was his concern. He was once again empty and cast out into the night.

Wesserman stood outside the door of his office. Brandon hung back as Wesserman hugged everyone all around. Then, a little shamefaced, he came up to Brandon. "Jeez, kid, tough day for you, I know. You had to be the cleanup guy, the chauffeur – hey, we'll get back on our feet again…" He read Brandon's misery and fell silent, then reached into his pocket. "You deserve a bonus – well, let's call it a prepayment bonus." Brandon felt paper slide into his hand, a crisply folded twenty-dollar bill.

Wesserman then spun from Brandon to Silvio and Soleil, his arms thrown wide to embrace both of them and draw them closer together. A way of protecting your assets.

It might have been okay, had Brandon's mind not in one despairing moment rejected everything he'd seen and heard. A shutter clicking and advancing the film to a clean frame. Silvio and Wesserman drew apart, and Brandon bounded up to Soleil and squeezed her around the waist. Her hips glided free. She turned to him with a curious but tired smile, as elusive as the half-purple tinge on the clouds in the twilight behind him.

"So you want to get together after the dinner?"

"I think it will be late, Brandon."

A note of begging crept into his voice. "I haven't seen you in three months, Soleil."

A streetlight flashed on and in that sodium glow, her face had an almost metallic indifference.

"Brandon, are you going to be silly?"

"Mr. Reed, shall I repeat the question?"

This Velasquez bitch – Vel, Worcek called her – was giving him the same kind of look, dark eyes pincering him down as her endless questions nipped at his defenses.

"Sorry, what did you say?"

"Did you go directly to junior college after high school?"

"No. Not for about five months."

"And what did you do during those five months?"

Brandon checked Worcek for a signal. He no longer had any idea which one of these tiny nibbling questions could draw blood. Worcek simply nodded.

"I worked at a local movie theater. Selling the popcorn and sodas."

Ms. Velasquez then forced him to remember his first year at the junior college, the courses he took and gradually abandoned. "So you weren't seriously pursuing a full-time education?"

Worcek was all over that one. "Objection! Leading, speculative..."

"I'll rephrase. How many courses did you take in the first semester."

"Four."

"And how many in the second?"

"Two."

And that was the time he'd picked up that Barcelona book, and realized that he wouldn't need night school business courses to take up this amazing passport of photography, to move in secret through castles and jungles and leave a wake of glittering visions. *The beach...the hotel...Soleil....* But Sheila was his only shelter back then. He wanted to help her, he had to help her. A fragment of a family constantly re-tuning the strings of their survival, they made an uneasy peace over a mix of vegetarian meals, walks in the park, and familiar t.v. shows watched in silence, until it all began to work somehow, and breaking through the boredom and the turbulence came moments of genuine love.

How could he remember who split what fucking expenses? Yes of course the expenses were split, he wasn't going to leech off his own sister, even with Barcelona beating like a trapped bird in his Hollywood head. But now that was taking points off his worker's comp score. Not really in school, sharing the bills - too partial a partial dependent. The questions relentlessly marched through his life, until it seemed his memories of Sheila were being taken away from him, impounded by the damn court case. Yes, of course there were arguments, there was stress in that life, and Miz Velasquez was trying to show that had meant Sheila's stress on the job, which caused her to blow her head off, was incidental. "Your honor, I'm simply trying to illustrate that AOE-COE doesn't apply here." AOE-COE. Sounds like a little kid ragging him in the park. Whole fucking worker's comp game takes him back to when he was running around the playground with that pudgy little asshole Steve Summerall, duking it out by the sandbox. A-oh-ee, C-oh-ee, nyaah nyaah nya-nyaah nyaah. Your sister's dea-ead. She got screw-ewed. You get no-thing.

Miz Velasquez finally shut up and rested. He saw Worcek looking at him with that useless professional pity, but he remained shut off in his own silence. Maybe they could steal his claim, but no one could take that wordless anger away from him.

He looked up and nailed the Chicana bitch with a look not of hatred but pure nonchalance. He congratulated her on the job she was doing "protecting her assets", said she deserved a bonus, and when his cocked finger floated before her, his hand dropped twenty dollars on the table. Yeah, that got her, she froze up all over with the insult. Worcek, embarrassed, jumped up to pocket the twenty.

Keep the change, motherfuckers. I'm gone.

Beneath Charlie's Samsonite chair was deposited his stack of reading material: the L.A. WEEKLY, back issues of THE ECONOMIST, and TATTOO magazine, the last a gift from Ellis, who had an eye for art practiced in dark corners (some of the tattoo work was gorgeous) and who'd playfully encouraged Charlie to use some of his new spare time to dabble in self-mutilation. But Charlie ignored these diversions as he munched on some "natural" snack food from the vending machine and looked around him at the packed waiting room of the Santa Monica Workers' Compensation Appeals Board.

How many times had he breezed through here in his lawyer's mufti, shunting all the applicants off into his mental blind spot as he focussed on the business at hand? They'd always looked like such losers – funny how they now looked like people who drove buses, managed offices, ran hospital wards.

The metal rim of the chair back grated against his tailbone, bunching up the khaki denim shorts and the butterfly-patterned silk shirt that Dana had joked made him look like a Malaysian tourist. On his feet was a pair of open-toed sandals. The important thing in the waiting room was air circulation.

Behind Charlie a massive old blue-collar worker with ponderous muscles hollowed out from illness sat and listened to his lawyer run down his prospects. Neither the big, knobbly hands nor the body moved, but the head rotated, tortoise-slow, to listen. Finally he seemed to set his calm aside like a weight he'd been carrying and wheezed "But what about the rash on my arms? That's not industrial?"

"Right now it doesn't go to the issue. Think permanent disability for the lungs. That's what I can get for you. That's not bad, huh? Get a lump sum payment to catch some sun in the rose garden? Here are the papers...Now you haven't worked since that downtown job?"

"Yeah, can't do the heavy stuff no more. And when I tried working security nights I came down with pneumonia, that's when I learned about the asbestosis."

The conversation slid below the babble of the room. The poor guy, Charlie knew, had stuck himself with a lowballer. The clowns who advertised on daytime t.v. with home movies of their clients cavorting on yachts, and then trooped down to the hearing rooms to bargain away lung cancer cases for peanuts.

Maybe, he thought, he should break into Worcek's conference. Cut right through the niceties. Let them all see one of their own dressed so down, shove his reality in Bert Silver's face and make him deal with it. But Charlie knew that that would only trip Worcek up, when he wanted desperately for her to succeed and bring his nightmarish dead time to an end. And besides, he blanched inwardly at the thought of seeing them all, because, despite everything, despite all the crap they'd put him through, he still felt he had done something wrong, had failed to shoulder the burden he'd accepted when he told Shackleton he could forge ahead and get past the shooting. As he looked around the room again, he realized that he probably shared that shame with every worker seated beside him, and every poor soul he'd ever faced down in a hearing room.

Behind him Charlie heard the attorney brightly suggest "Twenty-five thousand? Never hurts to ask." "How about forty thousand? I can't work again, ever, forty thousand ain't much."

Charlie had had enough. He wheeled around in his chair and eyeballed the laborer. "Listen. Your asbestosis is rated under LC4662 as a total non-apportionable 100% disability. Even with adjustments for age and occupation you could conceivably get $224 a month for the rest of your life! Plus you may be entitled to lifetime future medical, not to mention possible vocational rehab, and he's telling you to settle for $25,000 less his fifteen percent? Why don't you fire this slug and get yourself a real attorney?"

Before the other lawyer could stammer out a reply, Worcek barreled through the door, her aggressive stride nicked by high heels so that she cantered across the room like a worried horse. "That one'll give you some bang for your buck." Charlie exclaimed, just before Worcek beckoned him outside the waiting room. He grabbed his books, left the newspaper for the next claimant, and followed her into a rude blast of daylight.

"That ended quickly, Liz."

"Wasn't much to talk about." Worcek had worked herself up to a keen pitch of outrage. "Charlie, NONE of the doctors you saw at Hobart-Riis filed an initial med-legal report."

"You're kidding."

"Nope. No physician's first report, even from your shrink. Neither from before your awareness you were injured or since then. In their view, this was never a worker's comp claim, and this whole case is just post-termination vindictiveness on your part. The joke is that meanwhile they're claiming you're not p. & s.'d, you've still got the psych injury, the tinnitus, the whiplash, so we can't file our declaration of readiness. So of course, that's Judge Gabel's decision. Wait until you're p. & s.'d, then go to trial."

"Where's my temporary total disability payment if I'm not p. & s.'d?"

"Exactly. Your injuries are bullshit, but they still keep you from getting a hearing on whether your injuries are bullshit." She leaned against the wall, her energies briefly spent by the catch-22 machine in which she spent every day.

"Liz? Don't get gloomy and cynical on me. I hired a tank full of positive energy. Save me some of that piss and vinegar you've got left over from Brandon Reed."

"That one's going sour fast. Vel butchered the kid in her depo. Your narrow defense, thank you very much. I can't put him through this bullshit anymore. They pay him a grand to go away I'll suggest he take it and write the whole thing off." She flushed with renewed anger. "I gotta tell you, Charlie, I basically called Bert Silver a lying sack of shit, in a more ladylike fashion - well, marginally more ladylike - and, of course, that's what he said about you. Liz, he asks, didn't you very skillfully reveal Charlie's basic mendacity in your deposition? Cute as a sewer rat, that guy. But I'm sure you know that when this case gets to trial that's what's going to come out in your psychiatrist's testimony."

Charlie had expected that from Westphal but it was still infuriating, a coldly mechanical professional betrayal.

"That's what we're up against. Charlie Solomon is a liar by temperament and by profession, he got his treatment, he said he was okay, now he's trying to milk the system. You know how it is these days, Charlie. All a case has to be to be fucked up is a little complicated."

"I'm the liar? I'm the one playing games? I'm saying I'm injured, and they're saying I'm not injured but my injuries have to be signed off on before I can argue I'm injured! How do they have the nerve to argue junk like that?"

Worcek's voice sank to a rueful murmur. " You tell me, Charlie. You're the defense lawyer."

Calvin Toth's bearish frame had lost its ruggedness to backaches and muscle melt, and the gut that sat beneath his old knit sweater robbed his stride of its fluency, but in Calvin's fingers, as he swiftly rolled a joint for the guests, was the deftness and grace of youth. Marty Ammonds exclaimed with delight that Calvin must have been the class connection, while his wife Cassie brayed that she liked a man who could roll his own. Charlie knew there was nothing like the ritual appearance of pot at his mother's parties to bring back low sparks of forgotten sexuality and irreverence among her guests, or at least the catch phrases that triggered them.

"Nice spleef. Anyone watching for the fuzz?"

"Hey. We're safe. I've got gallstones."

Charlie looked into the kitchen where his mother was bent over arranging a few more sesame crackers around her mound of salmon-and-creamcheese pate. Gravity was turning her into a solid little earthen vase of a woman, a container of warmth and comfort that all those around her could borrow. Charlie glanced at Calvin, who was filching a great deal of his mother's comfort these days. As he watched him, with his usual bemused smirk, give one last transverse lick to the joint, he let pass a silent hope that, for his mother's sake, he was wrong about the cynical old bastard.

The tip of the jay reached its slow, clotted ignition, the roasted wood smoke and incense aroma pervaded the room, and his mother's friends passed it around, each taking a fat sucking hit. Charlie politely waved the joint off, along with the whole hokey pseudo-communal ritual. Camaraderie through shared smoke and saliva was something he'd never appreciated. He escaped to the kitchen and offered to help his mother, but as usual she urged him to relax and let her take care of everything. "The bruscetta - I just sprinkle the chopped tomato. The chicken's in the oven, what's there for you to do? Take the plate in and go have a good time."

By the time Charlie brought in the wheel of pate, the good time had sunk to its usual level of dissing everyone and everything in Los Angeles except the cozy circle present and accounted for who still happened to live there. Their eyes wheeled towards Charlie, lapping him up, his sharpness, his (relative) youth, and, this month, his ordeal. Just one more aspect of the perfidy of the city. The way Calvin's eyes were devouring him Charlie could tell he would be feeding several Toth bon mots.

"How's your case faring, Chazz?" Calvin's raised eyebrows barely nicked his perpetual bored disdain.

"Oh, I'm sure all of you know how lawsuits are. Slow and go - and pretty boring."

Ernie Harnick, a stern but charitable English professor who dressed like the carpenter he was in his spare time, shook his head dolefully. "You're really in the belly of the beast, aren't you?"

"Yes, and the beast has a strong stomach. You really have to be very indigestible to pass through. I ought to know. I fought for the beast once."

Charlie figured reminding Calvin that he was once on the other side might chill Calvin out and throw him off his favorite game, sympathizing with someone else's troubles through a polemic against his own personal demons. It didn't work. "You know," Calvin intoned, "it doesn't really matter. Worker's comp, HMO's, it's all one big set-up for the rationing of medical care when we all get hopelessly old. That's what it's all about, really. Beryl, when you and I get to that point, out on the ice floe for us."

Beryl, sitting down on the couch and laying down the salmon pate, shook her head. "Too cold," she muttered, with majestic common sense. "Besides, you know, I can never understand it. People killing themselves by walking out into the sea or onto ice – no really, it makes for good drama, but if I did it, halfway onto the ice floe I'd think, 'Gee, there's still some marzipan in the fridge', and that would be it."

Charlie grinned and laid a hand on her mother's shoulder. It seemed to spark a twinge of some kind of jealousy in Calvin, and he refused to let go of the conversation. "But Charlie, don't you think, this - this problem is absolutely the worst here in Los Angeles? This whole worker's comp and Health Murdering Organization mess?"

Calvin's voice was rising to that arch, inebriated bellow Charlie had grown to detest, and so he reached for another antidote to Calvin's biliousness: a little affirmation of hope. "Look, as far as my own case goes, this could be behind me in another three months, once the - you'll excuse the expression - dick-waving is over with, and we settle out with a schedule of payments."

207

Cass, the audacity of her high in full bloom, tried to bend it towards something like concern. "But Christ, Charlie, another three months. Don't you have a fairly pricey lifestyle to support?"

The room fell silent for a moment. Beryl squeezed Charlie's hand, and their exchange of glances gave her permission to speak for him. "Charlie's relinquishing his condo soon."

The group appropriately commiserated, and Charlie assured them that his voluntary surrender of property was a civilized process, not unlike a player folding his hand. "Although they do take away a couple of gold stars when you forfeit. It'll be tougher to get the next one."

"Well," Calvin replied, leaning back regally into his crooked forearms, "at least you've got a father in real estate. I'm sure he'll hook you up with some 'steal' or other." Cass reached over to pat Charlie's knee with the tips of her fingers and assured him they'd all been there. The talk now swirled through their various reversals, when Marty's land deal went bust, when Ernie was denied tenure at Harvard due to the machinations of some "deconstructivist bitch," and of course there was Calvin's triple whammy, the failed condo partnership auction, back taxes, and an abortive stab at writing features ("At least the selling out in t.v. was civilized. You could eat dinner with those guys!"). The more they tried to affirm solidarity with Charlie, the more the hilarity of the pot and the focus on their favorite bogeymen turned them self-consciously into themselves. They ceased to own up to their losses and became endlessly self-affirming losers. What would be the you-can't-win syndrome for tonight? The death of small intellectual and literary magazines? The end of public schools? Ageism in Hollywood? Every time his mother's friends got together they would get drunk or stoned and do their ghost dance for their vanished culture.

"Let's face it," Calvin exhaled with all the slowly settling weight of his adipose frame, "L.A. is fucked-out. It's a fucked-out bunch of whores being pimped to Asian investors by Anglo bagmen from the Valley."

Marty laughed hysterically, while Cassie chimed "He's on a roll!"

"Just one big whorehouse! The Jews are playing the pianos, the Hispanics are cleaning the toilets, and the blacks are mugging the johns on the way out!"

The laughter, caught somewhere between howls of appreciation and giggles of embarrassment, chorused around the table.

Charlie's ear was sirening now, and it was time for him to harmonize with it. "Actually, Calvin," Charlie muttered, "looking around the city, and you do get a chance, in my position, to do some looking around - the Koreans and Hispanics, for example, they don't look very fucked out to me, they look like they're fucking with great pleasure - so I think maybe it's just our little racial corner of the town that's tired, and I think, Calvin, bear with me, that it's so tired because of the dead weight of all you aging Boomers we have to drag around. We have to work to keep you in health clubs, and Viagra, and of course rehab, and then pay taxes for the Social Security system you're going to drag to the grave with you - and we have to do all this, Calvin, without any residuals from 'Here Comes Ratner!' Not that you haven't suffered, I know, but some of my friends would love the chance to tank on a Brentwood-adjacent condo deal, or trade a six-figure t.v. career for a shot at movies. Christ, Jack may never stop bartending, Ellis may never make partner, as for me - well, all bets are off, aren't they?"

He finally stopped when he felt the weight of the guests' chagrin and saw their smiles fight to retain their last bit of stoned goodwill. Christ, he was getting to be an expert at killing a room. He quickly shrugged off his tirade and darted off for a gin and tonic, taking a bottle from his mother's old wood-paneled liquor cabinet into the kitchen. Soon Beryl, on the pretense of checking the oven, was at his side.

Charlie crushed the wedge of lime over his gin and tonic and drank down half of it, the ice on his lips quickening the taste. That cool dry kick traveled through him, and as it did, he listened to the music from the stereo permeating the kitchen, the breathy sigh of the trumpet, like a rose with a faint soap-and-vanilla scent, washing over the brushed cymbals and the tiptoe of the bass.

"Chet Baker."

"Oh yes." His mother listened intently to the music. "The funniest thing. When we got here, and I was so homesick for New York, I found this thirty-year-old 'Pacific Jazz' record from back when Chet Baker was starting out, and I bought it, and I fell in love with it. I was kind of hoping L.A. would turn out to be like his music." His mother paused as the trumpet serenaded the kitchen. "Listen to him. He never pushes a note. He's so graceful, so utterly at ease with himself, really knowing who he is. That's genuine cool."

"It's music, Mom. Chet Baker wound up a junkie. Fell out a window."

"Please, don't go into that." Her mouth curled down and Charlie knew that he'd debunked a cherished myth cruelly. "The main thing is the music, Charlie. That's where he found peace."

Charlie stared out the window, where the ficus that overspread the pane of glass caught and muted the alley's motion-sensor light in its dark, shaggy foliage. "Good for Chet. I could use some peace now, Mom. This is all getting to me pretty bad. I can't find work in my field - I made a few inquiries, but even though all us worker's comp lawyers are a merry band of brothers and sisters and all that, no one's going to stick their own neck out for a potential employee who's damaged goods. And I really am injured, Mom. I really am fucked up, and I really can't get any more relief than the next guy. The truth is - they could grind me down to a welfare case."

"That won't happen, Charlie."

His mother's unshakable resolve, and a firm little squeeze of her hand, so unlike the usual clinging of her embrace, heartened him. As she stood quietly by the refrigerator respecting his anger and his dread, for a moment they were effortlessly united.

The crunch of chomped breadsticks shot through the kitchen. "Sorry, didn't mean to intrude." They both stepped back from the fridge as Calvin lumbered over to open the door, mused on the choice of brews, and groused about the absence of his favorite malt liquor. Beryl reminded him of his diet, and, as the mood eased, Charlie tried to make an apology for his rudeness, unable to avoid the man's bulky, offended presence any longer. "You know, Calvin, I never told you, but I liked that show of yours."

"'Ratner'? Well thanks, Charlie." He reflexively went into his apologia for his work. "Your basic it's-hard-to-be-a-schlep-in-the-city show, but we got some good haimish black humor into it."

"Didn't it get three seasons?"

"Yeah, we allowed ourselves to hope for syndication. At least it did well enough so I could take off for awhile when I needed it."

"Hey, you quit the game while you were ahead, and tried movies. Good job. Really."

Calvin leaned back and pondered Charlie's remark for what seemed an unusually long time, and then Charlie saw his mother wince in anticipation as Calvin angled his head towards Charlie, and pulled back a fold of skin from just below his ear. "Actually, I had a bit of a long hiatus." He pointed to thin purple lines that encircled his entire face.

Beryl looked glumly down at the floor, and then at Charlie. "After the show ended, Calvin -"

"Now Bitsy, I'm perfectly capable of relating my own tsouris. Always wants to be the little intercessor, your mom. See, Charlie, I had a plan for movies, but then I took a header through my car windshield." Charlie was dumbfounded, and Calvin, wanting to shock but not force a reply, accepted his silence and continued. "There was this young homeless woman who used to literally stagger through my neighborhood. Just a girl really. One night, coming back from a party, I didn't see her in time. The oddest thing - to have someone that close in your headlights where they've never been before. Such a - a violation somehow."

"You ran her over?"

"Almost. I swerved enough just to graze her, humped the curb and hit a telephone pole. Managed to get my arms in front of my face. I was very lucky. Totaled the old MG, but I could've lost an eye. And it's remarkable what they can do with grafts now. They grab skin off you from wherever they need it, they make skin. My arms look a little like a quilt, but on my chin they outdid themselves. Of course, I've been a little moon-faced ever since."

"Calvin's jaw was all wired, he had his nose reset -"

"Well it goes without saying it sucked, Bitsy."

"At least your doctors gave it their all. Calvin got the best of care, Charlie." Calvin was right, Charlie thought, his mother was irresistibly driven, with her girlish kindness, to arbitrate everything, to find the best even in the sheer viciousness of fate. "And Calvin made sure that that girl wasn't forgotten either."

"What happened to her?"

"She had a broken hip, but she recovered. I had my doctor pull her out of County. I heard someone finally flew in from Birmingham or wherever and paid some attention to her." Calvin took a deep pull off his beer. "I keep remembering that image of her in the headlights, like she'd just erupted out of the shadows. There was my usual street, and then there was this sad little girl bright as a torch, and then everything changed."

Charlie gazed with new respect at Calvin. Suddenly, with both of them unguarded as they contemplated the worst of their mishaps, he felt he could express something almost childish that had weighed on him for months. "And then after everything changes, it's hard to tell if anything makes any sense anymore. How do you know if it's ever going to make sense again?"

"Oh fuck that, Charlie!" Calvin roared. "I have no idea about questions like that!" He poured himself some white wine. "I went through a phase like you're going through now – angry at other people's high-class problems, trying to peer into the darkness a bit. But the only thing I'm really sure of about that accident is that it ended my career." He drank down his glass. "Glad you thought 'Ratner' was funny, Charlie."

Driving home that night, Charlie watched the path of his highbeams closely. That was one function a story like Calvin's performed: sharpening your driving skills.

He thought about Calvin, and about that zone where the girl Calvin had seen as a blot on the landscape suddenly got too close and bright to ever avoid again. And then he thought of that little half-smile Sheila had given him just before he'd shut his eyes and screamed but couldn't stop anything. The memory was clear now, clear as the white lines streaking down the corridor of light before him. A suicide's smile. A cold smile, but not vicious, almost forgiving. Where did it come from? Was it some kind of bliss she knew in consciously, willfully shedding her life - and at the same time one last taunt aimed at him, a little tug to let Charlie know he himself would soon fall into that net cast by the people in the road, the apparitions in the headlights?

For the past four months, whenever he'd thought about Sheila Reed, he'd banished it from his mind, the same way he'd shut the damn Dr. Casey notes away in a drawer. He'd forcibly shunted his thoughts back to the issue of his own case and compensation. But how in the world could he ever be truly compensated? He didn't have to have his face reconstructed, thank God, but his life was in shards and fragments, and where and in what form would come the will to put it back together?

And when he thought about that, he knew he could never erase his link with Sheila Reed, any more than Calvin could take back that night in the car.

He went to his computer and, for the first time since he'd met Dana, logged on to a chat group. After the blank monitor ornamented itself with the usual introductions, Charlie plunged in first, under his web pseudonym, Slice, and to the wraiths at the other end of cyberspace he typed it all out. When he finished his story the skittering responses across his monitor had pauses that couldn't be ascribed to the usual jam-ups. The toneless voices could not find the words. "I'll pray for you." "You need to just get work, any work." And one curious remark, "This worker's comp thing's getting like AIDS. It seems that everyone I know knows someone who's going through it."

Then the inevitable happened. "Bandit" went on a rant. Letting those fingers fly in the comfortable isolation of (as he put it) "my little Hollywood hovel," he flamed on and on about the growing underclass, the deterioration of the country into "a bunch of cozy mafias and legions of parasites", welcoming Charlie to the gulf, the pits. "Whatsamatta, can't find a yob?" Christ, what did he expect, seeking consolation and guidance on the Web? Going online these days was like trawling for junk mail. Charlie signed off in disgust.

Now with the screen dark and his fingers idle, in the air that seemed desiccated with loneliness, he really felt it, a volcanic burst of despair. An invisible C-clamp screwed tight around his rib cage, an ambush of raw terror. Once a law professor of his had looked over the class for what seemed like a full minute and said with startling passion "It was never truer than it is now. There are no second acts in American lives. You're about to select your particular path in the legal profession. Choose wisely. Build carefully. Because as surely as you can succeed, you can fail." Charlie had failed. Unchosen. Unbuilt. Fuck yeah, Calvin, I'm getting a glimpse of the darkness. All there was now was darkness, and fetid sweat and a future he didn't even want to imagine.

Trying to sleep was ludicrous. He tried taking a walk around the block to outrace his panic, find some calming silence, but he was chased by the oafish laughter of a loud party, the roar of the wind blowing clouds across a moon-lashed sky. He ran back to his bathroom to quench the long scrape of dryness in his throat. As he passed the answering machine, he saw someone had left a message and flicked it on.

"This is for Charlie Solomon. It's Theresa Calder. Please give me a call at work tomorrow. The Bernard-Duvall Group. I think you know the number."

He called her at the clinic the next morning, and she curtly gave him the name of a Mexican restaurant in the Santa Monica Mall where she wanted to meet him after work. Charlie underestimated the traffic and arrived fifteen minutes late. As he made his way through the happy hour crowd, past the metal trays of enchiladas and chile rellenos steaming under the orange heat lamps, he cursed himself for his tardiness. He was tempted to turn off the portable tape recorder whirring away concealed in his jacket pocket. She was probably gone. Drawing a few curious stares, he peered through the wrought iron gate and hanging asparagus ferns that surrounded the restaurant's stone fountain - and at last made out Theresa waving discreetly to him from the farthest corner of the room.

She shook his hand briskly as he joined her at her booth. The ruby glow of the glass-bulbed candle and its updraft of shadows brought into sharp relief her long, slim nose, the swooping planes of her face, and her lanceolate, almost Indian dark eyes. As she stirred her drink idly with her straw, the burgundy knit blouse she wore seemed to dissolve into the shadowy decor, and she became nothing but that glowing face and those eyes watching him with an ironical intensity and a hawklike alertness.

A waitress soon appeared and Theresa sharply told him "You should order the strawberry margarita. They're good here, not too sweet." Charlie thanked her for her suggestion and ordered the drink. As the waitress left, Theresa apologized for rushing him. "I'm sorry, it's just her hovering." Charlie thought this was an odd remark about normal waitress behavior, but said nothing. He knew that this was an encounter to be handled very gently.

"So this is a favorite restaurant of yours?"

214

"I suppose. Not bad for a spot in a mall."

"You like a drink after work?"

"I need a drink after work."

He asked her if there'd been any more hurling of objects at the clinic walls. She told him that with the last income and expense statement they'd become a little more respectful of the breakables, although more inclined to ranting and slamming their fists. Dr. Bernard, formerly the most civilized of the bunch, had gotten into the act, calling his Latina receptionist a pig and sending her straight out the door.

"How are they treating you?"

"Let's say I try not to get overdrawn at the scream bank. And I make my little alliances whenever I can." She laughed suddenly, a tinny, strident laugh, like a flashbulb going off at the wrong moment. Her darkly sardonic gaze lingered on him, then subsided and returned with a flash of contrition. "That moment in the street - that was really obnoxious of me. I owe you an apology."

"Theresa, I understand. When I spoke to you, I was practically deranged."

"So what? That didn't give me the right to bite your head off." Her hand made an involuntary move to shift the candle from her face. "Please forgive me."

"That was quite a door slam."

"Oh God!" Theresa threw back her head and laughed. She was still chuckling when the waitress brought Charlie's drink, but once the waitress stayed a beat too long, she looked away and waved her off.

"Hover, hover...Anyway, I felt pretty crappy after that, and then I found out you were fired."

Charlie was instantly alarmed. "How did you - did you call my office?"

"Relax, Charlie. The minute I heard 'He no longer works -,' I hung up. They never heard my name."

Charlie leaned forward and felt the little Sony tilt against his jacket pocket. "So what did you want to talk to me about, Theresa?"

Her grin turned vaguely malicious. "As in cut to the chase. Well, I'm about to be deposed by a Ms. Elizabeth Worcek, Esquire. The lawyer for Sheila's brother, right? Well, let's just say I wasn't crazy about my first

215

deposition and I don't want to repeat the experience." Her body stiffened, calling on further resolve in the face of deep revulsion. "And it won't help Ms. Worcek any, given the coaching factor." Charlie didn't even have to ask her what she meant. "I told that creep Sandoval last time I wasn't going to raise my hand in the air and then spout bullshit. But then - well, let's say my testimony was not as bad as they had feared."

"And not as truthful as you'd hoped?"

She turned away. "Deposing me will do her no good. That's that. And I figured – you could tell her for me."

Charlie felt his heartbeat against his tape recorder. "Theresa, Sheila went on and on about missing files. What do you know about that?"

She wilted back further against her banquette. "I figured you'd want a little quid pro quo. But honestly, I have no idea. There were a hell of a lot of them, though. During the remodel a whole shelf's worth just vanished."

"How do you know, Theresa?"

"Because I'd taken a big chunk of the past year's medical records and set them aside very carefully in another cabinet. Only Sandoval and I knew where they were, so when they went missing -"

She let him complete the thought, and his mind went far beyond it, pyramiding speculation upon conjecture in a dizzy combination of his old legal acumen and his new paranoia. This wasn't just losing – or hiding – a trickle of files here and there. This was a major disappearance of vital office records. Why go to that kind of trouble to drive one office manager from her position?

His mother's words came back. *"And to do it right with you there. Like it was meant for you somehow. Like she was trying to tell you something."*

"I should've known they'd all blame me for the missing files. *They'll have to blame somebody.*"

Theresa read his incipient exhilaration. "I couldn't reveal this in a deposition, Charlie. Not if I wanted a job the next morning. Understand that this is the only way you and this Ms. Worcek are getting this information."

He felt like thanking her profusely, but a professional reflex intervened. He bore down on his line of questions. "Do you know where all those files are now?"

216

"Not a clue." She took a long pull of her Margarita, and Charlie cornered her with his gaze, almost leery of his own boldness.

"And that's it, then? You have no idea why they deep-sixed the files."

Disdain shivered through her like a wave of vertigo from the drink. "Bastard and his stupid games. Sandoval thought he was so discreet and clever, but one time I'm just walking down the hall, and the door to his office was half open, like he forgot to close it, and he's forcing poor Sheila against the wall."

"He was making her have sex with him in the office?"

"No, not exactly, Charlie, for Chrissake, but he was doing that idiot macho thing, you know, kind of leaning full-body towards you when you're in a corner. Some Latin guys love that shit, it's like, 'I'm a force of nature and you better accept me.'"

"You said nothing?"

Her stare hardened. "I decided it was Sheila's problem and, thank God, not mine."

"And those vanished files - it was decided that was also Sheila's problem?"

"Oh yes. Sandoval insisted on it."

The hapless waitress picked that moment to step behind Theresa and ask if everything was okay and if they were ready for an appetizer. Theresa inhaled with a hiss and her whole body trembled. Charlie got the waitress' attention and ordered a plate of nachos.

"You read my mind," she muttered.

"About the nachos or the hovering?"

"Both." She looked him over with a weary tranquility. "You must be very attentive to your clients."

"I had only one client, Hobart-Riis."

"Really? You know, had I met you another way, I wouldn't've figured you for an insurance lawyer. You're a little more simpatico than that."

For a brief but vivid moment he resented her grudging compliment. "Getting fired opens you up a bit," he snapped.

Theresa backed off and eyed him with a glimmer of compassion, then glanced up at the waitress as she promptly ferried them their nachos. "Una mas vez on the rocks," she said, tapping the Margarita, "and one for my amigo here."

Charlie declined the second drink. "Theresa, I hope you don't have to drive home."

"No, I take the shuttle to Main Street and walk."

"You live in Venice." Charlie relaxed a little - something about Theresa finally made some sense.

"Yeah," she shrugged, " 'La Vie Boheme', that's me."

"Is it safe to walk back home there?"

"Far as I'm concerned, the real jungle is where I work." Charlie watched as she plucked out a chip, dunked it in guacamole and salsa, and dexterously munched it without spilling a drop. "It's amazing. When I first went to work at Bernard-Duvall, I thought, this is good, a highly-respected medical office, I mean, I was actually thinking of redirecting my career efforts to the health care field, as it were - and within a week, I see doctors throwing shitfits at nurses, ducking out on appointments to get to the track - they think it's their plantation and they treat the female workers like - I mean, I had to cool one of them out a month ago when visions of sugarplums danced in his head, and it's no damn fun, none at all. You feel really exposed and alone. But that passes, and you get used to it again, the whole rhythm, the office politics, the smarmy flattery, all the bullshit that wraps around you every day while you're just trying to do your job, and then one day you realize that part of that trivial nastiness has really crossed the line, and gone very badly wrong. Like the cockroaches in your kitchen turning to cobras." She daintily wiped her lips with her napkin. "So how'd you get fired anyway?"

"The last straw was when I talked to you."

"How would they know that?" Now it was her turn to be paranoid. "Oh Christ, Charlie! They saw you talking to me before -"

"They saw you slam the door in my face. You're Employee of the Month."

That logic piqued her ironical little smile again, but the residue of outrage seeped out of her. He glanced away from the accusation that lingered on her face to her fingers, which instantly sought motion, twirling her margarita straw. She finally asked him if he'd tried to find work, and Charlie

218

felt once again the chagrin that any memory of his former life brought. He had to explain that his own profession was a lost cause at this point, and a mid-career switch looked even more dismal. "I mean, I hadn't realized that every lousy administrative assistant position has its own computer literacy requirements. And even if I was willing to tackle that, I suppose," he admitted, "everything I've gone through has damaged me more than I thought."

"Of course," Theresa muttered sympathetically, "the trauma alone."

Charlie drank down the margarita; the tangy flavors were gone, and all he tasted was the alcohol. "But maybe it should've. Maybe it should've damaged me. I mean – at my deposition, Theresa – I couldn't even say she killed herself. I knew it, but…and then I get the evidence I told you about. She was totally suicidal, Theresa. That experience destroyed her."

"Yep," Theresa whispered, stirring her drink.

"And then – I come up with exactly the new wrinkle Hobart-Riis needs to bury Brandon Reed's case. My little parting gift on the way out to the street. I showed them how to destroy him with the letter of the law. The law…You know, none of this should have happened according to the law. But the law - it doesn't matter anymore. It's like a car alarm that goes off in a neighborhood that hates car alarms and doesn't even care about the guy breaking into the car. The clinic, the insurance company - they all broke the law, and it doesn't mean shit."

Theresa absorbed his words with rapt intensity. Someone at last was listening to him.

"There were so many bullshit worker's comp claims when I got into it – but now the pendulum has swung the other way. I mean way the other way. Workers get harassed and tormented on the job, injured on the job, driven off the job - and then the insurance company assumes every worker is a fraud, every claim becomes a denial. I mean, deny one worker's five thousand dollar claim, what the hell's that, deny another worker's ten-thousand dollar claim, still nothing – but if you deny hundreds of thousands of workers – hey, now you're talking about real money!" He took a pull of his drink. "Or you just delay. Endless delay. Justice delayed is justice denied, Theresa, and everyone plays along. I joined the System to stop fraud. Now it's all fraud, all of it."

Theresa let the silence linger for a moment, then said gently "You've grown a shit detector Charlie; Congratulations. Now maybe," she smiled ironically, "maybe you're thinking about it too much."

"Yeah. How about that?"

"Got any hobbies?" she asked, only half-kiddingly.

He appreciated her sardonic fellowship, her chocolate-dark gaze swinging back to him. "I was teaching a volunteer tennis class, but then I got into a car accident and -"

"You're a tennis jock?" She laughed softly. "Why am I not surprised?"

"Do you play?"

"I hate tennis." She laughed again, then draped his hand with her fingers, a gentle, apologetic touch. The contact startled him, and he shunted his eyes to her wrists.

"Those are really nice bracelets."

"Well, thanks. I guess I like my baubles, bangles and beads."

She seemed to shrug off his compliment, and he prodded the conversation back to business.

"Theresa, I'm sorry to go back to this -"

"Don't be so sorry all the time," she muttered, low-voiced and mocking.

"Fine. Theresa, I'm thinking of working with Worcek on this Brandon Reed case now. It's obvious Sheila Reed was maligned at work. It's obvious that injured her. And it's also possible that she was injured because of whatever was in those files. And I think there's a way you could be deposed by Worcek that wouldn't be so damaging for you and could tell her what you-"

"Goddammit!" she shouted, "why can't you try and show a little more fucking imagination?"

"Theresa, maybe we need less imagination here and more of the truth!"

"Oh go to hell!" She slammed her hand so hard on the table that the glasses rattled and the band, with the scrape of a violin bow, missed a beat. She dropped her head into the cradle of her left hand and looked ready to slump forward. "Christ, that was definitely one drink too many."

Charlie, alarmed, told her he could drive her home, and while she tried to decline the offer, the pallor of her skin told Charlie she would ultimately accept it. He paid the check and tip with his credit card. As he got up, the waitress dropped her mask and watched Theresa lurch away with smirking contempt. Charlie heard her remark to another waiter. "He should red-tag that bitch."

The dusk cut an orange gash beneath the strings of cloud over Santa Monica Bay, and a eucalyptus trapped sparks of saffron light in its maidenhair foliage. Palm trees rocked in the offshore breeze. Couples out for a stroll on the palisades sped up their walk in the evening chill, and passed the transients lying beneath their bags and shopping carts, who were trying to get some sleep before the nocturnal anti-loitering laws were enforced. Theresa picked at her drawn mouth as she stared at them. "Poor bastards," she murmured. Out over the bay the lights of the Santa Monica Pier's roller-coaster and ferris wheel came on, sprays of neon tinsel glinting to life.

Theresa lived on one of those charming, weather-beaten "Court" streets of Venice where Charlie had once considered renting an apartment until he'd realized how easily burglars could scoot through the alleys. Redbud trees overhung ramshackle wood fences, through which entwined heavenly blue morning glories and clumps of bougainvillea and lilac. The lengthening shadows melted the houses into a jumble of shaggy foliage and decaying wood, until streetlights once again marked their boundaries.

Charlie drove his car into the alley at the back of Theresa's block and she had him pull up before a 1970's Mercedes. She leaned back and closed her eyes. "I thought I knew my limit. Christ, if I don't have a cup of coffee I'll wake up tomorrow and puke."

"Sounds like you should have that coffee."

"You're invited to join me."

Charlie was astonished, especially after her reluctance to cooperate with him. He didn't know if it was loneliness talking, or some ploy of hers he hadn't anticipated. But as he searched for a reply she was instantly raking him over the coals. "Jesus, Charlie, I made a scene in a restaurant, so now I'm trying to be polite. But if I'm once again being rude, I apologize, and -"

"No. It's all right, Theresa. Thanks."

"I'll give you my parking space - they ticket like clockwork around here."

He watched her back out her old Mercedes. As Charlie moved his car into her space, he felt the weight of the tape recorder in his jacket. He bent down furtively, turned it off and slipped it under his floor mat. When he got up he saw Theresa already parked behind another person's car. An old woman's face stuck out of the window of the old bungalow; an exchange of pleasantries ensued, Theresa promising she wouldn't be parked there long, the old woman laughing and assuring her it was no problem. As Theresa arranged his parking and he felt the lightness in his breast pocket his heartbeat quickened. Beneath the cobalt evening sky Theresa's girlishly long fall of hair was carved of pure shadow, as earthy and mysterious as her bracelets. She slammed her car door so hard it shook, and walked towards him with a rangy, confident stride. She'd regained her equilibrium. She was inviting him in because she wanted to.

The apartment was pure Southwest, dominated by wood-frame couches plumped with cushions a soft dove-gray in color and striped with hatchet-mark insignias. Indian masks adorned the walls, along with one Oriental touch, some pastel-tinted Japanese fans. A finch slept in a wicker birdcage. Otherwise the place looked stripped. Orange crates supported a small t.v., there was a rattan basket of tapes on the floor next to a boom box, and a few shelves on the wall held a small library of books in English and Spanish. Theresa read his puzzled scrutiny of the living room.

"No, I'm not another Venice crime victim. Just working out a few debt problems."

"I didn't mean to pry."

"No, Charlie, of course not. You didn't say a thing. You're very well mannered, Charlie, your mother should be proud of you."

Charlie let the sarcasm pass - he realized by now it was just her normal way of talking. He watched her as she headed into a kitchen dominated by rows of ceramic jars - family heirlooms, it seemed, from their chipped, aged texture and their homey markings of "Tea", "Coffee" and "Sugar" - all surrounding a Proteo Barista cappuccino machine, its surfaces nubbly and blackened with constant use. "Debt or no debt, I wasn't about to part with the essentials." Soon the steamed milk gurgled, and the boiling water suffused the fresh ground roast coffee beans. Charlie savored the blend of scents both familiar and enticing, and with the strain of the interview with Theresa over he felt a pleasing lassitude sweep over him.

"So who was Spanish in your family?"

"My mother's side. She was a pure morena. My dad was major league WASP. That's not unusual where I come from. New Mexico's a real grab bag. Conquistadors and Zuni and Navajo and Georgia O'Keefe."

"Why didn't you stay in New Mexico?"

"What's there to do in New Mexico? Make belts for tourists? Why'd you leave wherever you came from?"

"New York? I didn't have much choice. I was a kid."

"When did you leave?"

"Fourteen years ago."

"So you've spent your whole adult life here, I suppose - what there is of it." She handed him a cappuccino and guided him to the living room. The cappuccino was just the way he liked it, not too frothy or sweet. She acknowledged his thanks, lay back on her couch and crossed her legs, and now the blood began to flutter in Charlie's temples. The caffeine and the closeness. It had been almost a month since Dana left him, and the presence of Theresa could no longer be tempered by thoughts of how inappropriate the conflict of interest was (they were on the same side now), or the age difference (what was it, ten years, tops?) or even how forbidding her temperament had been. His eyes involuntarily darted to the supple repose of those legs, hips straight, thighs swelling like the curves of twin musical clefs on the cushions.

"Theresa?" he asked, trying to mute the catch in his voice, "what did you mean when you said I had no imagination?"

"Oh, forget it. It was nothing. Maybe it was just that you were a lawyer being legal - kind of a bore."

"I guess I fall back on old reflexes that I'm comfortable with because - it's tough, it's - I'm trying to grapple with something much darker than I've ever experienced." He felt once again the haunting immensity of the event that had annealed a dying woman's last grimace of despair on his own face. "What do you do after something like this?"

"You have to change," she murmured. A long silence fell between them as she drank her coffee and stared into the bottom of the cup. "That's where you need the imagination. And a little cohones, that's for sure."

"But I liked who I was, Theresa."

"Give him a decent burial, and move on."

She got up a little unsteadily. "Mas. I definitely need mas." Charlie drank down his cappuccino and watched her head into the kitchen. She disappeared, and he heard water being run on the crockery, the squeak of the faucet, then silence that seemed to go on forever. He followed her now to where he could see her, worried about her silence, or feeling, warily, that it had summoned him. She was standing by the sink where she'd washed one of the dishes, and had turned away towards the dark window on the alley, head inclined as if she were listening for some code in the crickets and rustling leaves. Or maybe she was just giving way to the exhaustion that had dogged her for hours. With her face and its play of acerbic and taunting moods turned away from him, he found the courage to speak his mind.

"Theresa, Sheila said to Dr. Chesley that she should've known they'd blame her for the missing files. They'll have to blame somebody. Those were her words. I think this whole incident with the missing files was more than Sandoval driving her out over office politics. Do you think it was something bigger than that, Theresa?"

"Yes," she sighed. "Yes I do."

"You did a very brave thing talking to me today. I'm not that brave, and I'm not all that imaginative. But I am fairly clever, or so I've been told. I'll figure out a way to build on this."

Her voice was grave with impending sleep and sorrow. "I hope so, Charlie. I honestly hope so."

"And if I come up with something, and if it doesn't expose you, will you help me?"

She remained obstinately turned away, but her voice exhaled towards him. "Yes."

The echoes of that word, its husky, insinuating sadness, drew him towards her. A touch he meant to be comforting found her waist. His face dropped into her forest of hair scented with cinnamon as he planted a gentle kiss on her neck. The muscles tautened beneath his lips and as her face spun he leaned back and stiffened in anticipation of the slap he knew he deserved. Instead the flag of swirling hair caressed him. Her eyes fastened onto his, measured and challenged him, while her lips brushed, tickled, probed his own. Now he froze, remembering Dana, feeling alien in his own body, and so her mouth seized his to bring him back, the lips dry petals upturning to softness, and then a wet muscle burrowing into his mouth until their teeth clicked. His jaw slid open and her tongue flitted across his and that touch flushed her face. He smelled her warm blood and the faintly acrid musk of her skin. His hands, lunging for safety, found her hips, erect and sinuous, no, if he wanted to avert this that was not the way to do it...

"Theresa, if you - if you - I mean, this is pretty sudden and - now's the time to stop- because we'll be approaching that 'no' point pretty soon, so maybe we should stop right now."

He pulled back from her. She looked up at him, heavy-lidded and sullen. "Do you want me to stop?"

"We don't even have a relationship yet," he mumbled.

"Yeah. We do. I'll sign off on it."

She smothered his lips, and with a strength that emanated from her loins pulled him towards her bedroom. Charlie caught a brief glimpse of strangely childlike artifacts: old poetry books, framings of lacy dried flowers, a Renaissance picture of a saint, tender icons so at odds with the voracious incandescence of this woman's sexuality - his eyes sought out those kindly souvenirs as he felt himself going down to the futon below them. "I have one of these," he mumbled stupidly just before she pressed against him so hard he couldn't speak. His grasp found the knit shirt that with a wriggle of her hips slid free of her belt - in an instant she pulled it over her head. There was something vulnerable about her sun-pocked torso and small breasts, but she had the broad shoulders of a swimmer, and with her waist the sweep of flushed red womanliness began. It was with his eyes on her hips that Charlie felt the kernels of joy at answered lust popping and melting all through him.

"Do you have a jacket and tie rule for this as well, Charlie?"

He laughed, hearing in his own laugh both the shakes he couldn't hide and a deep pleasure whose heartiness astonished him, and he quickly shed and threw down his clothes, not caring if they fell in a wrinkled heap, not feeling the twinge in his neck, the room blissfully silent except for their breathing and the rustle of Theresa's clothes as she twisted her long suntanned flank, thumbed her belt and peeled off her tweed skirt. She smiled at Charlie's astonishment at how good a woman so much older than him could look, how firm her legs were without stockings, down to her tapered calves and flexed feet with their dark red toenails. He briefly wondered if this was a practiced routine with her, many young guys like him gaping in shock, but the sight and scent of her as she came to him naked chased his thoughts away, the two beautiful worlds of her, her chest lean and resilient, ribs showing, like some rueful but audacious modern painting, and then, below her hips, the warm glades of a Venetian fresco.

He sank to the bed with her, and now, around her eyes, he could see her age in the heavy, shadowy flesh, but that made her even more enticing, those garnet-flecked burning eyes touched with melancholy. But expecting her embrace to be soft and pillowed, his whole body shuddered against the leg clench, the arms that grappled him onto her, the fingers that almost stabbed at his groin as they put on the condom. He felt his own strength whip through him as he struggled to enter her, and then in a flash the roof of her loins was scraping against his own raw skin. Their hips pistoned each other; she hissed and groaned and, with a grateful sigh, deliquesced all around him; a tiny adjustment of her belly and their motion was long and sleek and gravid until a burning pullulation snaked all around Charlie that drew from his guts one long filament of a scream.

They lay there beneath the rumpled sheet and when she rested her cupped hand on his chest, and he felt not so much her affection as her testing of his presence, his solidity. He too stroked her back as if to confirm that this union actually had happened. He wondered if they were supposed to sleep now, but no one bothered to turn out the light. There was too much stinging sweat and roiling doubts for sleep to be any more than an absurdity. He watched her pad to the bathroom, her buttocks rolling and flexing beneath her sleek back - when she came out, she was brushing her hair. He could hear the hiss of static electricity in the brush, and as he watched her long black tresses part with glints of iridescence and caress the azure stones on her necklace he was burning for her all over again. She slid back in next to him and as he stroked

226

her hard, smooth abdomen and yawed on top of her, this time she pushed him on his back. This time she measured out every move, let him see and know what she could do. She arched herself expertly over his chest. The texture of her kneading muscles tearing at his skin while the percolating warmth kissed him through to his blood, the hair and breasts stroking - a million tiny stitches broke inside him and released a thick, resinous flow of delicious abandon until all he could do was close his eyes into his groaning and not let go.

He felt her still pulsing on him and he raised himself on his elbows and tongued her nipples, prolonging her breaths and her shudders, anything to give back as much as he could of that pleasure. She slowly subsided, wave upon wave of her.

He lay back, barely feeling her weight on his hips, and sank into the most lush repose he'd felt in a long time, until he felt the scalding splash on his chest.

He was wide-eyed in a second and staring at her tears. As her body folded over with sobs he took her down to him. He embraced her, and just let her talk, this shrewd, angry, knowing woman who now babbled like a child about how she'd been blind, blind, had no idea how tormented her friend was. "She came to me. I told her, Christ, just start looking around, you can get another job. She wanted to stay – very loyal somehow…but she felt she couldn't stop it, all of it…she so wanted my help…" And then Theresa had had to say, under oath, that Sheila wasn't that depressed, that Sheila had felt wrong in filing for medical treatment, that it was Sheila who'd lied and who'd lost the files. Sandoval was pushing her, and Theresa had to keep her job, what else could she do? "I really was Sheila's only friend and I sent her down."

Charlie kept hugging Theresa, and felt a grief so strong it rendered him invisible, a ghost.

She asked him if he would mind going home - after all, she hadn't intended to use the parking space all night. He hugged her and stroked her hair. She finally told him "I don't know where this came from, Charlie, but I think it'll be here when you get back."

The fog off the ocean cut right through him as he rushed to the car, laying a damp chill on the lingering scent of hungry musk still on his skin. The streetlamps were halating and their dim, elusive glow was everywhere. As he warmed up the Infiniti, he looked back into the mist - there she was, a shadow rushing out in a coat to move her car. The way people trusted the tolerant vibes in this seedy, crime-ridden neighborhood had always amazed him. She could be naked underneath that coat. He watched her go to the back door of her apartment building, jealously, protectively, making sure she was safe, and also keeping some kind of contact with that hidden face, that body. She saw him and waved to him before she vanished into the shadows and her door locked tight.

The minute she was gone he remembered. When he took the tape recorder out from under the mat he saw that it had run to the end - he had captured their whole conversation in the restaurant. For a moment he considered ejecting the tape and tossing it in the garbage, but then he remembered Sheila Reed, pocketed the tape, and drove down the fog-shrouded road.

-8-

treading water

Worcek's offices were tucked away in a small brick building in the Valley hard to spot amid the tawdry bustle of restaurants, beauty shops and chain stores on the Encino stretch of Ventura Boulevard. Charlie passed it right by, and had to fight his way back through lunch hour traffic to a parking spot several blocks from the office. He hurried through the ferocious heat into an alley fringed with hardy sea lavender and impatiens and ran up an exterior metal staircase whose every tremor and clang broadcast his humiliating lateness.

When the secretary finally buzzed him in and, making his apologies, he strode into Worcek's office, he instantly felt Brandon Reed's outrage. Worcek had probably prepared Brandon conscientiously, and explained how Charlie would be coming in not with some con-job of a settlement offer, but a genuine offer of help. But Charlie's late arrival had goosed the kid's suspicions - now Brandon had that cornered look, sparks about to fly, and Charlie would have to do a real tap dance to win him over.

"How are you doing, Brandon?"

"I don't have anything to say to you," he murmured.

"All right, then. I'm here to apologize, to admit some mistakes, and to-"

" Enough of that crap! All you got to do is take back what you said! That it wasn't a suicide! You want to help, like Liz says? That's what you do."

"Brandon," Worcek interrupted, "for all sorts of reasons, that's not feasible at this point. And you have to understand – Charlie and I both saw…that moment. And believe me, it was so frightening that neither of our impressions are to be trusted."

229

Those words seemed to calm Brandon down, and Charlie appreciated the charitableness behind them.

"Just listen to him, Brandon."

Charlie decided he wouldn't bring the kid up slowly, but really drive the case home. "The first thing I need to tell you, Brandon, has to do with what happened in the courtroom that day. We have a doctor's handwritten notes. I subpoenaed them, because I thought it would help our case against Sheila – well, actually, it was because I needed a delay..." Charlie realized he was losing control of the moment, and Brandon's eyes were blazing again, but he persisted. "Brandon, what these notes are about - Sheila spoke to the primary care gatekeeper at the clinic, and gave a complete description of the stress and harassment she was suffering on the job. We can use those notes in your case. They show the agony Sheila was in. She – she was clearly suicidal, Brandon. And they ignored their responsibility to her."

Brandon leaped towards Charlie, driving him into a corner of the couch.

"Then you did lie about her! You miserable piece of shit!"

"Brandon, sit down!" Worcek shouted. He stopped, befuddled, in the rebound of his fury, but then he snared Charlie's gaze with a flash of anguish Charlie couldn't look away from. "How can you be that cold? Lying about my sister's last moments..." His voice choked up. "Man, that must be a fucking talent."

Charlie could finally no longer hold it back. "I tell you what's a talent, Brandon! Your capacity for ignorance! Don't you see me here trying to talk to you, trying to work things out? What do you know about me? What the hell do you know about anything, junior college boy?" He scrambled up and stood toe-to-toe with Brandon. "You think I'm the enemy? The clinic, the insurance companies - they're just window-dressing, huh? Let's all fuck the lawyer up the ass! Gangbang the middleman!" Brandon took a step closer. He felt the kid's expectant breath, saw his eyes burning. "Like I'm the one who harassed Sheila at work? Refused her medical treatment? Put her through five years of shit? Like I'm the one who persuaded your sister she could fuck her way into saving her job?"

Charlie instantly knew he'd screwed up and wasn't surprised when Brandon went for him. But he didn't run, just tried to crouch down and raise his arm to intercept the blow from Brandon's fist, which still rammed into his mouth hard enough to make the lights spiderweb around him. He fell against the bookshelf and law books crashed at his feet. "You shut up about her or I'll kill you, you fuck!" Everything hung in one terrible moment that bled into the past, the gun smacking down on him, not icy metal now but knucklebone and nail, making him feel his flesh, not tearing him from it...

Worcek was shouting at Brandon, her partner Nadjari rushed in from adjoining office, and at last Brandon stopped, exhausted more by his own emotions than the effort of hitting Charlie. Charlie's vision swam, and he slumped down in the corner, dimly aware through the throb of his tinnitus of Worcek calling for First Aid. The brackish taste of his bleeding lip nauseated him, but he fought the sickness to a draw and stared at Brandon.

"Know something, Brandon? Maybe I had that coming. But you fuck up one more time, I walk out of here and you lose your only chance to beat this thing!"

The room finally came to a kind of order, and the meeting broke up while Charlie went to the bathroom, swabbed his lip with Mercurochrome and put a Band-Aid on it. He almost had to laugh: another day, another injury. When he returned to Worcek's office, she pulled out a chair with exaggerated courtesy for him. Brandon sat with his face turned away, hands tucked between his clenched knees, as if he was under orders to trap them.

"Okay, Brandon. We are now on the same side. Got that?" Charlie hurriedly laid out all that had happened to him, culminating in the termination four months ago. Brandon took it all in, and a lazy smile overspread his face.

"You got yours, didn't you?"

"You could say that."

"Yeah, you got yours." Brandon's grin fed on a deep well of malice. "You got yours. You sure fucking got yours!"

The repetition was getting old fast, but Charlie nodded in tune with it. Worcek finally interrupted him.

"Based on some new information that Mr. Solomon has brought us, I'm no longer recommending a settlement. Of course, it's your decision, Brandon, but I think you ought to listen to what Mr. Solomon has to say!"

Brandon was instantly resentful and wary. Just the syncopation of two lawyers' replies was enough to piss him off.

"Look, Brandon," Charlie continued, "I don't know all the details yet, but apparently a great many files went missing in the medical offices where your sister worked. That's nothing special in itself, but I have reason to believe these were fairly crucial files, and your sister was forced to take the blame for their loss - even though she never even touched them."

"How do you know that?" Brandon demanded.

"Let's just say I have an inside person at the medical office."

"So you want me to keep fighting the case? For the whole twenty-five grand?"

"Once you take the money, whether or not Sheila was illegally and brutally harassed out of her job, the book is closed. You have to decide how much you want to punish those involved."

Brandon mulled it over, unembarrassed by the public display of his slow, tortuous thinking, by the way he made them wait. Or perhaps that was deliberate, his revenge for their having thrown these reversals at him. Finally he leaned forward, his gangly frame taut with resentment.

"See, even two-thousand dollars could help me a lot now, even if it doesn't mean shit to you, Mr. Solomon."

Charlie could see the kid was getting skinny, his clothing threadbare. The last six months had done Brandon a world of bad. But Charlie was through playing nice or running scared. "In the first place, in case you weren't paying attention when I told you my story, in case you dumped all that data, I fully appreciate the value of two-thousand dollars at this point in my life, Brandon. But I'm trying to rescue something here! If we can prove files were hidden or even stolen and your sister was unfairly blamed and illegally harassed off her job, you just might get the whole twenty-five grand. Not to mention that we might just dig up evidence that the Clinic mishandled injured workers' medical records. Your case, because it's about everything that was done to your sister at Bernard-Duvall, just might bust that clinic for good."

Brandon looked down at his clasped hands. "Yeah. I could bring them down."

The simplicity of Brandon's remark reduced them to silence, and left them all contemplating the enormous but suddenly hopeful task before them. Worcek turned and spoke to Brandon with unusually hushed fervor. "If you give me the word, Brandon, I'll issue a set of subpoenas. Depose everyone in the clinic, Theresa, the doctors -"

"Not Theresa."

Worcek glowered at Charlie, while Brandon eyed him with curiosity. "The inside source, huh? How far inside, Charlie?" Brandon gave him a slight grin, and Charlie was disgusted. But for once Brandon backed off, and grew serious. "She was the only friend Sheila had at that fucking place."

"Exactly, " Charlie echoed, relieved. "And she came forward, she'll keep helping us, but not if she's exposed. She's no good to us if she loses her job."

"Well, Charlie," Worcek interrupted, "I suppose we can save Ms. Calder for last, and only if it's necessary"

Brandon sat bent over in his chair as if a strong wind had knocked him to the side, his eyes emptying out in contemplation of the new possibilities of his case. "If Charlie's right, maybe we're this close to digging this up. Fuck it, let's dig it up. Tell them to take their money and shove it up their ass."

Worcek smiled with relief as Brandon shook her hand. He turned to Charlie and chuckled as if Charlie had succeeded in getting some prank past him and he really appreciated the joke. "Nice dog-and-pony-show. You got me going now." Charlie almost cringed as Brandon's Little League grin stayed with him, lips parted with a breath of hope, the tossing of a lifeline it was now Charlie's burden to tow for better or worse.

"Good to have you working for me, Charlie."

Charlie's meeting with Brandon and Worcek had left him humming with dread, and literally whipped, but at least, he reflected sardonically, he felt like a lawyer again. That sliver of his old confidence was welcome, because once he swung open the oak door with the mullioned glass panes and entered the Camelot Inn he felt just like a kid. After all these years, he could find his way to his dad's table blindfolded, even through the murky red light - and there was Jonas beneath the bullshit Tudor coat-of-arms yelling on the cellphone.

233

"Jake, go up and look at that roof, that's all. I'm telling you the foam job's puckered to shit. When it rains you'll get puddles an inch deep. Sure we can seal up the baffles to the a.c. system but if you get a leak to the electrical room on the other side - well, it could short out the building, Jake, nobody wants that! Lemme talk to some people, get a competitive price. Yeah I know what a rebuild costs, I used to run a few buildings myself - all right, in the morning, we'll talk." He slammed the cellphone shut and seeing Charlie he vented on him the last word he'd failed to get in on the phone. "Guy's roof's falling apart but he figures he'll sell the building by the rainy season!"

"You're trying to fix a roof, Dad?" Charlie grinned. "I think you're mellowing in your old age."

"Wear-and-tear you tolerate. Atrocities you fix."

Jonas waved Charlie to the banquette and Charlie sat a careful distance away from him, for he and his dad were about to have a business conversation that neither of them would enjoy. Charlie might have felt a need to win the Brandon Reed case, but he had a greater need to save his car and keep a roof over his head, and both he and Jonas knew he couldn't go on forever without some kind of income.

"You'll like the Berger Princes, Charlie. That's what some people call Seth and Gregory. They're contemporaries of yours." Fueled initially by a hit of software company capital before the dot-coms died, their real estate firm was breezing along, they were buying and selling buildings right and left - and they were being sued by everybody. "They'd pay you as an independent contractor, Charlie, you understand, and for Chrissake at least you'd practice some kind of law."

Charlie knew what that kind of law was - his dad had mustered a parade of little shysters with gamey eyes and rumpled suits to wield it against his tenants in the '80's. "Forgive me, dad, if I don't seem terribly enthusiastic about revisiting the real estate scene."

His dad made no comment, but merely slipped his hand into his breast pocket for his ulcer pills, trying to make the motion as dapper as possible while hiding with a magisterially deep breath the belly pain that had prompted it. "Well," he exhaled scornfully, "I didn't expect you to hug my knees in gratitude." He swallowed his pills with an offhand motion and drank his water,

234

while his wounded glance seemed to transfer blame to Charlie for his ill health. "You're in your world-owes-me-a-living mode now. You're ready to retire."

"Dad -"

"Where you gonna draw the annuity, Charlie? The old man's portfolio ain't what it used to be."

"It never was. It was just a row of mortgages waiting for the right push."

Charlie waited for his dad to jump down his throat, but instead he gave a wistful shrug and leaned back into his banquette. "Yeah, maybe. What the hell…water under the bridge…."

Jonas subdued himself, his left hand waving the air with motions both dismissive and apologetic. "I was just making a suggestion. About the Bergers."

Charlie humbly relented. "It's a good suggestion. I accept the offer. Thanks, Dad."

"It's the Bergers' offer, son. Don't forget that." Charlie was touched by how his once-arrogant dad laid solemn emphasis on his own insignificance, on the gratitude Charlie needed to feel for the uber-Solomon powers-that-be.

"And I'm glad it's a legal job, Dad. No use letting the tools go rusty."

"That's right. All grist for the mill, son." Jonas peered at his lip. "Did you open up one of those cuts from the…you know."

"You might say that. But don't worry, I'm fine."

"Those bastards still burying your case?"

"They're doing their best."

"And I thought I'd dealt with some pricks in my day," his dad growled. "These guys would fuck over their own mothers for a dollar."

Charlie, touched by his sympathy, couldn't resist jibing at his righteousness. "You used to go to court and fight for every dime."

"I was staring at potential multi-million-dollar judgments." His voice softened with sadness at the memory of how much he once could've been taken for. "But these shitbags - a few thousand more dollars worth of therapy would be too much for these employers of yours, after you worked and slaved for them three years?" The thought galled Jonas so much he didn't even notice the waitress as she laid his liver and onions on toast points before him. "I'm no gentleman, Charlie, but I swear, if you and I negotiated a deal or shook hands on a job and you didn't screw up severely, then that was it. Your job was your job, your benefits were your benefits - none of this ground shifting under your feet all the time."

"Tennis without a net," Charlie murmured.

"Exactly." Jonas finally glanced down at his food. "They think they're such clever schmucks. Doctors, health insurance executives – people are players who shouldn't be playing."

Charlie impulsively reached over, his wrist butting the liver plate, and grabbed his dad's hand. The wedding ring indented his grasp. "Thanks again for setting me up with these guys. Really."

"Well, son, I'm not exactly leaving you an empire here in gold rush territory – least I can do is call in a favor when you're in a jam. And you should do well at this. You know, real estate, you never come down too hard on the guy – or gal – you happen to be suing, because next month, the smoke clears, you'll be doing a deal with them, understand?"

"I get the point."

Jonas beamed at Charlie with genuine pride. "That's one thing you got from the old man. You can cut a deal with the best of them. And you got your mother's – your mother's sweetness. You're smart, you got an edge, but you're a real gentleman. You got a nice soft touch, Charlie."

"Yep," Charlie muttered gravely, "that's me."

His dad smiled ruefully and clasped Charlie's hand.

"You're going to be a little down tomorrow."

The yellow light of the coffee shop's chandeliers fed into Theresa's warning. It took the swarthiness out of her skin, and drew a thin gray shadow where Charlie would normally look for that cheerfully defiant curl of her lower lip. But just then a waitress came over with two huge plates, and Charlie found himself staring at the biggest pancake he ever saw, grilled a robust brown at the center, crepe-thin at the edges, and bulging with apples. One forkful and his palate swam in maple syrup, brown sugar and cinnamon.

"This is a phenomenal pancake."

"A German apple pancake. The biggest. Best legal high I know, Charlie."

Charlie grinned at her in a blissful haze of gratitude. "I'd say second best."

They traded salacious smiles again, and once again Charlie thought: she's a magician. Or at least she knows all the hidden haunts where magic, even small, daily instances of magic, can happen. Like a breakfast feast at an old coffee shop called Dinah's that happened to serve the all-time humongous German Apple Pancake. Three hours later, she led him on a walk along the Grand Canal in Marina Del Rey and its marshy borders alive with zones of birds; the snowy egrets that tiptoed through the sedge while a pelican landed with a splash nearby; plovers jabbing their beaks into the mud pools; and in the shadows beneath a bridge, a great blue heron standing like a sentinel above the water.

Thanks to all the pleasure of the day she had provided, he could relax and talk to Theresa about the week he'd just gone through. He'd first met the Berger boys, his new bosses, across their huge L-shaped desk. Two intersecting slabs of black absolute granite mounted on bronze columns so that the brothers could work in tandem and subject anyone walking into the room to the crossfire of their brutally aggressive double-talk.

"Come in, Charlie. We were just discussing some of our recent litigation-"

"- a lis pendens we obtained on a property. We're saying the bank can't sell it to anyone but us, even if they can get a higher price elsewhere, because of our escrow agreement..."

"...we really had a sympathetic judge. Fuck it, we might not get as good on the appeal."

They were off, and Charlie was gleaning from their verbal badminton, as best as he could, one of his future tasks. Help the Berger Princes hold up a building sale to get leverage over the seller for a possible payoff. That's how the whole day was, catching the job on the fly as best he could. Always off-guard, one step behind, where the Bergers wanted him. They knew confusion well, and knew how to make it their friend.

Seth was short, hunched over in a permanent readiness to charge, with thick glasses resting on his hawk nose, a bushy red mane of hair, and a well-trimmed beard. Gregory was tall and emaciated, his prematurely grey hair moussed into brushed-up spikes that made it look like his scalp carried a static electric charge. The Princes were two faces of a spiraling real estate success. Framed pictures on the walls showed the Berger boys' fashionable homes, their parties, the steel-and-glass building they'd just constructed in the Valley overlooking a small airport.

"These legal files are hopeless. Charlie should put them together by category-"

"- or by year. I mean we never agreed on categories, or maybe -"

"He could just arrange it to his convenience. Figure it out. You the man, right Charlie?"

Charlie had started organizing their litigation files in the afternoon. Seth and Gregory had been in business only five years and their lawsuits occupied two file cabinets. Sewer companies, air-conditioning repairmen, contractors of all kinds. Former tenants who never got back their security deposits. A homeowner association. And meanwhile he could hear on the phone the Bergers' lacerating assault on some janitorial company's claim, or some locksmith's invoice, which would generate the next lawsuit. "The bill's outrageous...you want us to say no-way-Jose and just blow you off, stop doing business?...look we don't want to have to go to court...."

They looked on every bill or tenant's security deposit they received not as an obligation to pay, but as merely the first stage of a negotiation. Just step one in a drag-out battle where the claimant - and that's all a tenant or tradesman was to them, a claimant, a beggar, a chump - would have to take the Bergers to Small Claims or Superior Court. Six months, eight months, a year later, even if the vendor or the contractor won, the Bergers would appeal or sit out the judgment for another six months and get him to knock down the price by thirty percent or more as the cost of a settlement. Given what they shelled out on materials, contractors would often lose money on work done for the Berger Princes.

"Call our guy at Great Western, Charlie. You gotta know the bank accounts."

"....because sometimes we see a judgment levy coming down the pike - some case our last idiot attorney lost - and we have to close an account...fuck, I hope we won't have to close out the corporate account again..."

"That's what it comes down to sometimes, Charlie. One step ahead of the sheriff."

"Gregory thought that line was cool, Theresa. To him it's just a game, depleting corporate and partnership bank accounts to duck judgments in favor of the poor bastards they cheated."

She gently looked him over and threw an arm around him. "Don't lash out at anything prematurely, Charlie. Stay on the job. Think of the main game."

She wasn't making light of this little corner of mendacity he'd found himself trapped in, but her advice was free of any blame or condemnation. She'd weathered her own years of disappointment and betrayal, and absorbed those memories into a languorous cynicism that gave a bite to her wit and heft to her sympathy. With her hard-won tolerance she was smoothing his passage into the world of the fallen.

But as he drove Theresa back to his condo for the last night they would ever spend there he couldn't banish the memory of the middle of the day at the Bergers' offices. The workers trudged in, their bare arms heavy with scents of lead pipe and wet earth and paint, chunky and friendly and bravely struggling with English while the Berger boys screamed at them from both sides about the way their nine-dollar-an-hour labor was never done fast enough for them. "Benigno, what's going on? Where's my carpet in Suite 230?...my hallway light fixtures?...the countertop installation is all wrong! ...don't you know how to budget your time?...THIS IS A FUCKING JOKE!" Meanwhile Charlie would turn on the computer to begin work on the spreadsheet, and wait out all the virus and firewall programs that flagged intruders sent by the Berger Princes' many satisfied customers and friends.

Staring at the morning sun, listening to the Bergers wield the phone against their workers, he felt, as he'd never felt at Hobart-Riis, like a true predator, lowlife and thief.

There was a full moon that evening, and it shone down on the futon and limned the naked curves of Theresa's back. She turned to him at his touch and he fell upon her mouth, and let the lambent heat of her lips drag his tongue to hers. He rolled on top of her, instantly cradled in the spread of those strong hips, her groin softly clinging like some dark leaf bed. Smiling patiently, holding Charlie along the length of her body, she was like a river to him, her lungs moving her hard little breasts in a swaying current, her waist snaking to prepare to fit to him, her legs warm and alluvial, the richness of them pulling him onward to his climax and his rest.

Lying in each others arms, Charlie and Theresa took a good long look at the bare walls that had shed his pictures and posters, the boxes of books and records, the furniture lined up by the front door. "You're going to be a little down tomorrow." That was an understatement. The very act of moving upturned hopes best buried, dreams best forgotten.

"Yeah, moving always sucks, Charlie. I think my worst move was to Venice after my divorce."

"I can believe that. Leaving behind your whole married life."

"Except I couldn't," she muttered. "Not exactly."

And then she told him that though the divorce was amicable, surgically clean, and though she knew she'd feel the old marriage, the community of friends, the hope for children as a phantom limb, she wasn't prepared for the last part not being a phantom. A month after the breakup, she learned she and her ex had finally succeeded in conceiving a child. She didn't tell him, determined to bear the little girl alone. She'd worked so hard to nurture the baby, gotten amnio, sonograms, the whole bit. But her body rebelled against her, violated all her hopes in a gush of blood one Saturday afternoon after a walk to the grocery store for some sugar.

Afterwards the void she'd felt after the divorce came back as an endless trough, a gorge of bleakness and self-hatred that nothing, not the company of friends, not drinking, not exercising like a demon could help. A friend of hers who was into landyacht sailing drove her to a spot near Vegas where there was a dry lake and a casino. "That was it, Charlie. I declared a semi-permanent vacation and I spent three weeks in Vegas. If you can imagine staying in that town for more than three days – I mean, I'm not a white tiger fan - you can get some idea of just how out of my mind I was. I tried blackjack and craps and poker - but the main thing was the slots. You should've seen me frozen in front of those one-armed bandits. I was outlasting all the little old Chinese women

240

who practically camp out there. Two weeks just vanished - and so did every cent I ever saved in Los Angeles. So the third week was courtesy of the plastic. Only it's not much of a courtesy later on, I can tell you that. Another year, though, I'll be out of debt. Man oh man..."

"Your ex never helped you?"

"No, he moved on to the house and the Volvo and the honey-bunch in Brentwood. I was his sexual pit stop on the fast track. But at least that's behind me now."

"If you're sleeping with me, that's for sure. It's not like I've stopped in on my way to Paris."

"When you win, Charlie," she slyly pointed at him, "the Champs Elysees, April 18, 2002. Be there with your money." She turned away and grew serious as she stared up at the track of the moonlight on the wall. "You did come to me with an answer. Or at least a response to something that had really torn me apart. I guess - we all use each other, don't we?"

"I'm not using you, Theresa." His eyes searched hers for a response. She rolled on her side and stared at him. "I didn't mean 'using' in that way."

He stroked her hair. "Whatever you mean, this is a very nice way to get used."

"The only way, Charlie."

She let him lean his head on her breasts, kissed his forehead, and traced the moonlight with her finger where it fell in the crease between his ribs.

"You're so light."

What did that mean? Sometimes he thought her words were little knives she flicked at him, carving away at him. In some ways, she could never just leave him be. But tonight she wasn't challenging him. She seemed to simply relish the gentility of his body.

He yielded to her embrace, nested in the crook of her arms, and soon he breathed Theresa's slumbering warmth and followed her faint sighs into sleep. He fell into a thick and blissful shadow that only lifted when a patch of sunshine floated like smoke above the blinds, the hibiscus rapped on his window, and the hummingbird chittered in the courtyard for the last time in this phase of his life.

By early afternoon Charlie and his possessions were deposited in his new rental in the Fairfax district. When Charlie's whiplash had seized up on him, Theresa had redoubled her efforts to get him moved out quickly. Charlie had marveled at the startling strength with which Theresa, her frame now seeming as sturdy and compact as before it had been soft and supple, lifted carton after carton of Charlie's possessions and hustled them across the courtyard to the condo entrance. Her fingers sealing up the boxes, her whole body a force urging him to get on with it.

Now, in his bare room, she sat on the floor, exhausted. The building staff had not yet put up the blinds, and after only a few minutes in his new apartment Charlie was sweating. He stared down at the tiny kidney-shaped pool, where the sun, beating on the worn red tile, seemed to leach the life out of the potted oleander around the fence. A few old people basked in the sun, while a Russian family and their squalling kids jumped in and out of the pool, and on one of the balconies, another gray and ancient denizen peered suspiciously at the surging and caterwauling that breached his silence.

Charlie and Theresa stretched out beside each other on the futon.

"Theresa, this would've been unbearable without you. Thank you so much."

She squeezed his hand in response, and then asked him dryly if he wouldn't mind if they took a nap. He smiled and nodded, and within minutes sleep hit him as smartly as if someone had whacked him on the head.

He woke up to the last effulgence of the dusk vanishing from the bedroom walls. His piles of possessions seemed brooding and almost totemic, offerings to his ancestors at the start of some ritual trial. Theresa stirred by his side and, in the lingering grip of her slumber, had an expectation on her face that was almost childlike. In the growing darkness that wavered past the phosphorescence in Charlie's eyes, the planes of Theresa's face and her straight black hair were suddenly an unanswerable question to him, her alien heritage laid bare in the coming of the night until she seemed almost Aztec in her remoteness.

Charlie thought again, uneasily, about how she had said he was so light. He reached for her and embraced her again, needing to feel the crush of her clothes and the sheer resistance of her. She stirred gently, her torso sighing up to him, and he clung to her like a life raft in the silence presided over by the calming of his breath.

His own voice jolted him erect, his wryly casual greeting on the answering machine. Vel responded that she had important news and wanted to talk with him, as soon as possible.

She met Charlie in her little dark green Saturn in the health club parking lot near the hearing rooms. So that there was no risk of their being seen by colleagues she took him for a drive. As Vel smoothly accelerated her car onto Ocean Park Boulevard, he heard the music on her tape, a Bach harpsichord sonata, shivering filigrees of notes pleasantly serene but so intricate they seemed to rise to an inaccessible distance. Vel looked especially prim in a barrette and two austere gold and mother-of-pearl earrings. Her car, as Charlie had expected, was immaculate.

" The bottom line here, Charles - and I know you'll be surprised to hear this - is that no one, not even your nemesis, Bert Silver, is very pleased about your case."

"So I take it you're authorized to discuss settlement?"

"They're keeping me on a pretty tight leash, Charles. After all, you have been known to talk to me on occasion, which in their eyes makes you my biggest friend in the system. But I'm exploring a variety of options. Combinations of back disability payments, some extended treatment if you waive future medical and penalties, maybe even voc rehab if that's what you really want."

Charlie felt Vel's comradeship, nested in her assumption that he couldn't truly desire to leave their little worker's comp fraternity. But he pulled back from her, knowing what was at stake in the conversation, and his reply took on the lash of that recoil. "You know, Vel, the enticements of this job aren't exactly as dazzling as they once were. Even with you selling them."

"I'm not trying to 'sell' you, Charles."

"If I don't settle, will you take the case against me?"

"I would hope they wouldn't be foolish enough to put me in that position, and I would hope you wouldn't be foolish enough to court it."

"I can defend myself."

"Charles, they'll bring it all out. They'll accuse you of perjury in your deposition, using what's in your psych reports -"

"I know that."

"I don't want to go up against you, Charles - although I'll bet that we're already contending against each other."

Yes, of course Vel would guess he was working actively with Worcek on the Brandon Reed case. Still, her sagacity unnerved him, and he decided if she was going to try to bump him off his perch, he knew how to strike back while perhaps even extending some professional courtesy. The soft little slice that kills.

"Is that why you want to take me out of the picture? Because of what I might tell Worcek?"

"I didn't figure you would sit idly by once you landed on the other side, Charles."

"Vel, there's a lot more to this case than your new employers might have told you." Even as he made the remark, he knew he could only hint at what he'd discovered to his one remaining friend in the system. "The missing files and the mistreatment of Sheila Reed – we may be onto something pretty rank."

"Perhaps you're right, Charles. But whatever you might find, what could you turn up that will make it difficult to settle and return to your former employer? You see, last I checked, that wasn't the Bernard-Duvall Clinic, it was Hobart-Riis Insurance, where you were doing a pretty good job helping to stop waste and fraud."

"The Clinic is Hobart-Riis' client, Vel. And Hobart-Riis is backing them to the hilt."

"Whatever Hobart-Riis does or doesn't do with respect to Bernard-Duvall - what does that have to do with you? What does that have to do with me doing my bit to bring you back from career death, Charles?"

His politeness seized up on him as Vel's little pinpricks of logic finally goaded him to an explosion. "I don't know, Vel! I don't know anymore! This whole system - it's all one fucking pack of lies, isn't it?"

Vel kept her eyes firmly on the road, but he could tell from the flush on her cheek she had taken it all in. "Maybe it is all one fucking pack of lies. But you're forgetting one little player in this liar's poker game, Charles." She eased to a stop and focussed that dead level gaze of hers on him. "You know my encounter with Judge Minkin wasn't my first undercover experience in the System. My second week in my position, my boss sent me to the unemployment lines. I'm dressed up like some typical little Chicana hard case in torn jeans and an old T-shirt and I have a splint on my finger. I was on that line maybe five minutes when a capper comes up to me, hands me his card, and tells me how for just a few hours time with a doctor and a lawyer I can sue my employer's ass and be collecting benefits for years. So naturally I'm all 'dios mio, way to go, how do I get my ticket, my piece of the American dream.' It was quite an education. I was told about all the therapy I would receive for my... ", she wiggled her finger, "aggravated carpal tunnel syndrome, joint pain and accompanying stress. And the doctor and lawyer bills would cost me nothing. The insurance company would pick up the tab. I believe the capper even promised me a disabled bus pass. Ooh, I could even ride the RTD for free. So he gives me his employer's card and I go to the 'Administrative Law Offices' or some such nonsense, and they fill out all the forms for me, and send me to a doctor who tells me I've been injured and have a right to generous compensation. And when I said that all I did was sprain my finger, he asked me how it took place, and I said I jammed it on a fall, and he said where did I fall, and I said on the street, and he asked me where I fell again, and I said in the office on the way to going to the bathroom to cry my eyes out on the day I was fired. 'I like that,' he says. 'That's the way we'll go.' There would be therapy sessions, an easy lawsuit, and then, after a wait of no more than three months, this poor little wetback here would have enough money to buy herself a yacht."

Charlie had to smile. "Somehow or other I can't imagine you sailing, Vel."

"We put that bastard out of business. The Ventura Orthopedic/Neurological Group, or whatever they called themselves."

"That's right. They were all put out of business. The cappers, the doctor mills, all of them. They're no longer the problem. Christ, Vel, they're no more a danger than - than Reagan's old welfare queen in the Cadillac, for Chrissake."

"Oh really? You don't think they could come back? Charles, look around you. This is instant gratification town. Everyone's got Disney and

Vegas on their minds. You may have forgotten, but we fulfill a useful purpose in making sure people can't take their employers and the state for a free ride whenever they get angry at their boss, or just get angry at having to work for a living. If you'd seen the laziness, the disgusting stupidity..."

Charlie let Vel trail off, because he knew that she had spoken too much. Whatever dirty loutishness she was referring to, he could tell it wasn't the vulgar dreams of a bunch of people taking cards from a capper. Some other sensual impression of filth and crudity, some dark slice of the old country it would be best to let slide.

Vel regained her composure in an instant. "You can trust me, Charles. At least I hope you still can." The car stopped in front of the health club. Just across the street lawyers wheeled their carry-alls to his old appointed rounds. "Bert Silver's on a little power trip, everyone's gone a little crazy, and you've had to take a fall. But believe me, Charles, we can step back from all this together."

When it became clear that the firm of Worcek, Nadjari and Bellis had subpoenaed almost the entire staff of The Bernard-Duvall Clinic, Dr. Bernard finally had to make a speech. To the assembled associates and office staff, he promised that they would in all probability never have to see the inside of a lawyer's office.

But all that day fierce tantrums burst out of nowhere and made the walls of the executive offices shudder. It was no surprise to Theresa that the girls began to droop over to her on their breaks, craving some honest advice. She assured them that there would be many delays before they would actually be deposed. Before then the case would probably be settled. But if they were one day called in to tell a lawyer about their work at Bernard-Duvall and its relationship to Sheila Reed, all they would have to do would be to tell the truth, or say they didn't know, or they couldn't remember. She repeated the last phrase like a magic incantation to children. I don't remember. Still, every one of them left her office with that residue of reassurance already evaporating from her face, with fears of the skulking mysteries of American law still deep within them, and Theresa had a flash of anger at Charlie Solomon, and her own involvement in this whole affair.

That wasn't exactly rational, was it? The subpoenas were our side's strike, after all. But these were her workers, whom she steered through the little torments of every working day, and their qualms resonated within her. She hadn't realized how much of her emotions were invested with these women, and Charlie, lean and pliant in the throes of lovemaking, then cool and gentle as the moonlight beside her, now suddenly seemed another aggressive corporate male pulling his "moves" against her workforce.

Graphs and smothering piles of paper. She had a flash of her father in his world of instruments and charts, eyebrows beetling over his bifocals, blue ribbons of isobars from weather maps just over his head, foreshortened by her child's perspective so that they seemed to emit from his hair like waves of indifference towards her. The miles she and her mother had had to travel to receive that stingy excuse for a father's love. Their ancient station wagon barreling across the mesa. Shocks rattling with every gouge in the old highway. A few road runners and herds of cattle to spot, and then that bitter little eminence of a meteorological observatory, where her father, in the same way he peered into weather patterns, would coldly observe Theresa, and even as he tried to play childish games with her, would reduce her to something predictable, something to judge and to control.

Maybe that was why Theresa had rushed into her affair with Charlie. To make sure that with this cold, brainy, perfect little gentleman the control was hers. But there was so much tenderness for him too, because she knew what he was going through, what they shared together, and she sensed that even if he slipped away from her (hell, when he slipped away, this wasn't exactly kismet, she knew that), even free of her, Charlie, at least, couldn't and wouldn't judge her.

A woman who had let a trusting younger associate fall into a snare that had left her dead.

God it burned her to the core of the charity she possessed for all women like her, all the uncertain ones, all the ones trying on lives in the hopes that this job, this home, this man would be the one that fit - it twisted her up inside that she had done nothing on her watch while Sheila Reed, this hearty, suntanned, faithful woman, had plummeted into madness. You didn't succumb to that rage that took your life or another's through the pain, she knew that, but through the conviction that the pain was all there was, that you'd been cut off, shunned, betrayed. When Sheila's cheerfulness had been so blackened by "the injury" that she had called herself "W.O.E. - woman on the edge", that was when Theresa knew she was in trouble. Why didn't she try to help her then? Treachery, she knew, that was what killed.

Now she was thinking she'd betrayed her workers. Bullshit. Don't be wishy-washy now just when you should be tough. But all she could see now was the furtiveness clouding little Soong-Li's tranquil almond eyes as she came in to go over the week's inventory with her.

When they were running down how much tubing would need to be purchased, Theresa felt Soong-Li's fear as a constant tension waiting to be discharged. It was more than a vague worry about the legalities ahead of them. This woman had something to tell her.

Finally, Soong-Li muttered "I know Sheila was punished for missing files. Are they going to ask everyone about those files?"

Theresa answered carefully that there might be some questions having to do with medical records, but after all, neither she nor Theresa had anything to do with the records at that time. Then she gently asked Soong Li why she was so concerned.

"Because I think I see the files. I think they are not missing no more."

The phone rang and, since the Bergers had just fired the receptionist, Charlie picked it up, coldly answered "Berger and Berger", and was irked to hear Worcek's voice. Brusquely nosing out favors as always, she asked him point-blank for some tips on tenant law. Well, she figured, Charlie had been on the job two weeks, surely he'd picked up something that could help Brandon. The poor kid was doing pizza delivery and phone sales. He'd even said something about how he'd had to hock his camera. Now Brandon was telling Worcek that he was going to be evicted from his Hollywood dump any day now.

Charlie was in such a bilious mood that he was on the verge of firing off a quick goodbye and slamming the phone down, when he remembered some fine words he'd spoken to Theresa about putting his knowledge of the underbelly of real estate to good use. So he told Worcek that Brandon should

248

stay put, hang tough, that it would take at least a month to evict him. He should also look for code violations, anything from faultily repaired pipes to broken outdoor lights, or complain about his heating system - if he snooped around, or if he even contacted one of those Codewatcher groups, he could find something to hold over the landlord's head. At that point he should threaten to put the whole building into the city's mandatory Rent Reduction Program. He couldn't get in any more trouble than he already was in with the landlord, and maybe by making some noise he could pester the manager into cutting him some slack. Brandon should insist on his rights. As Charlie had found out cracking open a fortune cookie in his local six-dollar-a-plate Fast Wok, "The laws sometimes sleep, but never die."

"Any word on my case, Liz?"

"Vel and I are talking. But it's premature to discuss it at this point..." He let Worcek shuttle the conversation to a quick end.

Christ, Charlie thought, scanning his notes – I still have that talk with Inspector Santos ahead of me. The good Inspector had dropped by unannounced on the Berger Boys' Richmond Avenue property. The result was a staggering list of violations, including broken globes on the ceiling lights, dead lamps in the laundry area (a particular hazard to older tenants), exposed wires on the receiver for the garage clickers, and the pilot light flickering on the fire warning system that indicated the whole fire alarm had been allowed to go out. Charlie now had to call the city on behalf of the 1260 Richmond Partnership, arrange for some violations to be fixed and for most to be removed. "Charlie, just talk to the inspector...some of these guys have a burr up their ass about us but it's your job to deal with them..." Mr. Negotiator, Mr. Soft Touch. "And be sure to get the investigation fees knocked off...I dunno how, just do it...not gonna pay a fucking inspector to tell me what's wrong with my building..."

When the next call came for him he practically snarled the greeting – and apologized when he heard Theresa's voice. She in turn apologized for calling him at work, but told him she had to make sure that he would drop by that night.

He hugged her on the wooden steps to her apartment and was immediately disappointed as her big hoop earrings grazed his cheek. That was their little code that told him Theresa was having her period and there would be no sex for a week. But her almost girlish enthusiasm intrigued him as she led him to her garden out back. The landlady had let her fence off a plot of soil and Theresa had filled it with jasmine, oleander, purple solanea, and some potted plants that included a lovely mauve and gold-flecked plumeria. She playfully invited Charlie to sniff the blooms as they radiated their cool honeyed sent towards the twilight sun, and when he turned back to Theresa, he found she had put two glasses of wine and a file on the patio table.

"What's that?"

"One of the missing files. It came back." She pushed it towards him. "Sheila Reed's."

"And you brought it out of the office?" he exclaimed. He had a flash of her standing in the Venice night, naked except for her coat. The risks she took.

"Charlie, I was very discreet. And they're not going to know I'm poking around in suspect files. They slipped them back in a drawer and figured no one would notice. They forgot I knew they moved them originally. Why don't you take a look, Charlie?"

Charlie pored over the file in the fading light. He knew this file had been locked away somewhere because it was still an "open" file. No one had bothered to record the fact Sheila was dead. There was a DWDC report of injury, and a medical-legal form filled out by the Bernard-Duvall clinic. Charlie noticed that their dates went back years, and he wondered if they'd been manufactured and postdated. After all, at the beginning of Sheila Reed's stress case there was no physician's first report in the records - just a prescription for a mild tranquilizer. The Clinic had claimed they hadn't had to provide the necessary forms because they believed her whole claim was bullshit and would never be litigated.

Now suddenly here was a physician's first report, hastily scribbled, fresh and uncrumpled. It had all the earmarks of having been created "for file." And while the reports alluded to both stress and gastric complaints, they contained no copies of vital documents like Dr. Chesley's typewritten notes. To Charlie it looked like the contents of these files were enough to satisfy auditors from Hobart-Riis that the clinic was providing coverage, but not incurring the kind of claim that would raise premiums.

"It looks like they doctored this file, Theresa. They're covering their ass in case Hobart-Riis re-audits the file, or in case the files are subpoenaed."

But where had the trimmings of these surgically sliced files gone to? What had they done with the real reports?

"Theresa, you say there's a whole shelf of files like these?" Even as he asked this merely rhetorical question, he remembered the police report he'd looked at and Xeroxed at the clinic. "I wonder if they were first moved away the night the clinic was burglarized. The report said no sign of forced entry. Someone came in and in one night and took away all these files. All these patients. Why?" His mind combed through the Sargasso Sea of his past backlog of cases, trying to come up with names of worker's comp claimants Bernard-Duvall had examined. He remembered an old man hooked up to an oxygen tank. "Cozen. Lit-up diabetes. I wonder what his file looks like?"

"I'll pull it for you, Charlie. Whatever you need."

He stopped and turned to her to embrace her. "No. You can't take that kind of risk."

"We need to move forward, Charlie. Give me some names."

"All right. I will. But this time don't remove anything from the office. Make copies." His mind was racing. "There could be a hundred files like these. Before they go back in deep freeze we need to figure out what the hell's being done to them."

He looked at Theresa, and was thrilled to see her smile at him with what looked like a touch of pride. She leaned forward and kneaded his thighs, ruefully smiling at the obstacle her time of the month posed for both of them. They contented themselves with a long simmering kiss, and a pleasant excitement about what they were accomplishing as a team, wresting what appeared to be evidence of wrongdoing from the bowels of the System.

"Why not destroy the files?" That had been the first question Golan had asked in his brief meeting with Dr. Bernard and Bert Silver. All he'd gotten was a smartass remark from Silver that "we can't afford to have any more files turn up lost." What Silver, really meant, Golan knew, was that it would be too long and complicated to try and explain it to that coarse *muzhik* mind of his.

Well, let them play superior – he didn't need that knowledge for the job that awaited him and his associates Ogi and Daniel at this little house in Eagle Rock.

He enjoyed the Spanish neighborhoods. They were like Czech villages with their truck gardens and little backyard farms. And Oscar Mejia, the Bernard Duvall Clinic's Maintenance Supervisor, even kept some chickens in a pen in back. He was feeding and clucking to them when Golan and his associates strolled into the yard. Golan had a problem with the way even the men in this strange Latin Catholic culture wore little gold crosses around their necks. But he appreciated all the hard work close to the earth.

Oscar gave a little nod to his daughter and asked her to go help mama in the kitchen. Yeah, he knew the score. But Golan had to give him credit – he had enough spirit to stand close to Golan, even to look up into Ogi's eyes as the big brute towered above him. Oscar told them he was sick of dragging all those files around. One more time, Golan pleasantly assured him. Move the files from the clinic office to the warehouse, we'll take care of some other problems, and that will be that.

Then Oscar had to screw up by telling Golan never to come by his house again (as if Golan ever needed to do anything like that twice). He muttered something in Spanish, confident Golan wouldn't know the language. People were always assuming Golan knew so little.

Golan nodded to Ogi, who plucked at Oscar's arm, grabbed his hand between thumb and finger, and corkscrewed it the wrong way while placing the meaty flat of his other hand at the base of Oscar's elbow. Daniel clamped his hand over Oscar's mouth to stifle the scream of pain. Ogi pressed up harder on the elbow, gave the hand a slight twist, and the skin around Oscar's bulging eyes whitened.

By now Oscar was thinking of his arm being crunched, his life ruined as he fell into a puddle of shattered, useless, weeping pain in his own home in front of his family. Ogi twisted harder. Now Oscar wouldn't be thinking of his family anymore. All he'd be thinking about was the pain blasting up his arm and neck through his skull. Wishing like a baby it would just stop.

"I agree, Oscar." Golan told him. "You should be able to 'leave the shit from work behind you'" Golan then calmly told him in Spanish that, in that spirit, he expected Oscar to be totally silent about what went on today. In the corner of his eye Golan spotted the kitchen window, Oscar's wife and child looking on with anguish. Well, couldn't be helped. They'd just remind him to do what had to be done.

Another day, another game to run. Even though the day at work wiped him out, Charlie drove down to Little Santa Monica Boulevard in West L.A., and the black glass building where psychotherapist Dr. Will Laningham held group therapy sessions for what he called "victims of workplace traumas." It was part of Charlie's case that his psychological injury required therapy, so Worcek had arranged this appointment for him and he had to show up.

Laningham, a chain-smoker - he called two fifteen-minute outdoor breaks for this purpose - took his seat at the head of the circle, introduced him as "Charles" (the group was on a first-name basis only), and then slumped back in his chair with such a knotted and disheveled posture that Charlie could only imagine his back problems. His head was cocked back waiting to snare the circling flies of his patients' complaints, and he peered at the group from those sort of bushy elderly guy eyebrows that looked ready to scurry right off his head.

Except for Bill, a mournful but dignified middle-aged telephone-line repairman in a wheelchair, the entire group consisted of women. Charlie didn't think he was particularly sexist, but he found the composition of the group made him feel even more uncomfortable. He at least had sympathy for Sonya, the short, squat Russian woman who wore her hair up in an old country babushka kerchief. Her supervisor, who hated her, had forced her, while pregnant, to go from a sewing machine where she could sit to a workstation where she had to stand all day, which brought on a miscarriage. Charlie finally jumped in to advise Sonya to contact the sympathetic nurse who had treated her in the hospital. Have the nurse tell her employer that she'd heard about the work station transfer. There was no indication the employer knew what the supervisor was doing. Once he knew of the cruel treatment the employer might take Sonya's side and demand that the insurance company rehab her and get her back to work.

Sonya was deeply grateful for the suggestion, but Laningham was frowning at him. Charlie and Laningham had agreed he should be introduced as a laid-off lawyer with a case of post-traumatic stress disorder, but not (until Charlie chose to reveal it) a lawyer for the insurance companies. Perhaps Laningham thought that, with his free advice, Charlie had poached on his territory and violated their agreement.

Still, the only way Charlie could get through the session was playing Mr. Fixit. The telephone lineman brought up that the insurance company deemed his treatment for addiction to painkillers not compensable; he was a Vietnam vet, and his addictions were ruled to be pre-existing. Charlie, genuinely outraged, suggested that he write a letter directly to the Board threatening to publicize that ruling. By now the rest of the group seemed to open up with the hope Charlie would chime in and offer a solution for each one of them, but Charlie found no way to address their aimless chatter. A secretary, Martha, suing for stress over what had obviously been sexual harassment, spent her whole time complaining about her problems with men, which seemed fantastically inappropriate to Charlie. She found a willing soulmate in a lady-who-lunches type, Carrie, whose perfume had a killing radius of half an acre. A former dancer (she still could bring her leg up to her ear, she mentioned for no reason in particular), she'd tried working in an antique store until a fungus in this "sick building" had laid her up with (she claimed) crippling allergies – she talked about what "Philistines" her bosses were. This was constructive venting, some sort of working through of problems, this rehashing over and over of ruts and complaints and failures? These were his fellow claimants?

Charlie craved the only genuine therapy he knew: work on the case. He called Theresa the minute he left the building, wanting to drive down to her place right away, look at the additional files she'd retrieved, almost as eager as if he knew they would be jumping into bed. She answered his greeting sullenly, and the minute he heard her grief-corroded voice he knew the plans had changed.

Once again they sat on her patio, only this time there was a blender pitcher of homemade Margaritas on the table. The light of dusk through the yellow haze gave the plants a dry, waxy luster. Theresa pointed out a magnificent web that had appeared on her geranium bush, at the center of which a tiger-striped spider waited for his prey. "I was hosing the flowers down when I found this. Gorgeous, isn't he? And he'll help keep some of the pests away."

Her drunken appreciation of that spider, such a forced diversion from her gloom, told Charlie what he already suspected. "They caught you."

"Aah, fuck 'em, Charlie." She laughed that weird, off-kilter laugh of hers, and for a minute Charlie was worried she'd become hysterical. But she calmed herself and, pacing the garden in short, angry bursts, she told him how she'd gone in that morning to return the file, only to find an entirely different row of files in the drawer. And then she heard the soft tread of Dr. Bernard's loafers behind her, and turned to see him sucking on his pipe and examining her like some kind of lab specimen. He calmly told her to surrender the file and join him in his office for a cup of tea.

At least, Theresa felt, she'd seen through them all. Unlike poor Sheila, Theresa felt, she could not be shocked or humiliated. "But I was wrong about that, Charlie. Bernard was - he's smart, I have to admit it. He pointed out that the fact I wasn't subpoenaed along with the others got him suspicious. That was something we didn't think about, I guess, with all the brainpower at our disposal. Then he pops in a videotape on his monitor – and there I am, in glorious black and white, taking the file."

"He had surveillance in the office?"

"Yep. He plays the whole thing, just so I can see how ridiculous I look, checking over my shoulder while I peer through the files. Then I bend over to get poor Sheila's file and he freezes it. He smiles at the shot – it's showing some cleavage – and he leaves it on all through the meeting, just so I can feel especially humiliated. Then he starts talking about what a chance I blew here. And basically, the reason that his clinic was such a godsend to me, Charlie, was because I was just some little hustler a half-step away from the streets. No decent college degree, no real experience in office management, no class. The least I could've done was take orders. And if I wasn't going to take orders, then it was up to me, it was clearly up to me – the bastard tells me he'll give me a second chance, but I'll have to reconsider certain things I'd said to him before about our relationship. Well, at that point, I lost it. He couldn't even fire me in a way befitting a human being. I told him there was no way I'd sell myself for either the job or the body he was offering. So he gets right back into it, calling me a two-bit whore, and I almost fucking showed him what could be done to a flabby-ass weekend golfer by a woman who swims in the ocean every day of her life! But I said to myself it wasn't worth it. He had the security guard follow me on the way out and that was that."

"Theresa, I'm so sorry."

"You know, Charlie, I wouldn't go back now if I could. Now that I've seen how vile that place is." She stared down the alley and murmured with a chuckle, "I guess if you're gonna be washed up, be washed up on the beach."

She picked up her Margarita glass, and leaned her head against the beads of water on its surface, while reaching for a pile of papers on an adjacent chair and tossing it to him. "At least I made a copy of Sheila's file, Charlie. It's all yours."

"Thank you. Theresa, I - I don't know what to say. I feel that I made you -"

She slammed the glass down. "I knew it. I knew you'd get into that shit. Charlie, I'm not blaming you for this. I was a free agent, I did what I did, and that's that! Your candy-ass guilt makes me sick."

"All right, Theresa!"

She herself recoiled from her own remarks - with a tangible shiver she laid her head in her hands, then seemed to revel in a long sigh, as if it drew the poisons from her body. Her eyes met Charlie, and she smiled greedily. "You want to do something for me?" She got up in that slack-hipped way that whomped his heartbeat into overdrive. She beckoned him to her, he got up, and she snaked into his embrace.

"Theresa, you normally don't..."

"...not a normal day, is it?..." She exhaled hot breath into his ear and nibbled at it. "Maybe I'm too damn fastidious. It's not like not doing it will keep the wolves from the door, right? They like the smell of blood. Oh, I'm a bad girl now..." She was grabbing at his crotch, laughing into his mouth and driving him towards the planters - he threw a glance back at the geraniums wreathed in shade, but not before he stumbled on a planter and went crashing into the fence.

"Oh Christ, Charlie, I'm sorry, I'm such an idiot."

She helped him to his feet - he brushed the soil from his jacket and shook off of his fingers a strand of spiderweb.

"Oh, look at this, I ruined it."

"No, we just caught a corner of it." Odd thing to be doing in his life, he thought, soothing a grown woman over a fractured spiderweb. They could just make out the strands' vague iridescent glint in the last light of dusk, the big spider, despite Charlie's fall, still waiting at its imperturbable axis.

"Look at the symmetry of it, Charlie. I mean, you think about it. Any big bunch of those sticky strings will catch a fly. Why is it so beautiful? Well, it has to be big and spread out to catch the maximum amount of flies in all directions. And if the strands weren't widely spaced, maybe the flies would see them. It all makes such sense, and it's all so beautiful."

He gently touched the small of her back, and in a moment she collapsed on his shoulder, her strong arms crumpling like paper wings against his chest while her tears seeped onto his throat. He let her sob quietly, let the resonating body blows of her day loose their last shudders onto him. He thought of Theresa's half-empty rooms, of the debts she still hadn't paid. She didn't have to tell him she had no savings. The woman was two weeks away from the welfare line.

"Theresa, listen. Whoever played a shell game with the files that night – it's someone with access to the office who can be called down there at a moment's notice. That sounds like maintenance people. We'll find out who they are, talk to them. The Clinic, Hobart-Riis, they're nervous now. We've got them on the run, Theresa."

None of his words stopped her crying. He finally kept silent and held her like a child.

-9-
down in the flood

Amid the usual snacking and schmoozing of the Van Nuys Worker's Compensation Board cafeteria, Worcek and Vel grabbed some bagels and coffee and took a table away from the sunlight. The unseasonable heat had forced them out of their usual dark blazer outfits. Worcek wore a leopard-skin patterned tan silk blouse and a burgundy skirt, and Vel winced at the color scheme. Vel stuck with a black skirt and a white ruffled blouse, which struck Worcek as awfully starchy on someone so young.

Having each sized the other up as wardrobe-deficient, they got down to business. Charles Solomon vs. Hobart-Riis Insurance, Inc. Worcek asked Vel to at least concede that when a guy gets splattered with someone's brains, that's a trauma, and when he has ringing in his ears after a gun's gone off by the side of his head, there's no mystery about where that injury comes from. Vel immediately countered that "by the side of his head" would've deafened him, which was not the case, so there was a definite question as to whether the injury was physiological or psychological. Worcek was astonished, even impressed by Vel's clinical detachment and determination to fight over every dime in Solomon v. Hobart-Riis. There had been romance rumors about her and Charlie.

Well, it's not like Vel was the only grimly professional bitch in the room.

They plunged into the details. Charles Solomon, reeling from the scene of a suicide, ear-damaged or psych-damaged or both, was laid on the table and dissected. His attempt to be stoically macho about his injuries was both argued and lamented. The seeds of a compromise began to emerge: his disability rating

258

(with the exact nature of the tinnitus to be determined later), the amount of accumulated temporary total disability owed to him (Worcek was willing to go down about 25%), the nature of medical expenses that would be refunded to him. Vel insisted that Worcek waive any and all penalties against the insurance company and drop Charlie's 132A charge for harassment of a worker's comp claimant. Worcek grudgingly agreed. In a system that took seriously the principle that insurance companies would self-impose penalties, those penalties turned out to be a worthless bargaining chip.

"You wanna dance, you gotta pay the band, eh Vel? But there's one more factor here. Continuous trauma. The systematic isolation and termination he went through at the office. Happens in more worker's comp cases than I can tell you, Vel. Only in the case of our mutual friend Charlie, it was particularly odious."

"There's not a thing I can do about that."

"It was slow torture, Vel. Followed by one loss after another."

"Are we talking about industrial stress?" Vel inquired acidly, "or are we talking about life? There's no compensation for life, Liz."

"You know what I'm saying."

"Yes, and the imprecision of it disgusts me." Vel hastily took a bite of her bagel. "We're all subject to man's inhumanity to man. Talk about paying the band, Liz. I'm as sorry about what happened to Charles as you are, maybe even sorrier, but this 'continuous trauma' argument - it's your side going for the giveaway, and I'm not buying it."

"All right, let's not get our panties in a bunch...so to speak." Worcek was astonished by Vel's anger at her attempt to jimmy a few more benefits from Hobart-Riis. She knew she was pushing it, but Vel treated her argument as if it were a sacrilege. Oh well, she thought, sometimes you push people's buttons. At least this was a young woman, however strange a young woman, with whom she could deal.

"What about voc rehab, Vel?"

"Let's work out a buyout price."

"You're assuming Charlie's going to want to buy his way out of it?"

"You're assuming Charlie seriously wants to be retrained for another job?"

"Well, I don't know, Vel. Since his profession shat on him and he lost his condo, I haven't asked him. But I've seen people in his position chuck it all and head for Hawaii."

"I don't see Charles selling timeshares and scuba tours. Besides, you know what the system's like now. If Charles elects to pursue voc rehab, I can't guarantee that the insurance company won't cut him off at some point, and he'll have to fight in court for another year to get it reinstated."

Worcek eyed Vel with quizzical sarcasm. "So what's it like working for Hobart Riis?"

Vel shrugged the question off and Worcek continued. "I'll suggest a buyout to him. But don't assume he'll go for it. Charlie's head is getting to another place. I'm serious. What with helping Brandon Reed and this woman, Theresa Calder..."

"I'll admit this is a rough time for him. I'm sure he's just seeking companionship where he can find it."

Worcek thought she could hear it - a little shudder under the cool dismissal. She didn't know exactly why she was goading Vel. Maybe she wanted to crack that façade a hair, get Vel to admit to a twinge of raw emotion now and again. Not that any of that mattered. At the end of the day, all you could do was try to move the whole cartload of crap a little bit in your client's direction.

"So, Vel, while we're at it - the Brandon Reed case?"

"Nothing to talk about. The offer of one-thousand-five-hundred stands - and it's a gift, Liz."

"Some other time, then."

"Some other time."

The first thing Charlie revealed to the group seemed trivial enough. Just enough to play the game. The dampness. His new apartment had a dank, musty undertone of rot. There was a black mushroom in the corner of his closet, and he was worried that if he cut it out some fluid would ooze from under the nap of his carpet, revealing fungi all along the floor. There were now faint rust-colored stains on his white and beige shirts. God knows what would happen during the rainy season.

No one took back the discussion, so Charlie next told them about how difficult it was for him to sleep facing the courtyard, the leakage of t.v. noise and radios turned up by the half-deaf old people, the squalls of a colicky infant whose baby carriage (he'd seen it on one of the wooden patios one day) literally trembled from the force of the infant's cries. "All you can see is this little baby carriage with these horrible shrieks coming out of it."

After whatever sleep he got, he'd wake up and slog to work. Every day a little ball of calcined disgust and dread formed in his gut as he marched out the door. Charlie conceded an admission to the group: he could no longer deny to himself that he worked for " legalized sociopaths." Slipping into raconteur mode, Charlie related how he had defended the Bergers in court eight times. On one of those cases, arguing the janitorial company had baited and switched the poor Berger Princes on a low-bid agreement and then breached the contract to try to jack up the price, he'd actually won. On the others, like the case where the Bergers had held back a senile old woman's security deposit after she'd been moved to a nursing home, Charlie was forced to freeze his face into a mask of courtesy as judges attacked him as a total fraud. The Berger boys had figured he was falling down on the job as a lawyer, so when their latest property manager had quit in disgust, they'd made him de facto property manager, without the slightest raise in salary. "What the hell, Charlie, make a few deals, close 'em...a fixer like you can do that, right?..Yeah, Mr. Negotiator! Mr. Soft Touch!....otherwise, I mean, the legal thing, it's not exactly working out, and can you blame us for wanting value for our money?"

Out of the belly of the beast – and into its asshole. The rot overwhelmed him on every managerial trip he made to the Berger Boys' buildings. Leaks from the pipe joists. Busted pumps that caused garages to flood with every rainstorm. ("Get us cheaper bids on pumps, Charlie! Your responsibility!") Creaky elevators, ruined a/c systems, dirt and cobwebs over the shattered glass where uninspected fire extinguishers sat, or used to sit before they were stolen by the homeless. The apartment buildings smelled of carpet mold and uncollected trash. From south of Robertson to east of Fairfax, they all blended into the same evidence of airily dismissed infrastructure, of flagrant neglect. Maintenance just wasn't sexy for the Berger boys. And then of course, there had to be a bad roof, and unlike his dad, Charlie couldn't step in and fix that atrocity. He tried to point out that during the one freak rainstorm half the tenants had to put pails under the leaking vents and corners and cracks. "Charlie, how many months until the next rainy season?...now isn't the time...we'll tell you when it's the time, Charlie!"

Charlie remembered huddling with the Bergers' crew on a corner, giving them cash just like some payoff out of a mob movie, after he'd had them put in a PVC pipe alongside a tenant's ground floor office so it would channel the rain off and stop her office from flooding. The Berger boys had put off the repair for months, and he'd finally borrowed money from his dad to pay the crew himself. The Bergers were furious at him, but at least he'd had the satisfaction of doing one small task to allay a tenant's misery. And doling out the cash, he'd thought again, as he thought so many times – *what if one of my friends walks by and sees me doing this?*

Did he ever want to do more, Laningham quietly asked, then smuggle in an occasional service and fix the odd elevator bell or sink? Charlie resented the question. "I believe in rendering practical assistance." He could see Martha's nose wrinkle with disgust. He wanted to get pissed off back at her and stay that way. But another emotion was welling up within him, one he hadn't had to confront for months. The panic was back.

How could he have swerved into this awful trap?

He told the group that he'd successfully negotiated a hardship plea for the Bergers. Their partnership on the Richmond building was let off from massive fines and given more time to correct the abuses. *Getting the deal done, he'd almost heard his father's voice as he found the voice of his professional survival. What it would take to break the habits of two lifetimes?*

I'm shunned by my former profession. I've lost my inside person at the Clinic. Subpoenas and depositions take forever, and Hobart-Riis can wait forever.

This isn't my secret identity. This is my job.

He tried to be silent and let that silence hang. Someone else, out of sheer embarrassment, would have to take up the slack. But no one did. He had to admit that group therapy had a hell of a momentum. You start to reveal yourself and soon there's nowhere to hide. Through the dryness of his throat he had to keep talking. "You know, it's when the Berger Boys bring me in for

262

a friendly chat - hey, we're not bosses and employee here, we all went to the same schools, let's kick back, hang loose, talk about babes -"

"Oh, that must be charming," muttered Carrie.

"Anyway, it's when we're all relaxing, when they get chummy with me, that's the most dangerous point. That's when I want to really unload on them."

"Do that and you'll be fired, of course," Laningham weighed in.

"Obviously. But still - I mean you go through the day with this...this..."

What catches you when you fall this time?

"Welcome to the real world," Martha chuckled.

"Oh please, Martha! The goddamn fountain of wisdom. Just because you slogged away as a low-rent receptionist before you got canned doesn't mean that's the only reality!"

"Charlie, there's no need to -"

"I'm only doing this shit while I'm stuck with you all in this damn limbo waiting my case out!"

Laningham raised his hand to silence him, and leaned forward. "Just as long as you know, Charlie – it is real, and it's you who's doing it."

He waited for the elevator, obstinately silent while Carrie and Laura chattered away. How could he leak like that? That was the way he saw his performance in the group – one long repulsive unforced error. He thought he saw Carrie hastily conceal a grin at his discomfiture. Well what do you expect from them but to feast on your anguish like harpies? He'd had it with seeking guidance from this dysfunctional chatfest.

And yet, the leaking was honest. All his resolve of the past few weeks about busting the clinic and Hobart-Riis over a bunch of missing files suddenly seemed a shell, a brittle fabrication. He had chosen – or at least accepted – the Berger Boys as a way out. What was the way out of the way out?

I've lost my inside person.

When the others took the elevator, he took the stairs. As they left the building, he watched the women head to the corner to steal a quick smoke, and, no doubt, some gossip about the group. They huddled under the ficus trees in the planter, casting sidewise, quizzical glances at a thin young man who sat

263

calmly on the stone buttress checking out the front door. Charlie observed their little encounter, craned his neck to get the sunset glare out of his eyes, and the young man's features rudely startled him.

"Brandon?"

"Hey, Charlie. You look like you're surprised to see me. No, actually you look like you think I'm stalking you or something. Hey, it's cool. Worcek said I should check out this group."

"Worcek sent you."

"Yeah, but I dunno, I watched everyone go in, looked like a bunch of losers to me. And I'm not into that getting down with a bunch of strangers. But Worcek told me you were in the group, so that's why I stuck around. How else was I supposed to get in touch with you? I mean, you don't have to be so spooked, Charlie."

Brandon sprung down from the planter, all emaciated eagerness and burning loneliness, eyes arrowing in on Charlie in a way that filled him with dread.

"What do you want, Brandon?"

"I dunno." He rubbed his forehead nervously. "Just shoot the shit, maybe? There's a decent, cheap sports bar around here, the Fast Break."

Was he in the mood for buffalo chicken wings or roadside sliders with the brother of the woman who'd blown apart his life? Not exactly. But he didn't feel like going back to his lonely, noisy, musty new apartment, and Theresa, it was clear from her silence, was in a stubborn rut of depression these days. She wanted time alone while she desperately tried to get a job – and what was worse, she'd been unable to contact Oscar Mejia, the maintenance supervisor who, she believed, might know where the missing files were. Oscar's cellphone number had been changed, and, at his home there was now an answering machine screening all the calls.

He was concerned by how scared and alone Brandon obviously felt, and it wasn't just that Charlie was worried that Brandon would go sour on his lawsuit. Seven years of college and law school, and this kid was now his only true colleague. His one comrade-in-arms.

He soon found himself sitting at a tiny bar table beneath the video backwash of Dodger baseball. In that harsh effulgence Charlie could see that

Brandon was sallow and tired, his chin crusted with a livid rash. His wariness was gone, replaced by an almost desperate gratitude.

"So Charlie, did Worcek tell you? I'm still in my apartment!"

"Good to hear, Brandon."

"Word up, that advice you gave me - I really nailed my landlord. He got real sketchy, man, and I backed him right off. Guess he figures he better not fuck with a smart tenant. So thanks."

With an oddly quaint Boy Scout gesture he extended his hand for Charlie to shake.

"I'm glad the advice was useful to you."

"Think we could grab a snack maybe? I, um – I can't drink if I don't eat."

Charlie acquiesced with the inevitable "It's on me, Brandon."

They split the buffalo wings and roadside sliders. Whenever he tried to grab for a wing or a mini-burger and saw how fast the plate was dwindling, he realized how much Brandon needed him for a free meal. But as he watched Brandon gnaw greedily at the chicken bones, flecks of hot sauce and blue cheese spattering his t-shirt, a somber wave of fellow feeling swept over him. He ordered nachos for himself and another Dos Equis, and let Brandon eat as much as he wanted.

Still Charlie cringed as Brandon smeared his hand over the bowl and licked hot sauce off his fingers. He seemed to have no idea he was out in public. He'd become a rubbery spectre of tics and cravings. Charlie would've wondered if he were on drugs, except that when he finally spoke, his words made brutal sense. "Worcek's not gonna tell me what she really thinks my chances are. Her job is to just keep me on the hook, keep me going any way she can. But you're just as smart a lawyer as her, and you're in the shit with me now."

Charlie took a long pull of his Dos Equis. "Brandon, I wouldn't tell you to hang tough if I didn't think I had a chance."

"' You had a chance'," Brandon said softly, with a tiny smirk. He wolfed down another slider, grinning and talking while he ate. "That's what you wanted to say to me, right? But it came out 'I had a chance'. Is that the only reason you want me to keep going? Your own edge, Charlie?"

Flustered, Charlie spat out his reply. "Brandon, whether you lose or win your case has nothing to do with me." He continued tonelessly. "We've subpoenaed everyone we can about the missing files. Now we wait. You still expecting miracles from this process?"

Suddenly Brandon was in his face again. "You want to give me attitude? Look, you were the one who begged me to keep it going, okay? But now I think maybe I'm just getting fucked around. I mean, every night I go back to that rotten apartment, eat half a frozen dinner, then Ziploc the rest for breakfast, okay? And now my Nikon's sitting in a fucking pawnshop, and in a week that bastard's gonna sell it. My old Nikon camera! Sometimes I just figure I want to bail on all this shit forever!" He calmed down and sullenly curled back up over his beer. " You're backing me up for a reason. Worcek won't tell me dick so I gotta hear it from you."

Charlie knew he had to answer him – and he also knew he couldn't reveal to Brandon yet what he and Theresa had found out about the doctored files. The only words that came to Charlie seemed pompous but inevitable. "The truth. Lies killed your sister. I want the truth."

Brandon looked away with a smirk. "The truth. Wanna know what the truth was, Charlie? All she wanted to do was do her fucking job. She would keep walking around her room saying 'What have I done wrong, what have I'-"

"She didn't do anything wrong, Brandon. Someone should've listened to her. She should've gotten care. But the system .." - the words just emptied out of him - " it's fucking bullshit. Bullshit medical exams, bullshit files."

"What do you mean bullshit files?"

"What are you talking about? The files we're looking for."

"You didn't say missing files. You said bullshit files. You've seen something, haven't you?"

Charlie silently cursed himself for blurting that out. "Brandon," he replied crisply, "we don't have any proof of any wrongdoing yet."

Brandon stared down at the waxy surface of the bar, but even in his hooded stare Charlie could see the kindling of a battle fever that would be impossible to quench.

"Then let's just free the files."

"What?"

266

"The files Sheila got screwed over. We find out where the files are and get them."

"Look, Brandon, believe me, we depose everyone in that clinic, someone will say the wrong thing and -"

"There you go again! You just told me the system was bullshit! Why play games you can't win? You know there are files that have been fucked around with! Let's grab the files before the company destroys them!"

"Brandon, they won't destroy patient files. Those are worth money to them, they'll want to keep them around." Charlie stared at the scoreboard at the pulsing screen. "Look Brandon, I only know how to do what I know how to do. I'm a product of the system, okay? But one thing I do know is that we need to make smart moves, not foolhardy ones." He knew he had to be more specific. "Even if I knew where all the files were, which I don't, pulling some goddamn b & e job is not going to help us!"

Brandon turned away from him, staring at the great flat image of the major league pitcher in his windup. When he turned back to Charlie, out of his clasped hands one index finger rose accusingly towards him. "I should've figured you out. You got that sleepy-eyed thing."

"Yeah? And what does that mean?"

"You're gonna come up to the plate and strike out looking."

"Go to hell."

Brandon just laughed. "I can tell that you've never felt what it's like to really - connect. Bam! Just kiss that ball goodbye. Everything just - so strong it's almost on fire. Just a coupla months ago, man, I was almost there. Soleil, the movies..."

Oh great, Charlie thought, now he was on to his ex-lay, and it was time to be the crying towel. That was one reason he avoided one-on-ones in bars, even with his own friends. But at least he'd gotten Brandon off of freeing the files. Brandon stared at the beer glass and seemed to forget Charlie was even there. "I understand she wants to hook up with Glaudini for the career juice, but then she can come back. I'd take her back."

"I'm sure you would."

"She said I made her feel younger."

"And Glaudini makes her feel richer. Look, Brandon, maybe you should look at it like...Brandon, you ever talk it through with her? This on fire total connection you both had?"

"Didn't have to," Brandon muttered.

"Well, when you have a relationship, there comes a point when you do have to. You have to know what you're both about."

"Hey, Charlie, fuck your head games, okay? I made her scream. She took me out of myself. It was like - we were completely new creatures." His eyes tore through the shadows rebuffed from the video screen. "Soleil might have shined me on a little, left me for the Eurobucks, but she got something about me. She got it. Ever since my sister died, I've known that I'm supposed to change, really really change. There have been signs, okay? Soleil and I talked about that. That's what this case was about. And not just that twenty-five thousand gives me a new start. It's a lot more than that. Yeah, you don't know what's really happening here with this case, but I do, and you're not gonna take me out of it with your weak slimy lawyer bullshit!"

"Fine, Brandon. No way I can dissuade you from all these life lessons you've picked up from a soft-core porn actress." He tried to end with that sneering remark – but he had to keep going. "I've got everything at risk! Maybe I don't feel this is going to rock my world and change my life, but you better fucking believe I want to win!"

"You don't sound like it. You sound like...Mr. Sleepy."

"And you sound completely whacked out. You're into that jackpot garbage all the claimants get off on. When I cash in, I'll get it all. Get a grip! You win this case, maybe if all goes well, you can get a nice digital camera, get some video equipment maybe. But don't figure there's a magic bullet out there with your name on it."

Brandon raised his beer in a mock toast. "Here's to the magic bullet. It's better than thinking there's nothing out there but the same old shit. I bet you'd go running to the insurance company if they'd take you back. I bet you'll be waiting for their Christmas card."

Charlie was exhausted from arguing, and realized this night at the sports bar had in some way accomplished its purpose. There was no way the kid would abandon the case now. Charlie reached for the words that might snuff out the night for good. "Yeah, I'll wait for my boss' card while you're waiting for that love letter from Soleil."

Brandon took that remark like a blow he was prepared for, with a grim smile, and let its reverberations die away as he poured the rest of his beer into his glass. "I don't think I'll ever be with anyone like Soleil."

"No, probably not."

"Okay. That's something we can agree on, Charlie," Brandon chuckled. They drank the rest of their beers joined in an uneasy silence.

Charlie knew what was facing Theresa the following day, and told her he wanted to meet her that morning. Instead she invited him to come over to spend the night. "I need the strongest kind of consolation, Charlie."

They made love silently, caressing each other with a ritual tenderness, until the climax came so fast and sweet that she had to rush to catch up with him, but Charlie stayed with her, a little scraping pain, a few more pulsations, until at last she grabbed a shudder of pleasure with a sigh. She curled against him, with an instinctive grace that no weariness could overcome, and he relished the strong contours of her body. With Theresa trusting herself to his embrace, Charlie felt it like a gavel knocking on his heart, all the love in the world for this woman. He slid off into a dreamless sleep until, at seven in the morning, they were jolted awake by the alarm.

After they had breakfast, Theresa once again offered to go alone. Once again Charlie insisted on going with her. She'd sold her car two weeks ago and there was no way Charlie was going to let Theresa take the bus down there even if it was only in west L.A.

"Then you better park the Infiniti a few blocks down Pico Boulevard. You want to keep that hid."

So they walked five blocks to the squat little institutional building near Veteran Avenue. The cops waved them in through the metal detectors, giving them no more of a second glance than the shopping bags of the homeless piled against the glass doors. Theresa took her application and she and Charlie grabbed the last two seats in the back row of plastic chairs. She soon handed in the completed form at one of the windows. Two hours later, the sun was beating down on Pico Boulevard, but it seemed unable to penetrate the

269

fluorescent-lit space in which they sat, or dispel the muddy shadows that hugged the blue tile floors and peeling walls. The homeless who filed up to the postage window to get their mail, the applicants trudging out to the bathroom with sullen glances backwards as their seats vanished, the new arrivals filing through the doors, all merged into one endless crowd shuffling through the welfare office's grim routine.

After awhile the sounds and the glimpses of the place, no matter how hard Charlie tried to bury himself in his book, were inescapable. Two old Slavic women lamented to each other. A middle-aged bearded man, for some incomprehensible reason, was dressed in blue jeans and an old dirty nylon jacket bunched up to his chin, as if he were camping out. Every so often he would curse to himself loud enough to hear himself over his Walkman. The black kid next to Charlie, a big, limber teenager, sat placidly, elbows on his knees, staring at his open hands with a kind of sullen reproach. But the scrawny woman in front of Charlie would not stop babbling. She went on and on about the dirty buses, the bastard she met at the check-cashing place who was always after her, but she wouldn't look at him twice because he was a "dumb-as-paint senseless motherfucking throat-slit killer."

The chatter threatened to stifle the static-riddled p.a. system, and Charlie and Theresa had to listen hard to those tiny crackling speakers. The caseworkers read out the applicants' names in Spanish, Chinese and Russian accents and if you missed your name being read, you might not be called again for hours. Theresa and Charlie fought to listen against the brew of complaints, imprecations, and pointless laughter that engulfed them.

They ate all the Tostitos and drank the cooler of Pepsi Theresa had wisely packed for breakfast. Three hours later Charlie had wished they'd packed lunch. But he never felt sleepy. His eyes were frozen wide open. This is where you wound up when you fell through the brittle safety net that Social Security, worker's comp and the insurance companies had engineered. This was America's court of last resort, where the best you could hope for was a short term of imprisonment after you were judged guilty for having to go on living.

About three o'clock a bearded man in the nylon jacket threw his seizure. The head and back slid from view, and Charlie was almost knocked off his feet

270

by the rush of the crowd as its current forked against the convulsing victim, some shoving for a better view, some flailing in mindless panic. A bunch of kids chanted "Falling Down! Falling Down! Falling Down!" A nurse's aide rushed in to pillow his jacket beneath the sick man's head as the cops cleared the crowd away, and Theresa ran over to help her. The frantic activity finally ended when the paramedics whisked the man away on a stretcher - "he'll get three squares and a bath," someone muttered ruefully – but the functionaries behind the intake windows had dully, remorselessly kept calling the waiting applicants. Both Theresa and the helpful nurse's aide had missed their names.

It was another three hours, right until just before the building closed and the clerks told the remaining applicants to come back another day, when the p.a. spat out "Calder" and Theresa headed to the shadow zone in the rear of the building. Charlie followed her down a blue-gray corridor split longitudinally by an earthquake seam. A row of torpid caseworkers waited behind thick glass windows. Theresa conversed with her intake person and slipped beneath the window proof of who she was, where she lived, and how her car had been sold over thirty days ago. She could not get unemployment as her employer had fired her for cause. Stoical as Theresa was, Charlie could feel from her hushed, rapid replies how humiliating the interview was for her. Twenty minutes later, she finally clutched in her hand the papers that certified her general relief and food stamps.

She was silent during the drive back, except once when she scrutinized her explanation of benefits. "Three hundred fifteen dollars a month," she hissed. He would never forget the look on her face at that moment, a blank, steel-hard mask of utter betrayal. When they pulled into her old parking space by the Venice bungalow, and he took his hand off the steering wheel, she intercepted it and squeezed it hard.

"Thank you, Charlie," she whispered. "You're being there, it really helped." He cradled her hand silently as she looked again at her explanation of her meager benefits. "Now I've done it. Gone to the end of the line."

Theresa wanted no company that night, and ten minutes later, Charlie, fighting off a bone-numbing fatigue, was driving east on Venice Boulevard as fast as he could when the cellphone twittered. Its signal flooded Charlie with a profound sense of absurdity, the awareness after eight hours penned in the welfare office of the still untarnished upholstery of his car, the purr of Steely Dan, the fiberoptic and microwave ties that bind.

"Charlie, it's Vel. We've been trying to call you for hours."

"I've been busy. What's up?"

"We have numbers."

"Hold on, Vel." Charlie laid the phone aside and pulled off the road onto a quiet residential street near the Fairfax power station. He knew better than to ponder or to argue the terms of a settlement while driving down Venice Boulevard at night, especially when a dizzying fatigue was flooding through him, part relief, part the recoil of a deep, troubling uncertainty.

"Okay, what do we have?"

"Twenty-two grand, Charlie. That includes back t.t.d., and a buyout of your future medical and voc rehab."

"What do I give up?"

"The 132A. The penalties."

"That figures. Is there anything else?" However sharp a lawyerly knife Vel wielded, Charlie was confident she wouldn't aim it at his back. After all, she was contacting him directly before speaking to Worcek as normal protocol demanded, and they'd been friends too long.

"There's going to be a position opening in their San Francisco office. It looks like they want you to take it."

Charlie was astounded, and immediately suspicious. "What they want is for me to shut up and cooperate, Vel. Walk in like a happy camper as if all this had never happened. They want me to forget about the Brandon Reed case."

"As if that's been such a blessing in your life," Vel replied acidly.

"It's not something I can walk away from."

"You mean she's not something you can walk away from. Ms. Calder." Charlie, stung, let his silence serve as assent. "That would be truly unfortunate, Charles. We're talking here about returning you to your work, and this sort of distraction - look, why don't we meet at Nova Express and talk?"

"I don't want to talk about Theresa, Vel." He flinched at the snap of his own voice on that quiet street. The faint glow of the cellphone seemed to probe

272

him right down to the heart. "She's the best thing to happen to me in a long time."

"Bullshit," the phone hissed back. "There's your gringo jerk talking. I didn't expect that crap from you."

Charlie was genuinely shocked. The distance of the cellphone link had sprung Vel from her usual restraints. The venom across the airwaves stunned him.

"Vel, my relationship with Theresa is my business, and I don't think you can understand -"

"Please, Charlie, can't you see this is just a rebound scenario? I suppose you had every right to seek relief in your distress, and I'm sure she's very adept at that-"

"Is that all you think, Vel?"

"You're degrading yourself! And to continue to do so is worse than bad strategy, it's – you could ruin your life!"

"Theresa has raised up my life, Vel! She's taught me things, she –"

"Oh I'll bet! Christ, every guy I know in L.A. has had someone like her! Sexual priestess with deep inner wisdom - it's a job category out here! Is she into Taoism, Charles?"

"Goodnight, Vel."

"Wait! Charles, there are choices you make that you can't take back. Charles?" He heard her call his name one more time as he snapped off the phone. The firefly blip of the extinguished readout hung tremulously in the darkness.

"You know what's the worst thing about being on welfare?" Theresa snapped. "Well, one of the worst things? You're a dependent, and the state insists on treating you like one. You have to get yourself, and the buses are no fucking picnic, Charlie, to the prescribed check cashing place, to every little interview, to the spot where you and your fellow cases pick the roadsides clean. Actually that's not too bad. Kind of like summer camp, right, police the area? What the hell, honest work. But it doesn't leave you much time for a life of your own - not that you can muster up much of one on the scraps they toss

273

you. If Clara ever stops cutting me slack on the rent – I don't even want to think about it!"

Finally Theresa calmed down, and Charlie concentrated on his driving. He soon spotted the local Taco Bell, just one of hundreds of those fake stone huts with red shingle rooves that dotted the commercial neighborhoods of L.A.

"This is it, Theresa. This is the crack in the wall."

"I can't guarantee anything, Charlie. I had to beg him to come here. You're buying lunch."

Oscar Mejia stood waiting at the front door, a skinny workman with knotted muscles and a hawk-nosed peasant face, the cross on his chest glinting in the sun. He mumbled a refractory greeting and followed them to a corner table with all the cheerfulness of a prisoner in a holding cell. Charlie had come to know that resentment in the eyes of the Berger Princes' maintenance workers when they were bullied to rush a construction job, or made to work overtime - that obdurate up-against-the-wall shuffle that let the bosses know they'd get very little out of the crew that day.

Charlie went up to the counter and got them three tacos and Cokes. He waited for Oscar to consume half his meal in silence, and then, with Theresa helping with her flawless Spanish, he asked Oscar if he and his men had recently moved any files back and forth from the Bernard-Duvall Clinic. Oscar shook his head.

Charlie tried explaining to Oscar that those files might contain pertinent information in a worker's comp case. Information vitally important to the health of injured workers treated by the clinic. People like you, Oscar. Information that might have been criminally tampered with. Oscar finally grunted in reply that he had heard about missing files, but so far as he knew they were destroyed or taken away somewhere. He looked right through Theresa and kept his eye on Charlie.

"If they took them away, where did they take them, Oscar?" He waited tensely as Theresa pleaded with Oscar, then sat back and shook her head.

"Now he says they were destroyed."

"I don't believe it."

"Charlie," Theresa snapped, "isn't that what companies and governments do with incriminating files? Shred them?" She stared grimly down at her taco. "There's no reason to put Oscar through any more of this."

He was appalled as much by her quick surrender as her lack of logic. He leaned towards her and spoke urgently in a whisper. "Theresa, you heard him. First he says they're moved, then he says they're destroyed, he can't even keep the story straight! Besides, Hobart-Riis controls the medical care of every industrially injured person they send to the Bernard-Duvall Clinic for at least ninety days! And when Hobart-Riis has the clinic do a defense exam on a claimant they know they might need the records five years later. So those files are a legal and a money issue to the clinic and to Hobart-Riis. They don't just feed those files into a shredder!"

Oscar was still looking at Charlie, almost goading him to come at him.

"Theresa, just translate, okay?"

He bore down on Oscar and put as stern an edge on his voice as he could. "We're going to find out about those files, Oscar. I'll call you up before the judge. If you hid those files, you could go to jail. Your one chance is now! If you tell us where they are, we'll never bother you again! Help us, Oscar!"

He couldn't stop his final words from being a plea. He knew half of what he was shouting at Oscar was a bluff, and Oscar, if only through Theresa's flat, dispirited translation knew the score. The guy didn't scowl, didn't raise his voice, only repeated his denials, this time with a little more vehemence. He stuck to his story like a mantra. The files were destroyed.

They drove back silently to Theresa's apartment. After Charlie parked his car and got out with her, Theresa told him she wanted to take a stroll down to the Boardwalk.

"Sounds good. Maybe we should wait for the sunset."

"I'd like to be by myself, Charlie."

He felt a flash of resentment. She had her earrings on, so there would be no sex, but the trace of harshness in her voice stung him.

"Something wrong, Theresa? Do you want to talk about what just happened?"

"No, Charlie, it's not that, it's - I've just made some new friends on the Boardwalk, that's all."

"Oh really."

"We all have to show up at the same places to suck on the public tit, so we get to know each other."

"So you don't want to be by yourself?"

Theresa kept icily silent.

Charlie backtracked quickly. "Theresa, all this won't last much longer, you know that."

He caressed her hand as he said it, and he meant the words to comfort her, but she took them dreadfully wrong. " Well while I'm stuck in this crap I might as well make some friends. I know that doesn't register with you, Charlie. You seem to think a lot of people are beneath you. The way you treated Oscar –did you really expect him to cooperate? The man has a family –"

"Theresa I was - I - I got impatient with Oscar, I admit it. But I had to. He was giving me that typical blockhead silent treatment."

"Typical of what, Charlie?"

"Just of -"

"Or should I say what kind of people? My mother's people?"

"Oh, come on, Theresa! I work with your 'mother's people' every day. Don't accuse me of racism. What I meant was - isn't it obvious? He was lying!"

Theresa was suddenly in his face and shouting like a fishwife. "He is not lying! What he's saying might be a big disappointment to you and me, but he's not fucking lying!"

Two in-line skaters, their bare midriffs tanned to a deep mahogany glow, rattled by Charlie with a sneer, and he suddenly knew how ridiculous he looked, standing in his suit and tie being hollered at by a woman in denim shorts near Venice Beach.

"All right, Theresa." He backed off not just out of chagrin, but that astringent fear in the pit of his gut he'd felt not too long ago with Dana. In one searing moment the current of passion could dry up and a woman could be as remote and inaccessible as if she'd never entered your life. "We'll find another way," he muttered, and he reached out desperately for her, his arm tried to coax some answering rhythm from the small of her back. "Just stay with me a little. I don't feel too great right now. Take a walk with me."

In just a week, she had changed - he could almost smell the reluctance in her walk, her smoldering resentment towards him. Or maybe the problem was a vibration he was giving off that she could detect, that transmitted to her his one deep quandary, the issue he couldn't get away from - even Ellis knocking back his third beer had led Charlie's friends in a rousing chant of "Set-tle! Set-tle!" His job was going rotten fast. The Berger Boys had really turned on him - a deal had gone sour and just because Charlie had filed a document a little late (he was almost a one-man office now) they'd become lunatics, accusing him of trying to sabotage their business. And all that time, perhaps because Charlie didn't know how to handle the new third presence in his and Theresa's life - her absolute poverty, the regimen it imposed as surely as if she were a weekend convict - he hadn't even called her.

"Charlie, these people on the Boardwalk - I don't just hang with them for the fun of it. We've got a little barter network going. I can grow some tomatoes and zucchini. This one kid can steal me some shampoo. You have no idea, Charlie - it's illegal to use food stamps for shampoo, toothpaste, toilet paper, even tampons - I'll be running Maxi-Pad debts all over town! Look, Charlie, I don't want to talk about this - I have to go." She turned around and finally let it out. "What the fuck, Charlie, it's all so useless."

"No it isn't, Theresa." He kissed her gently on the forehead. "I'm telling you, one way or another, you won't have to put up with this much longer."

She relented. Her hand floated up and with a rueful smile she gently stroked his temple. "I hope so." He echoed that tenderness, hugging her just enough to let her feel a sympathy between them that could forgive anything and everything. But then, lingering in the embrace, he felt her stiffen, and then he realized - she could feel above his heart that thickness right through the fabric of his jacket. The alarm jolted through him and it sparked her to action. She pulled open his jacket and in a flash had the tape recorder in her hand.

"Theresa, look I - it's just a precaution, but I - I didn't record him!"

Standing there, transfixed by his little machine, she could have been a statue. She hit the rewind button, the motor whirred, and his panic rose.

"Look, I - if he'd started telling me anything I would've turned it on. Theresa, can you blame me? We needed some kind of evidence. Some kind of

277

leverage, okay? But I'm telling you, I didn't record him. There's nothing on that tape, Theresa!"

She clicked the tape to a stop. "You recorded something, Charlie. I can see it."

He tried to throttle back the panic in his voice. "It's not what you think. Will you please believe me - Oscar's not on that tape!"

She hit the play button.

"There were a hell of a lot of them though. During the remodel a whole shelf of them vanished."

"How do you know that, Theresa?"

"I'd taken a big chunk of the past year's medical records and set them aside very carefully in another cabinet. -"

Clicking the button off, she stared at the machine with a relaxed curiosity. With Charlie's recorder balanced in her hand, and the whole moment poised on the edge of an irrevocable explosion, Charlie felt that the recorder, this scene at the beach, their whole life together was suddenly more fragile than one of Theresa's spiderwebs.

"How was I supposed to know, Theresa? How could I predict how I would get to know you, how everything would change for us?"

She almost choked on the words. "After I committed myself to helping you, you kept this? All this time? Why? So you could always make sure I wouldn't have a choice? So you would always have 'leverage' on me? Don't you have faith in anything or anybody?"

"Of course I have faith in you, Theresa. This is just a –"

"And you accuse Oscar of lying? Lying is your every breath, Charlie."

"No, no Theresa, I - I'd forgotten this tape. It was past history. But you have to understand, I've been trying to get the truth here, Theresa! That's all that matters!"

"I'll say this much. You're more slippery than I thought, Charlie. You're not a complete cinch to control."

Her arm rose, ready to shatter the Aiwa on the pavement.

"Theresa! Keep the tape, just don't smash the recorder!"

She stopped, and threw back her head and laughed at him. He tried to acknowledge the absurdity of the moment. "Yeah, I know, how craven was that? But, Theresa, it's part of the work, part of the case..." Feeling a pit of humiliation open up below him, Charlie at last shut up.

"I know. Where would you be if you couldn't skulk around and steal people's words to use against them? Don't worry. I won't hurt your little tool, Charlie."

"Theresa, there's no need for -"

"But I'll keep the tape."

"Of course. You should," he babbled. "Or toss it, it means nothing. I would never do anything to hurt you, Theresa!"

She coldly pointed the tape recorder at him, thumbed the rewind switch, then hit "play." He cringed as his own voice came back at him, frightened, abjectly begging for her vanished love. "Yeah, I know, how craven was that? But, Theresa, it's part of the work, part of the case....Or toss it, it means nothing. I would never do anything to hurt you, Theresa!"

"How do you like it, you bastard?"

She popped out the tape, snatched it, then slapped the tape recorder into his hand so hard it stung him. He grabbed it and instantly glanced at it to see if it was broken - and in that moment Theresa had backed away from him.

"Theresa!"

"How do I know what else you've tape recorded? How do I know anything about you anymore? You don't change, Charlie! You're just another scumbag! Go to hell!"

"Theresa, please, just - just talk to me!" He wanted to run after her, but he knew it wouldn't work - and besides, he could barely stand. The surf was pounding in his head, but he knew that wasn't possible where they were - it was his tinnitus now that counterfeited the sound of a tidal wave that threatened to bury him.

He sat in his car and tried to calm down. The tinnitus subsided, and he could hear a blustery wind scatter palm fronds down a harsh track of sunlight in the alley. The dead leaves blew past the disheveled bums shambling by his car. Charlie suddenly wanted to drive a few blocks down to one of the beachside dives and knock back margaritas until the buzzing in his head stopped. Oh yeah, that's a great idea, he thought. Cap this fabulous day off with a d.u.i. citation. It was best just to get away from here, away from this sunburned, raucous horde that pitched and panhandled and insulted doctors and lawyers like him - a horde that now had claimed Theresa. Maybe, Charlie thought, she was always a part of this ragtag bunch of loafers and misfits - but if she was one of them then what was he, shorn of his old credentials, a hustling, wheedling little bagman for a pair of thieves with an office? And how could he be any more than that without her?

No. There was a limit to his errors. He was now trying to flush out criminals, unearth a crime. Why couldn't Theresa understand that? She was wrong, dead wrong about him.

But that didn't console Charlie as he sat in the car squinting against the glare, hoping that he would see her coming back to make peace with him. The need, the sheer need for her was clawing through his skin. Theresa's appearance in his life had been a total accident, and now his whole world cycled to her rhythm. He spent his days waiting for his nights with her. She had given him so many ways out of the desolation of the past year - and yet it was only a year, and it could be over right now, right this very second.

The noises were back, roaring, whistling, sizzling, a chorus of mockery that whirled around his thoughts. Maybe if he simply concentrated on driving they would relent. He broke free of the alley and drove home as fast as he could, trying to get back in time for happy hour. But the beach traffic was unbelievable and by the time he reached his neighborhood the sun was already setting.

Charlie took a long walk. Above the palm trees the sky faded from streaks of crimson to the color of glowing ashes, as lavender shadows moved across the Santa Monica Mountains. His tinnitus obediently sank down to a whisper in the dusk. Los Angeles sunsets were the most haunting he'd ever known, the way the big sky exhaled its colors into the tenuous branches of the trees, stucco walls retained the pink glimmer of the horizon, and the streetlights began to glow against the last purple radiance of the clouds.

Charlie was calmer now. He'd call Theresa, they'd make up, and he'd devise a new strategy. You don't master baseline play without learning tenacity. His emotions were reduced to a hard pit of grief that he knew he'd just have to live with for awhile. He stared at the darkening sky and the first stars and was so lost in contemplation of them that he didn't even notice the van until the ruddy face leaned out and grinned.

"Charlie?"

"Golan?"

"Pretty night, huh?"

The private eye was in a jovial mood, but alarms rang so sharply in Charlie's brain that his tinnitus woke back up, now a whoosh of a vacuum cracked open and sucking in fear.

"What can I do for you on this pretty night, Rody?"

"You can accept my apology. I'm sorry I have to keep my eye on you all this time."

Charlie tried to lightly tease him out. "You apologize for tailing me by dropping by at my apartment?"

Golan shrugged, heaved open the door so hard the whole van shuddered, and lumbered down to the pavement. With a jerk of his arm he reached down into his hip pocket and Charlie almost staggered from adrenaline shock - but all Golan produced was a hip flask. "You know my assistants and I, when work is over, we like to sip a little of this. Go on, please."

He accepted the flask, took a swig, and savored a pleasant plum wine taste before the kick of the liquor burned him down to his gut.

"Wo! Slivovitz!"

"How the Czechs survived Communism."

"I've been to Prague, you know."

"Oh yeah? Stood on the King Charles Bridge, watched the swans come down the river? Now tell me, are not Prague girls the most beautiful in the world?" Charlie nodded and laughed with relief at having connected so cordially with Golan. Golan took advantage of the moment to throw his arm around Charlie and lead him closer to the van. "You never see my office, do you?"

"Oh! The famous van! Or should I say infamous…"

Charlie knew that to refuse Golan would be not only rude, but also embarrassingly squeamish. Golan read his assent and with one yank of his rough red paw tugged the sliding door back open. Charlie leaped in. As his eyes adjusted to the darkness, the thick shadows that flanked him stirred and took the shapes of two other men.

"I don't think you ever meet my helpers, Ogi and Daniel." Charlie nodded to Ogi, a man with a sleepy, complacent demeanor whose trunk of a chest and massive arms blocked half the van. Daniel, considerably smaller, older, with a gnome-like squint to his eyes, crouched near the driver's seat. It was suddenly stifling in this little Russian encampment and Charlie changed his mind about staying. He was about to excuse himself when the door jolted shut behind him.

"These windows, you see, are one-way of course. No one sees or hears nothing inside here. And on this shelf we have our Nagra, our little mixer."

Charlie praised the complexity of the setup, and he was genuinely impressed that Golan could run more than one mike out of the van, that he had shotgun and omni-directional as well as radio mikes - he marveled at all of it as cheerfully as he could to keep down the quaver in his voice.

"So, Charlie, now you have some respect. You are smart, use the kopf, I know, but maybe you should appreciate things that I and Ogi and Daniel do more."

"I never took you for granted, Rody. You know how many times I've told you, all of you - you deliver."

Golan pulled a folding wooden panel down from the wall and sat on it gently. The bolts squeaked from his sheer muscular density. The man's gut, enormous without being the least bit soft, consumed the light all around him. Golan knew he was crowding Charlie, and knew exactly what Charlie was feeling as he made his approach. There was always that first moment when the subject knew his punisher, became intimate with the fear as it crept through his flesh. Americans - white Americans - were a little slow of course, stupefied by all their years of peace and television. Czechs and Russians knew it right away. The stinking little intellectuals there shuddered to attention at a moment like this, they knew in their history the smell of the hard sweat of the man who worked with his fists, the dank odor of their own piss, the grunts and howls they shared.

"Rody, anyway I - I gotta take off. I'm meeting a friend. But I appreciate the tour."

"Easy, Charlie. Right now I am on my own time. I do not work for you."

" Rody, I – you know we may be working together again soon," Charlie lamely improvised. "About to join forces again."

"I hope so. Problem is now, way I see - you stumble. Bump your head on something. You get a little woozy, a little meshuggeh, so this thing you bump your head on seem like great big wall when it's just a tiny little brick."

The dread sank in with a harder punch than the Slivovitz. Golan knew all about his meeting with Oscar. He had to somehow put him at ease, and lie, lie his way out of this trap, perhaps by reminding Golan of a political reality he could understand. "Golan, I don't know what you're trying to say and to do here, but look, you don't want me to settle with Hobart-Riis - and that's what my lawyer and I are talking about right now - you don't want me to come back and have a chat with Ted and tell him you're some kind of - loose cannon, are you? I mean, if something's bothering you - hey, all the times we worked together, I'm sure we can talk it out."

Golan glowered at him so hard Charlie had to steel himself to keep from shaking. But then Golan looked down at his knees, and finally spread his hands in a gesture of resignation. "You know, I think you're right. Now it's late. We need to talk, but we have that talk some other time. For now, we understand each other. Ogi, get up and let Mr. Solomon leave."

Ogi shifted to the side with a roll of his haunches. Charlie took a step to get around him and as he did Ogi flexed his back and a massive stone blasted through Charlie's rib cage. The force of the blow rammed him against the wall, his breath locked up on him.

"Oh God! Ogi, clumsy idiot, look what you did! I'm so sorry!"

The pain knifed through Charlie's guts. He couldn't believe how his body crumbled before it, how the taste of bile invaded the hot space of the agony and choked him. Was it an elbow, a fist? One effortless blow and he lay on the floor like jelly, and at the thought of another one a helpless moaning leaked through his gasps.

Ogi inspected him with a clinical detachment, while Golan fussily told him to relax, keep breathing. The pain still coiled like a rope in his chest, but at last he felt the air make it to his lungs. Still, he had no speech, no words for these apes glowering at him out of the darkness.

"Just lie here, Charlie. You be okay. This was so stupid accident."

"...no accident," Charlie finally gasped. "No accident, Golan."

"Charlie, what you say to me? I only try to help." He looked to his men, shrugged his shoulders ruefully, and then turned on Charlie. "What is this with you? Where is your mind, Charlie?" Golan's voice rose, and Charlie moaned, his momentary bravery snuffed out as he grappled with his terror for every breath. "I don't believe it, Charlie! How you say this to me! How you do this to your employer? How you do this to people who pay good money to you! You are on drugs? I can't believe it! Employers have no rights in this country! Someone is lazy and is fired and sues! Some bitch thinks the boss likes her ass, looks at her funny, doesn't matter if it's the President she sues! But employer he has no rights! Nothing! They hire you to help them! They give you opportunities - you get condo in Beverly Hills! Little apparatchnik like you! And now you want to poke around and poke around and destroy your employer? And you think you can destroy me too?"

"No, Rody, Rody, please - " He could feel the next blow being readied for him, he was almost crying, about to vomit, when Golan crouched down next to Charlie and patted his shoulder. "I understand. This Theresa woman - she is something. Real meat on the bones, eh, and smart. Knows things, eh?" The mention of Theresa finally prompted his goons to lascivious mutterings and laughter. "I can understand. Very, very nice.. But not worth losing it all, boychuk. Forget this," he pointed to the groin, and then tapped his head. "This is what you use, Charlie. The kopf, eh? Remember."

The door slid open, and moonlight struck the metal floor of the van, chill and precise on his rumpled suit pants, his legs supine before him. Charlie hastily pulled himself up and cried out from the caked bruises on his ribs. Golan helped him out of the van, again apologizing profusely for the accident.

Tonight the usually noisy building was silent. Charlie no longer wanted to get a drink, or listen to music, or even sleep. As he lay on his bed with a cold pack on his chest, the darkness flowed over him and brought a creeping paralysis that he almost welcomed. No emotion or desire could prick him now. At the bottom of the night, he would do what he must to breathe.

-10-
the west stops here

The children spotted the young deer. They crept towards it through the scrub pines, the massive purple bluffs of the Grand Canyon behind them, and as they inched ever closer, even if the deer would never let them touch its nose or its soft fur, their faces were bursting with happiness. Bert was particularly thrilled with this spread of pictures. It took up half the wall that Charlie's desk had once faced.

"Same old same old," Bert had told him, with all the cordiality he could scrape up, "some new faces, lot of activity." The tone was reassuring without a hint of irony. Yes, Charlie, I know you'll be pleased that since we kicked your ass out we've been doing just fine. Charlie accepted the man's sickening blandishments with an air of noblesse oblige. After all, as Worcek and Vel had both told him, he should consider that he won. Sixty cents on the dollar - not too many workers comp victims settle for that much.

And to top it off, he didn't even have to journey to the Van Nuys court to sign off on the settlement - no, they'd extended him the courtesy of a meeting in Century City, his old stomping grounds. The parties quickly adjourned to the District Manager's office. Shackleton's mahogany and oak enclave once again exuded its comforting solidity.

Charlie read the settlement papers. How do you measure it all? The poverty, humiliation, nightmares? How do you put a dollar value on such a plunge? And that final loathsome blow from Golan's thug – how do you factor that in? Had his colleagues themselves given the word? No, prim Maxine, starchy Shackleton, even Bert Silver, he couldn't figure them giving that order to Golan. Oscar, the hard-shelled mestizo poking his head out towards Charlie with nothing but resentment, Oscar had told Golan and Golan had made the decision without any intercession by the authorities. The slippery tactics of his former bosses were more geared to persuasion than terror. Straight fear and straight hatred had attacked him that night.

Charlie eyeballed the papers quickly. There were no surprises - the terms were just as Worcek and Vel had spelled them out over the phone. There was the lump sum, and the clause in which the applicant dismissed with prejudice the 132A serious and willful misconduct petitions against Hobart-Riis, as well as the wrongful termination petitions. The Compromise and Release in the matter of Charles Solomon vs. Hobart-Riis Insurance, Inc. was as it should be.

I've lost my inside person.

He let the pen pause in his hand for a minute. He could feel the watchful eyes of Worcek and Vel triangulating him. Then he looked at the other side, all those well scrubbed, professionally poised, but, just for one moment, itchily nervous bodies. Could one of them have told Golan, given his ordeal the final turn of the screw? For twenty-two thousand dollars, was he signing an agreement with people who consciously tortured him? What would Brandon say? Theresa? Sheila Reed?

He fired off his signature with one quick stroke of the pen.

Smatterings of conversation smoothed over a breakup of a meeting that, for everyone present, could not come too soon. Shackleton expressed gratitude that these difficult matters had been resolved, then sat back with a smile-on-hold that was an arrow pointing Charlie to the door. Worcek pleaded her busy schedule - yet there was a moment when Charlie, escorting her out the door, received a quick, fervent hug. "We'll be seeing you around the quad soon, Charlie, right?" Charlie patted her on the back. "Great work, counselor."

And then came one last afterthought of business, as Maxine Bunning not quite accidentally bumped into him in the hall.

"Well, Charlie, that wasn't so bad, was it?"

"Are you referring to the past hour, or the past year?"

Maxine didn't even quiver, and Charlie briefly reproached himself. She'd anticipated his spite, and he'd delivered it, with all the class of a dog salivating at a bell. He would try in his last few steps out the door to be civil.

"I'm glad this is all behind us, Maxine."

286

"Something to think about, perhaps, when the smoke clears, is that position in our San Francisco office. Don't say anything now, of course, in fact, maybe for a few days just put it out of your head, but it's yours for the taking, Charlie."

He realized how much discomfort this conversation was putting her through. "Thank you, Maxine. I'll give it serious thought."

"You know, I've been in this business seventeen years, now, and it still never seems to amaze me how these battles spring up and go way too far, as if they had a life of their own. But perhaps now we can all take a breath and assess the situation for what it is. We all know what you're capable of at your best, Charlie. And hopefully relocation isn't such an issue now that you rent."

No sooner were those words out than Maxine delicately repressed an inward shudder - yep, amazing how easy it is to be tactless in this kind of conversation. Charlie put an end to it quickly, with a bland goodbye and a quick march to the elevator.

He passed Silver's office. Funny thing about a space, it will always retain its old outlines if you're familiar with it, suspend you in double vision. There was his door, his desk, phantom furniture hovering just past the doorway where Vel stood listening to an unseen Bert Silver's parting words. They exchanged glances, and Charlie stood and waited for her to conclude the meeting.

Charlie walked Vel out to the west end of the blank white stone lozenge of a plaza that surrounded the building. They found the space oddly deserted for a weekday, and lingered by the geodesic fountain. Charlie searched for conversational words to lubricate the moment, but all that came to him was the first thing on both their minds.

"Maxine made the San Francisco offer."

"Take it, Charles. You know, the system is a lot less - abrasive up there."

"That's what I hear. And I am pretty unencumbered at this point."

Vel seemed to aim her glance deliberately at the pinwheels of water. "What about Ms. Calder?"

287

"That seems to have run its course. We're not speaking. I mean, her phone's been disconnected, so I figure if she hasn't made an effort to call me back...."

"I can't exactly say I'm sorry, Charles." Her scrutiny became, for a moment, compassionate. "Although I am sorry you were hurt."

"Less hurt than helped, Vel." Charlie squinted at the blinding white flagstones. "Theresa called it - she said maybe you try and use each other in the best possible way and get away clean."

Vel sat down on the black marble rim of the basin, as if the spray, though carefully engineered to not escape the fountain's radius, could cool her somehow. "There is love, Charles."

"Yeah? And when does that kick in?"

"Later. With someone else."

Charlie grinned knowingly at his friend. "Yep, you're doing that Mexican Zen thing with me now, Vel." He checked his watch. "Time to move on. I've still got to cram in a quick lunch and get back to work."

"I forgot about that dreadful job of yours."

"Looks like I will too very soon."

"You should celebrate. Go tie one on with your friends."

"Oh, I already did. Post-Theresa. Trying to forget, I suppose"

"Well - time to descend into that wonderfully confusing parking structure of yours."

He reached for her hand and clasped it hard. "I don't often find myself thanking opposing counsel, but-"

She squeezed his hand back, and laid her other hand, with almost a caress, on top of it. There was a small catch in her voice. "Go to San Francisco, Charles." And before he could respond to her she gave him her insouciant little wave and was smartly escaping across the plaza.

Frisco. City by the bay. Descending with measured grace down its old hills. Backed by skyscrapers, ringed with cypresses, veiled with fog and ocean surf, on its best days luminous with intelligence under pearl-blue western skies. A city with buses where everyone has a book in hand. Berkeley, Chez Panisse, Vanessi's, Chinatown.

288

Why not? Just thinking of it made his day roll on ball bearings. Of course, it was an excellent day in any case, what with calling Dr. Laningham to inform him he was leaving the worker's comp therapy group, and reporting to the Bergers to tell them this would be his last day at work. They subjected him to as many insults as possible during the eight hours, and shoved as much shitwork as they could onto his desk, but Charlie sailed through the spreadsheets, the threats from tenants and lawyers, the letters he had to write refusing to pay "outrageous" bills.

But finally, when they told him his sudden departure would make them look like schmucks, the words leaped out of Charlie. "That would be like making turds look like shit."

Seth eyed him with contempt. "Your dad is going to be so disgusted with you."

"At my recovery of my lost income? No, I think, overall, my father will approve. See, I settled my case today. Yes, Seth, Gregory, the laws sleep, but they never die. As I'm sure one day you'll find out, when you're in the prison bathroom on a double-date."

"Get the fuck out!"

"Yes I will, Seth. Soon as I do one thing. Get a check from you for the week's work. Otherwise you'll be speaking to my attorney." He let the pause have its proper weight. " Me."

"Theresa? Is that you? Where are you?"

"On the corner. Near a grocery store in Venice."

Even through the dead weight of his nap still upon him in the twilit room, he could feel the yearning for her clench at him so hard he wanted to drive to her that very minute. But the register of her voice disheartened him - she was in her taut, tight-lipped, dismissive mode.

"Charlie, I know you're pretty angry with me right now."

What was the right thing to say? What did that matter? "No, I thought a lot about what happened. I understand why you said what you said."

"I don't." There was a long beat of traffic rumble, the blare of a car horn. "I was a total shit to you. My judgment goes all to hell when I - I think things are being hidden from me. Listen, you have time to come over tonight,

289

maybe have a little talk?" A passing car pinched out her voice, but he thought he heard a dry chuckle, and then "....Ignatius said never change a resolution in a moment of despair."

"What?"

"St. Ignatius." When she repeated the quote again he thrilled to the meaning he dug out of it. She was admitting she was wrong when she'd changed her mind about pursuing the case, but especially about him. She was coming back to him.

"That fight we had. I'm not real proud of myself. I never meant for things to end that way, Charlie."

"No, of course not. I've got some very good news, Theresa. I have a way out of this for both of us."

"That's good, Charlie. I…" and the roar of a truck crunched down on her voice. He heard her quick goodbye and then the click of the receiver. As he clung to the phone in the silence, his head rang, not with tinnitus, but with a burst of joy. He knew San Francisco would now no longer be a blind retreat, but the beginning of a whole new life for him.

The cold pink clouds drifted in from the beach as night fell. They seemed to wear a penumbral charge from all the electricity that pulsed beneath them. New Mexico clouds were so different: their turbid oneness with the night sky broken by pale caverns of light from the moon. Shadowed with the wolf howl, laced with scents rising from the dust. Inviting all the senses to work as one, not to penetrate but to echo with that mystery.

Theresa had once thought there were no mysteries in L.A., had even embraced that as a cure for her drifting, treacherous hunger. But no, there were mysteries in this tarred and tainted city, and the biggest one was herself. Maybe that wasn't so strange. The city invited you to fragment, turn inside out, and then recognize yourself once you could only recognize yourself as lost.

Where had the desire to surrender grown from her appetite for control? What morality had stabbed through her cynicism? And at the axis of all these upheavals, a slim pallid young man who reminded her of the fragility and the remoteness of her own father.

That would really suck if all those pop psychologists were right. Women are always looking for the father, especially when the father had stunted their love and ruined their lives. Driving down the abuse trail, playing the old tapes. No, she thought, Charlie was not like her father. There was a warmth there, and a finely honed sensibility - and a sinewiness in the clinch, not that she could ever exactly know that about her father. About all that Charlie really shared with her dear old clueless weatherman dad was that blank abstractness around the eyes when he was making a decision.

And she needed that abstractness now. Just as she had once needed Charlie's empathy, now she needed Charlie's coolheadedness – and forgiveness. He had a wisdom beyond his years, even if he didn't know it, that she would have to tap into now. To help her figure out how to end all this so it would be right for Sheila and the other victims, right for Charlie, right for her.

Theresa passed the little park that sloped down to the boulevard, its lone elm tree steepling towards a crescent moon. Some vagabond from the beach waved heartily to her. Blues guitar scratched the chilly air from a nearby window. It suddenly occurred to Theresa that maybe she could never leave Venice, its arrhythmia of languor and madness set off by the balm of the distant surf, the deep purples of the morning glories and princess flowers that wreathed the courtyards' wooden fences, the moonlight laying down pathways in the alleys.

As always when she entered her court (funny thing, to name a tiny street, nothing more than a lane really, a court), she checked out her surroundings - here was where the visibility of the boulevard ended and the encroachment of the shadows began. She later realized that out of the corner of her eye she'd noted the van, for no other reason than that she hated the damn things, utility vehicles, vans, those big, stupid, gas-guzzling clunkers with none of the heart of your basic pickup truck. But at that point what really irked her was the racket of some kids partying just across the way, the grunge-punk-ska-whatever blasting in the alley, the cars illegally parked everywhere. Oh well, Venice. It's not like she and Charlie were going to go to sleep in an hour. In fact, she had a yen for coffee as strong as she could make it. She had decisions to make that could take all night.

When Clara was gone the rear entrance to the building had such a cheerless silence. The woman's natural gaiety was the reason that the apartment Theresa rented from her really felt like a home. She needed to dispel that silence, rush to the living room to turn on the music, start the cappuccino machine bubbling. She slipped inside and shut the door behind her, and very quickly in the darkness she knew that everything was different. Maybe it was the pocket of stifled silence from the finch's cage, or it was impossible not to sense the others' bulk, the alien breathing, but she knew what would happen even before the rough paw crushed her mouth and the gun was in her back.

Don't whimper into that acrid sweaty hand. What was the purpose? No choice but to move to the others' design (there was a second, she could sense him). They knew the geography, the pistol augered her spine towards the bedroom, her footsteps were like a child's, the blinds in her room were shut, all was ready for them. She could only coil down inside the dull earthy mass of herself like a snake, in the icy shadow - don't panic, don't panic, keep thinking, keep feeling, it's all falling apart in the howl of the darkness but stay intact - but she could feel that shell of flesh and muscle that was all she was now lose its power, as she was driven into a deeper and deeper hole. But in the burrow - oh god, where was it? - the footing, the fortress, the rock. Somewhere to be cornered, please God.

Hand whipping off her mouth, the wrenching of it spun her around and she was looking at the gun, the black skin-tight mask. Oh God, he knew how to do this. Place to stand, run - where was it? The hand was so quick ripping her blouse open. The cold metal pressed against her cheek froze her, and now as his fingers probed her belly, she knew some blow was coming, probably with the gun barrel, to get her down. Palpitating under his fingers, she could feel her damn sob begin, the helpless oh please get it over quickly - but suddenly the footing was there, in the quaking bowels of that hole, a tic of a smile, then a lascivious grin stealing over her face.

Theresa stared at the eyeholes in the mask. She whispered "You better be good."

Hand stopped. Eyes, somewhere, wavered - the whole evil metabolism thrown off, even as she found the pivot and she was whipping her knee and her leg up hard as she could. With the thick, curdling crunch of the impact the man screamed some curse in Russian and the gun was deflected and her fingers jabbed right for the eyeholes. Now there was more howling and a space to move and she hit as she'd been told not with her fist but her forearm and down he crashed. A view of the door - she hurtled towards it screaming for help. Her hair stopped her. The shock of the pain tore at her scalp - she flew backwards and the wall smashed the side of her face. Whirling around dizzily she saw the huge bulk before her and caught the blow right through every organ in her chest.

Her knees went like water to the floor and she wailed like a baby from the pain - oh how could anyone do that to her - but she knew to fight for breath, she needed it to scream again, she tried to crawl to her feet right up to the moment the back of his huge hand caught her mouth and smashed so hard through her jaws and her skull that she grayed out and sank to the floor. The footsteps doubled but there was nothing she could do as what she thought was the little man now kicked her in the ribs repeatedly. Her bones were going, snapping like harpstrings. She huddled into a ball to try and at least muffle the kicks. They stopped, but now the darkness fell harder than any blow, that grunting mammoth bulk was there again between her and the little man's shoes and a much stronger hand was on her mouth now, big as a boulder. She tried to bite it even with one of her teeth gone but it was no use, her skirt was torn away, she was hoisted by the belly like a rag doll and crunched against her own wall. With her last strength she tried to turn her legs, her haunches, her insides to stone, but it couldn't be stopped, the backs of her legs were crushed, and now it was piercing her, she had to open or it would tear her to pieces.

The walls were thundering. A heartbeat of sound resolved to clamoring voices, and though she couldn't raise her head to see the eyes trying to look through the blinds, she knew someone had heard her. A flashlight's beam snaked through and distracted her attacker, and her hand found space to yank at a table. The hand flinched off her mouth as the vase rolled to the floor and shattered like a thousand alarms.

She couldn't recognize her own bellow as she unleashed it but now there were shouts she understood, "What's going on? Are you all right?" and with grunts and hisses in that Slavic-sounding language again the weight was off her. Her door blasted open to the cool air. She tried to run after them but

293

her chest puckered in a hollow place, and her leg collapsed. Three-legged, misshapen from injury, she staggered out the door, ricocheted off the bungalow wall but kept in forward motion, howling with shouts and obscenities for their blood like the wolves when she was a child. She could see the mob in the light, the surfer kids, they all spurted out of the house towards the fleeing thugs, but the big man shouldered them off and then that little bastard fired the gun. The crack of it shook the alley, another blow to her crumpling insides. The kids in the crowd ducked, recoiled, fled. Theresa let herself fall to the cold pavement, slid against a clapboard wall, and at last the crowd's help could receive her, naked, bleeding and torn.

Unshaven. Unsleeping. Charlie felt like he'd been driving the freeway forever. Ever since, dressed in his new soft cotton shirt, slacks and shoes, hair carefully moussed just like the old days, he'd turned into the alley and almost run into the police lights.

Welfare case. Had to take her to County. Nothing else to say, nothing to tell him. Who are you? Next of kin?

"Russian men in a van...that's what I heard..."

Turning off into the slouching dark streets of all Los Angelinos' nightmares. Somewhere in his awful trance he'd come off the freeway and forgot the main boulevard. He dared not stop to check the map. All he could see, it seemed, was the iron gates and bristling wire of South Central. Stucco marked off with graffiti, feeble security lights everywhere and the curbs patrolled by packs of kids giving the eye to a cruising Infiniti. Low-riding car almost hit him, Christ, no accidents here. Find the main road. Copper chopper speared the alleys with its searchlight. He bore down in his mind on Theresa alone with her wounds in some hideous emergency room, and a tenacious calm stole upon him. Nothing could touch him. At last he was off the narrow streets, heading back to County General.

He found the monolith of the hospital in the haze of the acrid night, tried to find a space in the sodium-lit runnels of the parking lot, almost hitting another car - squeal of brakes, panicked family behind a window slashed with light. Emergency, emergency everywhere.

The room he ran to was one great sullen abattoir wrapped in shades of pain. Unlike all the other waiting rooms he'd known, this one was prodded to feverish life by trauma and terror; there were streaks of blood on shirtfronts, gnarled specters of agony in fitful movement, and that awful self-consuming smell and unending groan of humanity using the last of its strength. The walls were a dull green, the faces gray or black. Maybe she'd been taken inside, rushed to the head of the line somehow. But he couldn't be sure once he saw, reaching back into the pale glaucous blur of a fluorescent corridor, an endless line of gurneys.

They seemed to stretch on forever, white-sheeted jackstraw beds in a hall thronged by doctors, nurses and orderlies, who strode past the moans of the waiting patients with a well-crafted purposefulness. Hulks under the sheets. Tubed, bloody, strapped, caged, or just sitting there, head dropping down, lips working in a distended purple mouth, arm jackknifed to the side - it took him a long moment to even recognize her.

When he did he realized Theresa was staring at him. She had registered his horror, but she merely nodded as he took her hand. She didn't cry, didn't talk; obviously that was an excruciating effort to her. Finally she raised the hand of her uninjured arm to cover her face.

"It's okay, Theresa. It's okay."

She hung stupefied in the pain and grief. Charlie found it unendurable, and he finally couldn't stop himself from asking questions.

"Have they treated you at all, Theresa?"

She drew a long bitter breath. "Need a cast...for my ribs. Hurt like hell. Need to be examined."

"Who did this to you?"

"Russian - I think that's what they spoke...they had masks...I told the police, Charlie..."

"Oh god, did they -"

"No...it's okay...I stopped them...told the police everything I knew. "

He realized she was both reassuring him and begging him to be silent, and he had no choice, for his horror was overwhelming him. Russian men in a van. His next thought brought him down like a blow, his knees sagging as he bent over the bed in the midst of that corridor of misery.

"Theresa, if you'd never known me this would never have happened to you."

The shirt clung to Charlie in the tracks of his sweat. He'd sat in the car in the same brackish pools of perspiration ever since last night. God how the sun was beating down today. "Going to be a scorcher," Shackleton always said like clockwork. Going to be a scorcher in Century City.

The receptionist at Hobart-Riis, who had so often smiled at him, and had once shaken his hand, was a different creature now, half out of her chair to stop him. He demanded to see Shackleton and Silver. Police business, he babbled, figuring it would scare her, and it did - the stout entrance door with the huge metal lock issued its magisterial click.

His head was throbbing from sleeplessness. They'd released Theresa just before dawn, after checking her for injuries to her spleen and ovaries. They told her she had been extraordinarily brave and tough in preventing the rape, and also lucky - if the blow to the face had been angled differently he'd have shattered her jaw.

Charlie had driven her home, expecting her to be so frightened that she would inevitably ask him to sleep on the couch and stay with her. Instead, with a grim determination, she said she absolutely needed to spend the rest of the morning recuperating alone. Besides, she had to go to the police. She asked Charlie to come back late in the afternoon after she'd at least tried to get some sleep, and she told him he should also go back to bed.

Instead he was back at the office.

He broke right into the meeting - Shackleton chatting with Silver, coffee and Postex on the table, the morning pleasantries savagely interrupted.

"Why did you have them keep tailing us? I signed the goddamn settlement! What was the point of it? Tailing Theresa? You opened the door for the attack! It's on your head! On your head, you bastards!"

"Charlie," Shackleton shouted, genuinely bewildered, but already dreading his news, "what are you talking about?"

"What do you know? You don't know anything! Nobody knows anything, right? Deny, deny, deny!"

"Charlie, calm down," Bert hissed. "What exactly happened?"

296

What enraged him most was that Shackleton had no doubt forgotten Golan was still tailing Theresa. He knew from having worked these offices, slogged through the blizzard of paperwork every day, that you could forget a deposition, even a trial, let alone calling a tail job off. They had forgotten Theresa into hell. "You want to know, Ted? Why don't you pull in Golan? Question him yourself? Or just go down to the police station and talk to Theresa! About who attacked her and who sent them there!"

Bert hadn't forgotten. Bert knew exactly what Charley was saying, and what had to be said back to him. "Charlie, you're saying Rody Golan's associates attacked Theresa Calder? Do you have any evidence of that?"

"Theresa told the police. They were in a van. Speaking Russian, for Chrissake!"

"Do you have any hard evidence that their van was in that neighborhood and that they attacked Theresa Calder?"

"Go to hell, Bert!"

"Charlie, I'm going to give you a break because of what happened. Go home, and take a good long rest before you say or do something you may regret."

"Yeah, Bert? What the hell, in for a penny, in for a pound. So tell me, was it you who told Golan to give us both a little scare? Is that it? Is that it, Bert?"

Bert glanced at Shackleton, and received permission to escalate his warning.

"What we gave, Charlie, we can take away."

On the way to his car, Charlie yanked out his cellphone. Oblivious to the office personnel watching him, he punched in the number Theresa had told him, and asked to speak to Oscar Mejia.

"Yes?"

"Oscar, this is Charlie Solomon. Two men tried to rape and kill my friend Theresa last night."

"Que?", the gruff voice answered. But Charlie was sure he understood him.

"Two Russian men. In a van. I wanted to make sure you knew that."

He shut off the phone.

When Charlie came to the bungalow to meet Theresa she was moving stiffly and slowly on the axis of her cracked ribs and yet she insisted on taking a walk with him.

They headed down the long crescent beach from the Venice Pier towards Marina Del Rey. For a moment she seemed a much older woman to Charlie, the bruises like a crust of extra jowls on her face, her long denim dress swelling over her torso where they'd taped up her ribs. She steered herself gingerly over the sand, her arm raised over her sunglasses when the light glared her way. They had to walk slowly by the pounding surf, and Theresa couldn't dart ahead of the rising tide - she let the waves rush over her sandaled feet, and finally Charlie took off his sneakers and rolled up his pants' legs so he could keep walking alongside her. Contemplating her sudden slowness and fragility, he felt whole new emotions well up inside him, and cherished her more powerfully than ever before.

"I just wish - maybe if I'd been there."

"Oh, Christ, Charlie, be grateful you weren't."

He remembered Ogi's offhand blow that had almost caved in his chest. "Yeah. Yeah, you're right." He stared down at his toes as they squished into the soft lip of the beach.

"You settled, didn't you Charlie?"

Charlie couldn't quite bring himself to answer. "I gave them hell, you know. My old bosses. I told them they were responsible."

She looked at him with both tenderness and mild annoyance. "But you didn't endanger your settlement, I hope?"

"Well, Silver made some sort of smartass remark, but no, that's carved in stone. What had been on the table was a job offer in San Francisco."

She laughed and shook her head. "No shit. After all that."

"But I'm not going to take it. Not now."

"Are you gonna be okay, Charlie?"

He explained to her the details of the settlement, and how the amount of money, while not huge, would certainly keep him solvent and give him latitude to prepare his next move. His words quavered now, and not just because the offshore breeze whipping past them swept back into his throat - his mind was elaborating the businesslike details of his future even as something else was mounting within him, a great dare, his heart on the line. He kept talking as dryly as he could about how he would continue to help Worcek informally with Brandon's case. "Once I turn down their job offer, Hobart-Riis has no hold over me. And I want to help keep that case going." Theresa stood by the surf as it curled down the tracks of the late afternoon sun, and gently smiled at him. "But the main thing is - you don't have to live like this, Theresa. You deserve so much more and —and now I can give you at least - a place to recover. A little support. Not that you couldn't do it yourself, but..." He walked up to her, wanting to hug her but knowing her injuries made that impossible, so he laid his hands gently on her shoulders. "Let's just be together. Let's be together all the time. The adventure continues, right? I mean - I love you. I know it now. It could really work, Theresa."

Theresa's lips pursed, and for a moment Charlie thought that perhaps she was going to start weeping, but instead she just reached out and stroked his hair. "Do you feel responsible for me too, Charlie? Is that it?"

"No, it isn't that. I want you, Theresa, and I want you with me."

"Bit of an age difference, you know. I mean, over the long term."

"Hey, just think of me as your boy toy." He took her hand. "I don't care about that, Theresa."

"Charlie, I still think you feel responsible for me. Sheila had that too, you know. That sense of responsibility. But she didn't back it up. She was too scared."

"What do you mean?"

"She knew that whole thing with the missing files - that your instincts were absolutely right, Charlie. She had a feeling there was some improper procedure going on. She told me – but she didn't dare speak up. And then they destroyed her anyway. I think that was one thing in the back of her mind when she pulled the trigger."

Charlie was thrilled to have been granted that insight by Theresa. He also realized that they'd been on the brink of the deepest intimacy, and she'd stepped back. But she was still working intently with him on the case. From that tenacious bond other, deeper bonds would grow.

299

"When you came to me that night, Charlie - it was like you were coming with the little bit of courage Sheila never had. You were doing the rest of the job for her, Charlie."

"Finishing the point."

Theresa smiled tenderly at him. "Yes. That's it. And you drew me to you, Charlie, because you were right, and you knew it, and I needed to hear that. So one thing I am going to do is follow up with what we've always talked about. I've written down in detail everything I remember observing at that clinic, everything I know. I'm sure you can compose it in the form of an affidavit, do what needs to be done."

She pulled away from him and gazed at the breaking waves. Sandpipers raced the retreating slick of the water just past her still figure. Charlie was puzzled but something kept him from following to look at her face. "Theresa? The only thing is - if it comes to a trial, an affidavit carries much less weight than testimony from someone who shows up for cross-examination. Or why not at least have Worcek depose you? I mean, we can script the questions she'll ask from what you wrote down. What's wrong with that, Theresa?"

He could see her lower her head and rub her eyes in the haze of the sea spray. She turned to him with another kind of smile, lip trembling, helplessly asking forgiveness. "The reason I need to give you an affidavit is that I won't be here. I'm moving away, Charlie, and I'm never coming back."

He strode up to her, and the icy water sucking at his feet cut through to his bones. "What? Where are you going?"

"Smyrna, Georgia. If you can believe that. Well - at least it's warm. My big sister's willing to take me in for awhile. Hey, that's what a big sister's for, right? Besides - I need some kind of home, and L.A. - I just happened to come here. This is not a place to happen to come to, Charlie."

A plea, a prayer was clawing up through Charlie's throat, robbing him of his control, but he didn't care. "Theresa, you've got to listen to me. Welfare, all that shit - that's over! Right now! I can borrow money until my check arrives, and -"

"Oh, Charlie, I could've gotten that help a long time ago."

There was sorrow in her reply, but also a bitterness that left an opening, and sparked in him one last attempt to prove her wrong. "Theresa, was this

300

what you were going to talk to me about? When you called me from that pay phone? You talked about not changing a resolution in a moment of despair."

"I meant the investigation, Charlie. I meant the case. For awhile I thought that maybe I also meant staying here, but –"

"You do mean it, Theresa, you do mean staying here. You can't leave now. You've fought the bastards off. They're not going to touch you any more. And we can still win this case, and then make a life for ourselves here, where you can be - independent, not owing your sister, not owing anyone. Theresa, you said you would stick with this! To the end of the line!"

"Charlie, you're not going to judge me, are you. Because that's one of the things I loved about you - that you never judged me."

Her low, quiet plea for his compassion at last wrenched the words out of him. "Didn't you hear me say it, Theresa? I love you very, very much. Please stay."

She stroked his face and shook her head.

"My plane ticket's for tomorrow night, Charlie. I sent my things ahead to Georgia."

"So quick?"

"Not much to pack."

In a reflex he couldn't control he spurned her. He trudged up the beach, for one moment so infuriated that he could have thrown on his sneakers and raced back to his car. But in that same instant he felt a lethargy that robbed him even of the strength to climb the barrier of sand raised up to protect Ocean Avenue from the surf. He sat heavily down against one of the ridges that caught like a blanket the last warmth of the sun. Theresa walked up to him and carefully lowered herself beside him.

They sat long enough for gulls and terns to rest on the sand over their heads. The sun began its descent in a sky that was a wonderful soaring blue in the wake of a broken storm. Clouds lit with washes of silver opened up and swirled like the lunettes Charlie remembered on the ceilings of baroque churches, where God and his angels reached down and touched humanity.

Charlie's feet dried and chilled in the breeze and he put his socks and sneakers on, while Theresa drew her knees up and rubbed her toes to warm them. "This will be a gorgeous sunset. You know that's one of my first

301

memories? Walking out in the sunset in New Mexico? I remember the stones around the house turned blue. Blue stones."

"Blue stones. That's beautiful, blue stones."

Charlie looked down at the sand, and Theresa reached over to him with her good arm and drew his face to hers. He fought to keep his emotions in check, and her voice, so low and firm, was the restraint he needed. "Listen, Charlie. Listen to me. I know this feels either like something you did wrong or like a betrayal. It's not anything like that, Charlie. You and I just have to be in different places."

"We don't, Theresa, we -"

"Listen. There's something Jesus said that I learned in catechism that never left me. 'I would thou were hot or cold. If thou art lukewarm, I will spew thee out of my mouth.' If you're hot or cold, how do you feel? How do you really feel? What do you really, really want to do? That's what matters. At first I thought I wanted to leave L.A. because I was in despair - but I made the decision to leave after I fought for my life, Charlie. That's when you're pretty damn hot and cold at the same time. And it's not because of something you did or you didn't do or could or couldn't do, Charlie. I have to go."

"I'll go too."

"And do what? What the hell are you going to do in Smyrna, Georgia?" For the first time she was angry at him, but it passed quickly, and then he felt her lips against his, tenderly giving him love and taking it away at the same time. "You have to stay." She brushed her lips against his cheek. "You've got a job to do, remember? That's what you said when I grabbed your tape recorder, and you were right. And you've got the balance for it, Charlie. Never forget it. You've got - the ethics, you've got the strength, you've got work to do and you have to back it up, Charlie, and just - don't turn off to it, no matter how betrayed you feel, if people betray you because they're that way, or maybe they're just people who have no choice. And whatever you do, don't be lukewarm. Do it completely. You promise me that, Charlie."

"Yes, Theresa. I promise."

"Look over the ocean."

Charlie turned to face a sunset that had drawn a small crowd to stand all along the heaped-up sand berms. Bands of gold and crimson had bled out

302

of the horizon, and beneath them, its nimbus thrown onto the brooding clouds, the perfectly round sun emerged, the long red trail of its descent captured and reflected by one thin strand of cirrus before the ocean cupped its flame.

They knew the beach would darken fast and started the long walk back to the bungalow. By the time they arrived at her door Theresa was shivering with cold and Charlie held her to him just to warm her. He looked up at the window and saw a stocky woman with reddish hair but with Theresa's swooping nose glancing at them. She turned away and headed into the kitchen.

"Your sister? She's already here?"

"Yes. Charlie," Theresa sighed. "I don't think you should come in."

"Then this is it?"

Though she groaned from the effort she hugged him with both of her arms, swaying a little, and tried to be cheerful.

"Hey, scarecrow, I'll miss you most of all."

"I meant what I said. I'll always love you, Theresa."

"And I you. And that doesn't change. Vaya con dios, Charlie."

"God bless you, Theresa. Theresa - please write."

He knew she never would.

Is you am a dog
Is you got a dog
Is you am a dog
Oh close the jaw.

The tape Jack had given Charlie caught his desolation, spun it out and toyed with it for the length of the drive. Soul Coughing. Guys from New York crunching down bleak jazz-rap riffs. Bleats, creaks and wheezes to a thumping bass. Every tune a scavenger hunt.

How many cans must I stack up
To wash you out of my mind
Out of my consciousness?
How many times must I cash out
To bring you back the check fat
Off of my slenderness?

303

Dark-suited old derelicts. Ruins of black markets. Scenes gone bad and running down the alleys.

> You know that but you go on
> You know but that you go on
> You know that but you go on.

That deep bass thump crept like a batfish at the bottom of the pit inside him. He enjoyed the lyrics' mockery. Slim silver track in a view that was cold and bottomless.

Dinner was easy - first place with a happy hour. And afterwards, when the drinks slogged up on him, time to cut the murk with a little coffee. Then more drinks. He retreated to the Nova Express. There seemed a high babe concentration at the table tonight. He could take advantage of that.

No, that didn't help at all.

Nothing could chase the emptiness. Charlie found he wanted to cultivate it, and asked himself why. Maybe he could rush the moment when the new scrim of flesh arose under the picked scab, so clean and painless. Or maybe it was because he still couldn't believe Theresa had vanished, and in that blankness he could keep the evidence in dreamlike suspension. Walking down the sidestreets, past the Fairfax High School track and Television City, he looked up at the moon and its watery halo, a hole from which icy fragments of cloud scudded and fled. Now he really felt the cold on the street.

He trudged back home as fast as he could, and by the time he reached his apartment he was shivering and hungry again and yearning for his mail, and not just the settlement check from Hobart-Riis but anything practical, a communication from Worcek, a reply from one of the firms he'd contacted, anything to take his mind off the fact that Theresa Calder was no more.

The coarse thickly-taped envelope with the chicken-scrawled address on top of the mailbox seemed so out of place that at first he was scared of it, but then he laughed. What could it be, some kind of mini-letter bomb? Charlie realized he needed a definite cooling-out period from all this shit - when he got the check, he would treat himself to a vacation. He shook the envelope, and something in the little parcel gave a metallic rattle. What the hell was it anyway? As soon as Charlie was inside his apartment, he tore it open.

He stared at the crumpled, handwritten letter and the set of keys. "Oh shit," Charlie muttered to himself. These weren't your regular door keys, but big and rough, the type workmen carried around on their belts, keys that you really had to wrestle with because they fit huge steel trunks, or padlocks, or the doors of a warehouse.

The letter seemed written in haste - a trailing gray line indicated a point at which the pencil had actually broken. There was a Los Angeles Avenue address clumsily written out in the center, and around it the scrawl of a man getting rid of a demon. "I do not know what they do," Oscar Mejia wrote. Then he described the location where the files were stored in the best English he could muster - which wasn't very much. "They think I talk to you," Oscar wrote, and now he had his family "away on vacation" because of "terorise calls" "I get another job. No talk to me again. Bueno suerte, Oscar."

Whatever you do, do it completely.

Charlie laid the keys on his night table, and though it was only nine o'clock he crawled into his bed and under the covers as quickly as if a flu had struck him. He turned off the lights and the keys glinted in the green glow from his clock radio. Out in the distance a long trailing siren whooped to a stop. Now it was no longer part of the background. Now it had found a target.

Funny how he'd thought for one moment the envelope would literally blow up. Fear always ready to pounce. Oscar's fear when he'd tried to interview him had exasperated him. But what could be more basic and vital than the family man's fear of losing his job? Fear of not being able to provide, of watching the loved ones go hungry. Enterprises need workers, people need jobs. The most basic social contract we have. Get cut out of it and you're well and truly fucked. Maybe I should've realized that, Charlie thought, when I put all those workers through the months, years of waiting - that awful fear of joblessness. But Oscar had overcome his fear.

Fear of those keys. Fear of what they might set off. Scandal. Confusion. Armed guards springing out of the shadows to beat Charlie worse than they'd beaten Theresa. That iron piston of a hand boring into his rib cage, crushing his

305

guts. Yep, there was a lively image. Fear never lacked for a camera. Fear of fists, knives, guns. *The gun spoke to him.*

Continuous trauma. Stress, stress, stress. You could repeat a word until it emptied of all meaning, became a dull thudding incantation, a tribal grunt. You could get really pissed off at the hollow echo of the word. Why should he give a damn about stress? What was it really? An electric discharge, like the static before the first frame of a video? The fault line that detonates an earthquake. Stress. The hummingbird that natters at a cat and makes him leap to catch it. Also stress. What the hell did those have in common? Life - life is stress. More and more stress, and then you have "continuous trauma", a word that crumples into nonsense.

Until you learn to fear it.

One micro-burst of anxiety, frustration and anger after another that you try to ignore until, like a trickle of cave water depositing stone, it lays down its crust of pain in your gut, your nerves, your every thought.

Fear of the moment when everything snaps. Fear of that explosion at a dinner table, that crying baby. Or fear that nothing will snap, but the injustice, the wound, the torture will go on and on and on. No help from the law. Government of laws, not men. What is the law, are we not men?

Hovering over his bed, so much to be afraid of. Fear of getting up in the morning, time of most earthquakes and heart attacks. Fear on the roads. Fear of other drivers. Fear of the roads in the rain. Fear when you turn on the computer. Virus warnings come out and hundreds of businesses keep their computers dark. Even on a normal day, fear the computer will show you up, work you too hard, break you down, break down on you, paralyze you.

Fear of your new job. Fear of new jobs that never were. He realized how much he'd feared trial law. Civil law. Fear of hide-the-ball, sneak-attack, blood-on-the-floor. Not for Mr. Soft Touch. Fear of the hard evidence. Fear of losing. He'd chosen a gentleman's game of compromise. He'd tried to be the Jedi master of that. The split-the difference man. Fear of what he had become.

Fear of the other. The one that aims the blow to your heart. The one that takes your heart. Even though he had said the right words, all Theresa could feel from him was that goddamn fear. Fear of the wrong words, fear of the right words. Fear of the baggage of your traveling companion. Jesus and the desert.

306

What did the churches say as the holidays came? "Jesus is the reason for the season." Fear of what you were never raised to understand. Fear of the dry, iron-red, lightning-struck mesas of the unknown, even in the flow of sheer delight. Fear of what would happen if you did understand. Fear of the right path, even. The right woman. Fear of everything you had to give.

Fear of the open door, the stray car. Fear of even having another cat.

Charlie lay in bed soaked with every kind of fear he could name. Fear of your body. Yeah, the big one, fear of the tinnitus, paper dry throat, racing heartbeat. He raced to the sink, drank cup after cup even if it was L.A. tap water - fear of cancer, for Chrissake. There was light crepitating behind his eyes. Fear of a stroke. Fear of the hospital. Fear of the fucking bill. Fear of ruin, fear of death. He'd just seen an art exhibit, a mock Day of the Dead. Little clay ancestor statues and mock calaveras. Messages to and from the dead. Fake suicide notes. "The world is a non-stop hard-on and I will no longer remain erect." Try and hang on to the humor.

Fear of losing your soul.

Can't make an omelet without breaking eggs.

He would have to do it now, he'd always known it would have to be done very late at night, the streets abandoned by all but the real lurkers and predators - but no, the fear was savagely blasting right through him now, there were other ways to get the truth, through time-tested procedures, the law, the law...

I could move for the gun.

Lashing arm, terrible blows, crumpled against the wall, again, helpless. He shuts his eyes, and he cannot stop the blood.

Another face enters the dark. A twisted hatchet of a face, and as it approaches he wants to fear it but it's on him too fast. Charlie's ear shrieks, his heartbeat flies into his throat. There it is, his shoe pressing down on her neck, and that face beneath, the black blood shear over the eye in a wedge of fleshy grout, the mouth wrenched down, the cheek blown apart and caved in and twisted towards the peeled jawbone. He chokes with horror in the waking dream, but he cannot escape the face, jagged skull burning beneath his feet, Sheila at the blastpoint of her death. He opens his eyes and fights the scream down.

Slowly the image fades and vision is restored. He realizes his ear, his pulse is silent.

What do you really, really want to do, Charlie?

The women, dead and alive, had fled back to memory. The darkness full of life torn asunder generated a clear, cold space where for one brief moment there was nothing to fear.

Grab the keys. Reach for the phone.

"Don't get freaked, Charlie. Nothing's gonna happen."

"Thanks for the reassurance, Brandon." Leveled blocks and their afterthoughts of refuse rolled past Brandon and Charlie in the gutter light. Charlie drove the Infiniti through Skid Row and clubs appeared out of the darkness. On one block was a violet-shadowed conclave, scenesters lingering by a velvet rope, on another block a pair of quite different stragglers filed in beneath a cheap neon outline of a highball, red beaded curtains shielding the tribal whomp of a bass, bottles glinting in the alley.

"Son of a bitch, she ain't bad for street meat."

Brandon's exhilaration pissed him off. "Glad you're enjoying the tour." Would Charlie even find the warehouse in this subterranean gloom, with Brandon quite possibly fucked up and goofing on the scenery?

"You know, Charlie, I gotta hand it to you. I was just thinking last night about what a dickless wonder you were, and now - you really surprise me."

"What a difference a day makes," Charlie muttered sardonically, wishing that Brandon could downshift into some kind of serious intent and not make Charlie feel that he'd gambled his future and his safety on a joyride. Stopped at a light, Charlie watched a stray dog, a German sheperd, pad down the pavement, tongue hanging out. "You could get great low-light stuff down here."

"Brandon, will you look for the goddamn -"

"Okay! I'm looking!"

No, it wasn't joy coming out of Brandon, more like a yearning on the edge of hysteria as his revenge fantasy eluded him on dark corners heaped with garbage, past lone bodegas where the owner peeked out for his nightly one or two customers from behind a fortress of iron gates.

"Free the files, free the files, free the -"

"Will you shut up?"

Brandon shrugged and was silent. Charlie peered desperately down the street, and gave vent to his despair. "I don't know why I expected to find an address in this shitland. It could be anyone of these -"

"Stop! Back up!"

Oscar had described two "edificios board-up" and Brandon had spotted them, one-story brick warehouses whose shattered windows were nailed over with wood. Charlie could see an address on the old auto body shop across the street, an even number close to the one he had. He would have to get out and try his key.

As they hustled out of the Infiniti, and fetched two huge empty duffel bags out of the trunk, the car's door chimes rang serenely in the darkness. Charlie quickly slammed the door shut. He watched Brandon sling the empty bag over his shoulder, thinking that all this would look interesting on the police report: two burglars arriving in an Infiniti. The chain-link fence was porcupined with razor wire, the lock huge and knotted in chains. Charlie could barely fit the key in through the links. He wrenched it clockwise and it wouldn't budge. The chill in the air, the silence overhung with the roar of a distant overpass, the distant shriek of a siren, the desolate armor of the entire block sank Charlie into such a well of fear that his hands were shaking.

"Here, man, I'll hold the lock for you."

With Brandon cradling the lock in its bed of chains Charlie worked the key with concentration. He knew enough about that from showing spaces for landlords who never replaced their old locks - how to jiggle the key slowly, tilt it up and down until the tumblers engaged. Finally the teeth of the key caught and the padlock sprang open.

Charlie and Brandon opened the gate and raced to an annex of the warehouse divided into units of about four hundred square feet each, which some defunct mail-order company had once used as a shipping outpost. They found the reinforced metal door described in Oscar's letter. This key worked more easily, although when they tried to shove the metal door open, its hinges shrieked loudly enough to echo across the lot.

They squeezed past the door. The darkness was suffocating, as if they'd fallen into some deep and dust-choked hole. They switched on the flashlights and began to probe the skeletal iron cabinets, hunting for the right files. Pull-cord switches of the overhead bulbs brushed their necks like cobwebs. Just as Charlie had feared, boxes of files were stacked up everywhere, but at least some clerk had taken the time to label them, although Brandon and Charlie found themselves hauling down box after box so that the ones beneath them could be rotated with the labels facing forward. He found nothing but construction plans for the Clinic's new wing, and, inevitably, a box dedicated to lawsuits over that construction.

A black furry shape the size of a football wriggled across the room. " Oh Christ! " Charlie hissed, "is that a rat?" Brandon shone his light into the corner and laughed. A heart-shaped, weirdly fleshy face blinked up at them with a beseeching panic as the beast waddled into the corner, a tiny pup half squeezed out of its belly pouch.

"A fucking possum, man. How'd it get in here?" Brandon picked up a bottle and was about to hurl it at the animal.

"What are you doing? You throw that thing someone could hear it crash!"

"Okay, got it..."

"Besides, that's a baby in its pouch, asshole!"

Brandon squinted at the cowering beast. "You're right. Look at that." He lowered his bottle, and they both stared at the opossum until Charlie realized Brandon had fallen into one of his trances, the eyes hooded, mouth slack, adrift in synaptic misfire. He shouted at Brandon that they had to get back to the files.

They pulled down more boxes, riffled through endless folders, until at last they found the worker's comp records in the corner. Charlie quickly examined the Pendaflex tags, and he and Brandon pulled the files and manila folders of every name Charlie even vaguely remembered. Charlie felt the first pinch of hopelessness. So what if they were loading bags with files? This was an honest-to-God chance to expose the Clinic and Hobart-Riis, but he wasn't going to capitalize on it with this kind of indiscriminate snatching of paper. They worked silently, and the bags swelled up and grew more and more top-heavy. Now he could hear an undertone of squeaking and scratches along the walls, and he identified the smell that assaulted his nostrils as rat droppings.

"Got a little Hollywood menagerie in here, Chuck," Brandon drawled. Charlie fought off a wave of nausea as he scanned his flashlight along the files.

"Over there, Charlie! What's Lincoln Health?"

"Regular health insurance files."

Charlie turned back to the worker's comp files, then froze and followed Brandon's flashlight beam to the box. Regular health insurance files. "What the hell are they doing down here?"

He rushed over to inspect the files. He saw the name "Cozen", then probed back through at least fifty files towards the end of the alphabet. There it was. "Sheila Reed." He whipped through the file, and found the diagnosis. The minute he saw paragraph after paragraph, he knew.

"Get these files, Brandon!" he shouted. "All of them!"

They unloaded the box, and soon had the bags stuffed to capacity. When they shoved the empty box back Charlie saw the faint green flicker on Brandon's startled face. He was dizzy from a wave of panic even before he saw the light of the silent alarm winking in the corner.

Charlie and Brandon struggled to crush the duffel bags' U-shaped locks shut over the corners of the bulky files. Brandon could just manage to heft his bag over his shoulder, but Charlie couldn't even lift his, and had to drag it across the floor. Locking the door behind him, Charlie saw Brandon bent almost double under his duffel bag as he staggered towards the car. He dragged his own across the pavement, and felt for a moment he was in one of those dreams where your feet become mired in tar and the nerves of your legs start to die and you know you're going to lose your race against a deadly unseen enemy. The bag rasped horribly against the concrete as he backpedaled frantically to the gate.

"Just throw it in the trunk, Brandon! Quick!"

Brandon dumped his bag, grabbed the key, ran over to the gate and fought to shut the padlock as Charlie tried to hoist his own duffel bag into the trunk. Dammit, couldn't he have anticipated the two bags wouldn't fit? If the rent-a-cops were any good at their response time, they'd be here any minute. He yanked open the passenger door, shoved the seat forward, and groaning

311

from the effort tried to shoulder the squirming bag into the back seat. He felt Brandon throw himself against the bag beside him, and together they at last rolled it into the rear of the car.

"Let's book!"

They jumped into the car and as soon as Charlie gunned the accelerator, lights and bells winking mildly, headlights flared in their rearview mirror. He took off with a screech of tires, hoping against hope that the appearance of the car in back was just a coincidence until the brights tore through the windows.

"Charlie, pedal to the metal!"

He slammed the accelerator down and the Infiniti engines throbbed in protest. The automatic transmission always wanted to ease into the next gear, it wasn't built for what it would now have to take. But it was moving fast - suddenly the corner was upon them and Charlie wrenched the wheel. The car spun out sickeningly, but then the ABS brakes caught and he remembered to steer in the direction of the skid. Now the Infiniti was straight, but the vehicle behind him, a black van, was gaining.

"It's Golan!" Charlie glanced at the rearview mirror and quailed as he glimpsed that bull-nosed face behind the wheel, and the dour hulk beside him. "And he's got Ogi and Daniel with him, the guys are killers!"

"Charlie, stay cool, just drive! I'll try to -"

The sentence was slammed out of him by the crunch of the van's front bumper. Charlie lurched forward and could barely keep his hands on the wheel. In the rearview, Golan raised his hand, pointed to the side of the road. The street was still clear, but how long could he keep going? Reach for the cellular, call 911, then pull over and hope the police got there in time. He looked down at his phone and Brandon caught his eye.

"No! Eyes front, Charlie!"

The street was wider now, turning into some boulevard or frontage road, metal barriers and concrete berms on both sides, and the furious headlights were sidling away. Charlie heard the roar as the van came alongside him, and he couldn't believe it, Brandon was flung against him just as the next and much more powerful blow impacted the passenger side of the car. Now he was veering to the left, he fought to keep the wheel steady but he grazed the concrete, heard the metal shriek and spark on the barrier. Brandon was hooting

312

now, laughing hysterically, it felt like a howling last gasp, it felt like Charlie was being pincered and squeezed by some insane and insatiable force at the end of life. It was all he could do to make himself aim the car straight, keep driving somehow.

The cold air shot through him as Brandon opened the window.

"Brandon, what are you -"

"Fuck you, you stupid assholes! Yeah, you got a van, you got a horn? You pieces of shit! COME ON, MOTHERFUCKERS!"

If only he could reach for the phone, but he needed two hands on the wheel. He could see an overpass, a light, a street. Turn on it and they can't get alongside him, but it was too late, they were overtaking him now. Metal crunched and tore again, and this time he felt on his side of the car the barrier swipe through the door and bludgeon his ribs. He was past the street, couldn't turn, but there was another traffic light way up ahead. Turn off somewhere, park, beg for mercy, he couldn't take another impact like that. But they were coming up on them again, and Brandon was shrieking abuse at them, and Charlie had to look, and it was gray and glinting, that barrel, Brandon aiming it two-handed out the window at Golan's van. That gun.

"BRANDON, STOP!"

Brandon fired. A second shot, but no, that was a blowout. The van pulled away behind them like it was jerked and sucked back through some vacuum across the street. Charlie hit the brakes and the seatbelt gripped him, and Brandon was laughing exultantly. "Got 'em! Fucking got 'em!" They watched the Lincoln pirouette and smash into a streetlight. The light yawed from the impact, pitched forward steeply and descended in a long slow arc to the bulb's explosion in the street. The van humped into a vacant lot and broadsided a brick wall.

Charlie turned back to the road. He gunned the engine again, and winced as he heard an awful scraping from the driver's side of his car.

"Charlie, we gotta go back!"

Charlie's voice was surprisingly calm. "I'll be lucky if I can get us home in this car, Brandon. We're not going back."

313

"But we gotta check it out! We gotta – we gotta make sure they don't talk to the cops!" He clutched his gun two-handed and held it close to his breast, like a kid trying to be a desperado.

"Brandon, put the gun down. It's over."

Brandon was unconvinced. "But what if they talk to the police?" As if in answer to Brandon's unease, he heard the sirens blazing in their direction across the berm. "What about that, Charlie?"

"'Russian men in a van.' That's how Theresa described her attackers. Golan can try to explain Ogi and Daniel the best he can. I don't think he'll get very far."

Brandon thought about that and at last pulled his head back from outside the window.

"The side of the car – it's fucked up pretty bad, Charlie."

"Guess so."

"How's the radio?"

Charlie hit the button, and found the radio was still tuned to a rock station, still intact. The Mighty Mighty Bosstones thumped out of the speakers. Brandon listened to the ska music and began to laugh uncontrollably. Charlie felt the cool air wash over him as he paid attention to the Infiniti's rough but stable ride - and for once Charlie felt like laughing with him.

-11-
chapter eleven

When Worcek walked into the familiar stifling heat of the Van Nuys courtyard, she sensed the buzz among the claimants was different. Excitement leaked from tight circles, popped out in random outbursts, not the usual griping and fidgeting, but genuine enthusiasm. An overweight, red-haired ex-bricklayer raised a letter up above his head and shouted "They came clean! Bastards finally admitted they fucked up!"

And now came answering cries from all across the sunbaked courtyard, and other letters were waved in the air like flags, and the people on the benches, infected by the glee let loose in the usual sunny trough of despond, engaged in all sorts of funky behavior. Some banged their canes on the ground, some whooped and hollered, you could've been at a rock concert all of a sudden. Cellphones clicked off all over the courtyard, held at bay as the lawyers shared a moment of silent dread. Yes, this was it, this was the temblor in the crowd they'd always feared would erupt some sunny morning and destroy them. But the mob's clamor seemed self-contained, and it was almost as if, suddenly, the lawyers didn't matter. They were safe because they were out of the loop, and Worcek could tell, reading their faces, that their irrelevancy to whatever was happening disturbed them most of all.

Kaukonen, as always, seemed to have ferreted out the secret. He caught Worcek's eye, and as she came up to him, he was murmuring a line from an old Rolling Stones tune. "Maybe the last time, I don't know."

"What's going on, Jerry?"

Kaukonen bent towards her with full conspiratorial relish. "The Bernard-Duvall Clinic. One of our big defense mills. Looks like they fucked up big time. The claimant lawyer I'm having my M.S.C. with today just laid

315

this on me." Worcek took from him a letter on Hobart-Riis Insurance stationery. To her amazement, the Great Denier had sent a letter to the lawyer stating that they had reason to believe they were misled regarding the seriousness of his client's injuries, and would soon be taking the matter under consideration.

"So where's your letter, Jerry? The one from Hobart-Riis warning you that this was going to come down."

"Never got one. I'm trying to figure out why Bert Silver has it in for me - or how senile fucking Shackleton got all of a sudden. 'Bang-bang, my client shot me down.' Jeez, an old Sonny and Cher tune - now I'm even more depressed..."

There was a wolvish eagerness to the claimants' whoops of delight behind her. Worcek could pick out a familiar voice punctuated by coughs and wheezes. She laid a hand on Kaukonen's wrist to interrupt him and headed off to intercept Mr. Cozen, who was wheeling himself in his oxygen-tanked wheelchair with an alarming amount of energy. He thrust his letter into her hand and beamed with gratitude. "Look at this, Liz! They practically admit to the lit-up diabetes. I don't know how you did it, but I'm sorry I ever doubted you."

She accepted his praise, excused herself, and ran to the phones. There she was stalled for ten minutes by a brigade of lawyers fighting the phone staff at Hobart-Riis to confront, question and curse the executive board. When it was finally her turn, she called Charlie Solomon's home, then his cellular. At last the signal clicked in with a rumble of traffic noise.

"Charlie? It's Liz. We gotta talk."

His voice sounded crisp and almost relaxed. "I assume everybody got their mail."

"Charlie, whatever you're doing, I hope you can back it up. Legally."

"Let's just say the law has nothing to do with it."

"Where are you? Are you headed towards Van Nuys? Tell me where you're going, we have to meet."

"I don't have my car, Liz. It's a rolling total."

"What do you mean?"

"It means I suffered damage in excess of -"

316

"Oh Christ, I know what a rolling total is!"

"Look, I'm in a friend's car now. I'm fine, and I'm headed to Hobart-Riis. I have to get prepared, if you know what I mean."

Worcek sighed, filled with both admiration for Charlie and overwhelming uneasiness. The legal strategies they had worked on together had clearly been thrown by the wayside.

"Are you all right, Charlie? I mean, no injuries."

"I'm fine, Liz."

"And you got your settlement?"

"Deep in the bowels of the bank. They can't stop the check anymore."

"Be careful, Charlie. For all of us."

On the other end of the line, Charlie clicked off his phone and slipped it back into his jacket pocket. Vel cast him a swift inquiring glance as she coasted towards the bumper-to-bumper traffic at the intersection of Beverly and Santa Monica Boulevards.

"You'd think Worcek would be excited by all this. She sounded pretty down."

"She's a player, Charles. And you are breaking the rules big time. In case that hasn't sunk in."

They drove the long flat stretch of boulevard towards Century City in silence, until Vel abruptly shook her head and snickered. "We once owned all this."

"Who?"

"The Mexicans, Charles."

"True. But it was a desert back then."

"It was better off. Now there's a fantasy. The Mexican army comes back and levels Century City. You have a pristine desert again. Nice and clean."

"Vel, I know how disappointing this is to you, now that you've signed on as a staff counsel for Hobart-Riis. But believe me, you're not going to be touched."

Vel reached over and gave his hand a firm little tap - it seemed almost her equivalent of an athlete's well-wishing pat on the ass, and it startled him.

317

Her eyes were mischievous but a haunted sincerity flickered his way. "You do what you have to do, Charles."

"I know. And do it completely."

As Charlie trundled his new, fully loaded carryall to the elevators, he kept the lid on his nervousness by marshaling in his thoughts the names and the facts he would need to lay out his case. He was still so immersed in stoking up his presentation that he almost strode right past the new receptionist into the offices he had shared for so long. The receptionist shouted after him and eyed him like some alien life form, but when he announced his name, she immediately buzzed him in.

He found a way to steer the carry-all behind him with a kind of dignity and walked straight past the secretaries' desks towards Shackleton's office, pausing only to return a timid but nonetheless welcoming smile from Laura. She probably figured that he was here to finalize some details of his settlement, or even officially take on that San Francisco position that no doubt was the subject of the office's rumor mill. Would she be wishing him well, he reflected, if she knew what was about to come down? He wheeled the carryall around the corner and was abruptly face to face with Maxine Bunning, even more formal than usual in her blue blazer and skirt. With a grimace of embarrassment at her own inability to say anything to him, she directed him towards the conference room.

As always, Mavis Thorpe was ensconced behind the desk that flanked the massive oak doors of Hobart-Riis' inner sanctum. She actually waddled up to open them for Charlie, with an officious, hurried courtesy - she knew he was not exactly bearing gifts in those files.

The conference room never failed to impress Charlie with its star chamber effect. The immense green inlaid marble table stretched beneath the lozenges of fluorescence in the ceiling, which threw a faint sheen on the oil painting of Hobart, the one-time rancher, and the daguerreotype of Riis, the Dutch merchant with an eye for California shores. Those icons of a nurturing and smothering history that never wanted and never needed change frowned at him from the walls, a bulwark of disapproval behind Shackleton, Bunning, Silver, and, in the corner, Dr. Duvall, long-faced, haggard and remote, and Dr.

318

Bernard, chawing on his pipe, the gnome at his most testy looking more like a gargoyle.

The conference room, and the silent fury harbored by everyone in it, was soon working its bad juju – but Charlie was grateful for the intimidating size of the table as he slapped down the twenty sets of folders. Now he was making them fidget, he could tell, as he arranged one pair of files after another along the table, an unwanted croupier dealing them their nasty hands. Dr. Bernard didn't seem to realize what was going on until the last thick file smacked down before him.

"Those are our records. Goddam it, he stole our files!"

Silver, leaning back, chin resting in his hand, shot a warning glance in Bernard's direction. "Let's hear what he has to say."

Bernard was staring daggers at Silver, but was trapped into silence. Charlie cast one more glance at Sheila Reed's file, making sure he had separated out and left in the car Chesley's handwritten notes, which he'd subpoenaed in his capacity as Hobart-Riis' attorney and which Shackleton could conceivably lay claim to. No, Charlie had made no mistakes yet, he was safe, safe as he could be in this lion's den.

Silver shook his head, faintly amused. "So this is how you cooperate, Charlie? You are aware that your settlement was an implicit pledge to cooperate?"

"I'm cooperating the best possible way. Consider those letters I sent to those claimants a favor."

"Oh really, Charlie?"

"They're a shot across your bow, keeping you away from hostile territory. And once I'm finished here you can get rid of a client that sooner or later would've dragged you down."

Bernard brought the flat of his hand down on the table. "This clinic is not guilty of any wrongdoing whatsoever! The prosecutable crime here is that this impudent little snot stole our files!"

He subsided as Duvall shot him a calming, but distinctly chilly glance.

"Actually," Charlie replied, "I had a key. A key to an old warehouse in a terrible neighborhood. That's where these health insurance and worker's comp files are stored. And they were put there under such suspicious

319

circumstances, that the person who gave me this key," and Charlie plunked the heavy brace of keys on the polished green marble desk, "had his family spirited away on vacation to make sure they'd be safe."

Finally Dr. Duvall spoke up with a disapproving growl. "That's a lot of crap, Mr. Solomon."

"Seems to be, doesn't it? After all, what's so scary about a bunch of health insurance files? Why aren't these perfectly innocuous files just sitting at the Bernard/Duvall Clinic where anyone can find them? Why are they buried in a warehouse in an awful neighborhood in downtown L.A.?"

Charlie could see the worry creasing Shackleton's brow, and decided to arrow in on him. "And after all, these files are correct. I've met Dan Cozen." He picked up one of the files. "Just as this health insurance file says, he has diabetes and it was aggravated by an injury sustained at work." Charlie pulled out the second file from beneath the first. "The problem is, that's not what his worker's compensation file says. And here's where things get less than kosher. Oh, the file mentions heart problems, kidney problems, pre-existing complications, but nothing aggravated by an injury, nothing at all."

"The opinion of our doctor at the time is that the injury wasn't work-related. This is all perfectly legal!" Bernard shouted. Charlie couldn't help grinning. He could be cueing the bastard. And then, just as if he were orchestrating the entry of another instrument, a tremulous flute, Maxine Bunning turned to Bernard. "Yes, Dr. Bernard, but - was he examined by two different doctors? I don't understand..." And now Bert's voice echoed the quavering melody with a chord of impatience. "Charlie, let's get to the point."

Charlie rose from his chair, and turned as dramatically as he could to Maxine. "You gave these guys considerable power over the workers at the companies you insured. I'm sure you're aware of that. According worker's comp law, Hobart-Riis controls the medical care of thousands of patients in the first ninety days of their injury – in fact, any patient who doesn't name their treating physician - and you sent hundreds of them to Bernard/Duvall. And the ones you didn't send initially, you sent to Bernard/Duvall down the line when you wanted an opinion stating that a worker's comp claimant wasn't really injured, because they were your favorite defense clinic. And these guys were

320

pretty damn ingenious at telling their main customer exactly what that customer wanted to hear!"

Now Charlie was over the adrenaline clutch, and a delicious freedom crept into his presentation. He was departing from the prepared score, working the files like a jazz musician taking apart a standard. He recapitulated the procedures of the clinic's worker's comp mill. See the patient as a worker's comp injury. Fill out the first medical report. Then, in a handwritten note - he yanked a green-tagged note from the Cozen file - say it's "non-industrial", not a worker's comp injury, not compensable. Six weeks later write the full report - get about two grand - then bill Hobart-Riis for some minimal treatment. "The Clinic gets the money they need to keep their expansion going, Hobart-Riis gets to deny workers their benefits, everyone's happy, except, well, sometimes a few details about the patient's illness have to be removed from the worker's comp file." He plucked from the table his favorite case. The bouquet that stank the most obviously. "Mr. Jose Ramirez' worker's comp file shows a sprain in the clavicle area, a prescription for pain meds, a recommendation that he be returned to work. But in the health carrier file, lo and behold, an X-ray. A break in the collarbone. The guy's out there wolfing down his pain meds, not knowing why his sprain is still killing him, why it won't heal! It's because it's a broken bone, stupid!"

"I'm sure the patient received the treatment he required." Duvall's voice boomed across the room.

"Well, whatever the level of treatment, it's safe to say that one of these folders is a deliberate falsification! What about the rest? Over a hundred of them! Do you think medical experts, state investigators, do you think maybe they could spot any further altering, creating and distorting of medical records?"

Shackleton laid his head in his cupped hands, and his voice barely rose above a whisper. "My god, Charlie, that's a hell of an accusation."

Time to focus on his boss, Charlie realized, and a little more gently. "Look, I understand the clinic treated at least some worker's comp patients legitimately. They had credibility in your eyes, and there was no reason for you to assume -"

Shackleton interrupted Charlie and turned on Dr. Duvall. "Is that what you thought we contracted you for? Hide from us all evidence that the patients needed care?"

Charlie felt that Shackleton was now just about in his corner, and now, instinctively, he killed all the sympathy in his voice. "Why not, Ted? Didn't you just about commission them to be the ideal washout clinic? Deny, deny, right? Dr. Sandoval just took the process a notch up. Instituted a policy of complete advocacy. Nothing's wrong with any worker's comp claimant sent to the Bernard/Duvall clinic, and if there is, well then," and he took a long pause to let the hammer fall, "only the regular health insurance, who pays Bernard/Duvall Clinic for treatment the workers never get, ever needs to know."

"This is an insult... slanderous!" The shouts of both the doctors mixed with Bert Silver slamming the table with his fist, whether in disgust with Charlie or the scam Charlie couldn't tell. He looked over at Maxine, who silently clutched the edge of the table, pale, about to be sick. And Shackleton was perfectly still, his expression transparent. That was what Charlie wanted to see - someone, at last, ready to hear the whole story.

"I'm afraid this wasn't just slip some old lady some Valium and bill for a full exam." He broadened his gaze to take in the whole Hobart-Riis contingent. "Look at any of these files - in all of them, records of injury or illness in the worker's comp file have been removed and transferred to the health insurance file! Let's look at the case the closest to all of us, Sheila Reed's." He fought to control the shaking in his voice. "You can look at this health insurance file and see clear diagnoses and descriptions of incipient ulcerative colitis brought on by the acute stress Sandoval put her through when he psychologically and sexually harassed her before driving her off the job! The Bernard-Duvall Clinic buried those reports!" He pulled out a wrinkled green form from the health insurance file. "Here's the form she filled out at the doctor's office. You know the standard worker's comp form describing the injury. Here's where she indicated it was an industrial injury, because, remember, she'd already filed for worker's comp and they'd had her examined by one of their own doctors. They crossed out the entry about the industrial injury and put "private," to make sure to remind themselves that the health insurance company, not worker's comp, would be billed for her care." He

322

turned to Dr. Bernard and pointed to him with as much damning fervor as he could summon up from the memory of every lie and every insult he'd endured for so long. "What care? We know from her testimony at the trial they were not treating her for anything. You were blowing her off. Look what you did to Sheila Reed, one of your own! But at least you were being consistent. Your goal was not to cure and relieve, but to collect twice. You would double-bill for your patients' care, but not care for them. Any of them!"

Duvall stared down at the table, tipping his glasses a little farther up his head, and then, without a word, left the meeting. Bernard chose to stand his ground. "Oh for Chrissake, if an employees go the worker's comp route, they know what they're in for. The system is corrupt as Cairo! They're not seeking a serious, unbiased medical opinion with such an adversarial course. We know most of these patients are out to exaggerate or even create illness."

"So you created wellness?" Charlie exploded. "Gave clean bills of health to people in desperate need of medical care?"

Shackleton was trembling with indignation. "You're going to be in big trouble over this!" Even Silver was outraged. "How many defense exams did we throw you? You were our main goddamn provider! We are getting right on the horn to the Industrial Medical Council."

"Fuck you, Bert, I got the angel of death call already. What the hell, I'm better off out of this racket. Now if you'll excuse me..."

After Bernard left, Charlie could smell it in the room, in the odors of perfume and cologne kicked up a notch by that crepitation of the skin, that prickly sweat - he could actually smell the fear. Shackleton was slumped to the side, while Maxine was making a conscious effort at composure. Bert was the first to recover himself; he got up to shut the door after Bernard, then took his seat, planted his elbows on the table, and opened his palms like the pages of a new book.

"Well, Sandoval's little scheme won't be the first time we've dealt with risk management fraud." Charlie couldn't help but admire how quickly he took the meeting in hand. The motherfucker certainly was an executive. Right to the point of the spin control: Sandoval as the fall guy. But before they all got too damn complacent Charlie had one more point to make.

323

"I see. That's the strategy. Blame one disgraced middle manager we've never even seen who's now somewhere in Brazil. And I wouldn't mind seeing it as solely the Clinic's fault, except - well, Bert, isn't it possible you cut short an audit to let the files "go away" two weeks ago? Also, I'm sure if you talk to any lawyer on the Hobart-Riis staff - and I think state investigators will - they'll mention the missing defense clinic reports. I know there were several files of Bernard/Duvall records with no reports attached. Now maybe they all got misplaced - but if Hobart-Riis paid bills for which there were no reports, then it's almost as if Hobart-Riis didn't care about the content of the reports. Or didn't want to know."

The last words fell heavily from Charlie. Maybe the spirit of the room where once he'd worked so industriously had infected him, but it gave no joy to point out the company's possible complicity in Bernard-Duvall's scam. He sank into a cheerless silence, and Silver took advantage of his exhaustion.

"Enough of this shit, Charlie. You know damn well a carrier is not liable for the alleged malpractice of a doctor treating an industrial injury."

"But you can incur civil liability over activities following an injury. Investigation. Claims handling. Under the Unruh decision, because Rody Golan practiced fraud and deceit in terrorizing a witness like Oscar in the Sheila and Brandon Reed cases, Hobart-Riis is vulnerable to a suit. Not to mention the practice of fraud, deceit and invasion of privacy against all these patients."

"Shaky-shaky, Charlie."

"Jablonski vs. Royal Globe. Court of Appeals. An injured worker in a civil suit against a workers' comp insurance carrier stated the carrier wrongfully denied insurance coverage and destroyed evidence to deprive the employee of benefits. That was sufficient to bring the case to trial in civil court! The clinic's activities and Golan's practices lead right back to this room. I can prove that chain, Bert!"

Shackleton began shouting at Charlie. Charlie was worried - his old boss' chest rose and fell heavily, and for all the space that he took up, he suddenly seemed a tired old man. "What are you going to say, Charlie? You worked with us every day! Do you honestly believe that we mandated, or even tolerated such conduct? My god, I - I'm just a claims man from Iowa. I have to admit to being somewhat unsophisticated when it comes to clinic billing procedures - but I damn well know and understand fraud when I sniff it out, and I don't condone it. And don't you think it's bad enough that we must - must suffer the unintended consequences of these actions for the rest of our lives?"

"Maybe you shouldn't use such blunt instruments," Charlie replied coldly. "Giving carte blanche to Golan and his Russian street thugs, for Chrissake. Or maybe you should lay down your weapons altogether and stop fighting this war. Sheila Reed should never have been harassed. She should never have been exposed to potential physical and sexual violence in the workplace. And when she became ill, she should have been treated."

"That would've been simpler," Bert conceded.

"Charlie, let's move on." Shackleton regained his calm, and spread his hands almost prayerfully. "What is it you want? Adequate, even generous settlements for the poor victims of the Clinic? We can provide it." Bunning sighed into place behind Shackleton. "Of course, we want to work with you. But we can only settle on favorable terms with all these claimants if there's no suggestion that we were in any way involved with this atrocity."

"Yes," Shackleton chorused, "we can't risk the slightest chance of exposure."

"You need someone to surrender to you, Charlie," Bert quipped.

"Go ahead, Bert, make a joke out of it. Life's tough, laugh at the poor bastards who are the losers. Sheila Reed killed herself over this! A life was taken! And her brother is demanding justice!"

Now Silver was kindled with Charlie's righteous indignation. He got up, his face flushed, and circled the table until there was no distance between Charlie and him. "Look, you're to be commended for uncovering this scam. But you had better believe we had no idea this was happening. We regret that the pressure to counter claimant fraud and, yes, to maximize returns led us to these adversarial tactics. There could be a degree of validity in your argument that we were lax in our enforcement procedures. But try and put this ball in our court and you will lose. And don't drag out that old wheeze about a settlement for Brandon Reed. This ludicrous partial dependent case of his - you and Vel tore it to shreds, he almost agreed to settle, do you think we could give him a

325

gift of twenty-five grand and still maintain any credibility? If we're paying off her brother over nothing, we must be guilty of something!"

Charlie would ask himself later why he had blurted out Brandon Reed's case so prematurely. He had wanted to attach him to the general settlement once the process had begun, demand decent restitution for Brandon as his personal quid pro quo. Now, while he was still pushing for a global settlement, he had jumped the gun, and he could feel his plea for Brandon losing force even as he again spoke up for him. "Bert, you know damn well Sheila Reed was injured on the job and that Brandon should get his twenty-five grand!"

Bert was unfazed. "Charlie, here's the way it goes down. We're going to cooperate in every way with state investigators in busting Bernard-Duvall. Then we conduct our own internal investigation, find no evidence of wrongdoing, and settle these cases as discussed. We'll have to spend millions sorting out this mess. We're not giving dime one to Brandon Reed."

Shackleton and Bunning were silent, leaving Charlie with his thoughts, thoughts of the benefits he could bring a hundred people if one happened to be sacrificed.

"You've won major settlements for all these claimants. You busted a corrupt clinic. You're a hero, Charlie, okay? Forget Sheila Reed and her cretin brother."

At 7:30 that night, Charlie strolled into Orfeo, greeted the manager, and waited at a back table for Brandon. As always, the kid was late, and he looked hopelessly out of place amid the slickly dressed Thursday night crowd in his jeans, warm-up windbreaker, and faded plaid shirt. Charlie ordered them a couple of beers. He had kept on his suit and tie, and had his attaché case next to him on the seat where Brandon could see it. He wanted to have the appearance of having been on the job and fighting for Brandon right up to the moment he'd taken his seat at the table.

They quickly ordered some calamari, antipasto, shrimp scampi and lasagna - Brandon was already wolfing down the breadbasket - and Charlie launched into his presentation. He gave Brandon the dignity of as thoroughly and carefully orchestrated a speech as he would give to a major client, but he also wanted Brandon to be caught up in the story of the clinic bust, and realize

326

it was his own story as well. When Charlie had Shackleton and the others on the ropes, Brandon was also nailing them with a devastating punch. Charlie did his work deftly, and by the time he recalled how the doctors stormed out of the meeting, Brandon raised his beer to Charlie and drank it down in one long happy swallow.

"Way to go, Chazz!"

"Yep. We did it, Brandon. We secured wrongfully denied medical care for over a hundred people, and you better believe their lawyers will go for the kill with all their other clients."

"That clinic must be hurting pretty good."

"We've put them out of business. State investigators will shut them down, and Dr. Bernard will have so many lawsuits up his ass he's gonna need his staff proctologist to pull them out."

"Clinic's gonna pay, huh?"

"Hobart-Riis has the deep pockets. The clinic'll be hit with fines, but they'll go into Chapter 11, so it'll be -"

Brandon's eyes abruptly clouded. "Chapter 11, I know all about that. A way to protect your assets."

"Bottom line is, Brandon, the patients will be treated and compensated, like the law intends. No bullshit."

"Yeah." He took his darkening gaze off of Charlie, briefly contemplating the effervescent crowd at the nearby tables. "Too bad it comes too late for Sheila."

"Yes. Yes, it is. But Brandon - when those patients finally get the care they need, they'll owe it to her."

"Yeah. That's worth something." A smile flickered across Brandon's face again. "So when do I collect?"

Charlie took a pull of his beer. "I'm sure you realize that the patients needing the care have to be dealt with first-"

"Yeah, but - this has nothing to do with their care. 25 grand, straight up." Charlie said nothing, letting Brandon acquaint himself with the first ugly stirrings of the truth. "So what's the problem, Charlie?"

"We're going to have to take care of you a different way. We're going to do just what we planned to do." He made himself look Brandon squarely in the eye. "We're going to take your case to trial and win."

Brandon was silent, but Charlie could read the curl in his lip, his catlike hunch in his chair. Finally, he spoke up with surprising restraint. "Is this what you're going to lay on me, Charlie? After our night out there playing bumper-cars with Death? Is this the way it works? The clinic dodges the bullet? The insurance company pays their way out? Everybody gets well, and I get nothing, Charlie?"

Even though a part of him felt it was almost obscene, his professional reflex was to make light of Brandon's anger, to counterfeit the most free-and-easy possible confidence. "Brandon, there are so many ways we can go. Keep the pressure on to settle. Take them all the way to court. Hobart-Riis will have zero credibility with every judge in the system for a long time. All you need is a little patience."

"What I need is twenty-five grand!" Brandon twisted back and forth in his seat, chafing against invisible chains. "Does Worcek know about this?"

"Not yet. Since they're not offering anything to her, they didn't notify her. I'll tell her. Don't worry, she'll keep up the fight, and Brandon - Brandon, you'll get something, even if the best we can do, I admit, is a compromise."

"A compromise? No shit! Another compromise. It's always a compromise with you, Charlie."

"That's what it's like out there, Brandon, all right? There's no slam dunk, no closure. But look, in your case, we're only at the starting gate. You compromise a little, and then you start the fight again."

"Start over for what? To get to the next compromise? It never moves, don't you get it, Charlie? It never changes!"

Christ, there was just no defusing this kid once he got going. Well, what did it matter anyway? Charlie had just won, won big, and he was getting a little tired of Brandon's tirade.

"There are going to be plenty of changes. Don't you get it, Brandon? Some people may go to prison over this!"

"Yeah. For a minute." Brandon chuckled. "But you know the only thing that scares people? It just takes a day in prison to get buttfucked. Nobody's scared of the law, but those big tag team rapers reaming your punk ass...What the hell. Maybe my case was bogus anyway."

"No. It wasn't bogus. Worcek'll stay on it. I'll keep fighting it for you." Seeing Brandon so quiet, he once again felt pity for him, and knew he had to send him home with some hope. "You know why you're going to win, Brandon? Because Sheila's own words will destroy them." He reached over to the attaché case, and pulled out Sheila's file, making sure that Brandon could see the photocopies of Chesley's handwritten notes. "They don't even know about this. Remember I told you a doctor took down Sheila's description of possible wrongdoing at the clinic, her harassment, and her illness in her own words? Here it is. Trust me, Hobart-Riis will never want this to come to light. Brandon, you may have to wait, but - you'll get yours. You'll sure fucking get yours. I promise." He tried to smile, and was relieved when he got an answering grin from Brandon.

"Hey, I got nothing but time."

While Brandon devoured the rest of his lasagna, Charlie decided to order them both another round. Walking to the bar, he instinctively checked out the crowd for people he knew, and met the eye of a gorgeous young woman in a tight black dress. Time enough for that, he thought - first of all he'd be going on vacation. But he wouldn't head for Cancun or Cabo or any of the usual suspects. He'd already decided to fly to Santa Fe. Rent an old Ford Escort or Le Baron and do some driving down long dusty roads where the sun set over the mesas and lit up the blue stones. The unlikely wellspring of his love and enlightenment. Somewhere he could clear his head of all this noise and friction, and draw on the spirit of a memory that had become the better part of his being.

Brandon seemed to be amused by how neither of them had a car that night. Comradeship in L.A.: two guys actually walking. Charlie waited with Brandon at the bus stop until it was clear he was making the kid uncomfortable, then clapped him on the back and said he'd be seeing him. Brandon's handclasp was so sudden and intense it sent a shock through his arm, as he tipped forward into Brandon's quick impulsive hug. "We did good, Charlie," he whispered. "We really did good."

"Yes, Brandon." Charlie tried to find more words, but could only thank him and say goodnight. He headed down the street, and then, feeling oddly protective, took one last look back at Brandon waiting for the late night bus in the glare of the sodium lights. He wished he could hand the kid a check today. But there was always a tradeoff. Charlie knew that.

The calico kitten trotted to the door as Charlie opened it, swagging its little belly across the rug. Don't worry, a neighbor had told him, that same woman who'd helped him look for Gaucho. Aisha would probably start racing and bouncing off his walls any day now, and after a couple of weeks of that behavior she'd lose the belly, and he'd have a few broken dishes and a trim, beautiful little cat.

He pulled Sheila's files from his briefcase and threw them across his desk. They would sit on the back burner now, an extra item on his plate, for he'd been given reason to believe he'd have another job when he got back. Maybe Worcek's firm, maybe Remar's. He took his new purring little pet to bed with him and soon slipped off into a dream. In a forest glen, bent over a clear stream, suddenly a hand glided free of his grasp, and Theresa, naked, was diving into the water. Down the stream he walked, his toes scraping against pebbles and tiny twigs, captivated by the sight of the woman swimming effortlessly against the current until it seemed no more than a sheath that glided behind her and rippled to her every stroke. Now Charlie was swimming right beside Theresa. The water, warm as their blood, caressed them, and she turned to look at him, her Indian eyes wide open, calm and beneficent as they reflected the lapping of the water and the sunlight.

Her eyes scored into him, loading him with remorse. Take a piece of my anger. Come behind the "red curtain over my eyes." Brandon saw his sister's face again, more Irish than his from his father's side, eyes bloodshot, full of accusation. "I could grab the Drano off the sink and drink it but I don't want to leave a mess." Brandon could almost feel the Drano hissing through the membranes of his stomach. So hungry most nights he'd hear the Mexicans stomp outside and wonder what was in their cans. Lick that rim clean of pico de gallo, eke out the ramen noodles and Chef Boyardee. Better ration the grub than camp out with the midnight ramblers. Keep welfare away. Sheila proved you don't come back from it. "I try to meditate but it's all for shit." Yeah, keep it away, Sheila. But you couldn't keep it away from Dr. Chesley. The doctor

330

laid you bare - yeah, after that bastard laid you bare. "I'll have to let him do the nasty...I'll have to let him in the goddamn door." Open the goddamn door.

How many hours are going by, just him and these notes he stole from Charlie's briefcase? Night is turning, even the shouts of the drunks wiped out by the moon. But I know, Charlie, I know all through the night, compromise isn't the truth, asshole, compromise isn't the truth, right here on these pages, here's where it is. "Why doesn't he see? Why doesn't he see..."

> Down here in the pawnshop
> Down here in the pawn-shop-shop-shop!

Chugging reggae down in the valley of the dubmaster's echo. Brad Nowell called it out just like a fucking Jamaican. Bass hits, guitar licks, Sublime was a pretty hot band, but that Brad Nowell, he beat Kurt Cobain's asshole record by offing himself on heroin *before* he became famous. "Down there in the pawn-shop!" Brandon had just taken a walk and seen that niche in the window behind the iron gates, below a shelf of rings and watches and someone's old Stratocaster. His Nikon had sat there for two weeks, and now it was gone. Gone forever.

Gone with his sister. Yeah, Sheila Cobained. Asshole, asshole. They hid it from us, your sickness, your cry for help. It cost too much. Pain in the gut, no end, no hope.

> What has been sold
> Not strictly made of stone
> Please remember it's flesh and bone.

"Maybe Sandoval's right," Sheila wailed off the doctor's notes, "maybe I did lose the files, I fucked up, I'm a fuckup." You lose 'em, Sheila, but I got 'em. The files are power, Sheila. Power to show you didn't fuck up, not ever, sister, protector, dearest friend. "They just turn their back on things." No, won't, won't, not ever. "I wish I was dead. I wish I was dead. I just wish I was dead." She'd said she wished she was dead three times. They all knew how she felt – and they sold it.

331

Feel it clawing in my gut now, boiling corrosion in my tears. Tears of a man now, tears of a man with power. Or does the power bleed away into the welfare line, into Charlie the shithead's compromise?

A clear shaft of sunlight inflames the flowers in the plaza. Roman ruins by a hacienda, and near it all, that miracle of iron dragon wings and liquid stone. Soleil had told him he would be there. Just for a moment, Spain, Barcelona, Gaudi the magician, Casa Mila's walls rippling in their play like a charmed earthquake. The women step through the melting walls and the flowers with their arms wide open. The sun falling on the ageless city of his dreams.

Just remember that it's flesh and bone
Flesh and bone-bone-bone-bone-bone....

Sheila had opened up her belly to Sandoval. Put him in her pit. To fight back the sickness and seize the knowledge of her tormentor naked and helpless, and gain with that knowledge a chance to destroy him. Planned to put him down in that fire in her belly. That was what Brandon had to remember now. And as the sparks flew, the heat would rise faster, the fire's world would expand to become the whole world, and everything, everything would change.

The waiting room at Hobart-Riss was almost festive as Worcek, Remar, Barasch and two other claimant lawyers Charlie didn't recognize hobnobbed about their caseload and waited for their settlement bonanza. Barasch saw Charlie first, leaped up and hugged him, and shouted that Chanukkah was coming early this year. Remar did his usual grumbling about a client who'd fled the scene; this one had taken off for Alaska, believing her whole loan office worked for the Russian mob. Worcek, however, was not her usual effusive self, cautiously sizing Charlie up in what, after all, was his first moment on a new team. Charlie assured her he was doing just fine.

Vel patiently stood at Charlie's side as he accepted the backslaps of his peers. For Charlie, this would be a long day of crafting settlements, and he appreciated not only Vel's driving him to work but her willingness to sit with him in the meeting and help push the paper. He had to admit to himself, as he gave Vel a sidewise glance, that her forbidding presence was becoming more and more of a comfort lately.

332

He left his new claimant lawyer allies to their lively waiting room conversation and he and Vel made their way to the conference room. In the corner the files that Charlie had so ardently thrown in his bosses' faces two days ago were neatly stacked and properly tagged. There was a plate of lox, bagels and cream cheese and some jumbo canisters of coffee and decaf on the credenza. "We certainly know how to throw a wake in style," Vel cracked.

They contemplated the breakfast tableau for a second until the conference room door swung open and Bunning, Shackleton, and Jim Cotner, the young up-and-comer with the Keith Haring/Berlin Wall ties, drifted in to make strained small talk. Everyone seemed to be delaying the moment when the ground rules of the meeting would be formally charted. A fairly dry process of reviewing each case, laying out settlements, then meeting with the other side for the inevitable modifications - only this time, it was up to the Hobart-Riis legal staff to grin and bear it as they yielded step-by-step to a massive legal bloodletting. Charlie noticed no one was biting very lustily into the bagels, but he was famished. With an almost impudent enthusiasm he laid yet another spread on his plate. Vel shot him a cautionary glance, then simply smiled.

"I think I'll get myself some hot water for tea."

She headed out for the office kitchenette just as Bert Silver rushed into the meeting. He tossed off an apology for being late, then asked everyone's forbearance while he went to the bathroom. Yep, Charlie thought, Bert was nervous. And he was even more unconsciously self-protective than usual - Charlie noticed that he kept his attaché case with him even on the way to the john.

Shackleton buzzed the receptionist to send in Remar. Let the games begin. In the reception room, Worcek joked with her sallow, perpetually rankled colleague and told him to kick ass. "I hate to kick an ass when it's down," drawled Remar as he laid out his wallet and keys before the metal detector, then walked through. The gate beeped, and the guard waved him back and scanned him with his electronic wand. "Trust me, Julio," Barasch shouted, "I've seen him in trials, there's nothing up his sleeve." The guard laughed, then located the source of the problem, Remar's new watch, before motioning him to go ahead. Worcek was so distracted by the cheerful scene that Brandon had to tap her on the shoulder to get her attention.

333

She looked up and blanched at the sight of him. He was dressed in an old gray jacket, black pants and a black tie. One look at the outfit and she knew Brandon had some idea he was going to be able to get in on the meeting.

"Brandon, what are you doing here?"

"I heard about this from Charlie. I figured I'd join the party."

He was looking at the assembled lawyers but not really seeing them, until, catching the eye of the guard at the metal detector, his eyes took on that coldly amused look he always had when he was sizing someone up and finding something they said was worthless.

"Brandon, we have a lot to talk about, and I promise we'll discuss your case later this week, but right now, as I'm sure Charlie told you, I got a marathon run ahead of me with these settlements. We're gonna take them to the cleaners, Brandon. I'm gonna be all day in here. " Now she could see everyone looking at them. "Come on, Brandon, you know this isn't the way it's done."

"You're gonna have to convince 'em, Liz. You're my lawyer." He yanked the gun from his jacket pocket and aimed it at her mouth.

The other lawyers chat collapsed into silence as Brandon gripped Worcek's arm and forced her to her feet. He stuck the gun right in her chest. Worcek saw the muzzle push open her blouse beneath the button, felt its cold sting on her belly.

"Oh please, Brandon, you can't do -"

"Shut up!"

He pulled the gun off her, but only long enough to brandish it at the receptionist.

"Open the fucking door!"

Worcek saw the guard give the receptionist a look, as if he were imploring her to delay just a minute, but Brandon saw it too. He drove the gun into Worcek's ear and advanced on the gate, staring straight at the guy. Big guy, he knew, but thrown totally off guard, and knowing how badly he could screw up here. The guard was paralyzed as Brandon forced Worcek through the gate, right past its sonic whine.

"Brandon," Worcek cried, "didn't Charlie tell you? We're going to help you, Brandon. That's part of what this meeting is about!"

334

"Good! Then there's nothing wrong with my being there! All I want to do is listen!" But the guard didn't seem to be listening. He shouted above the screech of the alarm that if Brandon stopped now, nobody would be hurt.

"If you're so concerned for everyone's welfare, then tell the bitch behind me to open this door or some people in this room will be dead!"

The guard saw his eyes and stepped back. The door emitted its telltale click. Brandon pushed Worcek to the door and yanked it open.

The clerks and secretaries froze at their desks, some moaning softly, as Brandon maneuvered Worcek ahead of him. "Don't worry. I'm cool. See, got my lawyer." He chuckled at his own joke. "I just wanna talk, that's all. Listen and talk. Make a deal, maybe." He arrowed in on Laura, who was crouched back to the wall of her cubicle, already weeping. He took the gun off Worcek's chin and pointed it at the secretary.

"Where are they? Your bosses?"

Brandon drove the gun back under Worcek's chin even harder, feeling the gasp quiver through her back like the gills of a fish thrown in the bucket, the quake of her muscles as he inhaled her sour sweat. He shoved Worcek angrily towards Laura. Why the fuck is she so heavy? He should be gliding now, down the tunnel of his pure and unstoppable intent, but instead he felt he was pushing a big wooden puppet ahead of him, none of the joints behaving, her fat, slow terror pressing back so heavy it threatened to suffocate him. He brandished the gun at Laura again. "Tell me where your bosses are!"

"In the conference room!" Laura cried, and then her hand flew to her mouth and she broke down, shuddering and gasping as she sank to the floor.

He stared at Worcek, and Worcek knew she'd failed to keep the horror and repulsion out of her face. But he smiled at her without rancor. "Thanks for representing me. Now get out."

"Brandon, you can't possibly win this way. They've already called the police off their cellphones in the -"

"GO!"

He shoved her away from him. She tore off her high heels and ran back to the waiting room looking over her shoulder. But Brandon had forgotten her now. He was facing the clerks stationed just before the suite of the executive offices. In the corner cubicle, he had just seen one of them pull his hand from a speakerphone.

"Who did you call?"

"Nobody, I -"

"Tell me who you called!"

"I didn't do anything!"

"You call the police?" The dead weight was off him now, he was moving free, the gun leading, thrusting him forward.

"Please, I swear, I didn't-"

"TELL ME WHO YOU CALLED!" and Brandon grabbed him by the hair and shoved his face into the computer screen, the screen where Sheila's illness had been recorded and deleted, delete, delete, and he pressed the gun into the back of his skull, and the little nerd was sobbing and pissing and Brandon pushed harder just to really scare that piss out of him and it felt right until a great rubberband of black sound snapped his hand back so hard that he was catapulted into the cubicle wall and the pressboard caved in beneath him. He scrambled to his feet. No, this wasn't what he intended, all this howling and not a boss in sight, just that bizarre chimera of scrunched up nerd and head with the ragged black/red hole in back and a computer monitor where the face should be. Blood oozed down to the monitor's rim through the smashed frame of the glasses. The gun's heat pulsed through his hand and forced him to inspect the reality of it, the face rammed right through the screen.

"Log on, motherfucker."

"What is that?" Maxine repeated to the hushed conference room, and they could all hear her attempt to suppress the whimper in her voice. "Sounds like someone dropped something," Cotner mumbled. Charlie saw the guy actually trying to distract himself with his papers. It was ridiculous to Charlie, because even if the rest of his colleagues were bewildered, or trying their best to cling to their ignorance, Charlie could already hear the crying and he knew.

Brandon swept the gun around the room and the yowling, blubbering little people hit the floor, all except the guy walking out of the bathroom. Brandon grinned. Guy was probably taking a shit and flushing the toilet when the shot rang out. Brandon had gotten lucky. This asshole lawyer stranded and lost in the middle of the hallway. He banished his last tremor of shock and hesitation, calmly raised his gun in a two-handed grip, and walked right up to Bert Silver. He could see the shades of supplication flit across the man's face - first the lawyer's pompous, offended dignity, then the shock at the sight of the weapon fading down into a child's plea for mercy.

Silver rocked back and forth on his feet, staring haplessly at the gun. "What do you want?" he stammered.

"Twenty-five grand benefits for the death of my sister, Sheila Reed."

The lawyer in Bert Silver snapped back for one reflexive instant. "That's impossible."

"Nothing's impossible."

Silver just managed to scream and raise the attaché case to his chest when the two shots spat out. The case blew apart like cheap cardboard and shreds of its paper stuffing flew across the floor as it was blasted loose from Silver's arm. The momentum of the flying briefcase catapulted Silver onto his back and Brandon watched the impact of his shots, fascinated. The bulk of the man skidded across the floor until his head hit a cubicle and he stopped, his gut heaving out spurts of blood. The man's shrieks disgusted Brandon, and he coldly walked past them to the conference room.

There was no doubt about it now. Shackleton, some memory from old wartime service taking over, yelled at them to hit the ground. Charlie looked at the doorknob. No one was thinking about the lock. Or Mavis. Or Vel.

"What the hell is going on?" screamed Bunning. "Who's out there?"

"I know," muttered Charlie, and was already heading out the conference room, ignoring the shouts of protest behind him, of which only one, Cotner's plea to the others, emerged from the din. "Lock the fucking door!"

Brandon saw the glass wall in the corner and knew he was almost there, but what if someone sprang out of that hall leading to the right, those seemingly closed executive suites? Brandon briefly became cautious. He rushed into the hall, gun at the ready, and yes, someone was there, down the little hall in the kitchenette, he could see the faint woman's shadow on the wall. He had her cornered, and yes, yes, now he'd really got it. Payback would be simple and direct. The Chicana bitch who had lain her little knives into him on the witness stand. She stood there like a goddamn statue. He let it grow still within him, focus to its meaning, the purpose which would consecrate this

337

moment, for yes, he knew he was taking life, but he wasn't crazy, there had to be a purpose always. He gathered within himself the memory of Sheila's eyes, her words echoing on the doctor's pages, every insult and injury that was needed to pull the trigger.

Vel let loose a torrent of Spanish imprecations. The volcanic force of the cries drove him back. The curses pelted him like dung from unseen vermin and fouled his memory of Sheila, his vision, his reasons.

"Stop it! What the hell are you doing? Stop it!"

The sheer black flood of life in the words unnerved him. Kill it, kill it quickly-

"STOP IT!"

Not his own voice. He wheeled around, and saw Charlie standing in front of him, defenseless, pleading for him to stop, willing to do anything for it to stop. Yes, this was even better than he'd planned. Now Charlie would walk Brandon in to his masters.

But almost as soon as he laid eyes on Charlie, he could hear the running footsteps. Charlie automatically looked at Vel as she fled and in that same instant tried to wrench that tiny look back, but Brandon caught it. He wheeled around, steadied his arm, and Charlie screamed incoherently as if that could sever the chain that linked the immovable pistol with the woman fleeing endlessly down the long hall, but Charlie couldn't stop that gun from firing three times until Vel finally screamed, clutching her side, knocked against a desk and careened across the floor. She came to rest against one of the other desks, her hands flung in front of her as if reaching for a rope in a dark and freezing ocean.

"You bastard!" Charlie screamed. "You miserable piece of shit! What the hell have you done?"

Brandon's eyes went slack, and Charlie realized he had fatally lost control and was now one step from the abyss. He could be swallowed up by a gunshot at any moment. But Brandon hesitated, and for a moment seemed truly shaken. "She was brave. But - all wrong, all wrong...."

The gun arm drooped. And as it did, Charlie could hear the sound trailing way beneath the thick glass windows in the streets below. The sirens rising from the canyon of the city.

"Brandon, you hear that? They'll be here any minute." Brandon had heard it. He was waking up to it. The gun arm was slack.

He could go for the gun.

No. Not in a million years.

"Brandon, there's still time to -"

"Don't jam me, Charlie. You hear? Don't mess with my head! Don't get me any more turned around!" The gun arm tautened. "You all think you're so fucking clever!"

Charlie knew to instantly backpedal, not to even try to reason, cajole, beg, for Brandon was going to back Charlie into the conference room. Nothing could stop it, certainly not the sobs of Mavis Thorpe trapped behind her desk.

"Charlie, you got one chance. I don't want you. You know who I want. Open the door for me. Open it!"

"Brandon, I - I don't have the keys."

"That's right. You wouldn't have those keys. You don't even work here anymore. It's the gatekeeper. Old Katy. Katy-bar-the-door." Charlie saw him move on Mavis and the phrase began orbiting in his brain, like a gear trying desperately to spin a much bigger gear, any minute now, any minute the police will come, any minute now.

"It's Katy here I'm talking to." Brandon angled himself to look directly at Mavis. The fury of it, the black explosion and the wave of blood - nothing Charlie could do. This woman pleading for her life...any minute now. Any minute.

"I want your bosses. Give me the keys to that door!"

"I can't, no, I can't, I can't!"

Her obese frame palpitated with her cries as her loyalty to the end and her sheer terror paralyzed her behind the desk. Charlie, waiting helplessly for Brandon to shoot her, suddenly realized Brandon was stymied. This woman's agony, her panic, and her refusal to expose her bosses to harm had cast a spell on him.

He turned to Charlie. "C'mon, Mr. Mental, help me convince her! You really want me to kill you too, you stupid cow? I have to get them for Sheila, you understand? Not some clerk and a couple of fucking lawyers, I didn't mean for that, I have to get THEM! GIVE ME THE KEYS!"

339

He stopped, for they all could hear it, the charge of the footsteps coming closer.

"Brandon," Charlie managed to croak, "they're on their way. Put down the gun. Put your hands up. Come on, Brandon, you don't want to be holding that when they come in."

"Yeah," he whispered, finally comprehending it all. "I killed three people, Charlie. Three people are dead."

"They won't shoot you if you're unarmed. Just put down the gun."

"Take me for a good long time though." And Charlie saw for just a moment the most excruciating sadness cross Brandon's face as he turned towards Mavis.

"I told you all."

He planted his feet, raising his gun arm to Mavis' head. Charlie had one last view of Mavis squatting behind the desk, and then the space funneled between him and her. In one long leap he floated in that space until he slammed against the burning sweat-drenched fiber of her blouse and the sheer bulk of her, and drove her out of her chair. As he covered her he tried to drag her down flat but his shoulder split apart with a great racking pain that rode on a roar of sound. The roar multiplied, the wall fragmented all around him, and before he could even scream a terrible weight spiked through his back and pinned him to the floor. Waves of agony seized his flank and crushed the breath out of him, and as the hot blood seeped into his shirt he shut his eyes and waited for the blackness.

The weight was lifted off of him. He gasped for breath. Something turned him around and he was staring at the ceiling.

"Are you okay, son? Can you hear me?"

"Yeah, yeah..." he muttered, just as the pain spasmed again and he screamed.

"Careful with his arm!"

The officers propped Charlie up against the wall. He saw Mavis lying on the floor next to him, trying to get her breath back, a second pair of cops ministering to her. Next to her Brandon was also lying face down. His mouth was crushed into the carpet, where blood had pooled from his lips and turned the color of hard brown enamel. One eye faced Charlie, the gray shell of a last howling accusation sucked down into silence.

Mavis was pointing to Charlie and gasping between her sobs. "He saved my life!" She wriggled across the floor and tried to reach for his hand. "Charlie, you saved my life!"

"I'm all right. Let me get up." Mavis so wanted to clasp his hand, and he wanted to move closer to her, but the pain stabbed at him so hard he almost fainted, and he watched the rivulet of blood escape down his shirt.

"Jesus, his back -"

"No, the wound's in the shoulder! Get a stretcher down here!"

They laid him down and told him to wait for the paramedics. "Good work, son. You'll be fine." The cop squeezed his hand. He heard the conference room door creak open beside him, and as he let his head drop back the bulletholes in the door refacted the light towards his face. He could not take his eyes from the open door.

"Are they okay? Are they okay?"

The cop looked down at him. "Everyone looks all right."

They led out Shackleton, Bunning and Cotner, Bunning sagging into the arms of a patrolman, Cotner shaky, only Shackleton maintaining what seemed a steady, unswerving walk as they were led out of the conference room. He noticed that Shackleton also was the only one who did not avert his eyes from the body on the floor.

"How many dead?" he finally asked.

"Two, sir. Jim Hartley, one of the assistants out in the front room, and your counsel, Bert Silver."

Shackleton shook his head unbelievingly, and Charlie lifted his head towards the cop, trying desperately to get his attention. "Vel," Charlie croaked. "Elena Velasquez?"

The cop looked down at him. "She was shot in the leg, but she crawled to safety. They're taking her to the hospital. Looks like she'll be okay."

"Thank God...," Charlie whispered, and the phrase seemed to take him over, "thank God, thank God...," he kept muttering, until a new pair of hands were trundling him onto a stretcher. He surrendered to the force that swept him past Shackleton and the others staring down at him, down the corridor, past the

341

.uma specialists huddling with the office staff, through the glass doors of Hobart-Riis Insurance, Inc.

When they finally took him downstairs to the ambulance, a crowd of bystanders and news reporters had already massed behind the crime scene tape and the sawhorses. The sun was blinding - when he turned around on his stretcher to look back towards the monolith of the building, the glare washed over his vision and it seemed to disappear. He closed his eyes, winced and sucked in another breath against the pain of the wound. This time his own blood.